RAPTURE'S FANTASY

Suddenly Damian reached out to hold her face between his hands, rubbing his thumb gently across her parted lips. He leaned forward and kissed where his thumb had just traced, slowly increasing the pressure until Angelique moaned in newly-awakened passion. She clung to him, savoring the feel of his muscles rippling beneath her innocent, exploring hands. His lips moved from her mouth, slowly laying kisses along her jaw before gently nibbling on her earlobe.

"You're so beautiful," he whispered, his breath warm against her neck.

Dreamily, her eyes half-closed, Angelique felt Damian remove her wrapper while he left a burning trail of kisses where her silken skin was exposed. A fire raced through Angelique's veins. Every touch, every kiss heightened her desire for the unknown. He was taking possession of her mind and body and she couldn't resist—wouldn't resist. She clung to him as he eased her back on the bed. Damian moaned, drinking the sweetness of her lips, bringing her need to a fevered pitch.

The thought of finally being loved by Damian brought tears to Angelique's eyes. Her dream had at last come true, and she could only pray it would never end . . .

IRRESISTIBLE ROMANCE FROM ZEBRA!

Moonlight Angel

BY
CASEY
STUART

ZEBRA BOOKS
KENSINGTON PUBLISHING CORP.

ZEBRA BOOKS

are published by

Kensington Publishing Corp.
475 Park Avenue South
New York, NY 10016

Copyright © 1985 by Casey Stuart

First printing: April 1985

Printed in the United States of America

For Virgil Carrington Jones, who sparked my interest in the Civil War a long time ago, and is now a valued personal friend.

Author's Note

The historical facts depicted in this book are accurate. All characters are fictional, with the exception of those famous figures of the Civil War, mentioned to add authenticity.

If I have succeeded in making you want to read more about the Civil War period, then I would like to suggest the following sources I consulted: *The Civil War At Sea* by Virgil Carrington Jones; *Blockade Runners of the Confederacy*, by Hamilton Cochran; and *The Siege of Charleston*, by E. Milby Burton.

Foreword

On April 19, 1861, five days after the evacuation of Fort Sumter, President Lincoln proclaimed a blockade of the six Southern states which had seceded up to that time and which constituted the Confederate States of America: South Carolina, Georgia, Alabama, Florida, Mississippi and Texas. The proclamation declared them to be in a state of insurrection, and for this purpose, a competent force would be posted to prevent the entrance and exit of the vessels from these states. Eight days later, the president issued another decree, extending the blockade to include North Carolina and Virginia. This made the blockade of the South complete—from Cape Henry to the Mexican border, four thousand miles of coast line.

Chapter One

September 1862

It was pitch black as the slim silhouette of a ship made its way along the Carolina shoreline. Captain Damian Legare stood at the wheel of the *Sorceress*, an unlighted cheroot clamped between his teeth, his green eyes searching the blackness for any sign of the Union warships he knew were there. The crew stood ready, expecting any moment to see the flash of a Yankee gun or hear the roar of its explosion.

"We're getting close to the bar, Mr. Steele," Damian whispered to his companion. "If you're a religious man pray the wind holds."

"How could I not be a religious man in this business, sir?"

"On the starboard bow," Damian Legare whispered.

Steele strained his eyes to the starboard side, but

saw nothing. He started to say so, when he heard voices in the darkness. Not a man on board dared to breathe as the *Sorceress* passed within spitting distance of the Union ship. Damian spun the wheel, bringing the ship hard to port as another Union cruiser loomed ahead of them, crossed their bow, then disappeared in the darkness.

Steele stared behind them as they left two Union ships in their wake. "Hell's fire, Captain, I don't know how you do it."

"You promised me a bottle of France's finest brandy if we made it to Charleston without a shot being fired on us. That's what I did, Mr. Steele."

Tom Steele had been with Damian in the U.S. Navy and when Damian had resigned his commission Tom had done the same. He wasn't as familiar with the Carolina coast as Damian, but he was an expert at dealing with the everyday problems of a blockade runner. He made sure only first quality supplies were brought aboard, he hand-picked the crew and kept a critical eye on them, he kept the account book, and relieved Damian of the captain's duties when there was an emergency or Damian just needed a rest. Damian deeply appreciated his loyal friend and wondered how he would manage without him.

"I can almost taste that fine brandy, Tom."

Damian had no more than spoken when the sky was lit with the flare-like Drummond light. Damian called for silence. "It's another ship they're after. I can hear her engines. Proceed with caution."

Tom Steele watched through his spyglass for another Drummond light to brighten the sky. When it did, he spotted the other blockade runner following a short distance behind them. "Sir, take a look at this the next time they light up the sky. I think it's the *Petite Marie*."

Damian waited for the next light, then fixed the spyglass on the ship behind them. Steele was right. The bulky form of Beau Charbonne's French blockade runner was easy to identify.

"Now is when I'd like to have a few seven-inch guns," Damian said, still watching the outline of the Union vessel.

"Yes, but if we were captured we'd all be hung as pirates," Steele reminded Damian of the maritime law that while a blockade was in force, any ship entering or leaving a closed port is considered a hostile belligerent and is liable to be treated as such by being fired upon, and if captured, imprisoned, but if the ship is armed and fires in her own defense, her crew become pirates and can be hanged.

"We've got to take a chance. Fire your pistol in the air and see if we can create a diversion," Damian ordered.

A volley of fire rang out from Tom Steele's pistol, then there was silence. The Union ships were momentarily confused. Another Drummond light lit the sky, but not before the *Sorceress* had made its way into the harbor. When the Confederates manning the shore guns realized what was happening they joined the fight, shelling the Union ships with everything they had, giving both blockade runners a chance to enter port.

"Thank you, *mon ami*," Beau Charbonne greeted Damian with a bear hug after both ships had docked. "We watched you clear that course so neatly we thought we could do the same, but . . ."

Damian laughed. "It's those damned engines of yours, Beau. I keep telling you that."

"But they help me make the crossing so swiftly."

"It won't do you any good to make the crossing if you can't get through the blockade," Damian pointed out.

"Ah, but then I don't usually run the blockade. Lately I've been depositing my shipment in Nassau or Bermuda, picking up a load of cotton, and heading directly back to France. The profit has been much higher and there are very few risks."

"I should have known you were only in this for the profit," Damian said, unable to keep a touch of irritation from his voice.

"Now, Damian, I have no reason to feel about the Carolinas as you do. You are my only link in Charleston, the only reason I ever put in here." Beau threw his arm around Damian's shoulders. "Now come, let me buy you a drink and a night's pleasure. We can argue the point later—as we always do."

The two men caused quite a stir as they entered Miss Molly's establishment. Damian Legare was tall and muscular, with wide shoulders that tapered into a narrow waist. His hair and close cropped beard were sun-streaked blond, accenting emerald green

14

eyes. His face could almost be called classic with a straight nose and sensual mouth.

Beau Charbonne, on the other hand, was slightly shorter and stockier with black hair and gray eyes. Even though his features weren't as refined as Damian's, he had no trouble attracting the opposite sex.

Molly Flanagan, a plump red-haired beauty, greeted Damian at the door with an affectionate hug. "Where have you been keeping yourself, Damian? No, don't tell me. I know all about your mistress. You'd do better to stay with my girls." Molly smiled alluringly at Beau. "And who is this handsome gentleman?"

"I wondered if I was going to have a chance to introduce my friend. This is Beau Charbonne from France. We're both thirsty and dirty, so perhaps you can take care of us in that order."

Molly smiled again at Beau. "I know Damian's preference, but what about you, M'sieur? Blonde, brunette . . . ?"

"Personally I like redheads," he said winking at her.

"Get on with ye, Frenchman," she laughed as she beckoned forward a lovely blonde and an olive skinned Oriental girl. "This is Pearl," she said pushing the blonde toward Beau, "and this is Mai Lin," she said, introducing the girl to Damian. "Both these girls are experts at giving a bath—and anything else you might like."

"I'm sorry to disappoint you, Molly, but I'm only here for a drink and a bath. Perhaps my friend will stay."

"You're damned right I'm going to stay," Beau said putting his arm around the blonde, "and you can leave both girls."

Damian eased into one of the large brass tubs that had been prepared, while Mai Lin waited at his side to assist. He beckoned for the bottle of whiskey, slowly relaxing while Beau talked from another tub of steaming water.

"I was glad to hear you had finally given up your commission in the Confederate Navy to go into private blockade running, but now I hear you give your profits to the Little Sisters of Mercy Hospital here in Charleston. You know that makes all the rest of us look bad, *mon ami*?"

Damian laughed. "I don't need the money. I have Enchanteur and she's a good working plantation."

"If the Yankees invade Charleston you may wish you had kept some of that money."

"If the Yankees invade Charleston, money won't make a hell of a lot of difference."

"I guess that's true, *mon ami*. Tell me, what made you give up your commission? I was truly surprised to hear it."

"I guess the usual things that have turned a lot of career men away. When I joined the Confederate Navy after leaving the Union I had high hopes of being able to change things; of putting an end to this war swiftly. My first suggestion was to destroy the New York Navy Yard, but they wouldn't hear of it.

16

Then I suggested we purchase large quantities of arms, clothing, and provisions before the U.S. Navy did anything absurd, like blockading our ports, but again my suggestion was ignored. Then Jefferson Davis told me he didn't contemplate the Navy even being involved in the war, that if I really wanted to be active perhaps I should join Lee's forces in Virginia. It was about that time I decided I could be of better use to the Confederacy and Charleston by working on my own. Strangely enough, I find myself still working for the Confederate Navy."

"In what way?"

"I've become sort of an emissary between France, England and the South. I have a meeting in the morning with Secretary Mallory and I suspect I'll be asked to go back to Europe. But enough about me. Tell me about your family. How is *l'enfant terrible*?"

"My sister?" Beau laughed. "Angelique has grown into quite a lovely lady. She's still very independent and very stubborn. It will take a strong man to tame her."

"If she hasn't changed since she was twelve, taming is a very good word. I remember a time when your cousin was mistreating his pony and Angelique gave him a tongue lashing he'll probably never forget."

"I'm sure you're right. And Angelique is still very much the animal lover. Everyone in the village brings their sick animals to her. She has performed some rather miraculous cures, I must say."

Damian was enjoying the ministrations of the

lovely Oriental girl as he listened to his friend. "The last time I stopped at your home Angelique was attending a convent school."

"Ah, yes, but the nuns asked Father to come take her home. Seems she was teaching the other girls how to fire a musket."

Both men roared with laughter.

"She must be getting close to marrying age. Will Michel be able to find someone to take on such an independent girl?" Damian asked as Mai Lin poured hot water over his head and began to scrub his hair.

"She's had many suitors, but Father promised her he won't insist she marry anyone she doesn't want to, and so far she hasn't accepted anyone. She says the men are only interested in her money. This ploy has been successful for quite a while, but I'm afraid Father is getting impatient and plans to choose someone for her soon."

Damian laughed. "I pity your poor father."

Beau leaned his head back against the edge of the tub while Pearl's soft hands caressed his shoulders. He closed his eyes and listened while Damian recalled another of Angelique's escapades. He and Damian had enjoyed such great times when they were boys spending the summer together. Damian's love of the sea came from those summers.

The times hadn't always been good for Damian though. Damian had first come to Crozon when he was fourteen. Though his mother had deserted her family in Charleston for the gaiety of Paris society, her parents insisted on seeing their grandson. Colette

Legare was always busy with her social engagements, or her latest flirtation, so she was more than happy to let her friends, the Charbonnes, take Damian to Crozon.

After the first few summers, Damian didn't even bother going to Paris. He went directly to Crozon to stay with his second family. Occasionally, Beau went to Charleston to stay with Damian and his father, but both boys enjoyed being around ships, so most of their visits took place in France. Michel Charbonne taught both boys everything there was to know about ships and the sea. The Charbonnes had had been sailors and shipbuilders for four generations, so it had been assumed Beau would go into the shipbuilding business. However Damian's family were planters so everyone had been shocked when Damian announced that he had been selected to attend the Naval Academy in Annapolis. Damian's father had protested violently, insisting he was needed at the plantation, but Damian had been adamant. He was going to sea one way or the other. Unfortunately, this only served to widen the gap between father and son. When Colette had deserted them, instead of growing closer, they both kept their hurt inside, closing themselves off from showing their feelings even toward each other. Beau had suspected the old man loved and respected Damian, but he didn't think Damian realized it. When the old man died, the closest Damian came to showing emotion was to go into town and get drunk for three days.

"Are you staying here tonight?" Damian asked,

interrupting his friend's reverie.

Beau looked up at the honey-blonde who had just finished scrubbing his back. "I think I will. How about you?"

"I promised Kate I'd come by as soon as I got back. I'm sure by now she knows my ship is in the harbor."

"I didn't know you were still seeing Kate. I thought she had married old man Winston."

"She did, but Winston died a year ago. I met her at a restaurant in town shortly after that and, well, we had a few drinks."

"A few drinks, hell! I remember you telling me about Kate. She's always had her sights on you. Be careful, *mon ami*, or she'll have a ring in your nose."

"You know better than that. Can you imagine me a married man?" Damian brushed the girl aside as she attempted to dry him and began to briskly dry himself. Mai Lin was a lovely young girl, but he didn't want to disappoint Kate. Besides, she could do anything this girl could, and probably better.

He dressed quickly, then turned back to Beau who was now enjoying a massage by both women. "Why don't you meet me at the hotel dining room for coffee in the morning?"

"If I live through this," Beau grinned devilishly.

Damian crossed Meeting Street and headed toward the Winston house on the Battery. He paused out front, staring at the residence. Little Kate Monroe had done all right for herself. The Winston house was one of the most impressive on the street.

The door opened before he had a chance to knock, and a young black girl greeted him. "I thought that was you standing there, Captain Legare. Miss Kate will be purely happy to see you."

"Thank you, Nell." He handed her his hat.

"Who is it, Nell?" a lilting voice called from down the hallway.

Damian put his finger to his lips. "Shh. I want to surprise her."

"She's in the sitting room, sir. You go on in and I'll bring you a brandy."

Damian stood in the doorway watching Kate struggle with her needlepoint. Her silver blond hair hung loosely around her shoulders. She looked up, her blue eyes wide with surprise. "Damian," she exclaimed, dropping everything to the floor and rushing into his arms. "I heard your ship slipped into the harbor this evening and I was so hoping you would come."

"I stopped at Molly's place with a friend first."

"Oh," she said, her mouth set in a pout. "I hope you are not exhausted."

Damian threw back his head and laughed, his green eyes twinkling. "I only had a bath. Do you think I'd come to you after enjoying one of Molly's girls? I told you I'd be back to see you as soon as we docked," he reminded before kissing her deeply.

"Ah, excuse me, ma'am, but I thought Captain Legare would like some brandy."

21

"Brandy is not what I want," Damian whispered in Kate's ear.

"Why don't you put it in my room, Nell. We will have it a little later."

"Yes, ma'am," the girl smiled to herself as she left.

"Is my body all you crave, Captain. Surely you came for my stimulating conversation."

"You can talk all you want, love, but don't expect me to answer. I'm going to be too busy," he teased, nibbling at her neck.

"You're terrible, Damian," she complained, leading him upstairs. "What am I going to do with you?"

"I can think of a few things, but there's plenty of time for that."

Damian sat on the chaise lounge sipping brandy while he watched Kate undress. She slowly slipped her dress off, exposing ample breasts that nearly tumbled out of her chemise. Then she removed her silk stockings, stretching each leg provocatively, smiling at Damian's obvious anticipation. A moment later she stood naked before him, her eyes now a deep sapphire blue.

"I have something new to show you," she held a hand out for him to join her. "I bought it with you in mind."

"Really? And what would that be?" Damian asked as he kissed her neck and shoulders.

"You'll see in a moment," she promised as she undressed him. She stood back for a moment, savoring his hard, bronze body, lightly covered with gold hair.

"You are the most beautiful man I've ever seen. I love just looking at you."

"Are you trying to drive me crazy, woman?" He growled, pulling her into his arms.

Kate drew him down on top of her as she laid on the bed. Damian's hands and mouth began a slow exploration, leaving a burning trail everywhere he touched. "I can't stand it when you are away for so long," Kate murmured.

"Do you think about me and about the things I do to you?" he asked, still nuzzling her neck.

"You know I do," Kate answered as she aggressively rolled over on top of him. Damian opened his eyes, appreciating the abundant breasts that dangled before him, then his eyes widened as he looked beyond Kate to the canopy above them. It housed an elaborate mirror that reflected back their naked images.

"Do you like it?" she asked.

"How could I not like it?" he smiled, appreciating the way her derriere reflected in the opulent mirror. Kate laid back beside him, looking up at the reflection. She moved her hand slowly over his muscled chest and down his stomach. Damian's eyes were glued to the mirror watching her sensuous movements. Her silver blond hair spread out across his stomach as she moved down over him. He moaned as he not only felt, but saw as she took him in her mouth.

"Damn, but you're a beautiful whore," he moaned, gripping the back of her head as his pulse quickened.

* * *

"I'm not a whore, Damian," Kate said later as they lay in each other's arms beneath the mirror. "I only do that for you."

"I only meant that you are an expert at everything you do," Damian explained.

"I can't lie to you about my past. You've known me too long. I've had to do many things I didn't want to do to make it where I am, but now I'm a lady, Damian and I don't want to think about my past."

Damian rolled over and pulled her into his arms. "I wasn't referring to your past, Kate. Listen to me, I left a very obliging lady at Molly's tonight to come to you. I wouldn't have done that if I didn't want to be with you."

"Will anything ever come of our relationship, Damian?" Kate asked, impulsively knowing she shouldn't.

Damian rolled on his back, not answering for a moment. "Neither of us would be happy being chained to one another, Kate. I know that Philip Delacort spends a good deal of time here, and you know I'm not a saint when I'm away from Charleston. If you're not happy with our arrangement then I'll stay out of your life. I've told you before, I'm not interested in anything else, now or ever."

"It's because I let you have your way with me when we were kids," Kate said, turning her face away from him.

"You know better than that," Damian was becoming annoyed.

"I know I shouldn't have been so easy for you, but I

couldn't help it. I've always loved you, Damian."

"Really? Then how do you account for the string of men you've had?"

"You know damned well why," Kate answered, as she left the bed. "I was never invited to the same social functions as your snobbish friends. Your father wouldn't even let me in your house. Even that uppity slave woman Bessie treats me like dirt. So I wanted to teach you a lesson—to show you I had other admirers."

"It got a little out of hand, didn't it, sweet?" Damian asked sarcastically. "You slept with every friend I had."

"Damn it, Damian. You do hold my past against me."

"Why are we discussing this?" Damian asked angrily. "We're two grown people, Kate. I don't give a damn what you do when I'm not here or what your social position in Charleston is. I enjoy your company, and besides, you're the best damn woman I've ever had in bed. Now come on back here and stop acting like a spoiled child."

Kate suddenly forgot her anger. "Am I best you ever had?" she asked coquettishly.

"I said you were. Now come on back here and prove it."

Kate seductively ran her hands over her full breasts and down between her legs. "You'll always come back to me, Damian. None of your sweet, straight-laced lady friends will do the things for you I do."

"You're probably right," Damian agreed grabbing her around the waist and pulling her back on top of him. "Now shut up and do what you're so expert at."

Kate let her mind wander as she watched Damian sleep peacefully at her side. His incredibly handsome features never ceased to excite her, not since the first time she had seen him while she worked in the fields. He had been fourteen then, yet even at that young age he had been virile and handsome. She had set her sights on him that day. He had been attracted to her, too, but then his father discovered he was visiting a sharecropper's daughter and quickly tried to put a stop to it. But she had already had her first taste of Damian's lovemaking and she wasn't going to give him up.

Kate ran her hand over Damian's bronzed chest matted with fine gold hair. She wasn't sure why, but Damian had never married and she felt this gave her the upper hand. She had endured a sick old man's disgusting touch to get the money she always wanted. Now she had more than she'd ever need, but respectability hadn't come with it. Too many people in Charleston knew her background and knew how she had gained her present position. But things would change when she became mistress of Enchanteur.

Chapter Two

"Mademoiselle, 'tis none of my business, but doesn't your party start in two hours?" the groom asked as Angelique Charbonne mounted her gray mare.

"Yes, Sims, but I just have to ride for a few minutes," Angelique answered, her soft violet eyes seeking understanding from the groom who had taught her to ride as a child. "This is the third party this month. Papa says I must choose tonight or he will choose for me."

"He is only doing what he feels is best for you, Mademoiselle."

Angelique tied her long black hair back with a lavender ribbon. "Yes, I'm sure you're right, but I still have no heart for it. I wish Beau were here. He would be able to help."

The groom laughed. "You think your brother can help with everything! If you ask me, Beau Charbonne knew what he was doing when he sailed to America at this time. Now go on with your ride and be back quickly. I don't relish the idea of explaining to your father why I let you ride off just before your party."

"Thank you, Sims," Angelique flashed him a dimpled smile. "I'll be back before you know it."

"Just be back before your father knows it," he warned.

Angelique turned her mare into the wind and urged her to a full gallop, shamefully aware Sims would be in for a lecture from her father if she wasn't back in time to get ready for the party. But she had to get away, if only for a little while. She remembered her father's warning that tonight she must make a decision. She couldn't blame him; he had been more than patient, giving her time to choose a husband, but the fact was she didn't want to get married. She loved hunting, riding, and taking care of her animals, and she was sure none of the men her father presented would be as understanding as her family. She would be expected to sit silently, engrossed in her needlepoint, while her husband and his guests discussed the latest hunt. No, no, she couldn't do that. If she found a man who would treat her as an equal, one who accepted and enjoyed her independence and intelligence, then she would marry, but not until.

Oh, Papa, why can't I make you understand? she wondered mournfully.

Angelique pulled Gray Velvet to a halt at the stream running through the lower field. This was one of her favorite places. Here she could sit and read or just think without being disturbed. This was where Beau and Damian would come as boys—and where she would spy on them, until they had finally given in and made her a part of their discussions and deepest thoughts.

She patted the mare's soft neck affectionately, then dropped to the ground to remove her boots and stockings. A moment later she was wading in the crystal clear stream, her skirts hitched up between her legs. "I wonder what the gentlemen coming to my party would think if they saw me now," she laughed. "I dare say they'd probably hightail it away from Chateau Charbonne and poor Michel's strange daughter."

A twig snapped behind Angelique. She turned and faced a bushy-tailed red fox. "Well, there you are, my fine furry friend. How is your foot today?" Angelique asked as she dropped to one knee in front of the fox and gently ran her hand down its leg. "So, it is no longer sore . . . that is good. Now if you just stay away from the hunter's traps, you'll be fine." The fox licked her hand as if in understanding, then disappeared back into the woods.

"This is the way I would have it always," Angelique said to her horse. "Can't they see I am happy here? I need no husband to fulfill my life." Dropping to the warm grass, Angelique stretched out, her arms beneath her head. "If I had one wish," she whispered to the clouds, "I would wish for the love of my childhood. He and Beau were the only ones who ever understood me." Angelique covered her eyes and in a moment's time was asleep, dreaming about Damian Legare, her knight in shining armor.

"Please, Michel, do not be angry," Genevieve Charbonne pleaded, as they stood in the salon off the foyer. "Angelique is very unhappy right now. Sometimes I think we are making a terrible mistake forcing her to choose a husband. I know she is seventeen, but I don't think she is ready."

"She will never be ready if we don't insist. At least we are giving her a choice. She should be grateful, instead of riding all over the countryside while guests are arriving."

"I agree, Michel, but remember, Angelique is not like most girls and you have always said you were glad. Now when she shows the independence you've always admired, you are upset with her."

Michel's anger faded. "Of course, you are right, but what are we to do, Genevieve? If Angelique gets any older without a suitor, she will end up unmarriageable. I don't want that to happen. She may be happy with her life now, but as she gets older she will have a very lonely life."

"She has had many disappointments this year, Michel. It is only natural that she rebel," Genevieve reminded, tenderly touching the side of her husband's handsome face. "After all, she is your daughter."

"Of course you are speaking of my refusing to let

her tour as a pianist. Now, in all honesty, Genevieve, did you want her traveling all over Europe performing like a common musician?"

"No, of course not, dear. I was just pointing out her disappointments. We had to refuse her that, and then Beau went away. She misses him terribly."

Suddenly the door flew open with a bang and Angelique dashed up the stairs, unaware her parents had seen her.

"Wait just a moment, young lady!" her father bellowed.

Angelique froze in mid-step. She turned slowly, a sheepish grin on her lovely face. "I'm sorry, Papa. I fell asleep in the glen. But it won't take me long to get ready, my clothes are laid out."

Michel's frown softened. "Oh, Angelique, what am I going to do with you?"

Angelique rushed into his arms and hugged him. "Why not keep me around for amusement?" she suggested touching his face.

Michel's smile froze. "Genevieve, take your daughter upstairs and make her presentable. She will choose a husband tonight!"

"*Maman*, why?" Angelique asked as she soaked in a scented bath. "Why do I have to choose a husband and leave Crozon? I love it here."

"You will also love your new home, my dear. You are very young now, but when you get older you will understand why your father insists you marry."

"I will never understand!" Angelique answered, vigorously scrubbing her legs.

Angelique stood at the top of the stairs, hesitant to join the group below. She could tell the room was crowded from the din of conversation. Many couples had been invited, but the group consisted mainly of eligible bachelors. Has Papa missed a single bachelor in all of France? she wondered. This was the third party that had been given at Chateau Charbonne in the past month.

"Ah, there you are, my dear," Michel said catching sight of his daughter. "Come, I'd like you to meet some of our guests."

Angelique's pink satin gown swished as she descended the stairs. She appeared calm and self-assured, but she hated being put on display.

"Louis Bouche has been waiting to meet you," Michel said, leading her toward an elderly man engrossed in conversation with another guest. "Louis, I'd like you to meet my daughter, Angelique," Michel introduced proudly.

"Lovely," the white-haired gentleman said as he touched Angelique on the cheek. "Exquisite."

Angelique clung to her father's arm, willing herself to stand still as the old man devoured her with his eyes.

"Monsieur Bouche is one of Paris' leading businessmen," Michel pointed out, as if that would impress Angelique. "I'm sure you will enjoy talking with him," he said, untangling Angelique's arm from his own and leaving them alone.

"You must be a very busy man," Angelique commented, searching for something to say. "It was kind of you to take the time from your busy schedule to come to Chateau Charbonne for our little fête."

"It is my pleasure. Your father and I have been friends for a long time. I have met your brother, but have never had the privilege of meeting Michel's beautiful daughter. And, I must say, it was worth the long, tiring ride to see those lovely eyes."

"Thank you, Monsieur," Angelique looked past him, imploring her mother to come to her rescue.

"Why hasn't your father presented you in Paris? You would have been swept off your feet by every eligible bachelor. You are what every man looks for: innocence, yet a smoldering look in your eyes that says you will be . . ."

"Have you met my mother?" Angelique interrupted, pulling Genevieve toward them.

Bouche bowed over Genevieve's hand. "How nice to see you again, Madame. It is not hard to see where your daughter gets her beauty."

"That is very kind of you, Louis. Michel and I are very proud of Angelique. Not only for her beauty, but for her intelligence as well."

My God, she is doing it too, Angelique thought silently. She sounds like she is selling me. "Please excuse me, I see a friend I wish to speak with," Angelique lied, leaving them before her mother could protest.

Stopping to greet a neighbor, Angelique couldn't help but overhear a conversation behind her.

"I'm afraid Michel is going to have his hands full trying to marry off his daughter. She is an absolute beauty, but complicated, intelligent women are such a trial."

Angelique turned and faced the man who had spoken, a sweet smile on her face. "I don't believe we've met, sir, but then, if you're afraid of an intelligent woman, I imagine you've been avoiding me."

The unfortunate man had the decency to turn red and excuse himself, leaving Angelique alone with a tall, dark haired gentleman.

"Complicated, intelligent, and a venomous tongue to boot," he said with a smile that never seemed to reach his eyes.

"Are you also afraid of intelligent women?" she asked.

"Wary, but not afraid," he answered, openly assessing her from head to toe.

"Ah, Andre, I see you have already met my daughter," Michel said as he joined them. "I've just learned something very interesting I hadn't known before," Michel commented to Angelique. "Andre is Damian's stepbrother."

Chapter Three

Damian had guessed correctly. Secretary of the Navy Mallory did want him to go to Europe on a buying mission for ordnance stores and artillery. It seemed ironic that all the things he had suggested—no, begged—the Navy to do a year ago, they were now doing. Unfortunately, in a good many cases, it was too late. The Confederate Army was already feeling the pinch of the blockade. Along with the difficulty of having to bring supplies in from Europe, some of the unscrupulous blockade runners were not very particular when it came to purchasing needed weapons. Sixty thousand Austrian muskets just received were utterly worthless and unfortunately it wasn't the first time this had happened. Mallory gave Damian the impression that he wasn't sure any blockade runner could be trusted. Though Damian preferred staying on the coast running the blockade, if it meant securing decent weapons for the Army, he would go to Europe.

He would make Paris one of his stops this trip. It had been six years since he had seen his mother and brother. Perhaps he'd pay them a visit while there.

His mother . . . strange, how he tried to avoid thinking about her. Would he ever forgive her for deserting him and his father and taking his brother, Adam, from him all those years ago? As a boy he'd gone to France to spend time with them, but he usually ended up spending most of the time with Beau's parents. Then when his father died, his mother had married again, further widening the split between them. The last he had heard, Colette was widowed again and looking for a new husband. He wondered bitterly if there was any justice. She had made so many people's lives miserable, yet she always seemed to find a rich husband to give her everything she wanted. And still his poor father had died calling out her name. God how he hated her, yet he considered himself lucky for the experience; it taught him never to trust a woman, never to leave himself open for that kind of hurt again. He had learned very early in life to use women, and there were always plenty of women like Kate ready and waiting to be used. Why should he ever need a woman for anything else?

The aroma of chicory coffee bought Damian back to the present. He stood for a moment in front of the hotel. Going to France would mean seeing Beau's family and that was a pleasant prospect. The few happy memories he had as a boy involved Chateau

Charbonne.

Beau Charbonne was delighted to hear Damian's plans, as they drank coffee in the hotel dining room. When Damian mentioned that he had decided to leave the *Sorceress* in Tom Steele's capable hands so it could continue its runs, Beau insisted Damian travel back to Europe on the *Petite Marie*.

"I won't take no for an answer! Besides, it's time I went home for a visit. It will be like old times, *mon ami*. France's two most eligible bachelors together again."

Damian laughed, remembering the days when they thought nothing of spending hours going from one whorehouse to another.

Even though the business of war was the reason for the trip, perhaps it would do him good to enjoy Beau's company for awhile. He hadn't been in port longer than twenty-four hours at a time for almost a year. In fact, after a recent run when he had been on his feet so long his boots had to be cut off, Tom Steele had asked wryly if Damian was trying to win the war by himself. Maybe he was. God, it was a frustrating state of affairs, and he knew without a doubt the worst was yet to come.

The South had a lot of brave, dedicated men, but the North had the arms and ammunition. This trip to Europe was an example of the bad situation. If the Europeans decided against helping the South they might as well resort to throwing rocks. Ammunition was becoming that scarce, as well as clothing and food for the men. If every shipload he brought into

Charleston helped, he'd be damned if he'd stay in port longer than he had to. As it was, he probably brought in two shiploads to every one the other blockaders carried. Thank God for his dedicated crew. They all shared his feelings, even though he knew they needed a rest. Maybe this would be a good time to give them a week's leave before they sailed again. The ship could stand a quick overhaul.

"Are you thinking about all those French beauties who have been missing us?" Beau asked, a devilish grin on his handsome face.

"No, I was thinking about everything I have to do before we sail. I need to ride out to Enchanteur this morning. Able was sick the last time I was in port and if anything happens to him I might as well give the plantation to the Yankees right now."

"How about Bessie? Is she still running things at the house?"

"Ah, Bessie. Now there is a woman. Somehow she always knows when I'm in Charleston. I'd be willing to bet you she has cornbread and black-eyed peas ready for me when I get there," Damian said with a look of pride in his eyes. "Then she'll wrap me in those big brown arms and give me a hug that nearly breaks my bones."

"You sound like you're talking about your mother instead of your house servant."

Damian fixed his friend with a cold stare.

"I'm sorry, Damian. I didn't mean that the way it sounded. I know Bessie raised you."

"Bessie was more a mother to me than Colette ever

38

was," he answered bitterly. "I don't know what would have happened to Pa and me if we hadn't had Bessie and Able to look after us. My mother certainly never gave a thought to what it would do to a nine-year old boy to be deserted. I remember many a night Bessie held me when I woke screaming from a bad dream. Oh, hell," Damian swore, slamming his mug on the table. "I seem to be in the mood for reminiscing this morning. I've got to go if I'm going to get everything done. I'll meet you at the ship around midnight."

"Midnight it is, *mon ami*. Don't be late or I'll leave without you."

"I won't be late. I just hope you can get that boiler-maker across the bars of the harbor before the Yankees hear the racket she makes."

"Just wait, Damian. At this very minute the most beautiful ship ever to run the blockade is being built for me."

"Well I just hope you left those damned boilers off her."

"You will see, *mon ami*," was all Beau said, as his gray eyes glowed with the anticipation of his friend's envy.

The sun shone through the green leaves of the oak trees entangled with Spanish moss. Damian brought the horse to a stop and sat looking down the long drive. His father had built the present house, but in 1744 a French settler had planted the thirty-two live oak trees placed in two well-spaced rows. Enchanteur, his father had called the magnificent plantation. It was a shame his mother hadn't found it enchanting. Instead she complained of the heat, the loneliness, the people, the insects, anything to make his father feel guilty for taking her away from France.

Damian slowly rode down the tree-lined drive. One of the slaves trimming the well-kept lawn waved as he passed. Then the house came into view, taking his breath away. It was always such a beautiful sight. The two storied white house was surrounded by twenty-eight classical columns. The house had double doors and double windows to allow the natural flow of air to cool the rooms. The spacious veranda on the lower level and the gallery upstairs offered each room individual cooling and access. Like all great plantations, Enchanteur was a community in itself. A hundred yards behind the great house stood the kitchen, carriage house and a guest cottage for bachelors. Another hundred yards down the lane stood the rows of neat slave cabins, each with the doors and shutters painted in bright colors. The stables, where the Legares always prided themselves on having the best horseflesh raised in the Carolinas, was another fifty yards or so behind the cabins.

Sitting atop his horse, Damian savored the view. The fragrance and sights bedeviled his senses. It was such a beautiful place. Why did he find it so hard to be at peace here?

As Damian had expected, the entire household

staff waited on the steps of the veranda. Bessie, dressed in a gray dress with a white apron, beamed her approval as he stood tall and handsome in front of her.

"Are you going to just stand there, or am I going to get a proper greeting?" Damian asked, mischief in his green eyes.

Bessie threw her arms around Damian, wrapping him in a bear hug. "Boy, you is a sight for dese old eyes. When you missed spring planting we was plumb worried."

"I'm sorry, Bessie. I had no way of sending a message. I've had to make my last several runs into Savannah."

"Is you gonna let dat boy in de house, Bessie, or is you gonna keep him standing on his own front steps all day?" Able grinned, a gold tooth gleaming. "I'se got your favorite brandy waiting in de library, sir."

Damian hugged the gray haired man before following him into the house. While Damian settled in his favorite chair, Able poured the brandy.

"After you enjoy dat drink and relax a bit I have a little somedin cooked up for you," Bessie proudly announced.

"It wouldn't by any chance be cornbread and blackeyed peas, would it?"

"Why, sure it is," she laughed. "Lord knows we doan get much else what with giving so much to de army, but cornbread and peas we got. Now you jus relax and I'll have Tally freshen your room."

"No, don't bother, Bessie. I won't be staying. I

41

have to leave Charleston at midnight tonight."

"But you hasen't been here in months, suh. You need a rest. Why I never seen you with such dark circles under dem eyes."

"I know, Bessie, and hopefully I'll have a chance to rest on my way to Europe. I'm leaving tonight on Beau Charbonne's ship to take care of some government business in England and France. It will probably be midwinter before I return."

"Oh, Lordy, when will dis all end? Killing, starving, families broken up. I jus doan know what is to become of us," Bessie moaned.

"Now don't you worry your head about this war, Bessie. All you need to worry about is Enchanteur."

"Oh I worry about dat too, suh. And if you ain't careful dat Miss Kate gonna try to get her hands on it."

Damian stared at Bessie, a frown creasing his brow. "What are you talking about?"

"Jus last week she rides out here pretty as you please. She says she promised you she would check on de place since she was gonna be its mistress soon."

Damian threw back his head and laughed. "Don't worry about that. She will never be Enchanteur's mistress."

"I'se glad to hear dat. She said de first thing she would do was to sell me and Able."

"Did you tell her you and Able were given your freedom when Father died?"

"She doan care what I say, suh, she was too busy planning."

"Well, as I said, don't worry about her. Enchanteur has survived all these years without a mistress. I see no reason to change that, and you and Able know how I feel about you. You've been parents to me and without you this place would fall apart. Now come on, where are those blackeyed peas?"

Damian was silent as the ship slipped out of Charleston harbor toward the waiting Yankees, its deck piled high with tobacco and cotton bales. The crew crouched behind the rails, waiting any moment to see the flash of Yankee guns. On the bridge, Beau and Damian peered intently into the blackness ahead of them.

"We're over the bar, sir," the pilot whispered.

The ship crept through the darkness, the only sound being the paddle floats, still dangerously loud in spite of their snail's pace. A sudden rumble came as the sky lit up with lightning an instant before rain began to pelt the deck.

"That lightning is as bad as a Drummond light. I hope it doesn't give us away."

"The Yankees usually haul away off shore when the sea gets rough," Damian whispered. "Just don't run into one of them." The lightning flashed again and in that brief moment Damian saw the dark shape of a Federal cruiser.

"Cut the engines," Damian ordered.

Beau, knowing that Damian knew the coast and position of enemy ships like the back of his hand, didn't question the command. The ship rolled silently in the troughs of the waves. When the next bolt of lightning lit the sky they could see the cruiser far off their starboard side.

"Start the engines and proceed slowly," Damian ordered in a whisper.

A muttered order down the engine room tube brought the ship back to life. "Port two points and proceed with caution, Captain," Damian said, grinning at his friend in the darkness. "I'm going to go below to sleep until we get to France."

Storms and high seas were virtually as dangerous to the lightly built blockade runners as an enemy man-of-war, so when Beau, enjoying the first light of dawn, spotted a large side-wheeler about four miles astern in the heavy seas, he was naturally apprehensive. In another hour it would be full daylight and their chance of eluding the Federal ship would be less.

"Get those stokers piling on the fuel," he ordered.

Soon great billows of smoke spouted from the ship's twin stacks and she began to move faster through the choppy seas.

Damian had no more than drifted off when he felt the change in the ship's engines. He made his way up on deck through the busy crew. He didn't have to ask what was going on as he spotted the Federal cruiser closing in on them.

"What do you suggest, Damian? We're pouring everything into her right now."

"Bring her about in the wind. That will force them to do the same."

The other ship followed, but had to take in her sails, as Damian anticipated, and the Confederate ship gained a small advantage.

"We're gaining some, Damian. I just hope these heavy seas don't rip us apart. I don't know what would be worse, rotting in some damned Yankee prison or going to a watery grave."

Relentlessly the Federal cruiser shortened the distance between them. Damian next suggested they jettison the cargo and Beau ordered it done without question. Soon, along with the wake of foam, bobbed a trail of cotton bales worth four hundred dollars each. Relieved of the deck cargo the ship began to gain again. At times she was almost submerged by the green seas that swept her fore and aft. For most of the day they continued the grim cat and mouse game.

"If we can just stay away from them until dark we might be saved," Damian muttered, peering through the spyglass.

"I wonder why she hasn't fired on us? She has been close enough several times," Beau wondered aloud, staring out over the heavy seas.

"The captain is probably afraid his cannon will break loose from the lashings in these heavy seas."

"Captain Charbonne, my engines are going to blow if we don't stop soon and let them cool," Rap, the chief engineer, announced grimly.

"What now, *mon ami*?" Beau asked as Damian studied the skyline.

"Do you think they'll hold out for another thirty

minutes, Rap?" Damian asked.

"Who the hell knows. I thought they'd blow before now. They've been pushed full out for over thirteen hours. I can hear them grinding from up here. Not only that, but even if we do lose that bloody Yankee, we're going to have to stop in Nassau for coal. We've already used in one day what we expected to use in three."

"Damned steamship," Damian mumbled.

"Oh come now, Damian, you've got to admit she's done a fair job of staying ahead of that man-of-war."

"Sure, and if she hadn't been blowing sparks out of her stacks that ship would never have been able to follow us. You should at least be able to go to sails under certain conditions."

Beau's face lit up in a wide grin. "I agree, *mon ami*. I definitely agree."

The strained engines somehow continued to run. The deck flooring was so hot from the enormous strain, Damian could feel the heat through his boots. "Only a few minutes more," he said to himself.

Finally darkness came and the persistent Yankee couldn't be seen.

"Alter our course and lay to the port," Beau ordered. "Tell the chief engineer to get those damned engines cool fast."

The brief halt enabled the engineer and his crew to loosen the bearings and by using all the salad oil from the ship's stores they got them in working order again. After thirty minutes of lying silent, the engines were restored.

"Would you listen to that noise?" Damian exclaimed in exasperation. "If those Yankees are within ten miles, they'll hear us."

"Don't worry about a thing. I can almost smell the flowers of the islands."

Nassau, awakened from centuries of somnolence by the advent of blockade running, was a mixture of paradise and hell. The green islands, covered with poinsettia, hibiscus and bougainvillaea, were a treat to the sight and senses of the visitor. At the docks natives chanted in rhythmic cadence as they unloaded or loaded the ships with cotton that was already piled high on the wharves waiting to be moved.

"I fear the island has been taken over by riff-raff," Beau said with a grin as he watched a group of gaudily dressed young women waving to the ship.

"Yes, and I can see it really bothers you," Damian laughed. "Personally I prefer Bermuda. It doesn't seem quite so decadent."

"Ah, decadent. I love the sound of that word," Beau laughed. "Will you join me tonight for a little immoral activity?"

"Hell, why not? Traveling aboard this ship of yours I may never see France or America again."

It would be three days before the engines could be repaired and the ship stocked with coal and a new cargo of cotton. Beau and Damian decided to take advantage of the time and check into the Royal

Victoria Hotel for a few days of rest and relaxation. The hotel, opened the year before, boasted of bathrooms with water on tap, a glassed enclosed courtyard, and a dining room that would hold one hundred and fifty people. After an elegant dinner, Damian and Beau joined several other blockaders on the portico. They sipped brandy while watching a parade of women dressed in outlandish outfits, obviously showing their wares.

"Lord, would you look at that red-haired beauty?" Beau pointed out anxiously.

Damian turned to look at the woman standing in the doorway. Her startling blue eyes scanned the porch, then she smiled at them.

Beau let out a low whistle. "By God, Damian I think she's coming over here."

"Do you?" Damian asked with a low laugh. "I guess she couldn't resist your handsome face."

Beau was on his feet before the woman reached the table. She smiled at him, then turned her attention to Damian.

"It's so nice to see you again, Damian."

"It's nice to see you too, Lacey. You're looking as lovely as ever."

Beau cleared his throat, trying to attract Damian's attention. "Forgive my manners, this is Beau Charbonne. I'm traveling to Europe aboard his ship. Beau, this is Lacey Jamerson."

"Lacey. What a lovely name for a lovely lady," Beau kissed her hand.

"Oh, I do love Frenchmen," Lucy laughed seductively.

"Won't you join us for a drink, Lacey?" Damian invited.

"I would love to, if you're sure you want my company on your first evening in port?"

"I can't think of a nicer way to spend any evening in port."

"Why, thank you, Damian. I wish there were more gentlemen like yourself." Lacey's attention was drawn past Beau to the doorway of the porch. "Captain Charbonne, would you like me to ask my friend to join us? She's the blonde in the doorway."

"I can see I'm going to have to take second best to Damian, so I may as well meet her," Beau laughed.

A moment later Lacey was introducing Molly Devlin to the two men. Beau quickly forgot his disappointment and was absorbed in Molly's bubbly personality. So absorbed he didn't notice when Damian and Lacey got up to leave.

"You're different than most men," Lacey commented while lying in Damian's arms after their lovemaking.

Damian looked questioningly at her. "How is that, Lacey?"

She ran a long finger over his lips. "You make me feel like someone special. Most men expect a whore to be content with just pleasing them. You go to great extremes to make it really good for me."

"I don't think of you as a whore, Lacey. Maybe that's the difference."

"I thank you for that, Damian. I know you don't approve of what I choose to do, but at least you try to understand me."

"I know you think it is the only thing you could do after what happened, but you're wrong."

Lacey sat up excitedly, pulling the sheet under her chin. "I am going to try something else, Damian. As soon as I save enough money I'm going to open my own dress shop. I had thought about opening it right here in Nassau, but I think I may try Bermuda. I'm told the women there are a little more refined. Listen to me," she laughed. "you'd think I was a lady already."

"You've always been a lady, Lacey. You're the only one who didn't think so."

"Oh, Damian, I don't know what I did to deserve meeting you, but thank you," she said as tears filled her eyes.

Damian pulled her back into his arms. Her long red hair spilled across her white shoulders, making a very tempting picture. He lifted a strand of hair to kiss a pink nipple, then slowly rolled her over, pinning her with his leg while his hand caressed her silken flesh.

"Oh, Damian, if only . . ."

Damian quickly covered her mouth in a silencing kiss as he moved between her legs. When she moved to embrace him, he raised her arms above her head. He began a slow rhythm, teasing her as he moved in and out, denying her the pleasure of touching him, driving her to a frenzy of need as he slowly withdrew from her warmth, then plunged forward again. Lacey tossed her head back and forth on the pillow, trying not to beg for release of the exquisite torture, but she couldn't stand it any longer.

"Damian, please . . ."

"Now, my sweet Lacey?" he asked, his voice teasing, yet deep with desire.

"Yes, now, please," she begged as they both reached the peak together, then lay silently exhausted.

Lacey studied the man lying at her side. She had almost made the terrible mistake of revealing her feelings. She knew she would never see him again if she asked for any kind of commitment. It was enough to see him occasionally when he was on the island. She snuggled closer, running her fingers through the crisp gold hair on his chest. Oh God, who was she kidding? It wasn't enough, but it would have to do. Damian Legare wasn't about to be tied to one woman. Particularly a woman like her.

During the day Damian worked beside the crew, readying the ship for the remaining trip to France. The nights he spent with Lacey. They would sit and talk for hours, discussing politics, books, the war, whatever came to mind, then they would make love long into the night. He found himself dreading the end of this peaceful time. Despite the hard work of the last few days, he felt more rested than he had in a long time. He knew it had a good deal to do with Lacey's undemanding ways.

* * *

Lacey stood on the pier waving goodbye as the *Petite Marie* left the harbor. Damian stayed at the rail until he could no longer see her. He hoped when she discovered he had left her enough money to start that dress shop she wanted that she wouldn't be too proud to accept it.

He hadn't realized Beau stood beside him until he spoke. "Do you ever get tired of being alone? I mean, don't you sometimes wish you had just one woman waiting for you—one woman to come home to?"

"Hell no! You get chained to one woman and she'll use you. Use you until she's drained every last ounce of strength from you, then she'll go on to someone else."

Beau had thought Damian had lost some of the bitterness toward women as he had matured, but apparently the hurt hadn't eased in all these years.

"So you'll spend the rest of your life with whores?"

"At least you know where you stand with them."

"You seemed to enjoy Lacey's company. Not just at night, but during the day, too. I thought maybe there was something between you two."

"Lacey is different. She's very special to me."

"I wonder what makes a woman like her turn to prostitution?"

"I don't know about other women, but I know why Lacey did it. She was a nurse at the Federal prison at Point Lookout. She fell in love with a young Confederate officer who was being held there. When a Union guard got an inkling of the romance he raped Lacey in front of the lieutenant, then killed the man when he tried to stop what was happening. Lacey was then raped by all the guards on duty. Later that night she was found floating in the ocean, clinging to a piece of wood. No one knew if she had been thrown in the sea to drown or if she had tried to kill herself. Anyway, a Confederate patrol boat picked her up and took her to Nassau. She was more dead than alive and it was touch and go whether she would survive—particularly since she didn't care one way or the other. When she was better, no amount of talking could convince her what had happened wasn't her fault. She felt she was ruined and being a whore was the only thing left for her."

"How do you know that isn't just another story these girls make up to excuse what they're doing?" Beau asked.

"I was the captain of that patrol boat," Damian said as he turned and walked away.

Chapter Four

Damian stayed to himself the rest of the trip. Beau learned early in their relationship that it was best to leave him alone when he got in this mood. When they were boys, Damian's hurt at being deserted by his mother had taken the form of anger; often times violent anger. Then as Damian grew older he began to keep his feelings inside. Beau wondered if the outbursts of anger weren't better for his friend.

Beau strained to see through the fog. They should see the coast of Brittany soon. God, it would be good to see his family. Again he thought of Damian. How sad it was that his friend had no one to call family. His mother and brother were mere acquaintances. If only Damian could find someone to care for, someone who would care for him. But, how was that going to happen when Damian wouldn't let himself get involved with any woman?

"You're in very deep thought, my friend."

"Ah, Damian. I was just thinking this would be the first time we've been to Crozon together in a long time."

"I was thinking that myself. I believe the last time was six years ago. Angelique was twelve then."

"Yes, and we were two sophisticated, worldly men of nineteen," Beau laughed.

"Sophisticated? Then you forget what we did to *l'enfant* while she was giving a piano recital."

"How could I forget? I'll never forget the expression on Angelique's face when that mouse perched on top of the piano."

"And as usual, she turned the tables on us. We should have known she wouldn't be afraid of any four-legged creature."

"But still, the expression on her angelic face was priceless." Beau started laughing. "Do you remember the time she stole our clothes while we were swimming?"

Damian threw back his head in laughter. "I remember. I also remember it was you and I who got a taste of your father's belt when we chased her back to the Chateau *au natural*." Suddenly Damian became serious. "It will be good to see your family and *l'enfant* again."

"*L'enfant*, as you call her, has changed a great deal. I think you'll be pleasantly surprised."

"I find it difficult to think of her as anything but the brat who followed us around."

"When I left here last spring *Maman* was preparing to introduce Angelique to society. They had decided it was time someone else tried to, shall we say, control her."

"I pity the poor man," Damian laughed. "He certainly will have his hands full if she is still the same headstrong girl I remember."

Beau suddenly had a strange gleam in his eyes. "Yes, he'll have to be a very strong personality to handle her."

"Land ho!" came the call from the lookout.

Beau held the spyglass to his eye and scanned the rocky coastline. "There she is, Damian."

Damian scanned the cliffs, then spotted the chateau. It resembled a small medieval castle, standing like a feudal fortress on the craggy coast. Its dark stone walls and slate roof seemed to warn intruders away, yet inside Damian knew there was always warmth. Warmth from a warm, loving family. That was something that was always lacking at Enchanteur. No matter how beautiful the place was, it never seemed warm and homey, he thought bitterly.

The two men jumped on the back of a farmer's wagon and made the trip up the long hillside, waving and shouting to neighbors and acquaintances along the way. At the chateau, Genevieve Charbonne greeted Damian as warmly as her own son.

"My second son," she said affectionately. "Michel will be so happy to see you. We are always hearing of the exploits of Damian Legare, the famous blockade runner. I fear you and Beau both take too many chances. I don't know why you young men feel such need for excitement."

"Unlike me, Damian doesn't do it for excitement, *Maman*. He does it to help the Southern cause in its fight for independence. All the money he makes he gives to charity."

Genevieve stared at Damian with tears in her eyes. "You have always been such a fine young man, Damian. Your mother must be very proud."

Damian stared at her silently, then laughed awkwardly. "Yes, I'm sure. Now tell me, where is Angelique? I keep hearing about how lovely she is."

"Ah, that girl! She is at the caretaker's cottage treating a sick lamb. She will be home soon. Come, you must be famished. I'll have Marie fix something to hold you until this evening."

Damian and Beau were like young boys back in the element they enjoyed so much. For Damian, being at Chateau Charbonne was the only time he had been able to be a boy. He had loved his father dearly, yet Philip Legare had been a stern disciplinarian, expecting his son to learn and work as hard as he did. It made an extremely hard life for a young boy, yet he always tried to please his father. Even when Enchanteur became a prosperous plantation, with many slaves Damian never seemed to find time for frivolities.

"We were reminiscing about some of the pranks we played as children," Beau said between bites of cheese.

"Oh yes, I remember quite well the devil you boys

played. I remember also how you got that scar in your eyebrow," Genevieve touched Damian's face.

"*Maman*," Beau sternly reprimanded. "Don't bring up such things!"

"I had forgotten how Beau tried to kill me," Damian laughed. "If I remember correctly he was trying to show off for his cousin, Lael."

"Yes, and I remember how she rushed to you when you started bleeding," Beau interrupted with a snort. "I never have understood why a woman always goes to the defeated."

"She always did have good taste," Damian winked at Genevieve. "She knew which one of us was really the best."

"The best, hell!" Beau swore, then turned to his mother. "Forgive me, *Maman*. I forgot myself, but if this oafish Colonial thinks he can fence better than a true son of France, then I must challenge him." Beau was on his feet, stuffing the last piece of bread in his mouth while he danced around the table wielding an imaginary foil.

"Madame Charbonne," Damian bowed over her hand. "You must excuse us. I'm going to have to show your son what an oafish Colonial can do with a foil. If you're squeamish about the sight of blood," he winked at her, "I suggest you stay here."

"Now boys, do be careful," Genevieve called after the two men. "Be sure to wear the padded protectors."

"Is Beau really here?" Angelique asked, totally

out of breath from running halfway home. "Sims said he saw the ship in the harbor."

"Yes, my dear, he is here, and Damian Legare is with him."

Angelique's heart gave a leap. Damian . . . she hadn't seen him in six years. What would he be like now, she wondered. "Oh, look at me, *Maman.* I look a fright. I must get cleaned up. Where are they now?"

"Calm yourself, Angelique. They are on the terrace fencing, both of them acting quite insane."

"Fencing?" Angelique repeated breathlessly, her eyes lighting up with devilment. "Perhaps I will wait just a while before getting cleaned up," she called over her shoulder as she hurried toward the fencing equipment.

"Angelique, please remove those terrible breeches," Genevieve called after her.

Angelique tucked her long black hair into a bun and carefully donned the fencing mask. The black cloth covered her face and the top of her head and the white bib covered her throat. She adjusted the oversized vest, making sure her feminine figure was not too obvious.

Damian and Beau, both acting like idiots, were unaware of her presence. Damian had his back to her, retreating from Beau's attack when Beau noticed the fencer. He realized instantly it was Angelique.

"*En garde,*" Angelique commanded as deeply as she could.

Beau bowed and moved aside, leaving the new

opponent to face Damian.

"What the hell?" Damian swore, while sidestepping a skilled parry.

"You best do as *he* says, Damian. I'm told *he's* an expert."

Damian's opponent moved gracefully about him, perfecting a balestra while he counter-parried. They moved slowly as Damian discovered the rhythm of his opponent, then he feinted to evade a parry, their foils coming up and crossing in front of them. Damian was sure in these close quarters he could smell the scent of sweet flowers. He looked beyond his opponent to Beau, who was leaning casually against the steps, a grin splitting his face from ear to ear.

Something was amiss. "Angelique?" he inquired, as she disengaged her blade and swiftly stepped backward.

Angelique laughed as she tossed the mask aside, letting her black hair cascade around her shoulders. "Who did you think it was?" she asked jumping into his arms like she did when they were children. Damian twirled her around before they both fell to the floor laughing. He studied her, slowly taking in the violet eyes and black hair the color of a raven's wing. She wore riding breeches that showed long, slender legs, and a silk blouse open at the collar.

Damian looked up at an amused Beau. "It's not possible that such an ugly child turned into this beautiful ruffian."

"What do you mean—ugly child?" she asked punching him in the ribs.

Damian laughed. "One thing is for certain, Beau, she's still as mean as ever."

Angelique wrapped her arms around Damian's neck as they sat on the floor. "Why haven't you been back to see me? It's been six years."

"I stopped here four years ago, but you were away terrorizing the nuns at the convent."

"Oh, what a terrible thing to say," she pouted. "Do I look like I could terrorize anyone?" she queried, looking her most innocent.

Damian kissed her playfully on the lips, but the air suddenly bristled with electricity. He stared into her violet eyes, feeling as if he were lost in them.

Angelique felt foolishly flushed and confused. This was Damian, her brother's best friend whom she had known all her life. Why did she feel so strange?

"I don't want to interrupt anything," Beau said from above them, "but I would think you'd have a hug for your brother too."

Angelique forced herself to leave the warmth of Damian's arms and greeted her brother with a kiss and hug. "I'm so happy to see you both. It's like old times."

"Yes, and I can see you still plan to torment Damian and me like you always did."

"Torment? How dare you!" She grabbed her foil and faced her brother. "Be prepared to back up that insult!"

"Now hold on, Angelique," Damian interrupted, quickly getting to his feet. "I'm sure Beau only meant that in a loving way."

Beau and Angelique looked at each other, then began to laugh. "Nothing has changed after all these years," Beau said. "Damian is still playing the peacemaker."

The three laughed together and sat back down to discuss old times. When Angelique mentioned leaving to get cleaned up, Damian found he was reluctant to let her part their company.

"Tell me, Angelique, are you still treating all the sick animals in France?" he asked hoping to keep her beside him.

"All that come to my attention, Damian. Do you have one that needs my attention?"

"No, I just remembered how you took care of all the creatures. Beau tells me you still play the piano. Will you play for me soon?" he asked, his behavior surprising even himself. What in the world was the matter with him? He sounded like a fool.

"She doesn't just play, Damian. She is a virtuoso. M'sieur Valaine wanted Papa to let her go on a concert tour, but Papa wouldn't hear of it. He felt it wasn't proper for a young lady to be performing."

Damian studied Angelique while Beau spoke. He could tell from her suddenly drawn expression that she had wanted to perform.

"I'm sorry, Angelique," he said taking her hand. "I still hope you'll play for me."

Angelique attempted to make light of the situation, even though her heart was beating too rapidly. "If you promise there will be no mice."

"Don't promise anything, Damian," Beau

laughed. "If you do, we'll be at her mercy."

Angelique stood to leave. "Ah, but what you do not realize, my dear brother, is you are already at my mercy. Be sure you look in your bed before climbing in, and don't walk in any dark hallways," she laughed as she left the two men.

"My God, she is beautiful," Damian sighed.

"Easy, *mon ami*. Remember what a headstrong brat she can be," Beau warned, even though he was delighted at Damian's reaction to Angelique. What a pair they would make, he thought.

Damian leaned casually against the marble fireplace while he listened to Michel Charbonne discussing the ship he was building for Beau. Any other time Damian would have been glued to his every word, but tonight he kept thinking about Angelique. He smiled to himself as he thought of his old nickname for her. It certainly didn't fit any longer. She may still be a child in many ways, but she was also a woman in many ways.

Damian's attention was drawn to the top of the long wooden staircase as he heard feminine voices. His intake of breath was loud enough for all to hear.

Beau smiled at the expression on Damian's face as Angelique descended the stairs beside her mother. Her long black hair floated in a dark cloud around her shoulders, held only with a velvet ribbon. She wore a dress of lavender velvet trimmed with deep purple ribbon.

Angelique smiled at her brother, but then her violet eyes settled on Damian in a warm smile. She noticed, with admiration, the way his black velvet jacket stretched across his wide shoulders. "It is so wonderful to have everyone we love here," she smiled warmly.

"Does not Damian look wonderful, Michel?" Genevieve asked her husband.

"Yes, and, I must say, I'm surprised. After hearing of some of his exploits I was sure he would have a patch over one eye and carry a sword on his hip."

Damian laughed warmly. "I don't know what you've heard to make you think that. I do the same thing Beau does—only better."

Everyone laughed at Beau's feigned expression of insult, but dinner was announced before he had a chance to retort.

The meal was served in the large, darkly paneled dining room. Every candelabra was lit, flickering over the dark carved oak furniture, and a fire had been built in the hearth, giving the large room a cozy feeling.

The Charbonnes had many servants and even a family dinner was treated as a special affair. The first course consisted of a creamy potato and leek soup. After these dishes were cleared, platters of game hens and succulent roast beef were served on beds of wild rice with baby peas and mushrooms. Chateau Charbonne had its own vineyards and the wines served were renowned all over France.

Damian sat quietly enjoying the warm, wonderful

family atmosphere. This was the only family he had ever known. Michel Charbonne had taught him to love ships and the sea, and Genevieve had taught him to love good music and good books. Bitterly, he thought that the only thing his family had given him was Enchanteur, and sometimes he wondered if that hadn't been a curse. He loved the place, yet it was there he felt the loneliest. Perhaps if Enchanteur had a family like the Charbonne's . . . he mused. His eyes went back to Angelique. God, she had turned into a beauty. Her ebony hair hung in waves contrasting with her ivory skin. Her mouth was pink and begged to be kissed—and those eyes . . . what would it be like to teach her to be a woman and watch the wonderment in those pools of purple velvet.

"Damian, did you hear what I said?"

Damian quickly forced his attention back to Genevieve.

"How long will you be able to stay with us, dear," she repeated.

"A week, if you can put up with me that long. I have business in Paris I must take care of after that."

Damian glanced back toward Angelique. His eyes held hers from a moment, then she demurely looked away.

"Will you be visiting your mother while you're in Paris?" Michel asked.

Damian's smile froze on his face, but he forced an agreeable answer. "Yes, I plan to."

"We will be traveling to Paris next week for Angelique to be fitted for her trousseau. Perhaps you could travel with us."

The silence in the room was deafening. Angelique was unnerved by the look in Damian's eyes as he stared at her. She lifted her wine glass, but her hand trembled too much for her to take a drink.

"Didn't you know, Damian?" Genevieve asked.

"How could Damian know when I didn't know?" Beau asked abruptly. "It would be nice if I were kept informed of family matters."

"I'm sorry, son. You've been away so long. I thought perhaps Damian knew since Angelique's fiancé is his step-brother, Andre LaFrancois."

Damian couldn't tear his eyes from Angelique's face. Tears filled her eyes, making them look like pools of violet water.

"Surely you remember, Beau, that Angelique was being prepared for her introduction to society before you left," Michel continued. "She had many offers, but we felt Andre would suit her best."

Damian was silent as Beau began a furious tirade. Beau was fond of his sister, but it seemed to Damian there was something more to his protest. Perhaps Beau knew the chosen man and didn't like him. He was ignorant about this step-brother. He hadn't even known his mother had remarried again.

Genevieve tried unsuccessfully to change the subject, but Beau persisted. Finally Damian, unable to stand the look of pain on Angelique's face any longer, interrupted.

"Beau, this is very unpleasant for Angelique. Perhaps you should discuss this with your parents later."

Beau looked at his sister for the first time. "I'm sorry, Angelique. It's just that I had hoped . . . I just want the best for you, sweet."

"I know, Beau, and I thank you," she answered, her face flushed. "If you will excuse me, I believe I will get a breath of fresh air."

"Angelique, put on your cape and take Aimee with you," her mother called.

"I'll go with her and let you continue your family discussion," Damian suggested as he followed Angelique from the room. She had already disappeared through the door, alone and without a cape.

"Aimee, please get Mademoiselle a wrap," Damian requested of her maid. A moment later she returned with a warm velvet cape.

Damian walked out onto the terrace and found Angelique standing at one end, her back to him. The late summer evening was cool and crisp with the smell of fall in the air.

"You shouldn't be out here without this," Damian said placing the cape around her shoulders. Angelique was silent as he turned her to face him and fastened the hook under her chin.

"I am no longer a child, Damian."

"I'm quite aware of that, little one, but even grown women are susceptible to colds."

When Damian had finished, Angelique moved away and leaned against the rock wall. Even in the dark Damian could see her eyes glistening with tears.

"Are you all right, Angelique?"

"Yes, I'm just tired. So much has happened so

quickly. A month ago I had nothing on my mind other than playing the piano and tending my animals. Then suddenly I'm dressed like a princess and put on display for everyone to inspect. I tell you, Damian, I felt like a horse up for auction."

"Are you happy with the arrangement your family has made?"

"I don't know if I'm happy or not. I've only met the man twice. At least he is young. At one time my parents mentioned Louis Bouche, and he's almost sixty years old."

Angelique looked up at Damian and forced a smile. "Oh, Damian, I'm so glad you're here. I haven't had anyone to talk to."

"You do now, bright eyes," he said, playfully tweaking her nose. "We'll talk all night long if you want to."

"I'm not going to think about anything but having you and Beau here for a whole week. We'll go riding, and sailing, and we can walk on the beach." Suddenly Angelique's eyes filled with tears again. "I've got to make this week last a lifetime. I probably won't ever see you again, Damian."

Damian wanted to take her in his arms and tell her that now he'd found what a ravishing beauty she was that he wanted her with him, but he couldn't do that. "Tell me more about this concert tour you wanted to go on."

Angelique wiped the back of her hand across her eyes in a childlike gesture. "Oh, Damian, it would have been wonderful. M'sieur Valaine said we would tour all of Europe performing at the best concert halls. M'sieur was sure the King would invite me to play. He said I could take Aimee, but Papa wouldn't even listen to him. Papa said it was time I was married and had children."

Angelique looked up into Damian's soft gaze. "Why is it always what they want, Damian? I'm so tired of people telling me what to do."

Damian took her slender hand and brought it to his mouth, tenderly kissing the palm. "You're a woman, my pet, and a woman is born to be taken care of. First by her parents, then by her husband. Your father only wants what is best for you."

Angelique angrily pulled her hand away. "Oh . . . oh, damn!" she sputtered. "I thought you would be different, but you're just like the rest of them. I may have been born a woman, but I was also born with a brain. Why won't anyone let me use it?"

"Whoa, little one," Damian said placing his hands on her shoulders. "Why should there be anything wrong with a man wanting to take care of you?" He regarded her with mock censure for a moment, then gave up and laughed at her pouting expression. "You are so utterly charming. Any man who wouldn't want to take care of you would have to be dead."

"Do you want to take care of me, Damian?"

Damian was silent for a long moment. "You're a very special young lady," he said thinking to placate her.

"And you're a hypocrite! Do you think I haven't noticed the way you've been looking at me? As I said, Damian, I'm not stupid! Now you will excuse me."

Angelique stormed past Beau as he came through the door. He glanced back over his shoulder, letting out a low whistle. "I'm afraid I put her in a foul mood. Am I wrong to want the best for her?" he asked Damian. "She is such a special person."

"She has always been very special," Damian agreed as he lit a cheroot. "And no, I don't think it is wrong of you to want the best for her, but she hasn't actually said she doesn't want to marry LaFrancois."

"I wish we knew more about him," Beau mused.

"I'm sorry I can't help you. I didn't even know my mother had married again," Damian answered bitterly.

Beau turned and studied his friend. "You know, Damian, Angelique needs a strong man—a self-assured man who can accept a wife who is smart and talented. The little brat can actually outride and outshoot me, and I can tell you it's hard on the ego."

Damian laughed. "Where in the hell will you find a man like that?"

"Oh, I've found him," Beau smiled. "The problem is getting him to come around before it is too late." Beau pushed off the wall and stretched. "I think I'll retire now. I'm sure Angelique has big plans for us tomorrow."

Damian grabbed Beau by the arm. "Surely you're not thinking that I'm the man for Angelique?" Beau said nothing. "If you are, you're out of your mind." Beau still just smiled. "By God, no matter what this step-brother of mine is like, he has to make a better husband for Angelique than I would. I live a life of decadence—at my own choosing. My lust is serviced by whores. How could you even think I would make Angelique a good husband?" Damian continued, staring unbelieving at his friend. "You of all people know I can't—no, I won't let a woman get close to me. I'd make her life miserable."

"Simmer down, Damian. Did I say anything about it being you?" he smiled. "I'd have to be crazy to want you for a brother-in-law."

Chapter Five

Damian joined Beau and Michel Charbonne who were already having breakfast in the dining room. Damian was dressed in dark brown riding breeches tucked in rich cordovan leather boots and a loose fitting muslin shirt with full sleeves cuffed at the wrist.

"Good morning," Beau greeted cheerfully. "I see you got Angelique's message that we are to go riding this morning."

Damian laughed as he piled his plate high from the selection of food on the sideboard. "Yes, Aimee was at my door bright and early to give me the message."

"Good morning," Angelique greeted from the doorway. "Isn't it a beautiful morning?"

Damian was relieved to see no sign of last night's sorrow. She seemed happy enough, he thought—and beautiful in a forest green velvet riding habit.

Angelique took a cup of tea and a muffin and sat across from Damian. Now that she was closer he could see her eyes were red-rimmed from crying.

"I've asked Sims to saddle a new stallion that we've acquired. I think he will suit you," she agreed between bites.

"That will be fine," he said, studying her closely.

"I've also asked cook to fix a picnic lunch. It's so beautiful today, I thought we might take advantage of it," she suggested, looking from Beau to Damian.

"That sounds wonderful, but I have to stop at Jacques' cottage first," Beau announced. "He has been working on some special equipment for the ship and I want to check on his progress. It won't take long. Why don't you and Damian take in the sights for a bit and I'll meet you at the cove later?"

"If that's agreeable with you, Damian, we'll leave right after breakfast."

Damian stood with his mouth hanging open as Angelique mounted her horse like a man. She laughed at his expression.

"Before you say anything, just imagine how it would be to ride a horse side-saddle."

"I don't imagine it is very comfortable."

"No, it isn't. That is why I had my seamstress split my riding skirt and sew it into two sections. Now I can mount comfortably and ride with a little dignity."

"You haven't changed a bit," Damian laughed.

"Your prospective husband is going to have his hands full."

Angelique stared at Damian as if he had suddenly turned into a two-headed monster. She spurred her horse and galloped out of the stable yard leaving Damian and Sims, the trainer, looking after her.

"She's been a bit touchy lately, sir," Sims said. "I think talk of her marriage spooked her."

"Yes, I suppose you're right," Damian agreed, urging the big black stallion to follow Angelique's mare.

Damian quickly brought his horse alongside of her. They rode in silence for a long while, not slowing down until they neared the cliffs. Damian turned in his saddle and studied her face, but she pretended to concentrate on the scenery.

"Isn't the view magnificent, Damian?" she exclaimed looking over the coast where mauve granite cliffs jutted up from the ocean, some with flowers growing in their protected lee. "Sometimes I feel I'd like to set sail and let the sea just take me. Do you ever feel that way?"

"Often," Damian smiled warmly.

"Has Beau told you about this new and wonderful ship of his?"

"Just that it's unique," Damian answered, knowing she was trying too hard to be gay and cheerful.

"Perhaps tomorrow we will go to the ship works and see it. Do you remember the deserted monastery where we thought we saw ghosts?"

"How could I forget? You came flying out of there

74

so fast one time you knocked me over."

"Shall we see if there are any spirits still there?" she asked, urging her horse to a gallop.

A few minutes later they halted before a deserted gray church. The belfry, still reaching skyward was crumbling, yet beautiful stained glass windows were still intact.

Damian slid from his horse and raised his arms to help Angelique. "Are you sure you want to go exploring? This place gave you nightmares when you were a child."

Angelique's eyes held a dreamy look. "I've come back here often since then, Damian. I even spoke with a beautiful spirit once."

"Oh, come now, gamin," he protested, ruffling her hair.

"I did, Damian. I talked to her for a long time." Suddenly Angelique had a mischievous glint in her violet eyes. "Only she was in the body of a cat so she couldn't answer," she said over her shoulder as she dashed toward the church.

"You little devil," Damian shouted. "You sound like your brother now, telling stories of meeting Merlin the sorcerer in the forest."

Angelique stopped and faced him. "Don't make light of that, Damian. Beau truly believes it. Besides, it is said that King Arthur's knights came to Brittany in search of the Holy Grail, which supposedly lies in the Forest of Paimpont where Merlin made his home. So it isn't really that unlikely. Come on," she grabbed Damian's hand. "Let's see if we can find the cat."

An hour later, after exploring the ruins of the church, Damian and Angelique sat on the rocks overlooking a field of autumn wildflowers and heather.

"What is America like?" Angelique asked, as she sat with her arms wrapped about her knees. "Is it anything like Brittany?"

"There are places very much like Brittany's coastal area, but there aren't any old towns or ruins. America is still new and growing. Every man still has a chance to make a good life for himself."

"And every woman?" she questioned.

"I think women are pretty much the same. You'd be considered headstrong and stubborn even there."

Angelique looked across the field, saying nothing.

"Don't scowl. I was only teasing," he said flipping a black curl from her shoulder.

"I'm not scowling. I just wondered why a man says he likes a woman with spirit and yet does everything he can to break her."

Damian affectionately covered her hands with his large one. "I would hate to see you ever lose your spirit, bright eyes. I'm sure whoever you marry will have his hands full, but he'll love every minute of it."

"Humph . . . whomever I marry," she muttered beneath her breath. "Beau will probably be at the cove by now. Shall we ride on?"

"Have I offended you again?" he asked, puzzled as he gave her a hand up.

"Was it your intention to offend me?" she asked, one dark eyebrow raised.

"Never," he grinned. "I only live to see your violet eyes sparkle with laughter as I know they can."

"Oh, Damian," she laughed. "I'm so glad you're here. You make me feel so good. Have I told you this morning how handsome you look?"

"Is that your way of fishing for a compliment?" he mocked with laughter in his eyes. "Now I suppose I must tell you how beautiful you are?"

"Only if you want to—and truly mean it," she said, her eyes suddenly a deep purple.

"I do mean it, Angelique. You are so beautiful it takes my breath away."

Angelique could feel the heat rising in her face. "Come on, I'll race you back to the cliffs," she said, touching the mare with her heels.

Angelique rode leaning well forward over her gray mare, her black hair flying in the wind. The cliffs were in sight before the stallion passed her. When she brought the mare to a halt, Damian was waiting, his knee resting on the pommel of his saddle.

"What took you so long?"

"I'll have to remember to tell Sims to give you a slower horse," she laughed, her face flushed and vibrant, "or else I'll have to try that great, black stallion myself."

"He's a fine horse," Damian caressed the side of the stallion's neck.

"His name is Surcouf, for the famous Breton pirate who fought the English and Spanish."

"Surcouf the Pirate," Damian said stroking the horse. "It seems to suit him."

"And you," she said, a gleam in her violet eyes. "A pirate horse for a pirate man."

"You flatter me," Damian grinned. "I'm not a pirate, just a blockade runner. I've never plundered a ship for gold or jewels. Now, maybe for a beautiful, passionate woman a time or two, but never gold or jewels."

"Damian!" Angelique gasped. "I don't want to hear about your sordid life."

"Sordid life?" Damian laughed.

"Oh, stories of your exploits have made the rounds here for several years. Lael always has a new tale to tell me when she comes to visit."

"I thought you didn't want to hear about my sordid life," he teased.

"Well not from you, anyway."

"Why would anyone in France be interested in my life?" he questioned.

"*My dear Damian*, besides being a son of France, your mother is a duchess, so anything you do makes good gossip. Now come on, we're wasting time. If we don't picnic in the cove before long, the tide will be in."

Angelique clambered down the precarious path on the cliffside, holding onto the jagged rocks for support.

"Are you sure this is where we used to climb as children?" Damian asked from above her. "I don't remember it being this steep."

"Have you gotten soft, Damian?"

"Hey, I'm a pirate captain, remember. I have men

to do my hard work."

"Yes, I know," she said dropping to the white strip of sand at the base of the cliff. "You probably stay aboard your fancy ship entertaining the beautiful women you capture while your men do all the hard work."

Damian dropped beside her, his eyes gleaming mischievously. "Ah, but, my little one, none of them are as lovely or delectable as you."

Angelique's face reddened and she quickly walked away. "I wonder where Beau is?"

Damian settled himself on the sand, using a large boulder for a backrest. He watched Angelique walk along the beach, careful to avoid the waves. The wind whipped her hair, framing her face with wild, unruly curls. She closed her eyes and raised her arms skyward, taking a deep breath. Then she turned and slowly walked to where Damian lay.

"What were you thinking out there, Angelique?"

Angelique looked back toward the waves as they broke on the rocks. "I was wondering why things have to change. We were all so happy here."

"People have to change just as the tide does, little one."

"Are you happy, Damian?"

Her question caught him off guard. "I'm not sure I know what happiness is," he said, looking away from her.

"You lecture me on marriage, but you haven't married. Why, Damian?"

"I'm not the marrying kind," he laughed bitterly.

"How do you know? Tell me, Damian, so I will have some answers. I don't think I'm the marrying kind either, but no one will listen to me. I know I won't be happy in Paris. I have no one there except Lael and Tante Madeleine."

Damian turned and placed his hands on her shoulders. "You will have a husband who will surely adore you, and later you will have children to love."

Angelique's dark lashes fanned downward over her cheeks. Damian lifted her chin and stared into pools of violet. "I believe a man could lose his soul in those eyes," he whispered.

Angelique's heart was beating with a dizzying quickness at Damian's nearness. Why couldn't he see it was him she wanted. She wanted his children. "Kiss me, Damian," she begged, her hands tentatively moving to rest on his chest. His heart pounded against the palm of her hand. She could see the tension in his eyes and knew he was fighting with his conscience.

"Damian," she whispered, moving even closer. She stood on her toes and brushed her lips across his mouth, once, twice. He took a ragged breath before his hands grasped her hair and molded her body to his. He returned her kisses, a series of hard nips, then his lips parted over hers. His tongue teased the inner mouth, sending a wave of tremors through her body. He moaned something unintelligible, his breathing heavy.

Damian was fighting to get himself under control, but he was finding it difficult. She fit against him as if she was made for him. Her kisses, though innocent, were eagerly wanton. God, how he wanted her—but her family—Beau . . .

It was sheer torture, but he pulled away, smiling down into her eyes. He knew he had to handle this carefully. "Are you practicing your feminine wiles on me, Angelique?" he asked in a teasing tone.

A look of pain crossed her eyes, but before she could answer Beau called to them from above.

"Hey, down there. Did you save me any food?"

Angelique pulled away from Damian, but he captured one hand. "You are beautiful and desirable, little one, but . . ."

"And you are a fool, Damian," she said extricating her fingers from his. "It's about time you showed up," she shouted to Beau.

"I'm sorry," he said dropping to the sand, "I got tied up looking over plans." He looked from Damian to Angelique with a questioning look in his eyes. "Is everything all right?"

"Yes, of course," Angelique laughed. "Now, the two of you sit down and I shall spread this luscious repast for us. I know Damian must be starved," she continued gaily, almost feverish. "I've dragged him all over the place this morning. We went to the monastery. Do you remember the monastery, Beau?"

Damian stared at the violet-eyed beauty kneeling in front of him. What in the world was the matter with him? You don't trifle with a girl like Angelique unless you were prepared to . . .

"Won't you try a beef pie, Damian?" she asked

sweetly. "Cook makes such good ones."

The trio spent the rest of the afternoon exploring the beach and later an almost forgotten cave that led back to Chateau Charbonne. Angelique's sparkling chatter had turned to silence as the afternoon wore on. Damian felt her eyes on him many times when they stopped to talk. What was she thinking, he wondered, and what would have happened if Beau hadn't shown up?

That evening after dinner the family sat in the music room as Angelique prepared to play. The candelabra on the piano cast her in a gold light and Damian couldn't take his eyes off her even though he politely conversed with Genevieve. Beau whispered something in Angelique's ear and she laughed softly, smiling in Damian's direction.

"You did promise there would be no repeat of that mouse in the piano," she reminded Damian.

"I've never known you to be afraid of anything."

Angelique's eyes suddenly saddened. "Then I have become an accomplished actress," she said, lightly running her long fingers over the keys. "I thought I would start with some Chopin."

She began with a berceuse, a soft lilting lullaby that lulled the audience, then she went into a haunting polonaise with a melody that wove a spell over everyone. Damian was entranced as the music built to a crescendo, reverberating to the very core of his body. He couldn't take his eyes off her face. She was entranced by the music, her delicate hands moving over the keys as if they had a mind of their own.

When she finished, the room suddenly seemed cold and still. No one moved or said a word for a long moment.

"Papa, I think you've made a mistake," Beau observed. "I have never heard anyone play as well as Angelique."

"I have to agree, sir," Damian said, finally tearing his eyes from Angelique's face.

"I agree that Angelique has a gift, but she will use that gift to entertain her husband and children."

"But Papa," Beau persisted, "how can you deprive . . ."

"I don't want to hear any more, Beau. I will not have my daughter living out of a suitcase as she travels about the world like a gypsy. Now the subject is closed."

"Please excuse me," Angelique said, trying to hold back her tears. "I'm very tired."

While Beau argued with his father, Damian followed her from the music room. "Angelique, wait. Don't go to your room just yet. Why don't you get your cape and walk in the garden with me?"

"I don't think so, Damian . . ."

"The fresh air will make you feel better."

"All right," she smiled, "but just for a few minutes."

A few minutes later Angelique joined Damian. In the lee of the chateau there was a walled orchard of twisted apple trees and sheltered flower beds. They walked silently, slowly among the trees. Even the deep blue sky, the velvet background of billions of glittering stars, went unnoticed.

Damian wasn't sure what to say. Now that he had heard Angelique play he better understood her disappointment in not being allowed to pursue her musical talent. If she were a man there would be no question. But she wasn't a man, he told himself. She was a very beautiful, very desirable woman, that could definitely lead to problems if she went on tour. What the hell was he doing worrying about this anyway? It had nothing to do with him. Her father was quite capable of knowing what was best.

"I was playing for you tonight, Damian," she spoke so softly he wasn't sure he heard. Damian stopped walking. Angelique stood so close he could feel the warmth from her body.

"Were you, little one? It was beautiful, truly beautiful."

"Do you think my husband will appreciate my talent?" she asked bitterly.

For some reason unknown to Damian, he felt anger at the thought of her playing for anyone else. He pulled her to him by the shoulders. "Angelique, if there were anything I could do to help you, you know I would."

"Yes, I know you would, Damian," she agreed softly. "I'm sorry to keep complaining and worrying everyone. I'm sure when I get to know Andre I shall be happier with the situation. At the end of the week we will travel to Paris. Perhaps then I will have a chance to know him better."

"Yes, perhaps you will," Damian dropped his hands from her shoulders, as they slowly moved down the path again.

"I guess I've worried everyone with my anxiety. Poor *Maman* looks so distraught most of the time. I don't mean to worry her. I know she and Papa have always considered me to be headstrong and independent, but this time I can't help being apprehensive. It's the first time I've ever felt as if I had no control over my life. Does that make any sense, Damian?" she asked as she stopped and looked up into his face.

"Of course it does. I imagine everyone is apprehensive before they marry," Damian said, running his thumb along her jawline.

"It isn't just that, Damian. I've never known a man's touch—or a man's kiss—until yours today."

Damian was sure his heart stopped for a moment. He could feel the warmth of her body, smell the delicate scent of her perfume and it was driving him insane. He wanted to take her in his arms and teach her about a man's touch, not just a simple kiss, but God, he couldn't. This was Angelique, his best friend's sister—the child he had always thought of as a sister. He had already gone too far with her.

"Come on, little one, it's time I got you back inside."

Damian lay in the dark staring at the ceiling. He couldn't understand the emotions he was feeling. He just needed a woman, he told himself. Maybe he should go to Paris. No, he had told the Charbonnes he would escort them. What was it Angelique had said, he mused—she wanted to make this week last a lifetime? He couldn't disappoint her.

He smiled to himself in the darkness. How could one so innocent have such a depth of passion in those violet eyes. He felt an ache in his groin as he remembered the way her lips had parted under his, and the way her sweet body had molded itself to him. When she had looked up at him afterward her eyes were as deep a purple as he had ever seen.

His stepbrother was a lucky man, he thought bitterly. If it were ever in me to love someone . . . "Jesus, what am I thinking of?" he said aloud as he bolted from the bed. He lit a cheroot then stood at the window overlooking the courtyard. "It isn't in you to love, fool! You have to have been loved to know the emotion."

He desired Angelique, that much he admitted to himself, but that was all. A woman like Angelique would expect much more than a few passionate moments—and that was all he had to offer. She'd end up finding some dandy who would whisper sweet words to her and then she'd leave him without a second thought. No, a whore was what he needed to ease his ache. Not a woman who would want to possess him body and soul.

Damian finally returned to bed, determined to go into the village tomorrow and find a tavern wench to ease his needs. He was sure he would feel differently toward Angelique after that.

A short time later he woke with a start as he heard horses hooves clattering on the cobblestones below his window. It was just barely light, the faintest pink glow lit the room. He threw the covers aside and went to the window. He could see two people, one on horseback and the other holding the reins. As his eyes adjusted he realized it was Angelique on her gray mare talking to Sims. Then in a flash she was off, disappearing down the path into the forest.

Damian pulled on his pants and boots, then grabbed a leather fringed jacket and pulled it on over his bare skin.

"Where was she going at this hour?" he asked Sims as he threw a saddle on Surcouf.

"Little Dominique Neveux's mare is about to foal. Angelique gave the girl the horse last year and promised to help when the time came."

Damian relaxed a little, but was still concerned that she traveled alone through the forest. "Does she do things like this often?" he asked as he mounted.

"All the time," Sims laughed. "Why do you think M'sieur Charbonne is anxious to get her married? He's tried many times to stop her from riding off in the middle of the night every time someone needs her help, but she won't listen. Fact is, everyone in the village depends on her."

"How do I get to the Neveux cottage?" he asked as he climbed on the horse Sims held for him.

When Damian reached the Neveux stable, Angelique was already in action. He stood in the doorway for a moment watching her. The mare's water had already broken, scaring the young owner half to death.

"Now calm down, Dominique, and get me some fresh water," Angelique ordered.

"What can I do?" Damian asked from the doorway.

"Where did you come from? Angelique asked, startled.

"I saw you leave. I thought you might need help."

"Go on, Dominique, get the water, please."

"I am glad to see you, Damian. The foal is breech," Angelique continued calmly as she stroked the mare's side. "Dominique and her mother are the only ones here and I need someone strong to control the mare."

"Just tell me what you want me to do."

"I'm going to try to turn the foal. It doesn't seem badly breech. I think just a slight turn will do it."

Angelique watched as Damian slipped his leather jacket off. For a moment she was mesmerized. He hadn't worn a shirt under his jacket and his muscles rippled under his bronze skin. Her eyes lingered over his wide shoulders, across his chest covered with blond hair and down to his slim waist.

The horse suddenly gave a lurch, drawing her attention back to the problem at hand. "Lay your body across the top of her," Angelique instructed.

Damian did as she instructed, talking quietly to the frightened animal as he watched Angelique. Her arm disappeared into the horse as she attempted to turn the foal. The mare struggled to move, but Damian held her firm. Angelique withdrew her arm and dipped it into the bucket of water at her side.

"It's going to take a little more than I thought," she said wiping the perspiration from her forehead. "I'm going to try again."

Ten minutes later Angelique was still attempting to turn the foal. Her hair and face were wet with perspiration, but she continued undaunted. "Easy now, girl," she spoke to the mare. "You can relax your hold now, Damian. She'll have to do the rest on her own."

The forefeet of the foal, covered with a membrane appeared between the distended lips of the vulva. "Easy girl, easy," Angelique calmed as the mare attempted to get up. The mare continued to strain until the foal's head appeared. Angelique clasped each of the foal's forelegs firmly above the fetlock and pulled downward. As soon as the head and shoulders were free she broke the membrane over the foal's nose to allow air into the lungs. With another grunt the mare delivered her foal into the world.

Angelique's eyes met Damian's and for a moment she was surprised by the look she saw.

"Damned if you aren't something, Angel."

"Angel," she blushed as she laughed nervously. "No one ever called me that before."

"Well they should have. Look at this little beauty," Damian said, admiring the foal that now struggled to its feet. "It would have died and taken the mare with it if you hadn't done what you did."

"It's a gift," she said embarrassed as she scrubbed her hands and arms.

"It seems you have a lot of gifts," his eyes held hers for a disturbing moment.

Angelique felt her pulse throbbing with an unsteady erratic pace and found it difficult to breathe properly. She pushed her hair away from her face in a feminine gesture that didn't go with the dirty riding breeches or blood covered shirt. Nevertheless it made her look beautiful and vulnerable.

"Dominique's mother, Antoinette, will have some breakfast ready for us. I have a clean shirt in my saddle bags, so why don't you go in while I change? I'll join you in just a minute."

Damian gratefully accepted a strong brew of coffee while Antoinette explained that she was a widow struggling to raise a thirteen year old daughter on her own. Her husband, a fisherman, had drowned during a storm at sea. Michel Charbonne, at Angelique's urging, had given her a cottage that his gameskeeper had used for hunting at one time. In exchange for her seamstress chores he provided them with food and clothing. She proudly explained that for the last two years she made almost everything Angelique and Genevieve wore. The beautiful mare in the make-shift stable had been a gift to Dominique from Angelique, along with a continual supply of hay and oats.

"The girl is a saint," Antoinette described Angelique as she set a platter of scones in front of Damian. "I don't know what the villagers will do when she marries and goes off to Paris. Believe me, it will be a sad day for many of us. Old Pierre Lambert, the local innkeeper, has a daughter who can't walk. Poor Evette was born that way. Anyway, Mademoiselle Charbonne goes there at least once a week and has Pierre put Evette up on that beautiful mare of hers, then she walks her all over the village to places the poor girl would never see otherwise."

"Dominique is going to stay in the stable for awhile," Angelique said as she entered the door of the stone cottage. "I imagine you'll have trouble getting her to leave there for awhile."

Damian stood and pulled the bench back for her to sit. "Are you tired?" he asked.

"No, not really. It's exhilarating to witness the miracle of birth."

"Well, this miracle of birth had a little help from you." He gently squeezed her hand.

"And from you, Damian. I wouldn't have been able to do it without your help."

"I'm glad I saw you leave this morning. Antoinette was just telling me how many people depend on you here in the village. I think I'm beginning to understand why you don't want to leave Crozon."

"I'm fortunate to have many friends here," she agreed as she sipped her coffee.

"I'd say they are fortunate to have you." Unable to stop himself, he gently touched a smudge on the side of her face and lingered longer than necessary. She was so desirable at that very moment. *But, she is a child*, he reminded himself, *a child who needs love and understanding, not a quick romp in the hay.*

"I've got to go into the village," Damian announced abruptly. "If I'm not back to the chateau by dinner tell the family not to wait."

"Is everything all right, Damian?" Angelique asked, her violet eyes wide with puzzlement.

"Everything is just fine," he snorted.

"I wonder what is wrong with him," Angelique mused as Antoinette refilled her cup.

"I think he's a very bothered man."

"Bothered? What do you mean?"

"Just that he has a lot on his mind, sweet. Come now, eat up. You must be starved after all you've been through this morning."

"It's funny, I haven't been very hungry all week," Angelique said, still staring at the door.

Chapter Six

Damian entered the village inn. Since it wasn't yet noon, the place was deserted except for a couple of fishermen at a corner in the rear.

"Good morning, M'sieur," the barmaid greeted. "What can I get for you?"

"An ale to start," he smiled. Damian watched the girl pour his ale then walk seductively toward him. Placing the glass in front of him she leaned over, inviting him to view her full breasts.

"Will there be anything else, M'sieur?" she smiled.

"What is your name, sweet?"

"Helene, M'sieur."

"Have you someplace we can go, Helene?" he asked, pressing a coin in her hand.

"I have a room upstairs, M'sieur, but I cannot get away until tonight. Pierre would kill me if I disappeared now. Will you come then?" she asked hopefully.

"I'm not sure I'll still be in the village, but if I am you

can be sure I'll be back."

Damian downed the ale and ordered another. He watched the girl serving the men at the back of the room. Instead of seeing the buxom blonde that she was, he saw a lithe figure, with black hair swirling around her shoulders. He drew his eyes away, disgusted with himself for thinking of Angelique again.

"Here you are, *mon ami*," Beau said entering the inn. "I thought I might find you here. It's a little early for drinking, isn't it?"

Damian met his remark with a scowl.

"I understand you helped deliver Dominique's foal this morning."

"How did you know that?" Damian growled.

"I met Angelique as she was returning to the house. She told me you left quite suddenly."

"Yes, I guess I did. Is that a crime?"

Beau was thoroughly enjoying Damian's predicament and took great delight in annoying him. "Well, what did you think of my little sister in action?" he asked proudly.

"She was magnificent as she seems to be at everything," Damian said before downing the rest of his ale. "Where does a man get a woman during the day around this place?" he asked impatiently. "My friend, Helene, over there isn't off until tonight."

"Is that your problem?" Beau laughed. "Why didn't you say so? Come, *mon ami*, you don't need to wait for the barmaid. I have a friend who will more than please you."

Damian left enough coins to cover his ale, and a few extra for the girl, then followed Beau out into the morning sunlight. "Who is this friend?" he asked as they followed a winding road through the village.

"Her name is Alette. She's a whore, but a very discriminating one. Ah, what she can do for your body should be a sin," Beau recalled with a dreamy look on his face. "And you know," he said slapping Damian on the back, "it probably is!"

Damian laughed uproariously as they approached the gray stone cottage. Beau pounded loudly on the door. "She's probably still asleep. She usually does her business much later than this."

The door opened far enough for Damian to make out a dark haired girl with soft brown eyes. "Oh, M'sieur Charbonne, how wonderful to see you. Please come in."

"Hello, love," Beau greeted, kissing her firmly on the mouth. "My friend here needs a little of your attention."

Alette looked Damian up and down. "Ah, M'sieur, for that body I should pay," she teased, running her hand over Damian's wide chest.

"Enjoy yourself, *mon ami*," Beau laughed. "Meet me at the docks in a few hours and I'll show you my ship."

"All right," Damian answered, wondered if he hadn't made a mistake. He had no desire to bed this girl, even though she was beautiful. He was beginning to realize he wasn't going to be satisfied with anyone now that he had fallen under Angelique's spell. He found himself comparing every woman with the bewitching little minx, and all were coming up far short.

An hour later, Damian stood on the quay overlooking Beau's new ship. He had to admit she was a beauty, but he wasn't going to admit it to Beau just yet. The graceful hull showing only aout eight feet above the waterline, was painted blue-gray to merge with the horizon and become virtually invisible at night.

"She is 180 feet in length with a 22 foot beam," Beau explained as they boarded. "She has twin screw engines which will enable us to turn on a coin, and they will develop 250 horsepower. The propellers can be disconnected when under sail. And you'll notice the spars are proper enough to carry a full spread of canvas. I'll burn only anthracite coal so there won't be any sparks and if we have to blow off steam, it will be done under water to stifle the noise. My crew has been selected for their experience and courage."

All the while Beau talked, Damian examined the ship, saying nothing.

"The officers' and crews' quarters are large and comfortable so we won't go stir crazy if we're at sea for a long period of time. We'll carry a decent food supply and . . . For God's sake, Damian, aren't you going to tell me?"

Damian leaned against the railing, his arms folded across his chest. "Tell you what?" he pretended ignorance.

"What do you think of her?" Beau asked impatiently.

"Alette?" Damian teased. "Oh, she was quite enjoyable."

"Not Alette, you fool! The ship. What do you think of the ship?"

Damian laughed, throwing his arm around Beau's shoulder. "She is a bit of genius, my friend. A real beauty. I'd give my eye teeth to have her."

"Well forget it, *mon ami*," Beau warned proudly. "I've put up with your barbs about my ship for a long time. Now I'm going to enjoy seeing you drool."

"Ouch," Damian laughed. "You're a cruel friend."

"I'll tell you what, *mon ami*, another one is already in the works and she will be yours."

When it was time for the entourage to leave Chateau Charbonne for Paris, Beau had to stay in Crozon for another few days to handle the final preparations for his ship. He promised he would join the family as soon as possible.

The entourage consisted of two carriages, one carrying Genevieve, Michel, Angelique and Damian, and the second carrying servants and luggage. Damian had suggested several riding horses be led, and after being jostled and bounced about for several hours, Angelique understood why.

Damian and Michel had chosen to ride the horses the first part of the trip, leaving Angelique to listen to her mother's suggestions for a complete trousseau. Why can't I feel some excitement? she wondered. It had been bad enough before Beau and Damian arrived, but now it was much worse. Even the thought of seeing her cousin, Lael, did nothing to brighten her spirits. She glanced out the window and watched her father and Damian riding alongside the coach.

As a young girl, she had always dreamed she would one day marry Damian. What would it be like to be loved by him, she wondered as she observed him unnoticed. She wondered if any woman would ever be able to call him her own. She had neglected to tell him that some of the stories Lael related were not about his daring sea heroics, but about his reckless, arrogant manner with women.

"What are you thinking about, dear?" Genevieve inquired. "You look a thousand miles away."

"I was just thinking about Damian. He is such an enigma."

"Yes, I think his mother's desertion when he was nine years old left emotional scars that will probably never heal."

"Why do you think she took one son with her and left the other, *Maman*?"

"I can't imagine, dear. I remember hearing gossip that Philip Legare refused to let Colette take Damian, but no one really knows."

Angelique again stared through the carriage window. "I wonder if Colette realizes what her leaving did to Damian?"

"And to Adam," Genevieve added, then sighed. "Colette has never cared about anyone except herself. Even now she spends all her time and money trying to keep herself beautiful."

"Lael says she is still very beautiful."

"Yes, she is. At forty-five she can still draw the attention of every man in a room. But her beauty is all surface, Angelique. Inside she is a cold, selfish woman."

"It is little wonder that we hear so many stories about Damian hating women," Angelique mused.

"Oh, I don't think he hates women. I think he is just

afraid of being hurt. By associating with a lower class woman he feels safe from commitment. Perhaps someday the right woman will come along and there will be nothing he can do about his feelings. Your father was very much like Damian," Genevieve smiled. "He had planned to stay a bachelor, but I had other plans for him."

"Why, *Maman* you sound as if you trapped Papa!"

"I prefer to think I used my feminine wiles on him," Genevieve laughed.

The carriage halted slowly and Michel Charbonne appeared in the door. "Why don't you ride awhile, Angelique? Then when you're tired your mother can ride."

"All right, Papa. I must admit I'm looking forward to some fresh air and sunshine."

"Where is your split skirt?" Damian asked as Angelique struggled to mount in her long, flowing travel outfit.

"Papa doesn't approve of it away from the chateau," she commented, wrinkling her nose in distaste.

"Nevertheless, you look lovely," he added, giving her a warm smile as he reined his horse alongside of hers.

They exchanged light banter for miles, discussing the reason for Damian's trip to Europe, whom he was to meet, and what he hoped to accomplish. At midafternoon they stopped at an inn and had their meal. When they returned to the carriage Genevieve and Michel prepared to mount the saddle horses.

Angelique suddenly felt shy at the prospect of riding in the enclosed carriage alone with Damian.

"If you want to ride, Damian, please don't let me stop you."

Damian put his hand on her elbow and drew her toward the carriage. "You're not thinking of all those wild stories you've heard about me?" he teased.

"If I believed those stories, I wouldn't be traveling with you at all," she said flatly.

She took his hand and allowed herself to be boosted into the carriage. For some reason it seemed much smaller and more intimate than before. And to make it worse, with each movement of the carriage, some part of her leg touched Damian, sending shivers down her spine.

"Are you comfortable, Angelique?"

"Yes, thank you. I believe I'll just close my eyes and see if I can rest."

"Here then," he said moving beside her and propping his long legs on the opposite seat. "You may as well lean on my shoulder. With the jogging of the carriage you'll be thrown all about if you don't."

"This isn't really necessary . . ."

"Hush. Just close your eyes and sleep," he commanded gently.

Sleep? How could he be so foolish? Didn't he realize that his nearness made her heart pound erratically, that the smell of leather and tobacco assailed her senses, making her all too aware of his masculinity.

"You smell like a garden of jasmine and roses," he whispered hoarsely against her hair.

Angelique held her eyes tightly shut as he idly stroked the side of her neck with his thumb.

This was a mistake, he told himself. He should never have gotten into the carriage with her. His senses were beginning to swim alarmingly from her nearness. He was embarrassed as he shifted to hide the obvious signs of his desire. What in the world possessed him? He had always prided himself on controlling his feelings, but it seemed a losing battle where Angelique was concerned.

"I can't sleep," Angelique announced, suddenly sitting up straight.

"You're as jittery as a cat," Damian laughed. "I thought by now you'd be a quiet, sophisticated young lady, content to do needlepoint and indulge in idle chatter."

"I'm sorry to disappoint you, but I'll never be like that."

"No, I don't think you will be," he said smiling into her violet eyes, "but I'm not disappointed."

"Will you be staying with your mother while in Paris?" Angelique asked, for lack of anything else to say.

"No!" he answered too abruptly. "If I could avoid it, I wouldn't even see her."

Angelique held his brooding gaze. "Do you still hate her so?" she asked sadly.

"She left me when I was nine. How do you expect me to feel toward her? She betrayed my father and me, tore our family apart by taking my brother away. Why should my feelings ever change?"

Angelique reached out and touched Damian's face, something she had longed to do. "I understand how you feel, Damian, but you can't let hatred rule your life."

Damian averted his gaze and stared out the window. How could he make her understand how he hurt? She had a family who loved her.

Angelique sat for some minutes matching his silence with her own. Unconsciously she let her breath out in a small sigh.

Damian turned back to her with a sad smile and took her hand in his. "Don't try to take on my problems, Angel. They would overwhelm you. Besides, you have enough on your mind without worrying about me. I just want you to be happy with your new life. When you were a little girl you often told me that some day a knight would come riding out of the forest on a white stallion and whisk you away to live happily ever after. Well, perhaps this fiance of yours will be that knight."

Angelique stared into Damian's green eyes. How could she tell him he was her knight—he would always be the knight she dreamed of. "That was a child's dream," she said, looking away.

"Then you need another dream to take its place."

"I'm older and wiser now. I know better than to believe dreams can come true."

"Perhaps it is good you've learned that early. Nothing is as bitter as disillusionment."

"What about you, Damian? Isn't there someone you care for?" she asked timidly.

Damian stared at her for a long moment. "I've spent years learning to close myself off from people. It's easier that way."

"That's a coward's way," she said flatly.

"Yes, you're probably right," he agreed, "but I am what I am and I must suffer the consequences."

Damian again joined Michel when Genevieve tired of riding—and it was none too soon for him. Angelique had fallen into a moody silence after their conversation. He had the distinct impression she was angry with him, but he wasn't sure why.

Since the sky began to darken with the threat of rain, Michel Charbonne decided to bring the entourage to an early stop. They pulled into the courtyard of a busy local inn. While rooms were being prepared, they were shown to the dining room, already filled with weary travelers.

Damian took Angelique's elbow and led her through the crowd of leering men to a table near the end of the room, while Michel and Genevieve followed.

"Damn," Michel muttered irritably, as he noticed a dark, sinister man staring boldly at Angelique. "I should have asked for a private room. This place is filled with riff-raff."

Damian shifted his chair so that he was blocking Angelique from the man's view. "You can't blame a man for staring at a beautiful woman, Michel. I'm sure you'll have your hands full with two such beautiful women while you're in Paris."

"Ah, Damian, you're such a gentleman," Genevieve laughed. "It is good to have you with us."

They dined on shellfish soup with warm bread and ended the meal with fruit and cheese. Afterward they sipped tea and listened to Damian tell about the war between the states.

Angelique watched his face intently, realizing how dedicated he really was to his country, as he told how the people in the South were suffering from lack of food and clothing.

"It hasn't affected Charleston as badly as it has other parts of the South, particularly Virginia," Damian explained, "but I fear it won't be long."

"Dear, I'm very tired," Genevieve said. "Why don't you and I check on our rooms? I'm sure these young people have much to talk about."

Michel and Genevieve left, leaving Angelique and Damian alone. They were both silent for a long moment.

"Will we see you in Paris, Damian?" she asked, keeping her eyes on her cup.

"I don't know, Angel. I hope to quickly take care of the business I have there and then go on to England. Taking the time to visit with your family was really time I didn't have, but I couldn't pass up the opportunity to see you and your parents."

"I'm very glad you did take the time. I have so often thought of you and wondered what you were doing."

"I fear that is something I'm going to be doing for a long time, little one."

Angelique looked into his green eyes. "I don't understand."

"I'm going to be thinking about you, about those violet eyes and the way you laugh, and about the way you smell of roses and jasmine."

Angelique looked away, embarrassed. How could he

talk this way? Didn't he realize what he was doing to her?

"Do I embarrass you, Angel? I didn't mean to. I just want you to know, in case I don't have a chance to tell you in Paris, that I think you're the most beautiful woman I have ever known and I want you to be happy in your new life."

Angelique stared at him in disbelief. "Oh, Damian, how could you?"

Before Damian could guess what she intended, she grabbed her cape and dashed past him.

"Angelique, wait," he called. When he reached the door she was already at the top of the stairs leading to her room. He ran his hand through his hair, wondering what he had said that upset her. Damn. Would he ever understand women?

Chapter Seven

Angelique was tired and wilted when they finally reached Paris. The carriage stopped in front of the tall, narrow house belonging to Madeleine Moreau, Genevieve's widowed sister. Angelique dreaded the next few moments. She had made herself miserable by staying in the carriage, too embarrassed to talk to Damian. Now he would be saying goodbye to them and she would never see him again.

The carriage door opened and Michel offered a hand to Genevieve. Before Angelique had a chance to follow, Damian stood before the open door. He smiled as he offered her a hand. He looks happy to be ending his trip with us, she thought. How could I have ever thought he'd feel anything for me?

"I'm not going to say goodbye," he said, surprising her as he ran a finger along her jawline. Angelique swallowed, but said nothing. "I'll be coming back to the chateau before I leave for home. Michel said you

106

are planning to return home yourself by then."

"Yes, a few days in Paris and I'm always ready to get back to the country. By the way, you never did say where you'd be staying while you're in Paris," she said tentatively.

"I'll be staying at one of the clubs in the city."

"One of those wild and wicked places," Angelique tried to make her tone teasing, yet her knees had gone treacherously weak at his nearness.

"I guess some would say that." God, how he would love to take her in his arms and kiss her goodbye. The opportunity was taken from him as Lael rushed down the steps to embrace her cousin. Angelique looked back longingly to where Damian was saying goodbye to her father and mother.

"Angelique, who is that?" Lael asked in awe as she took in the lean, muscular figure of the man talking to her mother.

"Don't you remember Damian?" Angelique answered, not really wanting her cousin to become reacquainted with Damian. She remembered all too well, as a young girl, that Damian and Beau had both been infatuated with Lael.

"Oh my, he is handsome," her cousin whispered, staring openly at Damian. "I can see why women throw themselves at him. And you got to travel with him . . . oh, you must tell me everything," she whispered excitedly. "Angelique, he is coming this way . . ."

"Hello, Lael. It's nice to see you again."

"Thank you, Damian," Lael curtsied demurely. "You will be staying with us, won't you?" she asked hopefully.

"I'm afraid not. As I explained to your mother, I have business to take care of so I'll be staying at one of the clubs."

"Oh," she pouted prettily. "I was so hoping we could have a chance to talk over old times."

"I'm sorry, Lael, perhaps another time."

Damian turned his attention back to Angelique. "I hope you enjoy your visit in Paris, little one. I'll look forward to seeing you in Crozon before I leave for America."

"Thank you, Damian," she answered, unable to meet his eyes. "I hope your mission goes well."

Angelique sat in Lael's room talking late into the night. The girls hadn't seen each other in months and Angelique always loved to hear about everything that was going on in Paris. Tonight though, their subject was Damian Legare.

"Mother says he is a womanizer," Lael said, "and that I should stay clear of him, yet I find him intriguing. And believe me, if I have any say in the matter, I won't stay clear of him."

Angelique said nothing, feeling a pang of jealousy as she studied her cousin's fair beauty. Sometimes she wished she was as experienced and sophisticated as Lael. Perhaps if she had attended the fashionable schools in Europe like her cousin she wouldn't feel envious, but she hadn't really wanted to leave Crozon and Papa hadn't insisted. Now she wondered if she hadn't been foolish. Lael seemed so worldly. There was only two years difference between them, yet Angelique always felt like a child around her cousin. Lael drew her legs up under her in a very unsophisticated gesture. Angelique relaxed and sprawled out on the bed beside her. Perhaps her cousin really wasn't so different after all.

"I've heard it said Damian hates women," Lael continued. "I wonder why?"

"He has good reason," Angelique answered. "His mother deserted him when he was only a young boy."

"I wonder what could have happened to make her leave her husband and son?" Lael asked.

"I don't know," Angelique answered honestly, having wondered the same thing. "Papa says Charleston is a very sophisticated, cultural city."

"Yes," Lael answered, "but still it is the Colonies, and there are still savages."

Angelique let her thoughts drift a moment to Damian Legare. Everything about him exuded excitement. His looks, the way he moved, his occupation.

"Being a blockade runner must be very exciting," Lael exclaimed, as if she could read Angelique's thoughts.

"It's very much like being a pirate," Angelique answered, remembering their conversation on the beach.

"I wonder what it would be like to be held in those strong arms and be kissed by him?" Lael mused, looking dreamy-eyed.

Angelique got up from the bed and started vigorously brushing her long hair. "Now don't pretend innocence with me, Angelique. I know you've probably already wondered how it would be to kiss Damian."

"I didn't say I hadn't," Angelique answered, showing as little interest as possible.

"Can you imagine it, Angelique?" Lael asked, falling back on the bed and hugging herself. "Those sensuous lips closing over yours, his tongue gently parting, probing?"

"For God's sake, Lael! You sound like a strumpet." Angelique grabbed her brush. "I'm very tired. I think I'll go to bed," she said leaving her cousin's room as quickly as she could.

Angelique tossed and turned in bed. No matter how hard she tried she couldn't put Damian out of her mind. She could still feel the warmth of his hand touching her cheek, see his green eyes smiling at her. "Oh damn!" she swore, throwing the covers off. She'd be glad when he went back to America so she could put him out of her mind.

Damian turned away the advances of a beautiful demimondaine to sleep alone his first night at the club, but sleep was slow in coming. He lay in bed staring at the ceiling. He tried to think of his meeting with the French minister in the morning, but his mind kept going to Angelique. What was it about the little vixen that haunted him day and night? Was it her innocence, her spirit, or just her violet eyes? He turned over and punched his fist into the pillow, hoping to get comfortable so he could get some sleep. It certainly seemed like he hadn't had much of it lately.

* * *

Damian's meeting with the French minister was long and tiring, but in the end the Frenchman agreed to supply morphine, surgical instruments, quinine and some clothing. Weapons and ammunition were another matter. Damian had hoped to be able to acquire French LeMat pistols, but the minister was reluctant to promise them. After Damian reminded him that six hundred thousand people in France alone worked in textile mills that were dependent on Southern cotton, the minister promised he would meet with his council and would have an answer one way or the other in a few days.

Damian left the impressive government building, tired, but with hope. He hired a carriage, considered going to the Moreau home, but instead instructed the driver to take him to his mother's latest residence. He leaned back against the leather seat, deciding that after his visit with his mother was out of the way, he would spend the evening gambling and then, perhaps, invite one of the club's beautiful women to have supper with him.

The carriage came to a halt in front of an elegant brick house. Damian sat there for a few minutes. It had been years since he had seen his mother or brother. Six years to be precise. He wondered if she had changed much. After telling the driver to wait, he climbed the black iron steps. This wouldn't take long, he told himself.

He was ushered into a bright sitting room with windows overlooking a garden. He raised the lace curtain and stared down on the rose garden, remembering another garden his mother had started, but quickly neglected.

Damian turned as he heard footsteps on the marble floor. They stood silently for a moment, assessing each other. Damian was amazed that his mother was still beautiful.

"It is nice to see you, Damian. You are looking well," Colette finally said.

"I was thinking the same of you, Colette," he replied, making it a point to use her name as he had since he was ten. "It's amazing to me that you never seem to age."

Colette's face brightened. "That's very kind of you, dear. I do try to take care of myself. Please sit down. I've asked Jacques to bring you a brandy."

"I can't stay long."

"Surely you can stay long enough to have a brandy?" Jacques entered with a silver tea service and Damian's drink. "What brings you to Paris? Are you here to escape the American war?"

"I'm here on business for the Confederate States. I will be returning to Charleston in a few weeks."

"Pity," she said, her eyes assessing her son's tall, muscular physique. "I don't imagine it's very pleasant being in the South at this time."

"Where is Adam?" Damian asked, anxious to get his visit over and be on his way.

"He's at the hospital," she answered as she poured herself a cup of tea.

"The hospital?"

"Oh, you didn't know. Your brother is a doctor. He

has a very promising career in medicine. I'm very proud of him."

Damian ignored her barb at him. "I can remember a time when Adam got sick at the sight of blood."

"I guess we can all change," Colette said, as she studied her son's face.

"I doubt that, Colette. I've heard it said that a leopard can't change its spots."

Colette's face went red, but she quickly controlled herself. "Have you seen the Charbonnes?" she asked, straightening a pillow behind her.

"Yes, I've spent the last week at Crozon."

"Ah, then you know little Angelique is to marry my late husband's son."

"I believe that makes him your stepson, Colette, and yes, I know of the arrangement."

A fleeting look of annoyance crossed Colette's face. "If you knew Andre you would understand why I don't claim him."

"What is that supposed to mean?" Damian asked, trying to keep his annoyance at having to discuss Angelique's future husband from showing.

"Oh, it is nothing, really. The young man has never been taught to respect his elders—or anyone else for that matter. I'm sure Michel will take him in hand."

"Colette," Damian said between gritted teeth, "Michel Charbonne is not taking this young man, as you call him, under his wing to raise him. The man is marrying his only daughter and if there is something he should be warned of, you better damned well inform the family!"

Colette sipped her tea, watching her son over the brim of her cup. "You are right, Damian. I guess your brother is the only one who has changed. You and I still can't get along, so where does that leave us?"

"It leaves us where it always has," Damian said, downing his brandy. "With one of us leaving the other. I must go now. I just stopped by to be sure you were still able to take care of yourself."

"You need never worry about that," she said, lifting her chin proudly. "I have always been quite capable of taking care of myself."

"Yes, I know. I learned that lesson early. Good day, *Mother*," Damian said as he left the room.

Angelique's knees trembled as she followed Lael down the steps to the waiting carriage. Her parents had gone to the opera with Aunt Madeleine, thinking the girls and their escort were attending the theatre, chaperoned by Philippe Varnet, a distant cousin who was staying at the Moreau house. Instead the man had drunk himself into a stupor and couldn't be raised. Angelique knew it wasn't proper to go with Andre and his friend, but somehow she became caught up in Lael's excitement, and the next thing she knew, they were going to the infamous Lock and Key Club instead of the theatre. Lael's eyes sparkled with excitement at the mere mention of the club, but somehow Angelique felt she should try to talk her cousin out of this excursion.

"Lael, I must speak with you a moment," Angelique insisted, pulling her cousin aside. "Surely you don't mean to go to that place. It isn't only for gambling . . . it's . . . it's . . ."

"It's exciting," Lael exclaimed, "and a woman has to have an escort to even get in, so I'm not passing up this opportunity. Besides, Andre's friend is a count, and how many chances does a girl have to be seen with royalty!" she added.

"If Papa finds out I shall never be allowed out again," Angelique warned.

"Oh for heaven's sake, Angelique, you're about to be married, and I bet you've never done anything exciting. Where is your spirit?" she asked pulling her cousin back where Andre and Count Girard waited.

The gambling room of the Lock and Key Club buzzed with excitement as Damian won another hand. The blond woman at his shoulder leaned forward and raked the chips toward him, but he stayed her hand.

"Will M'sieur stay with black?" the croupier inquired.

"Let it ride," Damian answered without a second thought.

An audible sigh went up from the spectators as Damian won again.

"Damned if you don't have the luck of the devil," someone from across the table said.

Damian looked up into a pair of eyes the same emerald green color as his own. A smile crossed the handsome face. "Have you nothing to say to me, big brother?" The gentleman asked, a mischievous glint in his smiling eyes.

"Adam?" Damian asked, slowly leaving his seat. "I'll be damned," he said hugging his brother affectionately. "Look at you," he laughed holding him at arm's length. "What happened to my little brother?" Realizing everyone in the room was audience to this personal reunion, Damian turned to the croupier and asked for his chips to be cashed in. "Come, let me buy my favorite brother a drink in the salon. We have a lot to talk about."

"How did you know I was here?" Damian asked after they had talked for more than an hour.

"I wasn't really sure you would be, but the duchess said you stopped in on her today, so I just took the chance that you'd be staying at the most notorious club in Paris."

Damian laughed warmly. "I haven't seen you in almost six years, yet still you know my habits."

"Perhaps I know what you're doing because it's what I would wish to do." Adam laughed when he saw the puzzled expression on Damian's face. "It is sometimes called envy, dear brother."

"My God, how could you possibly envy me? You're a doctor, and from what Colette says, an excellent one."

"And you're a man fighting for your country, while I am a man without a country."

Damian didn't say anything for a long moment. Green eyes locked with green eyes. "When Mother chose to take you with her I always felt I was the deprived one. I never stopped to think how you felt."

"Yes, Mother chose to take me with her, and then sent me from one boarding school to another. I might

116

have spent as much as a month out of the year with her and whatever husband she was with. But worst of all, she robbed me of my father and brother, and my heritage. I have always considered myself an American, Damian, yet if I dared to claim to be an American, my French associates ridiculed me, and I *didn't want* to claim to be a Frenchman. Thus, a man without a country," he said with a defeated gesture of his hands.

Damian's eyes lit up with an inspiration. This man was his brother, but more than that, he liked him, felt a natural kinship with him. "Come back to Charleston with me, Adam. You have a home there and there is always need of a good doctor. It's high time you and I got to know each other."

"You can't imagine how often I've thought of doing just that, Damian. When I started hearing about the war and the desperate need for medical people I began thinking of going there, but then Mother was widowed again, so I put it out of my mind."

"Ha," Damian snorted, "Colette doesn't strike me as the type to need anyone, and she told me as much today."

"Whether she does or not, I don't know. But I don't think I'll have to worry about it for long. She is already talking about marrying again. Some duke from Alstairs this time. When that happens, perhaps I'll show up on your doorstep."

"Come on, Adam, don't put it off. I've at least a week of business in London, then I'll be heading back to Chateau Charbonne for another few days before sailing. Put your business in order and sail with me then."

Adam studied his drink, swirling the amber liquid against the side of the glass. "Is there something else keeping you here?" Damian asked. "Perhaps a girl?"

"No, I've been far too busy to meet anyone. Let me think on this while you're in London."

"All right, but send some word to the Charbonnes. And, if for some reason you decide not to sail with me, I'll expect to see you in Charleston in a few months."

Adam leaned across the table and shook hands with his brother. "If I take you up on your offer, will you promise to introduce me to some beautiful Southern . . ." Adam's voice trailed off as he looked past his brother to the entrance of the room. "Speaking of beautiful women," he whistled low.

Damian turned in his chair, laughing at his brother, but the sound froze in his throat. "Damn," he hissed between clenched teeth. "I ought to break her stupid neck."

Chapter Eight

Angelique found it difficult to breathe as they stood in the crimson and red receiving salon. What kind of place was this? she wondered, as a woman in a black, low cut gown laughed seductively while two men vied for her attention. Angelique turned to Lael in an attempt to talk some sense to her, but seeing the sparkle of excitement in her cousin's eyes she knew it was useless.

"Come, pigeon, let me show you around before we go to the gaming room," Andre LaFrancois suggested.

Angelique started to protest, but decided against it. There was something about this man that intimidated her, yet she couldn't put her finger on it. He was handsome enough with dark brown hair and an aristocratic nose, but the eyes . . . even though he smiled, his dark eyes remained cold.

Lael's inane conversation continued as they passed

the ballroom where a few couples danced to the sounds of a small group of musicians, then past the gambling room ablaze with dazzling chandeliers hanging over tables covered in dark green baize.

"We will return here shortly, but first let me show you the salon, then we will go upstairs to the private rooms," Andre said.

Angelique stood in the doorway of the elegant oak paneled salon with its gold velvet furnishings and blazing fireplace, but she saw only a blur. Her mind was reeling. Private rooms . . . it was time to put a stop to this. Papa would kill her.

"Are you all right, pigeon?" Andre asked taking her firmly by the arm while he led the group toward the richly carpeted stairs.

Angelique finally found her voice. "I do not wish to see the private rooms," she managed to blurt out, "and please stop calling me pigeon. I do not find it flattering."

"Ah, so my little bird does have spirit. I had heard as much. You needn't worry," he whispered near her ear, "I don't plan to seduce you—yet."

Angelique gasped with shock. "Andre, I wish to be taken back to my aunt's house. You are far too presumptuous."

Andre laughed. "Now surely you are not going to insult my intelligence by telling me you didn't come here tonight to have a good time."

What did you expect? she asked herself. What else would he think when you agreed to come to a place like this? She was sure no matter what she said, he wouldn't believe her anyway.

"Come on, Angelique, I want to see the private rooms," Lael urged. "Don't be such a stick in the mud."

Damian had watched the little scene at the doorway for a moment, hoping to give his anger time to cool. "Excuse me, Adam, but I must speak with the lady."

"Wait a minute, big brother. I agree the woman is beautiful, but her escort is Andre LaFrancois. He happens to be our step-brother."

"I don't give a damn who or what he is. He has no right bringing Angelique to a place like this."

Adam looked back toward the entrance, but the group had moved on. "Do you mean that beauty is Angelique? Angelique Charbonne?"

"One and the same."

"Well, that makes even less sense for you to intrude, Damian. She is Andre's fiancée. As much as I hate the bastard and would love to see him bested, I don't want to see you mixed up with him."

Adam suddenly had Damian's full attention. "Why do you hate him?"

"I had a good friend killed by terrorists a few months ago and it is a known fact Andre has some connection with the group. I've even heard rumors that he may be the leader, and this same group claims responsibility for several tragic bombings in Paris. I'm afraid he is living up to the nickname of *la terreur* given to him when we were at school."

"I've known the Charbonnes a long time. I can't believe they would chose him for Angelique's husband."

"They live in Brittany, probably far enough away not to have heard the stories of Andre's escapades. Besides, most parents would overlook such rumors to marry their daughter off to a duke."

"No! Michel Charbonne would never do that to Angelique. I want to know more about him, Adam. I had the distinct impression today that Colette didn't like him either."

"That's an understatement," Adam laughed. "Mother was left a very handsome portion of her late husband's estate. Andre tried to find some way of denying her the money, but fortunately Mother has very powerful friends. Andre inherited the estate in Cier, the title, and enough money to live a decent existence—if he doesn't throw his money away, but he's not happy with that. He wants it all, and for all I know, he may need it. I've heard that he has run up tremendous gambling debts and has tried to avoid paying them."

"And Angelique is very rich," Damian said, as he stared off toward the door.

"Leave it, Damian. You've been away a long time. Angelique must know what Andre is like if she is here with him. This place is one of his favorite haunts. He even has a room upstairs kept equipped for his personal . . ." Adam stopped, knowing he had said too much. Damian was already on his feet.

"Damian, wait!"

Angelique fled down the long stairway, her vision blurred by tears of humiliation and embarrassment. She didn't know where she was going, but she knew she had to get away from this place and from Andre LaFrancois.

"What the hell are you doing in a place like this?" Damian demanded as she ran headlong into him.

"Oh, Damian, I'm so glad to see you. Please, would you take me home?"

Without warning, he grasped her wrist and pulled her back up the stairs.

"What are you doing?" she gasped outraged.

"You're not going anyplace until I get some answers."

Angelique tried to pull her arm away, but found his grip only tightened. What was wrong with everyone tonight? Was the whole world going crazy or was she? "I don't have to answer to you, Damian. Kindly release me and I'll find my own way home."

Instead of being released, Angelique found herself in a small but exquisitely furnished room with a fire blazing in the grate.

"Papa isn't going to like this," she said childishly when Damian finally released her.

"That is an understatement, my pet," he replied sarcastically. "Now sit down while I pour some champagne. Then we're going to talk."

Angelique sat on a chair before the fire, but watched Damian out of the corner of her eye as he opened the bottle and poured two glasses full of bubbly liquid. His face was set in a frown and she again wondered what he could possibly be so angry about. She tried to force a semblance of gaiety to her manner as she began to chatter about the elegance of the room.

Damian gave her a black look as he handed her the glass. "A toast to your innocence," he sneered.

Angelique's eyes widened in shock. "Do you dare question my innocence?"

"What am I supposed to think when you frequent the most notorious club in Paris? And here I was fool enough to think I was the first man to kiss you."

"Did it matter to you that you were the first?" she asked, her eyes innocent and pleading for the truth.

Damian turned and stared into the fire. "That is not the point here, Angelique. I want to know what you were doing here?"

Angelique suddenly felt very tired. She just wanted to be home. "Even if it doesn't matter to you, I want you to know you were the first man to ever kiss me. At least kiss me like a man kisses a woman. Now please, Damian, I made a mistake coming here and I know it. It all happened so fast. Lael made these plans . . . we were going to the theatre with Tante Madeleine's cousin, but he became ill at the last minute. When it was suggested we come here, I knew it wasn't smart, but somehow I let myself get carried along by the excitement."

"Damn it, leave it to a man like LaFrancois to bring his fiancée to a place like this?" Damian shouted, his anger still unappeased.

Angelique drank the champagne in two gulps, then stood to leave. If Damian wasn't going to help her get home then she would just find her own way. "Thank you for the champagne," she said haughtily, before a noisy hiccup escaped.

Damian tried to keep a straight face, but at the look of embarrassment on Angelique's face, it was impossible.

She hadn't been prepared for his laughter. To her delicate state it only added more humiliation. She raised her hand to slap his face, but he grabbed her wrist before she made contact.

Tears welled up in her eyes. "How dare you . . . you drag me into this room, insult me, and then laugh at me when I am distressed."

He was staring at her as if he'd never seen her before. Suddenly he leaned forward and gently kissed her lips. He moaned her name, then placed a line of kisses along her jaw and down her neck.

She should pull away, she told herself. She should stop him, but instead she raised her mouth to his, eager to know more about the feelings his kisses and hands were evoking each time he touched her.

Everything within him warned him to thrust her away, but instead he pulled her even closer, feeling the soft rise and fall of her breast against his chest. God, she was the most desirable thing he had ever held in his arms.

Angelique gasped at the feel of his tongue roughly entering her mouth as he held her head secure with his hands entwined in her hair. This wasn't the same man who had been so gentle on the beach. He was demanding, forceful, even frightening, but still, she couldn't make herself stop him. He seemed to draw the breath from her, and it was setting her body on fire.

A part of him was sending warnings to his brain, reminding him who she was, but he was so aroused he ignored them. "Angel, Angel," he whispered against her ear. "What am I going to do with you?" His hands moved down her back, pulling her closer, but in the gown and crinolines he couldn't feel the outline of her body as he had on the beach. He stared down into her face, intoxicated by the look of passion in her eyes.

"I love you, Damian," she whispered.

He released her as suddenly as he had grabbed her. She looked up at him, searching his limitless green eyes for an explanation.

"I'm sorry, Angelique. I shouldn't have done that. I curse your fiance for putting you in a compromising situation and then I do the same."

Angelique's mouth worked, but no words came out.

"Straighten your dress and I'll see you home," he said turning his back to her.

"You are cruel," she sputtered with rage, feeling brutally rejected. "What kind of man are you?"

Damian closed his eyes against the anguished sound of her voice. What in the hell was the matter with him? This was his best friend's sister. How could he hurt her this way?

"I thought you wanted me," she whispered hoarsely.

With his back still to her he let out a sharp sound that wasn't quite a laugh. He poured himself another glass of champagne, then finally turned and faced her. "You deserve more than I can offer—more than I'm willing to give."

Tears clogged Angelique's throat. "I know you feel something for me. Why can't you admit it before it is too late? What are you afraid of?"

Damian shrugged his shoulders fatalistically. "I can't love, Angel. I'm sorry," he said before downing the contents of his glass. "Are you ready?"

"You never did tell me why you were fleeing your fiance in tears," Damian broke the long silence that hung between them as the carriage moved slowly toward the Moreau house.

"It was just a lover's quarrel," Angelique lied, unable to tell Damian what she had discovered in Andre's private room. Maybe she didn't know much about men, but Andre's tendencies just didn't seem healthy to her. Even Lael's face had gone white, but then she had claimed she was curious and had stayed behind. God, maybe she had been overprotected. She just didn't know. Perhaps all men had an interest in such things.

Again the deafening silence fell between them. When the carriage finally stopped in front of Lael's house, Angelique moved to get out.

"Wait just a moment, Angelique. I want to discuss something with you."

Angelique studied Damian's face in the darkness, daring to hope he had changed his mind.

"I'm sorry about what happened at the club. I was angry to find you there and I just lost my head."

"Are you saying you kissed me because you were angry?" Angelique asked incredulously. Even in the dark Angelique could see Damian run his hand through his hair in a gesture of frustration.

"Yes, something like that, but that isn't what I want to discuss with you."

"I'm listening."

"I think you should talk with your father about this fiancé of yours."

"And just what do you suggest we discuss?" she asked, a note of sarcasm in her voice.

"For God's sake, Angelique, do I have to spell it out for you? The man will not make a suitable husband!"

Angelique suddenly wanted to hurt him.

"Oh, I think you're mistaken, Damian. Andre is charming, considerate, and very exciting," she lied.

Damian laughed harshly. "Your life will be exciting for sure. The man has a reputation for being a sadistic bastard!"

Angelique said nothing, her eyes wide with pretended innocence.

"Damn it, Angelique, do you understand what I'm saying?"

She knew very well what he was saying, but she

shook her head no. "What foundation do you have for this accusation?"

"A damned good one, but aside from that, the fact that he took you to the Lock and Key Club and showed you upstairs is reason enough. You're not so innocent you don't know what those rooms are used for."

"Do you use those room, Damian?"

Shock her! Scare the hell out of her, he told himself. *Let her think you use those rooms. Put an end to this thing between you.* But he couldn't. "I use an occasional room, Angelique, but not for the reason Andre LaFrancois does. I'm no saint, but neither do I practice sexual perversion."

"You said you can't love, Damian. Does that stop you from taking a woman to your bed?"

"Angelique, we shouldn't be discussing this sort of thing. If you won't talk to your father, I will."

"You didn't answer my question, Damian. Can you make love to a woman?"

Damian shifted in the seat. "Yes, I can *make* love," he answered softly. "I stopped myself from going further with you because you deserve a man who can love you, not a quick tumble in bed. You need a man who will teach you to be a woman in a gentle way, teach you to understand your body and your desires. Not someone who will use you."

"Every time you touch me I feel . . . I don't know . . . something very special. I think if you were honest you'd admit you feel it too."

"Honesty? Is that what you want? All right, I'll be

129

honest. I've wanted you since the first day I saw you. I can't remember ever desiring a woman as much as I desire you, but I can't make love to you. You're different, Angelique. I respect you and would never do anything to hurt you or your family. That's why I know I have to put a stop to this before it goes any further."

"I envy you, Damian," Angelique said as she opened the carriage door. "It must be nice to be able to turn your feelings on and off at will."

"Angelique . . ."

"Goodbye, Damian. Thank you for the advice. I'll take it into consideration."

Damian watched Angelique run up the steps and disappear into the house. He sat for a long moment before giving the driver the signal to go on. Damn, he'd never met such an exasperating woman—or one as intriguing.

Chapter Nine

Damian sat in a crowded tavern in the harbor area, staring across the English Channel in the direction of France. He wondered if Adam had further considered going to America with him. He had never really had a chance to get to know his brother, yet he had a feeling they could be good friends. It was strange, Beau and Angelique had been his only family after Colette had deserted him and his father. Angelique, he mused. How he would like to be the one to teach her to be a woman—and she was ready—Oh God, was she ready. The little vixen had almost innocently seduced him. It had been almost two weeks since that night at the Lock and Key Club and still he couldn't stop thinking about her, about the way she had responded to his kiss.

A frown crossed Damian's handsome face. He hoped Beau had gotten his message about Andre LaFrancois. He would have liked to have waited for him to arrive in France so they could talk, but he just didn't have the time. Besides, this was a family matter. Beau would know how to handle it. The important thing was to break the engagement before Angelique got in any deeper with LaFrancois and his strange crowd.

At any rate, he would be back in Brittany in a few days since things had gone so well for him in London. The British had been much more sympathetics to the Confederate States than France, even though both countries desperately needed the South's cotton. His spirits had soared when he found that the best firms in England were eager and ready to furnish supplies, and accept the credit of the Confederate government.

Damian had discovered that the British found it galling that the Northerners thought they could tell everyone who could come and go on the high seas. Every day the war continued, the British became more pronounced in their Southern sympathies and louder in their denunciation of the Northerners' high-handed ways. He had found many British companies were outfitting their own vessels to enter the blockade running business. The excitement, narrow escapes and quick profits were front-rank topics of conversation every place he went. Officers in Her Britannic Majesty's Navy found the thrill of eluding Federal cruisers and dodging shot and shell exceedingly tempting. Many had applied for leaves of absence and many others planned to. No one was supposed to know these Britishers, fauntlessly attired in the height of civilian fashion, were actually naval officers on leave, using names quite different from those on their service records. Everyone in the South already assumed if Queen Victoria's government in England and the government of Napoleon the Third in France would recognize the Confederate States of America, the Northerners wouldn't stand a chance. Damian wasn't convinced that was the fact, but he sure as hell hoped so. The North had everything else going for it.

Damian took out his pocket watch and checked the time. He had another appointment with J. M. Mason, commissioner of the Confederate government in London, in an hour. At his suggestion Damian had contacted the Liverpool firm of Fraser, Trenholm and Company and they had agreed to conduct commercial transactions for the Confederate government through their branch in Charleston. The commissioner was now going to try to set up an appointment for Damian with a very successful Frenchman, who was residing in London at the present time, with the hope that he might be able to do the same thing for commercial transactions out of France.

Damian felt very pleased with the way the day had gone so far. He had already personally supervised the loading of the steamer *Fingal* with quartermaster and medical supplies as well as ordnance—and it was already on its way to the hard-pressed Confederate army. The cargo had included 8,000 Enfield rifles and 17,000 pounds of cannon powder. Now that his job was near an end he would head back to Brittany and then on to America. He had to admit, he looked forward to the return on Beau's new ship.

Beau, after deciding to act on Damian's warning without involving his parents, waited at the Cafe LaSalle for Andre LaFrancois to join him. He had done some investigating on his own, and Damian had been right about Andre having quite a reputation. Not only were his sexual appetites questionable, but he was also involved in some treasonous dealings against the emperor. One source told him that Andre was the leader of one of the ever-present revolutionary groups—a group who used terrorism to get what they wanted. What it was they wanted, no one was quite sure.

"You wanted to see me, Charbonne?"

Beau looked up from his seat to the impassive face of Andre. Behind him stood a pale, insipid looking character.

"Yes, alone if you don't mind," Beau answered indicating the one chair across from him.

Andre said something to the man, then took the seat. He leisurely pulled a cigar from his inner pocket and lit it, inhaled the smoke and blew it into the air. "What's on your mind, Charbonne?"

"While I was away, my parents chose you as a suitable husband for Angelique. I have learned some irrefutable facts that tell me otherwise."

"Is that right, Charbonne? Do you want to tell me what those facts are?"

"I think we both know what they are without

going into details. The way I see it, we have two courses of action. You can gracefully bow out of the engagement and nothing will be said about your politics or your sexual preferences, or I can challenge you to a duel."

"You're forgetting something, Charbonne. Suppose I win the duel?"

"It doesn't really matter, LaFrancois. If I win, the wedding is off. If you should win, the wedding is still off. You see, I know Angelique wouldn't marry the man who killed her brother."

The silence was heavy and long as the two men stared at each other. Suddenly Andre smiled, a smile that never touched his eyes. "I was already bored with your sister, Charbonne," he lied, "but I don't like being told what to do. Maybe you don't realize who you're dealing with," he added contemptuously.

Beau leaned forward, his face only inches away from Andre's. "That's the whole point, LaFrancois, I know exactly who I'm dealing with."

Andre slowly rose. "The Charbonne money was my only reason for marrying your sister, but now you've given me another reason. I'd love to see you lose everything."

"You won't live to get near her again, scum!"

"You think not? We shall see, *mon ami*. We shall see." Andre LaFrancois bowed, then turned and walked away, his thin friend falling in behind him.

Beau finished his drink, his thoughts on his family. His parents would have to be told about his conversation with LaFrancois, but he'd have to try to protect

Angelique from knowing what had taken place—or how close she had come to marrying the scum of the earth.

Angelique paced the room, her trunks packed and waiting for her parents to return. They were supposed to have left early this morning for home, but a message had been delivered from their solicitor informing them that he had to see them on urgent business before they left the city. That had been four hours ago and still there was no word. And where was Beau? He was supposed to have been here first thing this morning.

"It isn't like your parents not to send a message when something detains them," Tante Madeleine said, looking up from her needlepoint.

Angelique nervously checked the strap on the trunk containing her trousseau. She had decided against mentioning the night she had gone to the Lock and Key Club with Andre to her parents. After thinking about it, she realized she was more at fault for having gone, than Andre was for taking her. Besides if it were really such a terrible place, what were all those respectable people doing there? Andre had been very apologetic about his behavior when he arrived shortly after Damian had delivered her home safely. He explained he had imbibed too much before he arrived to pick her up and admitted his behavior was deplorable.

She had to admit, she hadn't really been herself

that night. The world they had entered frightened her. She had never been any place where inhibitions so quickly dissolved under the influence of drink, or where women were so openly promiscuous. It was really no wonder Andre had acted as he had. After all, she had agreed to go to that place.

At the sound of the knocker on the door everyone started. Angelique followed the butler to the door. Her knees turned to jelly as she saw a gendarme standing there, awkwardly turning his hat in his hands.

"What has happened?" she blurted out.

"Are you Mademoiselle Charbonne?"

"Yes," she answered, a consuming dread twisting her heart.

"I'm sorry to inform you . . . Monsieur and Madame Charbonne met with a terrible accident."

"What kind of accident?" Tante Madeleine asked, her voice trembling. "Are they . . ."

The gendarme looked sadly at Angelique then back to her aunt. "Perhaps the mademoiselle would care to sit down?"

"Please, what has happened?" Angelique begged, tears flowing down her cheeks.

"The carriage they were riding in exploded from a bomb. Apparently they were on their way here when it happened."

Angelique heard his words, but she was not reacting. She stared at the man talking, but knew it had to be a dream—a very bad dream.

"We don't understand it. It seems to have been the

work of the revolutionaries," he was saying, "yet we can find no reason for them to benefit by killing the Charbonnes."

As the full power of the gendarme's words finally sank in, a ragged sob tore itself from Angelique's throat. "Beau . . . was Beau . . ." Angelique tried unsuccessfully to get the question out.

Tante Madeleine slipped a motherly arm around Angelique's shoulders. "Angelique's brother was supposed to meet the family here this morning, but he has not arrived."

"I'm sure he will arrive soon. There were only two people in the carriage."

Chapter Ten

Angelique was devastated. The strength she always thought she possessed deserted her. For days she stayed in her room at Tante Madeleine's with the heavy drapes drawn, not wanting to admit such a cruel world existed on the outside. There was still no word of Beau, and even though the authorities reported that only her parents had died in the carriage, Angelique was convinced her brother had died with them. What other explanation could there be for his disappearing from the face of the earth?

She rocked back and forth, hugging her knees to her body. "Why, God? Why have you taken everyone from me?" she sobbed. "My mother and father were such good people. They were always helping others . . . and Beau . . . he was so young, so full of plans for the future . . ."

"Angelique, it is time," Tante Madeleine said, looking into the dark room. "Father Boitelle is waiting for you."

"It is time," Angelique repeated to herself as she straightened the black dress that had been borrowed for her. "It is time to put *Maman* and Papa to rest, but what about Beau?" she asked her aunt.

"Now child, we'll not be putting your brother in the grave until we know for sure what happened to him. I just have this feeling that he will be showing up any day now."

Angelique's tear-filled eyes brightened just a bit. "Do you really think so, Tante Madeleine?"

"I certainly do. Now come along, Andre is waiting to escort you to church."

Andre had been a daily visitor at the Moreau residence since the accident. Angelique had not seen him, but it was a comfort to know someone was there for her. Her future was an abyss now—she had not been able to think past the moment. God, if she could only turn back the hands of time.

Andre stared at the figure descending the stairs. She was thin and pale, and there was a faraway, haunted look in her violet eyes.

"You should have let me come to you, Angelique. I can tell by looking at you that you have not eaten."

"Please, Andre, don't worry about me. I will survive."

"Not if you stay locked in that dark room and don't eat."

"I cannot think of eating. Surely you can understand that," Angelique fought back tears. "I've lost everything."

"You have me, dear. I'm here to take care of you now,

but we will talk later this evening."

Angelique somehow made it through the funeral, clinging to Andre's arm like a child. When all the words had been said, they made their way back to the Moreau house. Tears burned behind Angelique's eyes and throbbed in her throat. All she wanted was to escape into the darkness of her room and cry, but Andre would not let her.

"We have to talk, Angelique. I cannot let you hide yourself away again. Let me share your grief, my dear. Believe me it helps to have someone at a time like this." Andre led Angelique to a chair and handed her a glass of red wine. "I have talked to your aunt and she agrees that we should be married right away. Now don't look so horrified. We will be married very quietly, but it is the only way, my dear. Unless you prefer to stay here and live with your aunt."

Angelique rubbed her temples. God, she had a splitting headache. Why couldn't everyone just go away and leave her alone? "Andre," she began, finding it difficult to even speak. "I have Chateau Charbonne. I will go there and wait for my brother to come home."

"But that is the point, cherie. You cannot go there alone. It simply is not proper. You are too young to stay on your own without a guardian, or a husband. So you see, if you insist on going you must have either your aunt with you or me. Now surely there is no reason to uproot your aunt, when we had planned to be married anyway."

"I don't know . . . I am so tired, Andre. I just want to go to my room."

"And you shall, my dear, just as soon as you give me your answer so I can make the arrangements."

Does it really make sense, or am I just tired? she wondered. She had no one. At least Andre would be there when she needed someone, and hadn't Papa chosen Andre for her husband. Suddenly Damian's image came to her mind. He had claimed Andre was not suited for her, but wouldn't say why. Damn him, if he had just committed himself it would be different. Angelique shook her head, trying to clear the cobwebs. She had always imagined herself in love with Damian, but he would never return that love. Now Andre offered her love and companionship—and she would be a fool to say no.

Angelique sat before the cheval glass, numbly watching as Aimee put the finishing touches to her hair. She had finally agreed to a small ceremony, but had insisted it be at the chapel of her home. Her parents and grandparents had been married there and she didn't want to break family tradition. Besides, she dared to hope Beau would show up at the chateau before the wedding took place.

"Do you like the pearls entwined through your hair, mademoiselle?"

"Yes, it's lovely," Angelique answered absent-mindedly. The face in the glass was hardly recognizable as her own. A white faced stranger with red-rimmed eyes stared back at her. It had been two weeks since her parents were killed and Beau had disappeared—two weeks of moving in a trance-like state, unable to understand or comprehend why her life had taken such a drastic turn. Her *maman* should be here, giving words of encouragement, telling her what would be expected of her; and Papa—Papa should be waiting to lead her down the narrow aisle of the chapel.

Lael burst into the room without knocking. Oblivious to Angelique's delicate state, she proceeded to model her frilly pale blue gown. "I'm not sure I should have chosen the blue. Perhaps the pink would have done more for my complexion," she said turning before the oblong mirror. "Of course there aren't enough people here to worry about how I look anyway. I really don't understand why you couldn't have a big wedding as originally planned. I'm sure your parents wouldn't have begrudged you a nice wedding. Oh well, it's too late now, isn't it? Aimee, could you do something with this stray curl?" Lael asked, tugging at a piece of hair her maid had meticulously worked on for an hour. "I don't know what is the matter with Gina lately. She doesn't do anything the way I like it. Well, I'd better check on *Maman*. Let me know if I can help you with anything, Angelique," she threw over her shoulder as she left the room.

"It's time to put your dress on, ma'am," Aimee said, relieved that they were alone again.

Angelique stared at the ivory satin gown Aimee held so delicately. It had been her mother's wedding gown, and Aimee had worked day and night to make it fit her tall, slim figure. Tears filled Angelique's eyes as she ran her hand over the cool satin. "It seems improper to wear this when I'm in mourning."

"I think your aunt was right when she insisted. Your mother would have wanted it."

143

Angelique rubbed her temples, a gesture she repeated often these days. "Everything has happened so fast. I wish I had time to be alone, to think . . ."

Aimee slid the satin material over Angelique's head, careful not to disturb her hair. "M'sieur LaFrancois says it is not good to think on the tragedy, ma'am. It will only make you feel worse."

"Everyone tells me what I should and shouldn't do," Angelique protested. "Will I never be allowed to have a thought of my own again?"

Moments later Angelique stared out the window, guiltily aware she was putting off going downstairs where Andre waited. What did she really know about this man she was about to marry? He was a nobleman, with the occasional pompous attitude most nobility seemed to possess. Lael had said he was in great demand by mothers looking to match their daughters with a title. Was that the reason my parents selected him, she wondered, laying her forehead against the cool glass of the window. She had been given a choice. She could have said no to Andre, but she hadn't—even after the fiasco at the Lock and Key Club—even after Damian had warned her.

Damian. She had tried not to think about him since Paris. He and Beau had planned to return to America on Beau's new ship, but the ship still sat in the harbor, a constant reminder of her brother's mysterious disappearance.

"Mademoiselle, it is time," Aimee urged softly. "You can't keep your guests waiting any longer."

A barely audible whisper went through the small

group of guests as Angelique appeared. Her eyes stood out like pools of purple velvet in contrast to her pale skin and black hair. She slowly moved down the aisle with faltering steps, the single white rose in her gloved hands trembling noticeably. She focused on Andre standing at the altar with the count beside him.

She didn't love him. Why was she going through with this? *I need him*, she told herself. *This isn't like you, Angelique, you've never needed anyone before. Oh, God, I feel as if I'm falling headlong into an abyss, yet I can't seem to do anything to prevent it.* As she moved closer, her eyes locked with Andre's dark eyes. *Why couldn't it be Damian standing there waiting for me? Why couldn't he return my love?*

Andre reached out to take her hand as she hesitated a few steps from him. Suddenly the door behind the altar was flung open and a gasp echoed throughout the chapel. Beau leaned heavily against the doorjamb, his eyes glazed with hatred.

"Beau," Angelique gasped. "Oh Beau, you're alive . . ."

"Just barely, thanks to LaFrancois," he growled pointing one of the two pistols he held at Andre.

Andre moved toward Beau, his hand going to the gun under his satin jacket. "You're a fool, Charbonne. You're in no shape to stop this marriage. This room is filled with my men, my friends."

"With the exception of one," Damian Legare's voice announced from the rear of the church.

"Make that two," Adam Legare said, falling in behind his brother.

145

Andre gave a nervous laugh. "Surely everyone here can see Beau is not himself. The shock of his parents' death has done something to his mind."

"If that is the case," Damian said, "then you won't mind postponing the wedding until he is well."

"No! Angelique and I will be married now. Take him," Andre ordered Count Girard. Before his friend had a chance to move, Adam had a gun in his side.

Angelique stood watching the scene unfold before her. The organist still played from the alcove at the back of the chapel and the candles lining the aisle and altar were dripping into grotesque shapes. Her eyes blurred as she stared at them, trying to make her brain work. Was she imagining that Beau stood on the altar brandishing a gun at her fiancé? Had the strain of the last few weeks finally become too much for her? She looked up into green eyes as Damian grasped her arm and pulled her along behind him. To the cave? Was that what he had whispered as she was propelled along?

The sound of a single shot brought her out of her stupor. "Where are we going?" she managed to ask.

"To the ship," Damian said, still pulling her along.

"Beau . . . where is Beau? We can't leave him behind. Why are we running?"

"Beau and Adam are right behind us, just keep moving. Damn that long dress! Why couldn't you have been in those breeches of yours? It certainly would have made it easier."

Oh God, she couldn't think straight. Too many things were happening too fast, everything crowding in on her . . . Beau was alive . . . Why had he held a gun on

Andre! . . . the hate on his face . . . why had Andre refused to postpone the wedding? Damian's hand was warm on hers. Were they children again, running through the caves? She could smell the salt air of the sea, hear the roar of the ocean. Would she wake up any minute now and find her parents' death had only been a nightmare?

Another shot reverberated against the walls of the cave. As a new paroxysm of hysterical fear took hold of her, her mind suddenly cleared. This wasn't a nightmare. They were running for their lives—running from Andre and his friends, but why?

"Come on, Angel, don't slow down now," Damian urged. "Do you want me to carry you?"

"No, I'm all right," she said, hefting the long train of her gown over her arm.

A longboat with two men waited at the water's edge. Damian paused, holding Angelique close to him, both of them breathing heavily. "I hear Beau and Adam right behind us."

Adam came out of the cave's entrance first, then Beau appeared, staggering as he hit the sand. Angelique was instantly at his side.

"Hurry, Damian, get him into the boat."

"No! I'm not going," he said surprising them. "Just listen for a minute," he insisted as everyone started arguing. "Angelique, I want you to go with Damian to America. I've got to stay here and straighten things out."

"I don't understand what is happening, but I will not leave you," Angelique said firmly.

"Angelique, Andre killed *Maman* and Papa."

Frozen, as if she had turned to stone, Angelique listened as Beau explained, as briefly as possible, how he had been drugged and held in the sewers of Paris by Andre's revolutionary friends. How they bragged of killing the Charbonnes and how they were going to kill him next. Fortunately, one man had taken pity on him and hid him out after telling Andre that he had killed him. Angelique only stared into Beau's gray eyes.

"Angelique, are you listening?" he asked shaking her roughly by the shoulders. Angelique nodded, unable to make her throat work. "I spent the week before *Maman* and Papa were killed investigating Andre. He's the leader of a band of cutthroats and even the radicals hate and fear him. He planned to get the Charbonne money by killing all of us, Angelique . . . even you."

Angelique threw her arms around Beau, holding to him for dear life. "We must go back and explain all this to the authorities."

"No, Angelique. Andre is no fool. He has thought all this through very carefully, and he has powerful friends. Right now I can't prove what I've told you, but I already have the promise of the man who saved me that he will help. Now you must go with Damian to America where you will be safe. I will let you know when you can return to Brittany."

"No," Angelique pleaded, "I won't go without you. I can help . . ."

"Angelique, we don't have time to argue. I have two very good friends waiting to help me. Now you must go with Damian!"

Damian interrupted for the first time. "I agree with

Angelique. I don't like the idea of leaving you here."

"Listen to me, both of you. If Andre somehow got his hands on Angelique again, I wouldn't stand a chance of proving what I've said. He'd marry her and kill her before I could prevent it. She's got to be out of his reach so I don't have to worry about her. Now we're out of time. Damian, take good care of her. Keep her safe, or you'll answer to me. I'll be in touch as soon as possible," Beau promised leading them toward the waiting long-boat. "And Damian, the ship is yours. Do me proud by her."

"Now hold on, Beau. I'll accept the loan of your ship, but that's all."

"We'll argue about that another time. For now she's yours." Beau turned and hugged Angelique to him, then shook hands with Damian. "God go with you."

Adam, who had been guarding the cave entrance came running across the sand. "Wait, I'm going with you," he shouted.

"Are you sure, Adam?"

"Of course. I had already decided to accept your offer. I just hadn't planned on leaving so abruptly."

Damian lifted a silent Angelique into the boat, then he and Adam began to shove it off the sand as Beau disappeared back into the cave.

"No! I can't," Angelique cried, attempting to get out of the boat. "I can't leave him."

"Angelique, for God's sake, sit down," Damian pleaded.

"No, I won't leave him here. I may be able to help him."

"Damn it, sit down before I have to tie you in the boat," Damian shouted as the boat tilted precariously.

"I can't leave him," she cried, jumping back into the water despite Damian's firm grip on her wrist.

The heavy wedding gown dragged her under the water instantly. Damian struggled against the incoming waves and the weight of her dress. The water sucked greedily at them, trying to drag them both under. Damian finally managed to get his footing and hauled Angelique up onto her feet. "Damn it, girl, your foolishness is going to get us all killed!"

Angelique was hysterical, pounding ineffectually against Damian's chest.

"I'm sorry, Angel, but I don't know any other way." Damian swiftly clipped Angelique on the chin, then picked her up as her knees buckled. He lifted her to Adam who was already in the boat, then climbed in beside them. He looked back toward the beach but it was already deserted.

Chapter Eleven

Damian was reluctant to give the order to sail. When he attempted to explain the circumstances to the crew, he found Beau had already given them orders to sail under him. They were ready and willing to follow his orders, but now he paced the bow, indecision nagging at him. He didn't like the idea of leaving Beau any more than Angelique did, yet it made sense getting her away to safety. But, God, if anything happened to Beau he'd never forgive himself.

"Angelique is resting now," Adam said, joining Damian at the rail. "She's still angry, but I don't think she'll try anything foolish." Adam realized the crew was standing at ease, still waiting for Damian's orders. "Shouldn't we be getting under way?"

"I'm going back to help Beau. You'll have to take Angelique on to South Carolina."

"Whoa, hold on a minute, big brother. I know nothing about ships. Besides, I don't think Beau would trust just anyone with his sister, particularly after he's gone through so much to protect her. It looks to me like he thought this through pretty carefully; the ship is stocked with provisions, Angelique's trunks have been brought aboard, the crew is prepared to sail under your orders . . ."

Damian ran his hand through his hair in a gesture of frustration. "I suppose you're right, but damn, I hate leaving him here!"

"I can go back," Adam volunteered. "Perhaps I could be of some help."

Damian studied this stranger that was his brother. He had no way of knowing what kind of man Adam was. If he let him go back would he be of any help to Beau or just get in the way?

Adam laughed at Damian's obvious reluctance. "I can defend myself, if that's what concerns you."

"I'm sorry, Adam. It's just that we don't know much about each other."

"No we don't, Damian, but I think we're both ready to remedy that."

"You're damned right we are," Damian agreed, slapping his brother on the back. "I don't know why I'm worrying about Beau. He's always been able to take care of himself."

"He did seem quite confident he could take care of everything once Angelique was out of the way," Adam pointed out.

"Mr. Maxwell, get her under way," Damian ordered the chief engineer. Within seconds the crew quickly and efficiently had the ship leaving the rocky coast of Brittany behind.

Rough seas on the first day out kept Adam in his cabin with an unmistakable case of seasickness, and kept Damian on a twenty-four hour vigil on deck. When he finally got a chance to check on Angelique he found her cabin empty. All kinds of thoughts went through his mind as he took the steps by threes.

"Have you seen Mademoiselle Charbonne?" he asked the first seaman he encountered.

"Not since I served her breakfast in your brother's cabin, sir."

Anger seized Damian in a vise-like grip as he headed for Adam's cabin. Here he had been fighting all his natural instincts to take Angelique to his bed, but had fought them like some knight in shining armor. Now his brother had . . .

He shoved the door open, letting it slam back against the wall. Angelique jumped from her seat beside the bunk, her eyes wide with shock. "For heaven's sake, try to be quiet. Adam just went to sleep."

Sheepishly Damian stood there trying to find something to say so he wouldn't look like such a fool. "What is wrong with him?" he finally asked.

"It would seem to me, you being a man of the sea, that you would know without asking," she answered in a clipped tone.

"How long has he been seasick?"

"Almost from the time we left the coast. The cook gave me quinine to give him, but it hasn't helped much," she replied, gently wiping Adam's forehead with a damp cloth.

Damian's muscles tensed as he watched the show of tenderness. He wanted to tell her to return to her cabin and stay away from Adam, but he knew he was acting like a jealous fool. What the hell was the matter with him?

"Adam told me he was ill on the crossing to France when he and your mother left America," Angelique added, feeling awkward with Damian's silence.

"There are some people who can never travel on the sea without being violently ill. It looks like Adam might be one of them," Damian said, thinking of the plans they had made for Adam to sail with him as a ship's doctor.

"Did you want something," Angelique asked without looking at Damian.

"I thought we should talk. I'd like to explain . . ."

"We have nothing to talk about," Angelique cut him short.

"Angelique, I'm sorry about what happened, but you were about to drown both of us."

Adam moaned and tossed on the bed. "Your brother needs his rest, Damian. Our talking is disturbing him."

"We will talk later then, Angelique," Damian said, leaving the cabin with his anger barely in control. It wasn't proper for her to be alone in the cabin with Adam, he told himself. *Who the hell are you kidding? a little voice asked. Since when did you ever worry about what was proper? Why can't you admit it made jealous seeing her tenderly administer to Adam?*

Damian slammed his fist on the polished wood of the

deck's railing. "I promised I'd protect your sister, Beau Charbonne, but I have a feeling it's going to be more than I bargained for."

The ship was everything Beau had boasted. They had been under steam ever since leaving the coast and Damian couldn't find any fault with her. She moved swiftly and almost silently through the heavy seas. By burning anthracite coal there were no sparks and very little smoke. As Beau had said, the crew was one of the best. They worked efficiently and amicably. Damian particularly liked Joshua Maxwell, an American who was the chief engineer. There was an easy, relaxed relationship between the two men ever since Damian stepped on the ship. For that reason, Damian didn't hesitate to ask him to have one of the crew keep an eye on Angelique. After that awkward day in the cabin, he only visited Adam when he knew Angelique had returned to her cabin. He also made it a point to eat with his crew, while Angelique usually took her meals in her cabin or with Adam.

Damian had successfully avoided her for several days, until late one night as he lay awake on his bunk, he heard a crash outside his door. He quickly pulled on his pants and boots and then slipped on a shirt without bothering to button it.

As he opened his cabin door he came face to face with the cook coming from Angelique's cabin. Behind him Angelique stood, clutching her robe of white wool to her.

"Sorry, Captain. I was bringing the mademoiselle some coffee and like the clumsy oaf I am I dropped the mug."

"It's all right, Sess. I was just worried it might be my brother." Damian turned back toward his cabin as Sess left to retrieve another mug, but Angelique's soft voice stopped him in his tracks.

"Damian, are you going to avoid me forever?"

"I thought that was what you wanted," he said turning to face her.

"I admit I was angry at first, but I've had time to realize you did what you thought was necessary. Besides, I need you as my friend, Damian."

"The last thing I want is to argue with you, Angelique."

"Please come inside, Damian," Angelique said, holding out her hand to him. "Have some coffee with me."

Once inside the cabin the silence was deafening. Angelique tried to avoid staring at Damian's bronzed, muscled chest under the open shirt. "Adam is improving," she said for lack of anything else.

"Yes, thanks to your fine nursing. I spoke with him earlier this evening."

"Is your jaw all right?" Damian asked, studying the fine features of her face. "I had intended to ask sooner, but never had a chance."

Angelique smiled as she tested her jaw between her thumb and forefinger. "I cursed you for days afterward, but it's fine now. Just be warned, don't ever try that again."

Damian laughed. "I'm warned."

Sess returned with two mugs, then again they were left alone. Angelique poured them coffee, then handed one mug to Damian. Their fingertips touched as he took the mug of steaming coffee.

Angelique quickly turned away and sat on the side of her bunk. "Damian, I've been very curious about how you came to be with Beau at the church."

"He met me when I returned to Crozon. He had been staying aboard his ship in the harbor, knowing I was due back. He told me the whole story and asked my help to stop the wedding. He didn't tell me the rest of his plan. I guess he knew I wouldn't have agreed to leaving him there."

"Do you think he will be all right?"

"Yes, I'm sure of it."

"What is to become of me?"

"What do you mean?"

"What do I do until Beau sends word I can return to Crozon? Where will I stay? Suddenly my whole life is turned upside down and no one tells me anything. I'm sailing to America and I'm not even sure why."

The bewildered look on Angelique's face tore at Damian's heart. He placed his mug on the table and sat next to her. Taking her hand in his, he began to explain. "Our first stop will be Bermuda. We'll load supplies there and then put Beau's ship to the test by running the blockade into Charleston."

"And once in Charleston?" she asked wide-eyed.

"You'll stay at my home. Bessie will love having someone around to pamper."

"Bessie?" Angelique repeated hesitantly, wondering if there was a woman in Damian's life.

"Bessie is the woman who raised me. You'll love her."

"God, Damian, sometimes I can't believe what has happened," Angelique whispered. "When I think about it I want to kill Andre myself, and I swear, if he harms Beau I will kill him."

"You'll have to stand in line, Angel, but put it out of your mind. Beau will be fine."

"It's so strange, Damian, I keep thinking when I return to Crozon *Maman* and Papa will be waiting, but they won't be, and it's all my fault."

Damian drew her into his arms, caressing the back of her neck. "Don't ever think that way, Angel. Andre had Michel and Genevieve fooled, or they wouldn't have chosen him as a suitable husband for you."

"How could he have done such terrible things?" she asked, pain contorting her face, "and he planned to kill me too."

"Please, try not to think about it, he said. "You are safe."

Suddenly he held her face between his hands, rubbing his thumb across her parted lips. He leaned forward and gently touched where his thumb had just traced, slowly increasing the pressure until his tongue touched her tongue. A moan escaped Angelique from deep within her throat. She clung to him, savoring the feel of his muscles rippling beneath her innocent exploring hands. His lips moved from her mouth, slowly laying kisses along her jaw before gently nibbling on her ear lobe.

"You're so beautiful," he whispered, his breath warm against her neck.

Dreamily, her eyes half-closed, Angelique felt Damian remove her wrapper while he left a burning trail of kisses where the skin was exposed. One hand caressed her bare waist, while the other teased one nipple, sending a fire racing through Angelique's veins. Every touch, every kiss heightened her desire for the unknown. He was taking possession of her mind and body and she couldn't resist—wouldn't resist. She clung to him like a drowning person as he gently pushed her back on the bed. Moving beneath his aroused body, she could feel his rigid manhood against her thigh. Her hips raised instinctively, craving satisfaction. Damian moaned, drinking the sweetness of her mouth, bringing her desire to a fevered pitch.

The thought of finally being loved by Damian brought tears to Angelique's eyes. As Damian's lips moved along her face he tasted the saltiness of those tears. "Oh God," he moaned.

Angelique instantly sensed the change in him. He pulled from her embrace and sat on the side of the bed, his head in his hands. "I'm sorry, Angelique," he said without looking at her. "Your brother entrusted your safety to me and here I'm the one you need protecting from."

"This is the last time you play these games with me, Damian," she shouted as he headed for the door. "I swear, if you leave me I don't ever want to see you again. Why are you so hateful," she sobbed. "Are you trying to drive me insane?"

"I'm sorry," was all he said before leaving.

As they neared the islands the weather turned calm and warmer. Adam, still weak and a little green from his bout with seasickness, managed to come on deck with Angelique's help.

Angelique took a deep breath, inhaling the smell of the early morning air. What a beautiful morning, she thought raising her face to the sun. It was almost as if she could feel the jubilance and strength of freedom through the rise and fall of the deck. You could almost sense the pride of the crew as they put their strength and skill to work in tandem with nature's energy. For the first time in her life she realized why her father and brother loved the sea. The fresh salt air had a way of clearing one's mind and soul.

Damian walked past them, engrossed in conversation with one of the seamen. He nodded in their direction, but said nothing.

"What is the matter with him?" Adam asked, staring after his brother.

"I really wouldn't know," Angelique answered, busying herself by wrapping a wool blanket around Adam's shoulders.

"No." Adam removed the blanket. "Thank you, Angelique, but I really don't need that. I'm afraid my brother already thinks little of me as a man."

"Oh no, Adam. Damian's attitude doesn't have anything to do with you."

Adam smiled at Angelique's flustered state. "Then you do know what's wrong with my brother?"

"Yes . . . I'm afraid Damian finds me a burden."

"I find that hard to believe. I've seen that special light in his eyes when he speaks of you."

"I wish that were true, Adam," she answered staring

out to sea. "If you promise not to laugh at me I'll confide something to you," Angelique said, suddenly needing someone to talk to.

"We are friends, Angelique, and I would be honored if you confided in me."

Angelique leaned back against the railing watching Damian as he worked with his men. "I've loved Damian since I was a child. I always dreamed he would be the one that I would marry. Sometimes I think he feels something for me, then other times he closes himself off. Several times he has kissed me, and I think he is . . . well, you know . . . but every time he pulls back. I don't understand him, Adam. I love him. Why can't he return that love? He is driving me crazy."

"All right. I have a plan. You and I are going to make my brother see the light."

Angelique's eyes sparkled mischievously. "What do you mean?"

"There is nothing like jealousy to make a man realize what he wants."

"Oh, Adam," Angelique giggled. "Would we dare?"

"I think he is already peeved that you've spent so much time with me. He feels reasonably safe though since I've been sick. But, now . . ." he said, holding out his arm to her. "My dear Mademoiselle Charbonne, would you honor me with a stroll around the deck?"

"I would love to, Dr. Legare," she answered a warm smile brightening her face.

Damian let the rope he held drop, and the sails began flopping wildly as he stared at the couple strolling casually below him like lovers in a park. Angelique was looking into Adam's face, hanging on his every word.

"This is no place for a Sunday stroll," he bellowed. "I suggest you go below and stay out of the way of my men."

Angelique had to turn her face away to keep from laughing. "Sorry, Damian," Adam shouted. "Angelique and I have not had a chance to get much fresh air."

Damian looked embarrassed. He busied himself by gathering in the stray sails. "We'll be on the island in a few hours," he said before turning his back to the couple below him.

"What did I tell you?" Adam laughed as he and Angelique crossed the deck. "Jealousy rears its ugly head in all of us—even the infallible Damian Legare."

Chapter Twelve

Adam stood on the deck with Damian as they headed into the picturesque harbor of St. George. There were already more than a dozen blockade runners lying in the harbor, all deserted while their crews enjoyed the island.

"God, this is beautiful. I've never seen such color," Adam exclaimed.

"Those reefs provide a barrier of protection from the seas, but they can also lay open a ship from her bow to her stern in a matter of seconds. Look over the side and you'll see what I mean."

Adam leaned over the railing and was stunned by what he saw. The penetrating sunlight revealed towering pinnacles of coral just below the surface in the incredibly clear water.

"Bermuda was originally called the Isle of Devils because of those devilish reefs," Damian informed Adam. "In the early days it was a happy event for the islanders when a ship wrecked on the reefs. The people turned into vultures, stripping the vessels down to the last nail. Those speechless, hidden coral devils have even managed to snatch a few blockade runners. They almost got me one night."

"One night? My God, what were you doing coming in here at night?"

"We had spent twelve hours with a Yankee man-of-war in our wake, and we didn't lose him until dark. By the time we reached Bermuda we were all ready to get drunk. There wasn't one of us who wanted to sit out here beyond the reefs where we could see the lights of the island. With a little encouragement I tried it. We hung up right over there," Damian said pointing to a place where the coral was exposed. "Fortunately we just grazed it. We made it into port with very little damage."

"What a reckless life you blockade runners lead. I've been listening to the crew telling stories, and it sounds to me like you lead the life of a pirate— drinking, eating, orgies. I don't know how you've stayed alive this long."

Damian laughed. "The crew tends to exaggerate. It's true, we do enjoy living high on the hog when we're here, but the islanders expect us to. You'll see what I mean when we check into the hotel. Blockade runners are treated like royalty, but believe me, at the exorbitant prices, we pay for it."

"Sounds like an interesting place," Adam commented.

"Now, if you want interesting," Damian laughed,

"I'll take you to Shinbone Alley. You can buy any kind of diversion there, and the best damned rum you ever tasted."

"All I want right now is to feel firm ground under my feet. Once I get off this ship you're going to have a hell of a time getting me back on it."

The hotel was a beautiful white limestone building with bright green shutters. The grounds bloomed profusely with bright flowers that scented the air with their fragrance. As Damian had predicted, they were given a warm welcome.

"Angelique and I are going to have dinner in the hotel dining room," Adam announced, winking at Angelique. "Would you like to join us?"

Damian stared at the two of them for a moment. "No thanks, I've got to meet with John Bourne tonight and try to expedite the loading of the ship."

"Well, if you should change your mind, you know where you can find us."

Damian stared after the two of them as they left him standing at the desk. Just where would he find them later, he wondered.

The hotel dining room was a wall of windows overlooking St. George's harbor. When Damian entered the room with his guest, the agent for the Confederate States of America, Angelique and Adam were already finishing their dinner and engrossed in

conversation. Damian found it very difficult to concentrate on his conversation with John Bourne as he
watched the two of them. Angelique was gorgeous in
a green silk gown, with a heart shaped neckline,
exposing her creamy flesh. She leaned forward, showing even more of herself as she laughed at something
Adam said. Damian had an ache in his groin as he
watched her smile at Adam.

"What do you think, Captain Legare," Bourne
asked.

"I'm sorry, what did you say those figures were?"

Bourne laughed. "I see the young lady you're
eyeing. She is very beautiful, but I'd be willing to bet
the gentleman is her husband."

Damian almost choked on his drink. "What were
those figures again?"

"I think it's hopeless, Adam. Damian isn't interested in me. He is making it very obvious. I'm
wasting your time when you could be with someone
else."

"I don't want to be with anyone else, Angelique.
I'm thoroughly enjoying myself. I keep hoping that
you'll see what a charming, handsome devil I am and
fall head over heels in love with me."

"Oh, Adam," Angelique giggled, "you are a dear,
sweet friend. You have a way of making me feel so
good."

"Well, that dashes my hopes," he answered good
naturedly. "If it makes you feel any better, Damian

has been glaring at me ever since he came in."

"Has he really?" she asked hopefully.

Adam lifted her hand and placed a kiss on her palm. "Keep talking. This should drive him crazy."

"Adam, there is something I've been wanting to talk to you about."

"Yes, what is it?"

"I'd like you to teach me all about medicine."

"Teach you medicine," he repeated.

"I'm serious, Adam. Damian needs someone to sail with him who knows about doctoring. Since you won't be able to, I will."

"Whoa, young lady, I feel bad enough about not being able to sail with Damian, but don't make it worse."

"Oh, Adam, I'm sorry. It wasn't my intention to make you feel bad. It's just that I want to be able to help. I've always had a gift for treating animals—why not people? Surely you can teach me to dress wounds and treat fevers, or whatever else a seaman might encounter. I watched you the other day when you treated the man who burned his hand. I could have done the same."

Adam shook his head. "Angelique, I spent years studying medicine. How do you think I can teach you all I know in just a few days?"

"Please, Adam."

"Even if I tried, there is no way Damian is going to let you sail with him."

"Let me worry about that," she smiled confidently.

* * *

Gritting his teeth, Damian watched as Adam and Angelique seemed to be absorbed in an intimate conversation.

"Well, that about covers everything," Bourne finished. "You didn't touch your dinner, Captain. Was there something wrong with it?"

"No, I wasn't very hungry," Damian answered, watching Adam and Angelique heading toward the exit holding hands. "John, if you will excuse me, I just remembered some very important business. I'll be at your office first thing in the morning."

The sun was setting, turning the sea into molten gold, but Damian was in too big a hurry to escape the hotel and return to his ship to notice. What was the problem, he asked himself as he sat on the bow staring back toward the hotel. Adam was a fine man. He would be just the type of man the Charbonnes would want Angelique to marry. Why then did it bother him so much? Angrily he threw his cigar over the side. Damn it, he promised to protect Angelique and he wasn't doing a very good job of it. It was time he found out just what Adam's intentions were.

He tried not to show his obvious relief when he found Adam in his room reading a medical journal.

"Did you get your business taken care of?" Adam asked, looking up from his book.

"Not all of it, but I'm meeting Bourne again in the morning."

"I think I'm going to visit the hospital tomorrow," Adam said. "Who knows, maybe I'll stay on the island and avoid ever having to sail again."

Damian studied his brother for a moment. "I want to talk to you about Angelique."

"Of course," Adam said, laying his book aside. "What do you want to talk about?"

"I'd like to know what your intentions are," he said, knowing how foolish he sounded.

"Right now we're just friends, but who knows what it will lead to," Adam answered, enjoying the look on Damian's face. "Do you have any objection? I mean, if you care for her, just tell me and I'll stay away."

"Of course I care for her," Damian answered angrily. "I'd have to be made of stone not to, but I promised Beau I'd look after her. What the hell am I supposed to do?"

"I'd say you've got a problem, big brother, but if you're worried about me, don't. My intentions are purely honorable."

Damian glared at Adam for a moment. "If you haven't already included Angelique in your tour of the hospital, I'd like to show her around the island tomorrow."

"That's fine with me, but you'd better check with the lady. Don't forget we're invited to Mount Wyndham tomorrow night. Captain Russell tells me we're very lucky to have arrived on the island in time for this party. It seems Mrs. Darrell feels it is her duty to entertain the Confederate blockade runners when they're on the island, and she does it with real style."

"Yes, I know. I've been to a couple of her parties. She invites all the beautiful women of the island.

Maybe you'll find one to your liking."

"I've already found one to my liking," Adam grinned.

"Adam . . ."

Adam held up his hands in mock surrender. "I told you, all you have to do is tell me to stay away from her."

"The lady has a mind of her own, Adam. I have no doubt she'll see whoever she wants. I'm going to turn in now. I have to be at Bourne's early tomorrow. Why don't we plan to meet here for dinner and then go on to the party together?"

"And that way you can keep an eye on me, right, big brother?"

"Exactly," Damian laughed. "Will you see Angelique in the morning?"

"Yes, I'm having breakfast with her."

"I thought as much. Would you mind telling her my plans and ask her to wait for me. I should be there by ten."

"Afraid she'd say no if you asked her yourself?" Adam laughed at the look on his brother's face. "All right, I'll tell her."

Angelique didn't tell Adam, but she had no intention of waiting for Damian. She was tired of being torn apart by his indecision.

Thirty minutes before he was to arrive Angelique headed for the garden. The hotel sat on a hill overlooking the harbor, and from where she stood the colors of nature were magnificent. The sea was shades of jade and turquoise under a bright blue sky laced with clouds of fleecy white. Mesmerized by the sights and scents, she didn't hear Damian approach.

"Why didn't you wait for me?" he asked. "Did Adam tell you I'd be here?"

"He told me," she said walking away from him.

"Angelique, if one of the staff hadn't seen you come out here I wouldn't have found you," he said getting impatient with her attitude.

"You weren't supposed to find me," she answered nonchalantly.

Damian grabbed her by the shoulders and turned her to face him. "All right, Angelique, I understand why you're mad at me, and I'm sorry. I warned you I wasn't an easy person to get along with. Now, why don't we call a truce. We're going to be thrown together for quite awhile and it isn't going to be very pleasant if we can't even talk to each other."

Angelique was silent, then she smiled up at him. "Is Charleston this beautiful?"

"It is beautiful in a different way." Damian answered, remembering how his mother had hated the lovely city.

"I've always dreamed of seeing America. I just never imagined it would be like this."

"Things don't always go as we plan, little one, but you have to make the best of whatever happens."

Angelique walked away, staring out over the sea. "Adam said you wanted to show me around the island."

"That's right. I have a carriage waiting. I thought we would start with a ride on the far side of the island and then stop for a bite to eat. I don't want to make too long a day of it since we're going to a party tonight."

Angelique stopped and faced Damian. "I really am not in the mood for partying, Damian. I wish you and Adam would go without me."

"Absolutely not. We'll only be on the island for a few days and I'm not going to let you miss this party."

"I understand all the eligible young women of the island attend. Why should you care if I'm there?"

"I care, Angelique. Now come on, the driver won't wait forever."

"The island is only twenty-two miles from end to end," Damian explained as the carriage moved slowly along. "It was named for Juan de Bermudez, a Spanish navigator who discovered it in 1503. A group of English later settled here after their ship wrecked on the reefs."

Angelique found herself relaxing as she listened to Damian. He seemed to know everything about the island. He showed her a beautiful lagoon, then the gardens of one of the plantations. Afterward they stopped for a lunch of lobster and champagne.

"I've never seen anything quite like this island," Angelique said. "It is so beautiful, and the people are so friendly." The carriage moved past houses painted every color of the rainbow. One in particular caught Angelique's attention. "Please, Damian, can we stop? I want to see that beautiful place."

Damian had the driver stop in front of the tree-lined drive. The house at the end was pale, shell pink with an immense lawn spreading down to the sea. The driver told them the house had belonged to an artist from New York, but since the war it had been for sale.

"My sister used to cook for de man," he informed them. "If you would like to see de house, the key is under de flower pot."

"What do you say? Shall we take the tour," Damian asked, seeing the anticipation in Angelique's eyes.

"Let's do. It will be a fitting end to our day."

The driver opened the house and then left them alone to wander around. The living room windows overlooked the sea. Angelique stood mesmerized.

"It's beautiful. Just beautiful," she sighed. "I would put a piano right here in front of the doors, and a big chair right there where I could sit and look at the view. Look, Damian, I can see the ship from here."

Damian leaned against the doorjamb, taking in every expression on Angelique's face. What would it be like to have a wife and family, he wondered for a brief moment. He felt so good around her.

"Come, I want to see the rest of the house," Angelique said excitedly. "The view from upstairs must be magnificent."

"You had quite a view at the chateau," he laughed.

"Yes, but it was different. The chateau seemed closed off from the sea. Here you feel a part of it."

Angelique floated happily through the house, humming softly. She opened the French doors in the bedroom and let the warm breeze caress her.

Damian watched, his eyes feasting on her breasts rising and falling with excitement. What in the hell was he going to do. He wanted her—he ached with it. If he kept up with this big brother act he'd probably end up raping her to ease his pain, but he didn't want that. You fool, what do you want, he silently asked himself. You know damned well what you want.

"I would put my bed right here where I could see the sun come up and enjoy the stars at night."

Damian had to turn away so she wouldn't see his obvious desire. "We better get going, Angelique. I don't want to keep Adam waiting."

Angelique stared after him as he left the room. She sighed as she closed the glass doors. What an unpredictable man, she thought. He had been so warm and pleasant all afternoon, then without warning he became cold and distant.

Angelique looked questioningly at Damian as she reached the door. He smiled at her. "I'm sorry to rush you, but I told Adam we would meet him at the hotel for dinner. I'm sure you want to rest before then."

Angelique said nothing as she accepted his hand into the carriage. As soon as they reached the hotel she quickly escaped to her room where she ordered a bath. Afterward, lying across the bed, she stared at the ceiling thinking about her feelings. She was crazy to want to get mixed up with a man as unpredictable as Damian, she told herself. He was cold and arrogant, without a sensitive bone in his body. Adam was sweet and considerate. Why couldn't she love him? she asked herself, as she brushed away a tear. "Why do I have to love Damian?" she asked aloud.

Chapter Thirteen

Dressed in a lilac gown of shot silk trimmed with a deeper shade of lavender, and cut very low across her breasts, Angelique turned every head as she entered the dining room. She smiled as Adam told her how beautiful she was, but said nothing.

After Adam and Damian realized Angelique wasn't in the mood for small talk, they also fell silent. The silence prevailed as the carriage made its way up the drive of Mount Wyndham.

The Darrells' home was bright with candles and lanterns, giving it a warm, inviting look and chasing away a little of Angelique's depression. Mrs. Darrell, a charming hostess, greeted them at the door and ushered them into the salon.

Angelique found herself enchanted by the elegance of the house. The furniture was cherry wood and upholstered in pale colors, with each piece picking up the beautiful colors of the magnificent paintings that hung everywhere. The doors dividing the room from the parlor had been opened, making one grand room that opened into the courtyard and garden where guests danced.

As Damian spoke with another officer, Adam pulled Angelique aside. "What happened today, Angelique? You've been so quiet all evening."

"I came to a very important decision today, Adam. Somehow I'm going to put Damian out of my thoughts."

Angelique looked across the room to where Damian was now surrounded by women. He was so breathtakingly handsome, his tall, muscular frame turned out in a brown suit and white silk shirt, with a vest of gold brocade. He looked every inch the successful man, yet his expression was one of weary disdain. Suddenly she realized he was staring back at her, and she was instantly aware of a trembling in her legs. Damn him for having that effect on me, she cursed silently, giving him a scathing look before turning back to Adam. Out of the corner of her eyes she could see Damian heading toward her. "I need some air," she said, but Damian was there before she escaped.

"Would you like to dance?" he asked as he rejoined them.

"Thank you, Damian, but Adam just asked me."

If Adam was surprised by her statement, he didn't show it. They left Damian and headed toward the garden where other couples danced. Angelique glanced back into the room and saw Damian leaning against the doorway watching them. His face was set in a grim expression, his mouth taut with suppressed emotion.

"I have a feeling I'm caught in the middle of some turbulence," Adam said, his eyes showing concern. "Are you going to tell me what happened today?"

"Nothing, Adam. Absolutely nothing. Damian was an excellent guide, and on the whole it was a very pleasant day. The only problem was that at the end of it he turned into a stranger."

"You've known all along what Damian is like. It didn't stop you from loving him before."

Before Angelique had a chance to answer Damian was at Adam's shoulder. "May I?" Adam stepped aside as Damian swept Angelique into his arms. Stunned and just a little breathless, she tried to close her mind to him, but found it hopeless. His hand was warm at her waist, holding her closer than custom approved. She could feel his tenseness; the anger he was trying to control.

"Why did you refuse me back there? Adam hadn't asked you to dance."

Angelique took a deep breath before answering. "You have made it quite clear how you feel toward me. Why shouldn't I prefer the company of someone who cares for me?"

For a moment Damian didn't answer. "I never said I didn't care for you."

Looking up, Angelique found his eyes studying her, his expression serious. "I believe it was you who told me to find a man who could teach me to understand my body and my desires."

Damian's green eyes widened in shock. "You didn't. Tell me you didn't."

"Excuse me, Captain, may I break in?" a young British officer asked.

"No!" Damian growled.

"Damian, don't be rude," Angelique said sweetly as she moved into the officer's arms.

Why did you let him think you had allowed Adam to become intimate, she chided herself. He will take his anger out on his brother. Over her partner's shoulder she could see Damian talking with Adam. His expression was angry, but Adam remained calm, shrugging his shoulders as Damian talked. While Angelique was engrossed in what was taking place across the room, another officer broke in.

"You looked as if you were bored to death," her new partner said. "I can remedy that."

"I beg your pardon?"

"Give me a chance and I'll liven this party up for you. We can walk further into the garden and . . ."

"Release me!" Angelique ordered.

"Now come on, sweetie, I just want to show you a good time."

"All right, Blake, go find yourself another partner," Damian ordered. "This lady belongs to me."

"Sorry, Legare, I didn't know. Excuse me, ma'am. No offense was meant."

Angelique turned to walk away, but Damian grabbed her wrist. "I'm not amused by your lies, Angelique."

"Just what is that supposed to mean?"

"You let me think you and Adam had . . ."

"Yes?" she asked, smiling sweetly.

"Damn, you infuriate me. One of these days you're going to push me too far," he threatened softly as he pulled her into his arms. She tried to pull away, but he held her firm. Their eyes were locked, dueling without words. The overwhelming physical power of his maleness dulled her senses. She suddenly relaxed, leaning into his hard body as they slowly moved to the music.

For the next two hours Damian never left her side. They danced, drank champagne, and walked in the garden. Angelique was in heaven. He had said she belonged to him. Maybe it was only for the night, but she would make the most of it.

"Are you having a good time?" he asked as they stopped for another glass of champagne.

"Yes, a wonderful time, but if I have one more glass of champagne you'll have to carry me home."

"That sounds like a fascinating prospect," he grinned.

"I say, old man, you've been keeping the most beautiful lady here to yourself all night. It's time you give someone else a chance."

"How are you, Taylor," Damian shook hands with the grinning officer. "I was sorry to hear you lost the *Banshee* last month."

"You're avoiding the subject, chap. Introduce me to your lovely lady."

Damian laughed good naturedly. "Tom Taylor, this

is Mademoiselle Angelique Charbonne."

The officer bowed, kissing Angelique's hand in a formal gesture. "I have watched the good captain occupy your entire evening. You must be bored to tears."

"No, not really, Angelique laughed.

"Then he is improving with age," he declared. "I've always heard he had a way of boring all the ladies."

Adam joined the trio and before long the talk was of the war. Damian stayed closed to Angelique, occasionally touching her in a possessive way. Her mind reeled with his closensss. She had given up hope, but now . . .

There was a commotion in the room as a group of people arrived. The woman, a beautiful redhead dressed in an oyster white gown, was quickly surrounded by young officers vying for her attention. Suddenly everyone cleared a path as she made her way toward them. Angelique looked at Damian and her heart stopped at the look of admiration on his face.

"Damian, I must speak with you," the woman said, as if no one else was there.

"Hello, Lacey. You're looking well."

"Please," she said, tears shimmering in her blue eyes. She held her hand out to him, and Damian followed without a word of explanation; only that he would be right back.

"I want to leave," Angelique said to Adam who had been as surprised as her at the little scene that had just taken place.

"Shouldn't we wait for Damian. He did say he'd be right back."

"I'm sure he'll be quite busy the rest of the evening."

Adam quickly gave up attempting conversation as they rode back to the hotel. He left Angelique at her room, wishing there was something that he could say or do to ease her pain. What was the matter with Damian, he wondered. How could he be so insensitive to Angelique's feelings?

The room was too warm to wear anything to bed, so Angelique slipped nude between the sheets. She tried not to think of the way the evening had ended. It had been so perfect until the redhead had walked in. How could she compete with someone like that? she asked herself. The woman was one of the most beautiful she had ever seen, and she also saw the way Damian had looked at her. It was as if he were taking credit for the way she looked—almost as if she belonged to him . . . no, she wouldn't think of it. She must sleep, she told herself, throwing her arm across her eyes as she tried to block out all thoughts. She had almost dozed off, when a pounding on her door bought her out of the daze.

"Open the door, Angelique," Damian ordered.

"Go away!"

"I mean it, open the door before I kick it in."

Angelique didn't answer. He wouldn't she told herself.

With one swift kick the lock gave. Angelique

grasped the sheet to her, staring unbelievingly as Damian stood in the doorway, his face dark with anger.

"Where is Adam?"

"How should I know?" she answered indignantly.

"Damn it woman, you push me to the limits. Do you mind telling me why you didn't wait for me? Were you so anxious to get back here with my brother?"

"I don't have to tell you anything," she answered defiantly.

"I thought you were enjoying yourself. Why did you leave?"

"Did you really think I was going to stay there while you went off with one of your . . . your girlfriends? I've lost most of my pride where you're concerned, Damian, but not all of it."

Damian's expression softened. He moved toward the bed and sat on the foot of it. Running his hand through his hair, he laughed. "I thought Adam would be here with you. I think I would have killed him with my bare hands."

Angelique swallowed, finding it difficult to speak. "Damian, I can't take much more of this. You've got to tell me what you want."

Damian moved closer to sit next to her. "I want you, Angel. Oh God, how I want you, but I don't want to be remembered as the man who tore your life to pieces."

As Angelique touched the side of his face, the sheet slipped, exposing her breasts. "I want you,

Angel, I want to whisper sweet words of love, feel your body next to mine, skin touching skin . . ." Suddenly he stood in a swift, frustrated move. "I'm sorry. I've got to get out of here."

"Damian," her voice stopped him before he reached the door. "If you leave me this time you may as well as say goodbye." Slowly he turned. She was bathed in moonlight, her dark hair the only thing that covered her breasts. He removed his jacket, then his shirt, never taking his eyes from her.

"I can't promise . . ."

"Hush," she ordered, as she held out her hand to him.

He lifted her chin with his finger, drawing her face upward. His warm lips touched hers gently, then he ran his tongue along her lips. A small moan escaped her as his fingers touched her skin. His mouth, still infinitely tender, consumed her breath with the barest trace of unleashed passion.

"I want you," he whispered against her mouth. "Oh God, how I want you."

"I want you too," she answered, her voice hoarse with desire, while her fingers explored his upper body, assessing the texture and muscles.

Damian ran his hand over the curve of her hips and across her firm stomach. Never had he experienced such a turbulence of emotion. She was an innocent, willing to give him her gift of love with no stipulations. Could he compromise her without giving some part of himself? But what did he have to offer?

Angelique sensed the change in Damian. His hand still moved over her skin, but suddenly the passion seemed to be tempered. She was afraid she wasn't doing what was expected.

"Tell me what to do, Damian," she said touching his chest.

He kissed her hand and placed it at her side. "Just lie still. I want to make it good for you." He laid a trail of kisses across her shoulder and down to her breasts, concentrating for a moment on each rosy peak before moving down over her stomach.

"Roll over," he commanded. Angelique did as ordered, shivering as his lips touched the small of her back then the back of her knees. She gripped the bed in sweet torment. She was alive with an all consuming need that only he could fill.

"Damian, I can't take much more," she moaned.

He rolled her back to face him. His hand moved from her hip to the triangle of dark hair between her legs. The heat from his fingers seemed to sear her vulnerable flesh. He leaned forward, taking one rigid nipple between his teeth as his hand caressed her most sensitive area. She arched her body off the bed, meeting the pressure of his hands, seeking satisfaction.

Angelique opened her eyes, pleading for him to come to her. Suddenly she realized he was still partially dressed. As inexperienced as she was, she knew instinctively what he was doing. He had no intention of taking her virginity. He still meant to keep his promise to her brother.

"Don't do this to me," she begged. "I need you."

"It's best this way, love. Relax, you're so close."

She was close. Her pulse pounded, threatening to explode, begging for release, but not like this. Not this impersonal violation.

"I will never forgive you," she said choking back a sob.

"Will you ever forgive me if I take you?" he asked, cradling her in his arms.

"You won't be taking anything I haven't offered, Damian. Don't you understand, I want you."

For a long moment Damian searched her eyes, then he began to remove his remaining clothes. The weight of his body lowered gently on her, pushing her deep into the feather mattress. "Temptress," he groaned as he gently parted her legs. Her hips raised instinctively seeking him. Her eyes were luminous with desire, begging him to take her.

"Easy, love, I don't want to hurt you." He entered her, quickly breaking the only barrier that safeguarded her virginity. He deliberately slowed his pace, prolonging the agonizing sweetness, delaying the exquisite release that would bring them both back to reality.

Angelique was beyond patience. When she moaned softly with pleasure, Damian forgot everything but the feel of her warm flesh joined with his. He could feel the tremors begin in her body as she rocked her head back and forth. The spiralling intense pleasure jolted through her. He met her passion with a final thrust, feeling as if the intenseness would consume him.

"You are exquisite," he whispered as they lay side by side.

Looking into Damian's eyes, Angelique thought she saw sadness. "You're not sorry?" she asked.

"You've given me the most beautiful gift a woman can give. I just hope you won't regret it in the light of day."

"I've given it to the man I've always loved," she said, touching his face. "No matter what happens, I'll never regret that."

Angelique quickly fell asleep nestled in Damian's arms, but Damian wasn't as lucky. His mind was much too active to let him sleep. The beautiful, passionate woman in his arms was Angelique: little Angelique who used to make his life miserable when they were children. Come to think of it, he smiled, she had also been making his life miserable for the last month. Miserable because he had wanted her so badly. Now what? he asked himself. Would his life ever be the same? If he faced the truth, did he really want it to be?

Chapter Fourteen

Angelique stretched like a cat, a contented smile on her face. She slowly rolled onto her side to study the man sleeping beside her. She touched a curl, thinking an artist would love to paint Damian. His profile was classical, with a full sensual mouth, and golden curls framed his bronze face. What beautiful children he would produce. If his seed grew within her, would the child look like him, she wondered as she touched his lips with the tip of her finger. Suddenly Damian's eyes opened. She wasn't sure what to say until he smiled at her.

"Good morning. I trust you slept well," she said.

"What little sleep you let me have," he teased.

Angelique turned red, remembering the wanton way she had reacted to their lovemaking. "I'm sorry."

"Don't be sorry, little one. You were a very pleasant surprise," Damian said, his voice soft with satisfaction as he nuzzled her neck.

"I must admit, I was pleasantly surprised myself. I didn't realize it would be like that."

"Not every woman finds it pleasurable," Damian said, as his lips traveled down her shoulder to her upper arm. "Most women are told from the time they are born that it is their lot in life and they have to bear it."

"Oh, I knew better than that," Angelique answered. "*Maman* always told me it would be special if I loved the man."

Angelique felt Damian tense before she finished her sentence. She was a fool, she told herself. You were no more than a way to pass the night. Don't expect him to feel what you feel. She lowered her lashes, suddenly unable to look into his face. "You needn't worry, Damian. I fully understand last night was nothing but amusement for you."

"Amusement?" he asked lifting her chin, forcing her to look into his eyes. "Is that what you thought it was?"

"That is what I think it was to you."

Before Damian could answer there was a knock at the door and Adam's voice followed. "Are you awake, Angelique?"

A strangled cry caught in Angelique's throat at the thought of Adam finding her in bed with Damian.

"Tell him you'll be downstairs shortly," Damian whispered, understanding her embarrassment. "I better leave you to get dressed," he said after Adam had left. "We'll talk later."

Angelique watched in silence as Damian dressed.

She couldn't think of anything to say. Why did Adam's timing have to be so bad? Damian had been about to tell her how he felt, but now . . .

When Damian finished dressing he stood at the foot of the bed looking at Angelique. God, she looked so young. He cursed himself silently for taking her without regard for her feelings or reputation. "I'll be back around noon. We'll talk then," he said leaning forward and placing a brief kiss on her lips.

Adam watched Angelique as she moved the croissant around her plate, with no intention of eating it. There was something definitely gnawing at her, and he wondered if she was still irritated at Damian for going off to talk to the beautiful redhead, who arrived late at the party.

"Did you sleep well?" he asked.

"Why do you ask that?" she asked guiltily.

Adam laughed. "I was just making conversation. You haven't had much to say this morning."

"I'm sorry, Adam. I'm afraid I have an awful lot on my mind."

"Can I help?"

"You've already been more help than you know, just being my friend. I don't want to burden you with more."

"Angelique," Adam said taking her hand, "friendship is never a burden. Now tell me what is wrong."

"I'm afraid, Adam. I feel as if I've been set adrift and have no idea where I'll end up—or if I will survive. What is to become of me, Adam?"

"Nothing is going to happen to you, sweet. You have Damian and me to take care of you. As soon as we hear from your brother, you can go on with your life."

Go on with my life, she pondered. After last night could she do that? "Adam, I'm going back to my room and rest for awhile. I really didn't sleep very well last night."

"All right, Angelique. I think I'll go see how the loading of the ship is coming along. Damian mentioned we might be ready to sail tomorrow."

Angelique paced her room, the events of the past month closing in on her. Her life had changed so drastically she found it difficult to think straight. Where would this strange turn of events lead her now? She had willingly given her virginity to Damian, knowing he would never make a commitment to her. That made her no better than a whore— except for the fact that she loved him. Oh, God, how she loved him, she admitted to herself, clutching the balcony railing until her knuckles turned white.

Looking down the path that led to the hotel, she could see Damian coming toward her. She felt a tingling sensation in the pit of her stomach as she watched him. He smiled and waved before disappearing into the hotel. A moment later he was knocking at the door. Angelique took a deep breath before answering. He stood, one hand inside his jacket, grinning like a Cheshire cat.

"I have a gift for you," he said, carefully removing

a small brown and black puppy from inside his jacket.

"Oh, he's darling. Where did you get him?" she asked taking the puppy and hugging it to her neck.

"A friend of mine, who sails out of Savannah, has the mother dog. She gave birth to these pups on his last run to the islands, and he has been trying to find homes for them before he sails again. When I saw them I had a feeling you'd like one."

"Oh, Damian, there is nothing you could have given me I would like more," she said still nuzzling the puppy. "He's so soft and cuddly."

"I'm not sure he'll stay that way. He will be a big dog. Probably as much as a hundred pounds."

"He'll still be soft and cuddly," Angelique said, kissing the top of the puppy's furry head.

Damian was silent as he watched Angelique talking to the puppy. She had so much love for everything, even for him, and he wasn't worth it. That was why he couldn't marry her. Her life would be miserable without love in return. Oh, he could give her passion—there would be plenty of passion. He couldn't look at her without wanting her, but what else could he offer her? If the war didn't go in favor of the South, he would lose Enchanteur, and everything that went with it. No, he wouldn't think of that. He would take things one day at a time.

"Damian, are you all right?" Angelique asked, noticing the pensive expression on Damian's handsome face.

"Yes, I'm fine," he answered, shaking the oppressive mood off. "What would you think about you and me, and your furry friend taking a picnic lunch to that pretty little pink cottage we found yesterday? I don't think anyone would mind us using that lovely expanse of green lawn for a picnic."

Damian had the kitchen prepare them a picnic of cold chicken, fruit and a bottle of white wine. They rode the short distance to the house in a rented carriage, chatting about the flowers that bloomed profusely on the island.

"It's strange," Angelique said as they pulled into the driveway. "It makes me sad coming here and seeing this house sit empty. It should be filled with a happy family."

Damian didn't say anything. He thought about Enchanteur and wondered if that was why it had never been a happy place. Perhaps if he and Angelique filled it with happy, laughing children . . . God, what was the matter with him? One night with her and he was talking about children.

"Over there, Damian. Under that tree would be perfect," Angelique instructed.

The puppy romped across the wide expanse of lawn while Damian and Angelique sat on a quilt and watched. Angelique clapped her hands for the puppy as he ran too far from them.

"You'll have to give him a name," Damian said.

"I've been thinking about it, but nothing appropriate has come to mind. Do you have any suggestions?"

"When I was watching the two of you together earlier he wouldn't leave your heels. How about Shadow?"

At that moment the puppy climbed into Angelique's lap and snuggled down to sleep. "Yes, I think Shadow is perfect," she laughed.

Damian lay back, his arms beneath his head. The sky was a brilliant blue with white fluffy clouds moving slowly above. It was hard to think about sailing tomorrow for the Carolina war-torn coast when it was so peaceful here. He dreaded exposing Angelique to the blockade and the hardships, and wished there were some other way.

"Adam says we will probably sail soon," Angelique said as if reading his mind.

"Tomorrow," he acknowledged, then said no more.

"I can see the ship from here," Angelique said after a few more moments of silence.

Damian leaned up on one elbow and stared toward the harbor. "She really is riding low with all the supplies aboard."

"Shouldn't you give her a name, Damian? You always refer to it as she."

"It's Beau's ship. I'm sure he will want to name it."

"Beau has given the ship to you, Damian. I think he would be offended if you didn't name it."

"We'll compromise. Why don't you name her."

Angelique studied the streamlined gray ship riding at anchor in the harbor. "She looks like a ghost ship," she mused.

"Please, no ghostly names," Damian laughed. "Seamen are superstitious enough."

"When we were under way I thought she looked like she was dancing on the water . . . and you say you only run the blockade at night," she mused. "How about *Moonlight Dancer*?"

"*Moonlight Dancer*," Damian repeated. "Yes, I like it, and I think Beau would like it."

"Good, then it is settled. Tomorrow *Moonlight Dancer* heads for Charleston. Doesn't that sound better than saying she?" Angelique asked.

Instead of answering, Damian had a worried expression on his face. "Angelique, I'd like to try to find someone on the island for you to stay with."

"No! Absolutely not. The plan was for me to go to Charleston with you."

"It could get bad, Angelique. This morning one of the blockaders told me that the Union has doubled the ships guarding the harbor."

"I don't care, Damian. I will not stay here."

"All right, we'll say no more about it for now. It's too pretty a day for us to argue," Damian conceded.

They lay in the sun on the hillside and talked away the afternoon. There was so much they didn't know about each other. Angelique felt something stir within her as she listened to Damian talk about the South's dedication to the war. Perhaps it was envy. Damian had a purpose in life. He knew where he belonged and where he was going. She suddenly felt insignificant and without purpose.

"There will be another lady traveling with us," Damian said suddenly, breaking into Angelique's train of thought. "She will be company for you."

"Oh?" was all Angelique said, waiting for Damian's next words and dreading them before they came.

"You met her briefly last night," he said, not meeting her eyes. "Lacey Jamerson is her name."

Angelique knew exactly who he meant—and she thought she knew why he wanted to leave her behind on the island. She quickly stood and brushed off her skirt. "I'd like to return to the hotel now," she said walking toward the carriage.

Damian was on his feet before she got very far. "What is wrong with you?" he asked angrily.

"I'm not stupid, Damian. I know why you wanted me to stay behind. I was a disappointment to you last night so you want that redhead with you for the remainder of the trip."

Damian's anger was gone. This was an innocent he was dealing with, and he had to tread softly. "I wanted you to stay behind for your safety," he answered softly. "And as for last night, it was beautiful . . ."

Angelique wasn't listening. Tears filled her eyes. "I didn't ask you for a commitment. I would have accepted whatever relationship you offered, but I never imagined you would need someone else while you had me. What kind of a man are you, Damian?" she asked with a ragged sob.

Damian pulled her into his arms. "You are so wrong, so naive, my beautiful Angel," he sighed as he stroked her hair, waiting for her sobs to cease. "Give me time, Angel," he whispered. "At this moment I don't know what the future holds for me. Believe me, I want you with me. More than that I can't promise. I've spent years closing myself off from feeling anything for anyone. I can't change that overnight."

Angelique studied Damian's face. She knew the emotional scars he carried were from being deserted by his mother. "I would wait forever if I thought . . ."

"If you thought what?" Damian prompted.

"If I thought you would make a commitment to me and only me. I am not the type of woman to put up with infidelity, even if we are not married."

"And you think Lacey is traveling with us for my amusement?"

"I don't know what I think."

"Come back and sit down," Damian insisted, pulling her back to the quilt. "I've known Lacey for a long time. I saved her life after the man she loved was killed while trying to stop her from being brutally raped in a Union prison. She was a nurse, and a damned good one I understand, but her self-esteem is gone. She turned to prostitution for awhile, but now she is ready to try to pick up the pieces of her life. I want to try to help her, Angel. I hope you'll understand. That is what she wanted to talk to me about last night. She came to Bermuda from the Bahamas hoping no one would know the kind of life she had been leading, but unfortunately several of the seamen recognized her. Now she's decided to return to Charleston. Will you help me make her welcome, Angel? She really needs friends."

"Have you and she been lovers?" Angelique asked, knowing she shouldn't.

"No questions, Angel. If we are to have a chance, there are to be no questions. Agreed?" he asked lifting her chin so she had to look at him.

"Agreed," she answered before he claimed her mouth in a possessive kiss.

Chapter Fifteen

Angelique had made up her mind to dislike Lacey Jamerson, but that changed as soon as the two women met. The Lacey Jamerson who boarded the ship was a sweet, freckled-face young lady, instead of the beautiful sophisticated siren Angelique had pictured at the party in Bermuda. In less than an hour the two of them were oblivious to the admiring stares of the seamen around them as they discussed the latest fashions in Europe.

Damian watched them with suspicion. He knew one wrong word from either of them and all hell could break loose.

"You're not feeling a little apprehensive about the two of them being together, are you, big brother?" Adam asked, a knowing grin splitting his handsome face.

"I don't need your humor right now, Adam."

"No, I don't guess you do, but I find it very

difficult to sympathize with a man who has two of the most beautiful women I've ever seen in love with him."

"Don't you have medical supplies to check?" Damian asked before walking away.

"Big brother, I have a feeling running the blockade is going to be a picnic compared to the fireworks that could erupt right here on your own deck."

But they didn't erupt. Angelique had noticed the way Lacey looked at Damian from the moment she boarded the ship and instantly realized the beautiful redhead was also in love with Damian. Yet for some reason she couldn't hate her for it. That night, as they shared a cabin, they discussed their love for Damian.

"You have nothing to fear from me, Angelique," Lacey promised. "I saw the way Damian looked at you and I knew he had finally given his heart to someone. I'm happy for him."

"I wish I could believe that, Lacey. It always seems as if he is keeping me at arm's length."

"I don't believe Damian has ever loved anyone before, Angelique. The feelings are still new to him. So many times I wanted to tell him how I felt, but he'd disappear from my life as soon as I'd try to get close. I finally learned just to enjoy him while I had him," Lacey admitted, then realized she was getting too personal about her relationship with Damian. "I'm sorry Angelique. Your love for Damian is still so new. Perhaps it isn't wise to be so open."

"My love for Damian isn't new, Lacey. I've loved

Damian since I was eleven."

The two women spent half the night talking. Angelique felt closer to Lacey in that short period than she ever had any other friend. There was a special bond between them—the bond of love for the same man.

The next morning was dark with storm clouds when Angelique and Lacey came up on deck. Adam was scanning the horizon while Damian pointed something out to him. "Good morning," Lacey greeted.

Damian turned and his eyes met Angelique's. "I trust you ladies found your accommodations to your liking," he said, still looking only at Angelique.

"Oh, yes, much nicer than expected," Lacey answered, knowing Damian had eyes only for Angelique. "Doctor Legare, Angelique tells me you have suffered with seasickness, but have conquered it. Perhaps you can tell me how. I've had this unsettling feeling . . ."

Lacey and Adam moved a short distance away, leaving Angelique and Damian alone. Damian leaned back against the railing, his arms folded across his chest as he studied the beauty before him. "The sea agrees with you," he said.

"I have to admit I enjoy it. It's a shame today is so overcast."

"On the contrary, it's a blessing," Damian corrected. "If it stays this way it will give us better cover when we run the blockade tonight."

"Tonight? I hadn't realized it would be that soon."

"We've already seen a couple of Yankee cruisers,

but they didn't see us. With our low silhouette, camouflaged paint and smokeless coal, we're practically invisible."

"I think you're pleased with Beau's design," Angelique said proudly.

"I think your brother is a genius, but don't ever tell him I said that. He's already difficult enough," Damian laughed.

The expression on Angelique's face was one of sadness. "When you talk like that I really believe I'll see him again."

"Of course you'll see him again. You don't think he's going to let me just sail away with you?"

If the truth were known, Damian Legare, I think Beau wanted just that, Angelique thought to herself.

"Are you getting along all right with Lacey?" Damian asked.

"Oh yes, very well. I already feel as if I've known her all my life."

"I thought you would. Lacey had a bad time of it, but she's a very special person."

"She says she never would have made it without you."

Damian stared at Angelique for a moment. "Lacey tends to exaggerate. She pictures me as a knight in shining armor and I'm not."

"That's funny you should say that. That is exactly how I've always pictured you," Angelique said softly.

"I'd rather you picture me as a man like any other man. I have faults, I've made mistakes, and I can be hurt."

"I'll try never to hurt you, Damian."

Damian reached out and took her hand. "I'll never intentionally hurt you, Angel, but don't expect too much from me. I've never had any experience with a woman like you."

"I'll stop thinking of you as my knight in shining armor if you'll stop thinking of me as a fragile saint."

Damian's laughter echoed across the water. "Touché, little one." He leaned closer to her. "But I'll tell you something, after the other night I find it difficult to think of you as a saint or as fragile. You were a delight."

Angelique felt her skin flush, but she was enjoying this pleasant bantering too much to play coy. "When will we have a chance to be together again?" she asked softly.

"Ah, so you crave my body," he teased.

"Yes, I crave your body," she admitted honestly. "I lie in bed at night remembering how it was."

"So do I, little one, so do I," Damian answered, his eyes turning a deep emerald green.

"Damian, come see this," Adam shouted as he looked through the spyglass.

Lacey joined Angelique while the two men discussed what Adam saw. "You actually glow when he is around," she teased.

"I don't mean for it to be so obvious," Angelique answered, embarrassed.

"Don't ever apologize for being in love, Angelique," Lacey said sternly. "Particularly when a man like Damian Legare returns that love. But you're

203

going to have to be strong and secure in that love. Never doubt him or you'll lose him." When Lacey saw the expression on Angelique's face she realized she didn't understand. "Listen to me, my sweet. Damian would never lie to you about his past, but then I doubt he'll ever tell you anything about it either. You're not so innocent you don't realize a man like Damian has had many women. But they've been women who've never meant anything to him. More than one has tried to put a claim on him, including myself, but he has never fallen—until now. You're going to be meeting these women everytime you turn around. They will most likely do everything in their power to spoil your love for Damian, but don't let them! If you forget Damian's past, he will forget it. Always believe in him. He needs love, but he also needs to know you're going to be loyal to him."

Lacey's eyes had filled with tears as she spoke. Angelique clutched both of her friend's hands in her own. "You are a dear friend, Lacey Jamerson. I'll never forget it. Knowing how you feel about Damian makes your friendship and advice all the more valuable to me."

"Lacey," Adam called. "There are whales out there. Come take a look."

"I think Adam may be infatuated," Angelique teased. "He certainly does his best to impress you."

"Are you trying to play matchmaker?" Lacey laughed. "What would a respectable doctor want with someone like me?"

"Adam is wonderful and sensitive, Lacey. Just like

Damian. And he's almost as handsome. Take a careful look at him," Angelique encouraged.

"You don't have to convince me, sweet. I've already had my eye on the nice doctor."

"There are whales ahead," Damian announced as the two women joined them.

Angelique studied the area where he pointed. Then she saw one break the surface, sending a spout of silvery water over its blue back. "It is beautiful," she said, awed by its size. "I had no idea they were so large."

"Captain, Yankee cruiser spotted off the port," Damian's first-mate interrupted.

Damian scanned the horizon, then focused in on what seemed like a dot on the surface. "Increase speed," he ordered. "Stay on course."

Angelique watched the other ship, gripping the railing in anticipation, while Damian lazily leaned on the railing watching. "I'm beginning to believe this ship really is invisible," he said after a few minutes. "This is the fourth time today we've gone unnoticed. I hope we're as lucky tonight."

They weren't. There was no moon, giving them a false sense of security. Every man, dressed in gray to be as invisible as their ghostly ship, waited and listened. The engine room hatchways were screened with tarpaulins, and the binnacle was covered, dousing all light. On the bridge Damian and Roget peered intently into the blackness ahead.

"It's time to cast the lead," Damian ordered. "I

think we're getting close." A muttered order down the engine room tube was given and the ship suddenly lay silent in the water. One of the seamen moved forward to cast the lead.

"Seventeen fathoms—sandy bottom with black specks," the seaman announced.

"We've still a distance to go," Damian said, "and we're too far southward. Port two points and proceed."

An hour later another sounding was taken and Damian was satisfied it was time to head for shore. "Starboard, and ahead easy," he ordered, hoping the tide and wind would drive them silently forward.

Moonlight Dancer moved past the first line of blockaders without being seen, drifting by two of them at a distance of less than three hundred feet. She moved on, like a veritable phantom ship as they glided past two more Union ships less than a hundred feet away. As she passed through the midst of the blockading squadron, every man held his breath, not daring to breathe for fear some Yankee would make it his last. They moved past the wreck of the *Minho*, past Sullivan Island, sliding gently over one of the treacherous sand bars. Still unobserved, they crept quietly on, then all of a sudden a Yankee cruiser loomed ahead of them, steering slowly across their bow.

"Stop her!" Damian ordered, but too late. The sound of metal shattering the wood hull of the Union ship broke the silence like an explosion. "Back off! Back off!" Damian yelled down the tube.

Shouts and curses filled the air from the Union ship, still unaware what had hit them. "Full steam ahead," Damian ordered when they had dislodged from the Union cruiser. Rockets lit the black sky, highlighting the commotion on the Union ship, but *Moonlight Dancer* had already disappeared like the mist that had mysteriously enveloped her long enough for her to move away undetected. Just below Sumter, two barge loads of Confederates stationed on picket duty opened fire on the Union ship, giving *Moonlight Dancer* the chance to enter the harbor safely to the cheering of the blockade runners already anchored in the harbor.

The usually subdued men aboard *Moonlight Dancer* began cheering, the tension of the last hours finally released. Damian grinned as some of the men broke into song. Seamen on the ships anchored in the harbor shouted their welcome and a job well done.

"Break out the whiskey," Damian ordered. "The men deserve a celebration. It had been close—too close and he didn't want to think of the danger he had put Angelique in. After he had her settled he was going to get good and drunk himself.

"Captain, will you and your lady friend be joining us for our celebration?" Maxwell asked.

"Lady friend?" Damian repeated angrily, knowing the seaman referred to mistresses as lady friends. "What the hell are you talking about?"

"Sir, I meant no offense. I just thought Mademoiselle Charbonne and Miss Jamerson would be joining the celebration," Maxwell answered, wondering why the captain was so upset.

"For your information, and for the information of the rest of the crew, Mademoiselle Charbonne is not my lady friend. She happens to be my . . . my ward. Her family placed her in my safekeeping!"

"I'm sorry, sir. I didn't realize the situation," Maxwell said, still wondering what he had done to deserve the captain's wrath.

Adam heard the last part of the conversation as he joined his brother, and wondered what precipitated it.

"When we're anchored I want you to take the ladies to the Charleston Hotel. Arrange for a room for them to share and a room for us to share. I'll join you later."

"Yes, sir!" Adam saluted.

Damian ran his hand through his hair. "I'm sorry, Adam. I didn't mean to bite your head off."

"What did Maxwell say that upset you?" Adam asked.

"He thought Angelique was my mistress," Damian growled.

"And that was reason enough to bite his head off."

"Hell yes! I won't have anyone debasing Angelique's name."

"Forgive me for saying so, brother, but haven't you taken the lady to your bed?"

Damian grabbed Adam by the lapels of his jacket and shoved him back against the rail. "Stay out of my business, Adam! Do you understand?"

"No!" Adam broke Damian's hold. "I don't understand. You've got a problem, Damian, and I'll be glad to listen if you want to talk."

Damian stared at his brother for a long moment. "I'm sorry, Adam. You're right. I do have a problem," he admitted reluctantly, "but I don't know if talking would help a damned thing. I have to work this out myself."

Adam watched his brother walk away. I'm afraid Mother left deeper scars on you than you'll ever know, brother, Adam thought to himself.

Chapter Sixteen

It was a dark moonless night, yet the activity around the wharf was as busy as if it were the middle of the day. Torches lit the way for workers unloading ships that had successfully run the blockade, while other ships were being loaded with cotton for the run back through the lines the next night. There was barely a space to walk for the bales of cotton stacked everywhere. A mood of merriment prevailed, and *Moonlight Dancer*, making such a daring run was just another excuse to celebrate. The new design of the ship was of interest to all the blockaders, for they were always looking for ways to make their run less dangerous.

All of this was new and exciting to Angelique, yet her excitement was dampened by Damian's absence. She had been frightened when their ship had collided with the Union ship. Clinging together, she and Lacey had waited, wondering what was happening on the strangely silent ship. When they heard the cheers of the crew a few minutes later they knew they had made it, but still Damian hadn't come. Adam had finally arrived to escort them to the hotel.

Lying in bed later, she cuddled with Shadow and wondered if she would ever have any semblance of peace and stability in her life again. The only thing she was sure of was her love for Damian and that seemed to be one-sided. She listened to Lacey's soft breathing as she slept soundly. At least Lacey and Adam seemed to be getting along.

Damian stood in the darkness across the street from Kate Winston's house. He drew deeply on his cheroot. What the hell was he doing here? He didn't want Kate. He wanted Angelique. With a derisive snort, he threw the cigar aside and headed toward the hotel. He didn't like this situation a bit. Why couldn't he be indifferent to Angelique's feelings? In all his life he had never cared what another person thought. He had done enough already to ruin her reputation, but somehow he had to correct that. In Charleston a woman's reputation meant everything. She would end up like Kate if he didn't protect her, and he wasn't going to let that happen. He had told Maxwell she was his ward. Perhaps he could convince the good people of Charleston the same thing. The damage to the ship would take a few days to repair. That would give him time to get Angelique settled before he sailed. In the meantime he would talk to Lacey and try to convince her to act as chaperone to Angelique.

Damian received a very cool reception when he joined the ladies for breakfast the next morning. Angelique seemed more interested in her melon than in his description of the damage to the ship.

"We won't be able to travel to Enchanteur until tomorrow morning so I thought if it was agreeable with you ladies, we'd take in Mr. Arthur's play and then have a late dinner."

"That sounds wonderful," Lacey exclaimed. "Don't you think so, Angelique?"

Angelique looked up from her melon for the first time. "If that is what everyone else wants to do, it's fine with me."

Damian stirred his coffee, wondering how to bring up the next subject. He hadn't expected this to be easy, but . . . "There is something I need to discuss with both of you," he began and was met with silent stares. "Angelique, since I gave Beau my word I would look after you, I feel we have to be very careful to make sure there is no question as to your reputation." Still no one said anything. "I think the easiest way to accomplish that is to introduce you as my ward and Lacey as your companion."

Angelique dropped her fork. "Your ward! You can't be serious!"

"I'm very serious. Charleston is extremely socially conscious and the ladies wouldn't have anything to do with you if they thought . . ."

"If they thought what?" Angelique interrupted. "If they thought we were lovers?"

"Angelique, lower your voice," Damian ordered.

"I don't believe this. I thought I knew you, but I don't."

"Angelique, calm down."

"You can go to hell!" she spat, as she shoved her chair away from the table. "You can just go to hell," she repeated, the strain of the last few weeks showing on her pale face before she dashed from the room.

Damian caught up with her outside her room. Grabbing her by the arm he angrily shoved her through the door. "That was quite a scene, Angelique. That most certainly will give the gossips something to talk about," he growled.

"I don't care about gossips or society, or anything else in Charleston," she shouted back.

"You're being unreasonable. Stop and think how hard Lacey is trying to gain back some shred of decency. Do you want to just throw your reputation away?"

Angelique turned and faced him, her eyes soft with yearning. "It doesn't have to be that way. I love you, Damian."

"No! Don't say that," he groaned. "You don't mean that."

"I do mean it. Why can't you accept my love? I know you have feelings for me. Be honest with yourself."

"I'll be honest, Angelique. I want you and I desire

you, but I have no love to offer and you must accept that."

"All right, Damian. I accept that. But if you desire me then I want to be with you. If you need me I want to be there for you."

"Oh, God," Damian moaned defeatedly. "What am I going to do with you?"

"Hold me, Damian," Angelique begged softly.

"Please, Angel, don't do this to me. I already feel guilty enough for what I've done to you."

"Guilty?" Angelique asked, unbelieving. "Is that what you feel? It's strange, I've always heard the woman was the one who regretted losing her virginity. Here I am throwing myself at you and you're telling me you feel guilty."

"You're making this worse than it need be."

"My whole world is falling apart—has been falling apart for the past several months, and you can stand there and tell me I'm making this worse than it is? I think it's time you get out of my room. I'm tired of listening to your excuses."

"No. I won't leave until I make you understand—until I make you see that what I suggest is for the best. I tried to warn you all along that I couldn't love; I can't open myself up to that hurt."

"Do you call never loving, never committing yourself, living?" she asked, her eyes blazing with anger.

Damian returned her stare, his expression impenetrable. After a long, uncomfortable silence, during which Angelique refused to look away, he said only, "I can't."

"You can't?" she asked sarcastically. "Unable to? Incapable of? What is it, Damian? Is the great, brave hero who runs the blockade with nerves of steel afraid to give his heart to a woman who only wants to love him?"

At the shaken look on Damian's face, Angelique softened her tone. "Oh, Damian, I know why you don't think you can love, but I think you're wrong. You've never given yourself a chance. Put all thoughts of your mother out of your mind. Other people have been deserted by a parent or a loved one and they still find it in them to love. Let me help you," she begged, reaching out to him.

"Spare me your sympathy," he growled, as he turned on his heel and left the room.

"Damn you, Damian Legare. I will not give up," Angelique shouted at the closed door. "You're going to find you've met your match in stubbornness!"

The people of Charleston had a knack for being able to go on with life even though the war was on their doorstep. There may be a lack of food, and the women may have to wear mended gowns, but they continued to hold social balls and attend the theatre at least once a month. This didn't mean that they didn't do their part for the war. Women of South Carolina, particularly Charleston, sold their diamonds, gold, silver, paintings, vases, and anything else they could sell or raffle, and raised enough money for a gunboat to protect Charleston's harbor.

This proved conclusively to the many people who criticized them for their continued social activities that they were wholeheartedly behind their men, the war effort, and the cause for which they fought.

Heads turned as Damian and Adam escorted the two beautiful women into the theatre. The women whispered about the elegance of their gowns while the men just stared in admiration. One woman in particular hadn't missed the stir made by the party's entrance.

After they took their places in one of the elegant boxes, Angelique took the time to look over the audience. Suddenly her eyes locked with the icy blue stare of a woman in the lower seats. She was taken aback by the hate she saw and quickly looked away. She would have liked to ask Damian if he knew who the woman was, but she was trying to remain aloof.

Damian had seen the looks Kate was sending him, but he ignored them. Instead he spent the entire first half watching Angelique enjoy the comedy. Her laugh was enchanting and he found himself thinking about the night he had made love to her. She had been so warm and willing; so innocent, yet filled with a fire. It was that damned innocence that kept him at arm's length. She needed a man who would love her, give her a home and a future. He had nothing to offer. Enchanteur was all he owned and she would probably hate that isolated place like his mother had.

The applause at the end of the first half brought Damian back to reality. Adam and the two girls were ebullient about the play and were engrossed in repeating some of the dialogue as they headed toward the lobby for refreshment.

"Damian," a feminine voice called out. Damian had no choice but to acknowledge the woman and her escort. "I had no idea you were in town, *darling*," she said as she stood on tiptoe to kiss him. "Shame on you for not letting me know." Kate studied Angelique with cold regard that missed no slight detail as she talked.

Damian could tell Kate's anger was barely suppressed and he took perverse pleasure in it. "Kate, this is Angelique, my ward; Lacey, her companion, and my brother, Adam. This is Kate Winston and my neighbor, Philip Delacort."

Angelique's face flamed at the introduction, but she managed to acknowledge the woman who had been staring at her before the show. God, Lacey must be right, she thought, Damian has a woman in every port. This one was attractive enough, yet she didn't have the soft, refined looks Lacey possessed. Still, she could see how a man would be attracted to her. It was more her actions than her looks.

"My word," Kate drawled, "you left here a few months ago alone and come back with a full entourage. You must tell me about it—soon, darling," she said coolly. "Perhaps tonight after the play."

"I'll see what I can work out, Kate. Now you must excuse me, I promised the ladies some refreshment," Damian said, wanting to escape. "Would you care for something?"

"Don't bother yourself, darling," Kate stayed him

by wrapping her arm in his. "Philip will get us all something. Won't you dear?"

Philip, who had been explaining to Adam that his plantation bordered Enchanteur, looked embarrassed, but hurried off to do Kate's bidding.

"So, you're Damian's ward," Kate commented, turning her attention back to Angelique. "How delightful for you," she said sarcastically.

"Yes, Uncle Damian positively dotes on me," Angelique answered laconically as she gave Damian a scathing look.

Damian knew he should be furious with her for not taking the situation seriously, yet he had to fight down his impulse to laugh. God how Kate paled next to Angelique, he thought.

"How did you come to be Damian's ward?" Kate asked.

"I don't see how my relationship with Damian is any of your business," Angelique answered curtly.

"Angelique," Damian warned.

Philip broke the tension of the moment as he returned with cups of punch and the conversation turned to the war. Adam asked about the Stone Fleet, a fleet of ships loaded with granite and sunk in Charleston's channel to paralyze the city.

"The London Times said people who would do an act like this would pluck the sun out of heaven and put their enemies in darkness," Adam informed them. "The European nations were stunned that the Union would do such a thing."

Damian explained that even though the Union

considered their mission a success, the sunken fleet had disappeared into the mud five days after they had been sunk. Not only had they disappeared, but the high tides and strong winds carved out new channels and navigation had been quickly resumed.

Angelique knew Kate was still assessing her as the men talked. She met her eyes in an uncompromising stare. Let her know she doesn't frighten me, she thought.

The theatre bell rang, calling the audience back to their seats. As they were heading back into the theatre Kate laid her hand on Angelique's arm and drew her aside. Damian was engrossed in conversation with the men and didn't notice.

"My dear child, you would be wise not to antagonize me. One day soon I will be married to Damian, and if you really are his ward, I could make your life miserable."

Angelique didn't hear anything Kate said after that. Her ears rang with the blood pounding in her head. No wonder Damian wouldn't make a commitment to her—he had already made a commitment.

Kate turned back to her escort, leaving Angelique to numbly follow Lacey into the theatre. She didn't hear a single word of the rest of the play. Once when she looked down at Kate Winston, the women smiled at her triumphantly.

"Angelique, are you all right?" Lacey asked. "You look so pale."

Angelique shook her head, but couldn't say anything. She would not give Kate Winston the benefit of seeing her hurt. A grim determination illuminated her face as she stared back at her.

Adam and Lacey walked arm and arm a short distance ahead as they walked down Church Street the short distance back to the hotel. Damian knew Angelique was upset. She hadn't paid any attention to the second half. Leave it to Kate to leave no doubt that their relationship was more than just friendship, but it was best this way, he told himself. Now maybe Angelique would realize what he meant about his way of life. Why wasn't that a comforting thought, he wondered. Damn it! Why couldn't he make up his mind? Either he wanted to protect Angelique or he didn't. It was as simple as that. No, it wasn't that simple. Even if he did decide to commit himself to her, she would never be happy at Enchanteur. He wasn't going to let happen to him what happened to his father. He wasn't going to be left a broken man by some woman—he had to put a distance between them.

Damian looked down at Angelique's profile. She had an allure, an innocent sensuality that made a man want to possess her. God, he had to stop thinking this way.

"Did you enjoy the play?" he asked, trying to take his mind off his disturbing thoughts.

"Yes, very much."

"My favorite part was about the monkey."

"Yes, mine too," Angelique answered, her mind

still on Kate's warning.

"All right, do you want to tell me why you didn't pay any attention to the second half?"

"Of course I did."

"Angelique, there was no mention of a monkey in the play."

Making a valiant effort to shake off her despondency, Angelique forced a smile. "I knew that. I thought you had gone senile on me and I was just humoring you, *Uncle Damian*."

"Very funny," he said exasperatedly. "I should be angry with you for that display at the theatre. I keep trying to save your reputation and you keep throwing it back in my face."

"I've never been one to worry about what other people think, Damian. If they don't like me for what I am, then they're not worth worrying about."

"That might work in a lot of places, Angelique, but not in Charleston. People here are very conscious of propriety."

"Then perhaps I won't like it here after all."

Her words only reassured Damian that he was doing the right thing. Angelique wouldn't fit in here. She was too honest, too open.

When they reached the hotel Angelique made her excuses to see to Shadow, but she had no intention of joining Damian for dinner. Instead she took Shadow to the lawn at the back of the hotel. She was engrossed in throwing a stick for the puppy and didn't hear Damian approach.

"There you are. You gave me a scare. I didn't

know what had happened to you. We've been waiting for you over an hour."

"Order without me. I'm not hungry."

"For God's sake, Angelique, you scared the hell out of me. Now why don't you tell me what this is all about?"

"Just go on to your friend's house, Damian. I certainly don't want to delay your little rendezvous."

Damian sat on the step below her. "You're acting like a child, Angelique," he said softly. "Now come and have dinner. Lacey and Adam are waiting."

His condescending tone infuriated her. "Why couldn't you have been honest with me? Why did you have to let me make such a fool of myself?"

"What are you talking about?" he asked in an exasperated tone.

"Why couldn't you have told me that you had a fiancée waiting here in Charleston? Instead you lied to me, giving me hope that we had something special so you could take me to your bed." Angelique's voice trembled, but she would not let him see her cry. "I thought all the stories about you were lies. I remembered you as an honorable man."

Damian turned away from her accusing look, but said nothing in his defense.

"You don't deny it?" she gasped, hoping he would tell her she was wrong—praying he would tell her.

Damian turned and faced her, his voice cold and deliberate. "I never lied to you. I tried to tell you I wasn't the man for you."

"Yes, I have to admit, you didn't lie about that,"

she said in disgust as she scooped Shadow up in her arms and left Damian sitting alone on the steps.

Adam stepped from the shadows and stood above Damian. "Is it true? Is that woman your fiancée?"

Damian laughed, ridding his voice of any betraying emotion. "No, she's not my fiancée."

"Then, why didn't you tell Angelique the truth?"

"It's better this way."

"Have you gone mad, Damian?" Adam asked angrily. "It may be better for you, but Angelique doesn't deserve this kind of treatment, and you damned well know it."

"I know what she deserves, and that's why it's better this way."

"I can't believe this! I know you love her."

"Love?" Damian snorted. "You and I had the same mother. How would you know any more about love than I do?"

Adam placed one foot on the step and leaned his arm across his knee. "Let me tell you something, Damian. If I thought Angelique would return my feelings, I'd have no trouble showing her my love—and Mother doesn't have a damned thing to do with it!"

Chapter Seventeen

Angelique stood at the window watching Damian cross the street below, leaving little doubt in her mind what he would be doing tonight.

"Why, Damian, why?" she asked, leaning her forehead against the cool pane of glass. "You're a fool, Angelique Charbonne. How could you possibly still want the man? He lied to you—took advantage of you!" *Or was it the other way around?* a little voice reminded. "It doesn't matter," she said aloud. "I'll make him sorry. He'll beg me to come to him. But I won't . . . no matter how badly I want him."

"I can only stay for a few minutes, Kate," Damian explained as she ushered him into her sitting room. "We start for Enchanteur in the morning."

"What do you mean, you can't stay?" Kate turned on him angrily. "I don't want a few minutes of your time. I want you here with me!"

"I'm sorry, Kate. Things have changed in my life. I have other people to consider now."

"Oh, yes," she sneered. "That infant you called your ward. Who do you think you're kidding? It is obvious she's your latest mistress."

Damian stepped menacingly toward her, then checked himself. "I came to try to explain, Kate, but I should have known better. When we parted the last time, I think you and I both knew it was over. Now there should be no doubt." Damian headed toward the door, but Kate stopped him.

"Please, please, Damian, don't leave like this. We were so good together."

"We were good in bed, Kate. There was never anything else."

Kate's blue eyes blazed angrily. "And does that child satisfy all your needs?"

"Goodbye, Kate," Damian said as he opened the door and walked down the wrought iron steps.

Damian walked slowly back to the hotel trying to sort out his feelings. He had hoped that once back in Charleston, the availability of Kate's charms would put Angelique out of his mind, but instead it worked just the opposite. The two were like night and day. Kate was blond and fair, with a full figure, while Angelique was tall and slim, with the most beautiful long legs. Kate was an expert at seduction, but then she had practiced it so long she should be. Angelique was innocent of her charms, yet a look from her violet eyes let you know exactly what she was thinking. What was he going to do? The more he fought it, the worse his longings were.

Damian had no sooner slammed the door before Philip sauntered out of the library, a glass of bourbon in his hand. He leaned against the banister, a pleased smile on his handsome face. "Looks like you won't be mistress of Enchanteur after all, sweet."

"Shut up!" Kate screamed. "Just shut up! I have to think."

"You might as well face it, Kate. You've lost him."

"Not yet, I haven't," she smiled deviously. "Damian thinks to protect his little Angelique's reputation by calling her his ward, but when I'm finished with her no one in Charleston will have anything to do with her, including Damian."

Philip felt a twinge of sympathy for the girl, but he said nothing.

"Damian will be leaving again soon. When he does you will become a regular visitor to Enchanteur. Take your sister along the first time and make it look as if you're just being neighborly. Then you will become the smitten suitor."

"That's ridiculous, Kate. I'm on the verge of losing Bellemeade and you think I should go courting. Besides, why should I do this? You know I'd just as soon see you forget Damian."

"And you know I'll never forget him, so you might as well enjoy the money I give you without complaining. Listen, Philip, this means a lot to me, and I'm willing to pay handsomely for your help. I'll see that you have enough to save your precious Bellemeade, if you do the job well."

"This might be very pleasant," Philip mused. "I've never been paid to court a beautiful woman."

"A child!" Kate screamed. "She's nothing but a child."

It was a beautiful clear morning for traveling. The colors of autumn burned in the trees in shades of claret and amber. November weather like this was something new to Angelique. In Brittany November was cold and damp, keeping most people indoors.

Damian was polite, explaining sights they would see on the way, and joking with Adam about a time he had chased a dog into a field, only to be chased himself by a bull who didn't care for trespassers.

After letting Shadow run for a few minutes, the ladies climbed into the carriage. "Have you ever been to Enchanteur, Lacey?" Angelique asked with apprehension in her voice.

"No, I haven't. This will be a new experience for both of us."

"I've had enough new experiences to last me a lifetime," Angelique said wearily.

"I know that feeling, Angelique," Lacey answered.

Hearing the emotion in Lacey's voice, Angelique turned and looked at her friend. "I'm sorry, Lacey. I'm feeling sorry for myself."

"Do you want to talk about it?"

"I guess it was being introduced as Damian's ward, and then last night Kate Winston pulled me aside and told me she and Damian were planning to be married."

"I warned you things like that would happen. Kate Winston just wishes Damian was going to marry her. From what I hear she's been trying to get her hooks in him for a long time."

"I think she might have succeeded this time. When I asked Damian about it, he didn't deny it."

Lacey didn't have an answer for Angelique. Why was Damian doing this to this sweet girl? she wondered. She was sure he loved Angelique. Why couldn't the fool admit it? "Be patient with him, he'll come around."

"I really think it best if I just forget all about Damian. I must put him out of my mind and get on with my life. As soon as I hear from Beau I will be going home."

Lacey didn't know what to say. She couldn't give Angelique false hope because she wasn't sure what Damian would do. Even if he loved Angelique, he might just abandon her as he had all the other women in his life.

Enchanteur was a two hour trip by carriage. Angelique and Lacey passed the first hour talking, but now Lacey peered out the window, silently watching the scenery go by. The road, which was usually deserted, was now traveled by soldiers, some heading home on leave, or to recuperate from injuries, while others were returning to their units.

"They are so young," Angelique said, as they passed a group who stepped off to the side of the road to let them pass.

"War doesn't discriminate," Lacey laughed bitterly. "Most of them will die before they ever have a chance to love a woman or hold a child in their arms. But then, maybe they are the lucky ones. They won't know what they've missed."

Angelique was startled by her friend's words. "You sound very bitter, Lacey."

Lacey turned away from the soldiers and faced Angelique. "I hate this war, Angelique. It's a terrible waste. Men are dying by the thousands, and for what? It isn't going to accomplish anything. We've been involved in it for two years and the South is just barely holding its own. Are they going to continue until there are no Southern men left?"

"I hadn't given the war much thought," Angelique said looking back toward the soldiers. "When we ran the blockade I realized for the first time how dangerous Damian's occupation was. Before that, I had always thought running the blockade was an exciting thing to do. Still, I'm glad he is not one of those soldiers. They look so tired and hungry."

"The blockaders usually live much better than the soldiers, and most will come out of this war a whole lot richer—if they live. What they do is just as dangerous as facing a Yankee on the battlefield. They just don't have to do it quite as often."

"It's strange, back in France the stories of the war all sounded so glamorous."

"That's what most Southerners thought when the war first started. They thought they'd ride off in glory, fight a few battles, and come home heroes. It's been a rude awakening to most of them. Whole families have been obliterated. Brothers are fighting against brothers, fathers against sons, and still, we put the sword in the hands of the children." Lacey's voice was rising in hysteria as she watched a soldier on crutches, with a bloody bandage on his head wave to her. "Oh God, why did I come back? I don't think I can go through this again. I thought it would be different, but it isn't. Seeing those desolate faces reminds me . . ." Lacey began to cry. "I don't want to be here. I can't be here," she screamed, trying to wrench open the carriage door.

"Damian," Angelique screamed. "Stop! Stop the carriage," she shouted, trying to hold Lacey in her seat.

Damian was in the carriage before it stopped. "Calm down, it's going to be all right," he said, shaking Lacey.

"It won't. It will never be all right," she screamed. "I've got to get away from here."

Angelique gasped as Damian slapped Lacey soundly across the face. Lacey stared at him, then collapsed sobbing against his chest. "It's all right, love," he murmured, "try to forget it. You're among friends here. We love you."

Adam stood at the door of the carriage feeling helpless. Damian had explained about Lacey's past, but he had no idea she still suffered from the experiences.

Angelique sat silently, feeling desperately sorry for

her friend, yet at the same time fighting the pain of jealousy at seeing how Damian comforted her, telling her she was loved. A thousand unsought visions of him possessing Lacey flitted across her mind, but she forced them away . . .

"Damian, what can I do to help her?" Angelique asked, forcing her attention back to Lacey.

"I'm all right now," Lacey smiled weakly, pulling a handkerchief from her sleeve. "I'm so sorry. I don't know what came over me."

"Are you sure you're all right?" Damian asked. "Perhaps you'd like to walk a little."

Lacey could still see the soldiers filing by. "No! I want to go on."

Damian turned to Angelique, who sat clutching Shadow to her chest. "Are you all right?" he asked softly, while affectionately rubbing Shadow's head.

"Yes, I'm fine. Is it much further?"

"No, less than an hour. We'll quicken the pace if you don't think you will be too uncomfortable."

"I'll be all right, if Angelique will," Lacey pleaded. "Let's just get there."

Angelique nodded her head at Damian's questioning look. "We'll be fine."

The sound of the wheels clattering across a wooden bridge woke Angelique from her slumber. She leaned out the window to ask where they were. Her intake of breath brought Lacey beside her.

"What is it?"

"The most beautiful place I have ever seen," Angelique answered in awe. She looked around for Damian, but there was no sign of him.

"He has gone on ahead," Adam shouted, coming alongside of the carriage. "God, I forgot how beautiful this place was," he exclaimed.

They had passed several plantations on the way here, but none that equalled Enchanteur. Terraced lawns stretched from the front of the house down to the edge of the river. Live oaks, draped with Spanish moss lined the drive, their twisting limbs forming a canopy overhead. At the end of the drive they circled a rose garden before coming to a halt in front of the house. Damian stood on the steps with his arms around a beaming black couple. Adam swung off his horse and rushed toward the woman, meeting in a hearty embrace, while the man pounded him on the back in a good-natured welcome.

"Lordy, Mister Adam, we never expected to see you again," the black woman exclaimed, wiping tears from her eyes.

"Did you really think I could do without your cornbread for the rest of my life?" he laughed still hugging the couple.

By this time the carriage was surrounded by black children, all wanting to see Shadow who was barking over the commotion. "Doan jus stand here boys, help the ladies down. Where are your manners?"

Adam helped Lacey from the carriage and turned to assist Angelique, but Damian was already there. Bessie and Able welcomed Lacey warmly, then turned their attention to Angelique.

"Lordy, you look like that devil of a brother of

yours," Bessie cackled. "I hope you doan give me de trouble dat boy do with his teasing."

"I'll try not to," Angelique laughed.

Bessie grew serious as she noticed Damian's regard for Angelique. In the few minutes he had before the carriage arrived, he had explained about Angelique's tragedy. "You are safe here with us," she assured. "Now come on, both of you ladies must be plumb tuckered."

Bessie gave orders to a young girl standing on the steps, then led Angelique and Lacey into the large foyer. They both gazed around in awe. The dark wooden floors shone with a satin sheen and smelled of beeswax. Landscapes hung on the cream colored walls and a large crystal chandelier glistened overhead.

"After you ladies rest I'm sure Mister Damian will want to show you around. He is very proud of dis house," Bessie said as they climbed a large curved stairway. "Now Miss Lacey, dis is your room," Bessie said opening a door into a beautiful room done in shades of green. "Tally will hang your clothes when one of de boys unload your trunks. She will also bring you hot water for a bath."

Angelique followed Bessie further down the hall. "Mister Damian thought you would like dis room," she announced proudly as she opened the door. Angelique stood mesmerized. The room looked like sunshine. Carpets of off-white with yellow and blue flowers covered the dark wooden floor. Drapes of yellow velvet criss-crossed French doors that led onto the balcony. The four-posted canopied bed was covered in a damask of yellow and white.

"Dis room is soft and honey like you," Bessie smiled. "I think Mister Damian knows dat."

Angelique looked at Bessie in surprise. "What did he tell you about me?" Angelique asked.

"Oh, he told me you was his ward, but I seen de way he look at you," Bessie answered as she opened the French doors to let air in the room. "And he was most particular about the things he wanted done for you. He doan say nothing bout the other lady."

"I wish you were right, Bessie, but I'm afraid Damian has made up his mind to treat me as a ward."

"Do you love him, child?"

"Yes," Angelique smiled, "I've loved him since I was a young girl."

"You will be good for him. He needs someone to love him. Now you jus be patient. You got ole Bessie on your side now."

After Bessie left, Angelique was too restless to take advantage of the bed that had been invitingly turned down. Instead she walked out onto the balcony that surrounded the second floor of the house. This side of the house overlooked the river, giving her a breathtaking view. She wondered how Colette could have given this up—this and her son.

"Is your room to your liking?" Damian asked, startling her. "I'm sorry, I didn't mean to startle you."

"I didn't hear you behind me," she laughed, knowing she had been lost in thoughts. "Yes, the room is beautiful. Was it . . . was it your mother's room?"

"Yes, but I had it totally redecorated. It is nothing like she had it."

No, I guess you wouldn't keep any reminders of her, Angelique thought. Noticing the doors to the room next to hers open, she asked, "Is that your room?"

"Yes. Do you mind my being so close? I am supposed to be protecting you . . ."

"No, no of course not," she answered, feeling a flush come to her cheeks. "It doesn't matter to me where you stay." She wouldn't let it bother her. She would put him out of her mind by reminding herself he belonged to Kate.

Angelique's mouth was set in a pout, a look of determination on her face. Damian had an irresistible impulse to lean forward and touch her lips, but with an effort he restrained himself. The silence continued.

"I must go now. I have a bath waiting," Angelique said, anxious to escape the penetrating looks Damian was giving her.

"Sounds interesting," Damian drawled, with a mischievous gleam in his green eyes.

Angelique's eyes flashed with anger. "How dare you play your stupid games with me. If you think because you're away from your fiancée that I'm going to fall into your arms again, you're mistaken!"

Damian laughed and pulled her into his arms. "It wouldn't matter if I had a wife, little one. I want you every time I'm near you."

"Leave me alone," she struggled, trying to free herself. "Go to your whore if you want to play games."

Damian picked her up in his strong arms and headed into her room. "Your water awaits, Mademoiselle," he said setting her on her feet.

Angelique waited for him to leave, but he didn't. Instead he flopped down on the bed to watch her.

"If you think . . ."

"If you don't want your bath, then I assume you want to come to me now . . ."

"Damian, you said . . ."

"Forget what I said. All I know is I want you."

"If you want me you'll have to take me by force. I won't willingly submit to you again."

How dare the little minx stand there so defiantly, Damian thought. She is daring me to strip the clothes off her back. Their eyes locked, violet and green, neither giving ground.

Damian moved from the bed and stood in front of her. "I don't ever want to hurt you, love."

She closed her eyes, her body taut, knowing that if she looked at him she would give in. "Please go away."

"No," he whispered sharply, as he swung her body up in his arms. He gently lowered her to the bed, then began to remove her clothes. She steeled herself against his first intimate touch, but instead when she was nude he picked her up again and set her in the tub of warm, scented water. Picking the sponge up he began to scrub her back.

She couldn't stop trembling as his hands roved over her body. Never in her life had she ever experienced the painful pleasure he was giving her. He brushed his fingers across her taut breasts, making the nipples spring to prominence.

She moaned softly as his hands moved between her legs. "Do you want me, Angel? Do you want to feel me there, loving you?"

"No," she whispered, shaking her head back and forth.

He ignored her protests and pulled one long, slim leg up out of the water and gently, teasingly rubbed it from the sole of her foot to her hip. "You are beautiful, my little tease. Just thinking about you drives me crazy." He began the same process on the other leg, but she fought to get out.

"Please, I can't stand this, Damian. Love me. For God's sake, just love me," she begged.

Damian laughed softly, picking her up from the tub. He put her down on the bed and quickly undressed. She watched him, remembering her words a few minutes before, but it didn't make any difference. He made her crazy for him, and he knew it. There was nothing she could do. His flesh was warm against her wet skin. He kissed her soft mouth, parting her trembling lips, until she kissed him back, teasing his tongue and inner mouth with her own. She tangled her fingers in his curls, plundering his mouth as he had done hers. But then he began his exploration of her body with his tongue. First her breasts, then lower to her navel. Then he came back to her mouth, kissing her deeply as his hardness disappeared inside her. Her legs twisted around his, clutching him to her as the world began spinning, turning everything around her in a rainbow of colors until she thought she would surely die.

When Damian moved she turned her back to him. "Angel, what is wrong?"

"Please leave now. I'm going to catch pneumonia if I don't get dressed."

Damian sat up and began to pull his clothes on. "You can pretend all you want that you didn't enjoy that, my pet, but you and I both know differently."

"You forced me," Angelique hissed, knowing her words were hollow.

"Hell," Damian swore, "you forget you begged me to take you. What a hypocrite you are."

"Hypocrite?" she shouted. "How can you talk about anybody being a hypocrite when you have a fiancée."

"You'd better get some rest, Angelique. I think the trip was too hard on you."

"You bastard!" she screamed as Damian left the room.

"Damn you, damn you," she whispered. "Why do I love you so?"

Chapter Eighteen

Damian stood at the foot of the stairs and watched Angelique descend. She wore a pale blue gown with an overlay of white lace, trimmed in blue satin ribbons. It draped low, baring her lovely shoulders. Her black hair was pulled back with the white camellia that he had asked Bessie to give to her.

"You look lovely," Damian said, giving her his arm. "This house has never been graced by such beauty."

"Save your gallantry for your fiancée," Angelique snapped.

Damian's handsome features were carefully controlled. "I assure you I have enough compliments for both of you," he said forcing an indifferent tone.

Angelique bit back her retort as they joined Lacey and Adam on the veranda.

"Oh, Angelique, you must try Bessie's peach brandy," Lacey exclaimed, holding up a crystal goblet of amber liquid.

Before Damian had a chance to offer it, Adam handed Angelique a glass.

"For a beautiful lady," he said in a very seductive voice.

"Ah, kind sir, you are a flatterer," Angelique answered, performing a little curtsy.

Damian gritted his teeth as the two of them continued their banter.

"Lacey, have you seen the garden?" Damian asked. "There is a lovely gazebo."

"I would love to see it," she agreed, winking at Adam as they walked past.

"What are you two up to?" Angelique asked, knowing Adam and Lacey's relationship had been growing into something very special.

"We've agreed we want to do this, Angelique, and nothing you say will change our minds."

"Do what?"

"I'm going to sweep you off your feet with so much attention you're going to be dizzy. We're going to make Damian furious, and hopefully he'll come to his senses."

Angelique had to laugh. "And what does Lacey think about you courting me?"

"She knows it's only temporary. I've had no trouble professing my love to Lacey. I want my brother to be as fortunate."

Angelique had to walk away from Adam as she fought to control the tears that threatened to flow.

"I didn't mean to upset you, Angelique," Adam

apologized.

"You didn't, Adam. It's just you and Lacey are so sweet to want to do this, but I'm afraid it's a waste of time."

"I don't agree with you, Angelique. Just watch my brother's face tonight while I charm you and you'll see what I mean."

"No. No, really . . . we've been through this before . . ."

Adam cut off her further protests by tucking her arm in his and walking toward Damian and Lacey. "Just watch," he whispered.

Angelique did notice the stiff set of Damian's wide shoulders as she laughed at something Adam said.

"I thought you and Adam were beginning to get close," Damian said bitterly, watching Angelique enjoy herself with his brother.

"No," Lacey answered, looking as dejected as possible, "I'm afraid it has always been Angelique."

"We thought we'd take a walk down toward the stables," Adam announced.

"No!" Damian said. "I mean, it gets dark here very fast and I'm sure Bessie will be serving dinner in just a few minutes. Why don't you do that tomorrow?"

Adam squeezed Angelique's arm. "I suppose we can wait until then. Will that be all right with you, *my love*?"

Angelique had to look at Adam before she realized he was talking to her. "Yes, that will be fine, *dear*."

When dinner was announced, Adam kept his hold

241

on Angelique's arm even when Damian moved toward her.

With a knot of tension in her stomach, she tried to concentrate on the smoked ham, blackeyed peas and boiled potatoes on her plate. Adam was still playing his part to the hilt, whispering intimate little tidbits in her ear. His eyes seldom left her face and he pretended to hang on her every word. Angelique noticed a twitch of muscle in Damian's jaw when Adam suggested that he show her the garden by moonlight, yet his conversation with Lacey never faltered. Another time Adam covered her hand with his while he leaned close to hear something she was saying. She took perverse pleasure when she noticed Damian's discomfiture as he refilled his glass with wine a third time.

"I think you should give the three of us a tour of Enchanteur before you head back to Charleston," Adam suggested.

Damian stared at Adam as if he were going to refuse, then he smiled. "I have to leave day after tomorrow, so if the ladies are up to it, we'll plan to do it tomorrow."

"I'm sure I will be," Lacey assured. "All I need is a good night's sleep."

Damian turned to Angelique. "I suggest you also get a good night's sleep."

The look Angelique gave Damian would have cowered a lesser man. "I assure you, Damian, *I have a clear conscience*. I will have no trouble sleeping. Adam, could we take that walk now?" Angelique asked, turning her shoulder to Damian.

Angelique drank the precious coffee Damian had brought in on his last run, while Bessie helped her dress. Contrary to her statement about sleeping well, she hadn't. It had been the early hours of morning before she finally drifted off. Now she rushed, so the others wouldn't have to wait.

"I should just let them go on without me, but I won't give him the satisfaction of saying I wasn't up to the outing."

"Give who the satisfaction," Bessie asked, knowing full well who Angelique meant.

"You know who, Bessie," Angelique said placing the green velvet hat on her head at a cocky angle. "There, I'm ready." Angelique paused at the door. "Thank you for your help, Bessie. I couldn't have made it without you."

"It's nice to have a lady to wait on," Bessie smiled. "Now get on with you."

"Good morning, everyone," Angelique greeted cheerfully. "I hope everyone slept well."

Damian mumbled something as he strode past her toward the stable, but she couldn't make out what he said. "Your horse is over here," he shouted back over his shoulder.

Adam winked at Angelique as she followed Damian toward the stables. She wondered why her horse wasn't in the yard. Lacey and Adam were already mounted. Suddenly she stopped in her tracks. In front of her stood a beautiful white Arabian mare.

"Oh, Damian, she is beautiful! The most beautiful horse I've ever seen."

"I thought you'd appreciate her," Damian smiled. "A friend stationed in Egypt arranged to ship a matched pair to me by way of Nassau. The stallion is magnificent, but I haven't been here long enough to break him. My thought was to breed them, but not while this damned war continues." As Damian spoke he was tightening the cinch on the saddle. "Well, what is it going to be, side saddle or . . ."

Angelique smiled and displayed the split legs, then suddenly the expression on her face changed. They stared at each other for a long moment, both remembering the first time Angelique had explained the skirt. Angelique remembered Damian saying that her husband would have his hands full.

"A hand please," she asked softly, bringing them both back to the present. "What is she named?" she asked, stroking the silky white mane.

"Magic Lady," he answered, staring up at her. "Magic Lady," he repeated softly, before turning away to mount his own horse.

"Take good care of Shadow for me," Angelique instructed the small black boy who held the squirming puppy in his arms.

"Yes em, I sure will," he beamed, proud that he had been chosen to take care of the nice lady's dog.

Damian took the lead and Lacey quickly maneuvered her horse to fall in beside him, leaving Angelique and Adam to follow.

The atmosphere of tension seemed to dissolve as Damian proudly pointed out the cotton barns, and the boat landing where the cotton was transported down river. Further on Damian pointed out the fields where the stock roamed. In the distance they could see the white stallion grazing. It was a breathtaking place, with fields and fields of fertile land. A lot of hard work had gone into making it what it was. Angelique remembered the conversation they had had at dinner about the Yankees burning all the plantations in the South and she shuddered. How terrible it would be to take a man's life-work and destroy it. Lacey was right, there was nothing good about war—no matter what the outcome—everyone was a loser.

They toured the plantation until the noon hour when Damian led the way to a clearing at the river's edge where they would picnic. Adam tied his horse to a limb and circled the area.

"I remember this place. This is where we used to swim," he said as if he had discovered some lost treasure. "Able used to bring us here with his boys."

Damian laughed. "You should remember it. You almost drowned here while learning to swim."

Adam looked at his brother, his eyes bright with remembrance. "And you saved me. I remember another time on that old plow mule . . ."

Angelique and Lacey spread the cloth Bessie had packed in their basket while they listened to Adam and Damian reminisce.

"Can you imagine how it must have hurt them to

be separated?" Angelique whispered sadly.

"Their mother had to be a very selfish woman to have done such a thing," Lacey agreed. "If she wanted to leave why didn't she just do it and leave the boys together with their father?"

"No one has ever been able to figure that out," Angelique said, watching the brothers laugh about something they recalled. "At least it didn't leave such emotional scars on Adam," Angelique mused.

"I would imagine that the father's hurt left an indelible impression on Damian."

"Yes, Damian mentioned one time that his father was never the same."

"No, I don't imagine he was. That is probably the reason Damian is afraid to trust his heart to any woman. He saw how it could destroy a man."

Lacey leaned closer to Angelique. "Speaking of that, how is our plan going?"

"I'm getting a lot of black looks, but nothing else," Angelique confided. "If Damian realizes what we are doing he will be furious."

"He won't find out for awhile. Then it will be too late. Shh, here they come."

"Are you hungry?" Lacey asked.

"Why don't you and Damian go on and eat," Adam said. "I want to show Angelique the path by the river." Before Angelique had a chance to refuse Adam took her hand pulled her to her feet. "Just leave us something."

Damian stared after the two of them as they disappeared on the tree-lined path.

"A piece of ham?" Lacey asked, offering Damian a plate.

Damian looked back at Lacey, a puzzled look on his face. "Doesn't it bother you that they are carrying on this way? I thought you had some feelings for Adam?"

"I guess I wasn't his type," Lacey said biting into an apple. "If you remember, I also had feelings for you."

"Oh, come on, Lacey, what we had was a brief affair. Adam flipped over you the first time he saw you in Bermuda. Why all of a sudden is he smitten with Angelique?"

"Perhaps he didn't realize you weren't interested in her."

"What is that supposed to mean?" he said leaning back on his elbows.

"On the ship it was understood that Angelique was your woman. Then all of a sudden in Charleston this fiancée shows up. I guess that made Adam realize he had a chance with Angelique. I understand his change toward me. Angelique is a lady, someone very special."

"Don't put yourself down, Lacey. You're also someone very special, and I was really hoping things would go well for you and Adam."

"Thank you, Damian. That's very kind of you. Now come on, eat something. Those two lovebirds could be awhile."

Damian was about to take a bite of ham, but instead he tossed it aside. "I'm going to find them.

Adam has probably forgotten about the snakes in this area."

Lacey watched Damian stride off down the path. "I think the plan is working very well," she smiled to herself.

As Damian turned a crook in the path he saw them. Angelique was sitting on a rock while Adam had his hand on the calf of her leg. Damian's first impulse was to throttle his brother, but he thought better of it. Angelique had her foot on Adam's thigh while he laced her boot, but to Damian it looked like he was massaging the calf of her leg.

"I think it would be wise for us to stay together," he announced through gritted teeth. "You never know what kind of animal you're likely to meet out here."

Adam, with his back to Damian, stifled a laugh. "Of course, Damian. Just let me finish tying Angelique's boot."

Damian didn't answer before stalking back down the path.

"We've gone too far, Adam. He's not jealous, he's angry, and at both of us. I can't let you go on with this. I won't let you jeopardize your newfound relationship with your brother."

"Our plan is working, Angelique," Adam assured, leading her back down the path. "Just a little more time."

"No, Adam. I remember very well the temper Damian has, and I will not subject you to his anger."

"All right, but let's continue our little charade for

the rest of the day. If he doesn't come around I'll back off."

Reluctantly Angelique agreed, but the look she had seen in Damian's eyes had frightened her—and well it should have.

While Angelique and Lacey explored the river banks for wildflowers Damian and Adam sat on the bank talking about the plantation and the effect the war was having on it.

"Every time I return, more of the livestock has disappeared. We don't have enough help to watch over things anymore. So far they've only taken small stock that they can carry, but it won't be long before they're leading off our horses and cows, and I can't blame them. The army is not supplying them with enough food and they have to steal what they can."

"What will the outcome be, Damian? Will the South be able to hold her own?"

Damian was silent for a long time. "The North found its future in factories, and that is extremely important to her now. The South clung to their pastoral way of life, living by agriculture and depending on slave labor, which isn't any help to her now. The Union has seventy percent of the railroads, most of the fighting ships, and most of the money. In all honesty, the only thing I'd say the South has going for her is faith—faith and a consummate will to fight to defend one's honor and homeland."

"Will that be enough?" Adam asked.

"Who knows? We did all right at Bull Run and Cedar Mountain, but sometimes I wonder if that hasn't given us false hope. You saw those soldiers on the road. Did they look like victors to you?"

Adam shook his head. "To the contrary, most of them didn't even have shoes."

"I can remember when the cheering crowds lined the streets of Charleston to bid farewell to those very same soldiers, then decked out in fine uniforms. They were off to win a quick and glorious victory and return home heroes—or so they thought. Those were the good days, but unfortunately they were few. It didn't take long for them to realize the stakes were life or death."

"I'm going to offer my services, Damian. I'm sure they can use another doctor."

Damian stared at his brother. "This isn't your war, Adam."

"What do you mean, it isn't my war. I'm an American. I was born right here on Enchanteur. Why shouldn't I want to be involved?"

Damian ran his hand through his hair in the familiar gesture of frustration. "I would never have encouraged you to come here if I thought you'd want to get involved in this damned war."

"Aw, come on big brother, what did you think I was going to do, become a gentleman farmer?"

"Gentleman farmer?" Lacey asked as the women joined the men. "Who is a gentleman farmer?"

"We were both saying that is what we'd like to be," Adam laughed. "Now come here, Angelique, sit be-

250

side me. I've been missing you."

"It's time for us to move on," Damian said abruptly. "There's a storm brewing."

"Yes, in more ways than one," Adam whispered to Angelique as he helped her mount.

Chapter Nineteen

The sky was a menacing yellow-gray back toward the house. Before they were mounted the wind began to blow, making the branches of the trees seem to droop and cower.

"There is no shelter between here and the stables. We're going to have to ride," Damian shouted over the thunder.

The first large drops of rain came before they reached the clearing, and within minutes Angelique was soaked to the skin. Her hat drooped, obstructing her vision. She tossed it away, but there was nothing she could do about the weighted riding habit clinging to her. An extraordinarily loud clap of thunder frightened the horses. Lacey's horse reared up, its front legs pawing the air, then it bolted back toward the woods with Lacey holding on for dear life. Before anyone else had a chance to react Adam was beside Lacey. With a quick move, he snatched the loose reins and brought the frightened horse to a halt. Angelique and Damian watched as Adam pulled Lacey from the horse and held her tightly in his arms. Angelique glanced toward Damian and found him staring at her. Before she had a chance to say anything, another crack of lightning sent her horse nervously dancing sideways.

"Follow me," Damian ordered. "It isn't much further."

Later, alone in her room, Angelique had time to think about the day, and about the way Damian had lifted her from her horse and gently carried her into the house where he insisted she drink brandy to chase the chills away. Then he gave her over to Bessie, who had a steaming tub of water waiting. Angelique had soaked for nearly an hour with Bessie standing by to replenish the hot water before it could cool. Then she had climbed into the inviting bed, under the feather quilts and slept, but not without disturbing dreams of Damian—of the way his hands had lingered at her waist and how his eyes had held hers, silently saying he knew what his touch did to her. He wanted her. She was sure of it. She pushed her supper tray aside, still feeling queasy from the brandy she had drunk earlier. She was glad Bessie had insisted she stay in her room and rest for the rest of the day. She felt drained. She picked up the copy of *Vanity Fair* that Bessie had left her and read for a few minutes, but that didn't satisfy her. Finally sitting at the dressing table, she began to pull the brush through her long, ebony hair. Her thoughts were again on the afternoon when her attention was drawn to a movement at the French doors behind her. She met Damian's green eyes in the mirror as he leaned against the doorjamb watching her.

"You enjoyed yourself today, didn't you?" he asked, his speech slurred from drinking.

"I don't know what you mean," she answered as she resumed brushing her hair.

"Of course you do," he laughed bitterly. "You and my brother were trying to make me see the error of my ways."

"You don't think Adam could be interested in me?" she questioned.

"Oh, I'm sure he could be, but today's performance was a little overacted, and then when Lacey's horse became uncontrollable, it was obvious how he felt about her."

Angelique didn't say anything as she watched Damian move to stand behind her. He lifted a handful of hair and let it run through his fingers. "If your little act was to make me jealous, you succeeded."

"Why should you be jealous of me? You have a fiancée."

"Don't play games with me, Angelique."

"I don't play games!" she said turning to face him.

In one swift move Damian grabbed her by the shoulders and pulled her to stand in front of him. His eyes blazed with a mixture of anger and desire.

"Neither do I," he said before his mouth took possession of hers.

For a moment Angelique struggled, then she gave in to the pleasurable feeling of her senses inflamed by his touch.

"I want you, Angel . . . God, how I want you," he whispered hoarsely. "You are in my every thought . . . in my blood."

"You are drunk," she hissed, pushing him away.

"Maybe," he admitted, "but that doesn't change a thing."

"I won't be used again, Damian," she whispered as he undid her wrapper. "No! I won't let you do this," she said pulling away as she realized her body was reacting to his touch.

Damian moved toward her again, taking her in his arms. "You've been driving me crazy these last few weeks," he whispered, as he buried his face in her hair, "and the past two days seeing you with Adam have been hell."

"Why should it bother you?" she asked breathlessly, as his lips roamed her neck. Stop this now, she willed herself, but instead her arms came up to wrap themselves around his neck.

"You belong to me," he whispered, his breath warm against her ear. "Why can't I make you see that?"

Angelique wasn't sure she heard him. She tried to pull back, to have him repeat what he said, but his mouth took possession of hers, exploring with growing intensity. "Ease the pain I have, love," he pleaded as he swept her up in his arms and took her to the bed. He lowered her gently, his eyes locked with hers, then as he started to remove his shirt she rolled to the side of the bed and jumped off. "No! I won't lie with you again while you're engaged to someone else. I might be a fool where you're concerned, but I do have principles." Angelique stood naked before him, her hands on her slender hips. Her high-pointed breasts rose and fell as she faced him.

At that moment it would have taken the whole Union army to sway Damian's intentions. As he took a step toward her she took a step backward.

"I mean it, Damian Legare, just stay away from me. Things have changed between us!"

"Nothing has changed between us, Angel. Your eyes are dark with passion, and your lovely nipples are rigid with desire."

"Stop it, Damian!" Angelique ordered as she pulled the sheet from the bed and wrapped it around herself.

"That isn't going to do you any good, love."

"You lied to me and I hate you for it."

Damian moved another step closer, giving no sign he heard her angry words. His hands were on her shoulders, slipping away the sheet, slipping away her defenses. At the same time the stark realization of his feelings for her made him tremble as he pulled her to his chest. His own heart was beating so rapidly the sound of it seemed to fill the room. "Oh God, Angel," he whispered against her ear, "I thought I was so smart . . ."

Angelique pulled back and looked up into his eyes. He smiled at her, yet there was something disquieting too.

"You're so beautiful, so desirable. I want you, Angel."

"Damian," she murmured, her sigh signaling total surrender.

When he picked her up she wrapped her arms around his neck, feeling the muscles ripple beneath his skin as he leaned forward to lay her on the bed. This time he sat beside her as he removed his own clothes, then he stretched his body out alongside of her. He brushed his lips across her eyes and ears before finally moving to take possession of her mouth—and her soul.

"You're a sorceress," he whispered, nibbling on her lower lip, "an enchantress, a witch who has cast her spell over me."

Angelique moved her hands up Damian's arms and across his chest, but he captured her hands, placing a kiss in each palm, then placing them at her side.

"Just lie there. I want to make love to you." His lips enclosed the peak of one breast, then the other, until both throbbed with exquisite sensation. Angelique's breath caught in her throat as his tongue made warm, wet patterns around her navel, then down the inside of her trembling thigh. She groaned with a frustrated, excited intensity that was almost Damian's undoing. Slowly he came back to her mouth. "I can't prolong this any longer, love. I want you now."

Angelique ran her hand down his flat, muscular stomach, enjoying his words, as she gently ran her fingers through the crisp curly hair at the base of his stomach. Tentatively she touched him. His breath was uneven and ragged as she explored this strange and forbidden part of a man's body. She was weaving a sensual web that Damian would never escape from—would never want to escape from. Enduring her exquisite caresses as long as he could, Damian rolled over on top of her. Catching her bottom lip between his teeth he moaned. "I can stand no more of this torment, my temptress." With a slow, expert move he filled her. Their bodies blended, making them one. Damian moved in a slow, easy rhythm as Angelique arched her hips to meet his thrusts. She closed her eyes, letting Damian feed the fires that threatened to consume her.

"Open your eyes, love. I want to lose myself in them as we reach heaven together." At that moment, with eyes locked, hands embraced, and bodies one, Damian knew he never wanted any other woman but Angelique. She belonged to him, body and soul.

"*Je t'aime*, Damian," she cried out, twisted her fingers in his blond hair. She arched her body as the fires raced toward her loins, crying out in surrender.

It was a few minutes later before Damian spoke. "You're all fire and passion, my sweet Angel." Angelique reached up and ran her finger over the smoothness of his full sensual lips, while his hand still roamed over her smooth skin. "I've never wanted to touch a woman the way I want to touch you. Your skin is like velvet."

Angelique closed her eyes, contented to enjoy this feeling of belonging to Damian. "Don't go to sleep yet, love. We have to talk," he whispered.

Angelique was too exhausted to open her eyes. "Ummn," she murmured, snuggling even closer.

"Come on, sleepy head, wake up. I have to leave in the morning and I don't want to leave with matters unsettled."

Angelique opened her eyes to Damian's troubled face. "What matters?" she asked, touching his blond sideburns.

"First, I have no fiancée." Angelique started up, her eyes wide with surprise, but Damian stopped her. "Now just hear me out. Kate lied to you for her own devious reasons. At the time I thought it would be better for you if we ended whatever there was between us. Now I realize that isn't possible, Angel. When you're with me I can't keep my eyes or my hands off you. When I'm away I can't think of anything but you." Suddenly Damian rolled over on his back and stared at the ceiling, still stunned by his own feelings. Angelique was silent, waiting for him to go on. "What I'm trying to say is for the first time in my life I feel love—and it scares the hell out of me, yet I know in my heart you belong to me."

Angelique's hand moved from Damian's arm to lie on his chest. "I've known that all along, love. Ever since I was a little girl following you and Beau around. When Papa began to talk of marriage I hoped and prayed you would come to take me away." Angelique's eyes darkened with remembered pain. "If only it hadn't happened like it did . . ."

"I know, love," Damian said pulling her into his arms. "But I know Genevieve and Michel would approve. All we have to do is make Beau understand.. That might take some persuasion since Beau knows the kind of life I have led."

Angelique rolled over to look into Damian's face. "You have nothing to worry about, my love. Beau has always said you and I would be a perfect match."

Damian laughed. "He probably said that because we are both so stubborn and strongwilled."

"Perhaps, my love," Angelique said, as she laid kisses along Damian's chest, "but my stubbornness paid off this time."

Chapter Twenty

On the twenty-second of November Damian sailed under the dark of the moon. Angelique threw herself into learning everything she could about the plantation, hoping it would make the days pass swiftly.

The relationship between Adam and Lacey progressed rapidly. It was no surprise to Angelique when Adam announced that they would be married as soon as Damian returned.

Angelique and Bessie were working on the side porch filling lamps with whale oil while they talked about the wedding.

"Perhaps it be a double wedding," Bessie suggested.

"Oh, Bessie," Angelique laughed, "we're making progress, but I'm not sure Damian is ready to think about marriage."

"Maybe he fool you. He sure was a different man when he left here," Bessie grinned knowingly.

Angelique didn't say anything, but her smile told of memories of the morning Damian had left. He had admitted to her that she had held him with velvet chains from the moment she had jumped into his arms after crossing swords with him. Angelique's reverie was interrupted by the sound of a carriage coming up the drive.

"My heavens, Adam and Lacey weren't supposed to be back until late," she said wiping her hands on her apron.

"That's not our carriage," Bessie said. "Looks like we is goan to have company."

"Oh no! Just look at me," Angelique exclaimed, already pulling the checked scarf from her hair.

"I told you dis ain't no job for a lady," Bessie laughed. "I jus hope it's not dat Winston woman."

Bessie's statement sent Angelique scurrying to her room to try to quickly make herself presentable. Minutes later she stood at the top step, hesitating as she heard a man's voice coming from below. She prepared herself to face Kate Winston, but was relieved when the guests turned out to be Philip Delacort and his sister. Philip came forward to kiss her hand and for the first time Angelique noticed he walked with a limp.

"I hope you don't mind us stopping in on you uninvited, Mademoiselle, but once Patrice learned there were ladies here at Enchanteur she wouldn't hear of not welcoming you."

"Please, call me Angelique," she said, not missing the strange look Patrice gave her brother before picking up the conversation.

"Yes, I've always wished Damian had a sister. It can get very lonely living on a plantation with no other women."

"Yes, I'm sure it can," Angelique answered, wondering what this visit was all about. As Bessie entered with tea, Angelique studied Patrice. Her pink satin gown was patched in several places and the slippers she tried to keep hidden under her hem were very badly worn. Still she was a lovely blonde with exquisite green eyes which had a sad expression even when she smiled.

"Our plantation, Bellemeade, borders Enchanteur. We are your closest neighbor," Philip explained.

"Yes, I believe you told me that the other night at the theatre."

"Philip has talked of nothing but you since that night," Patrice added.

Why in the world would he talk about me, Angelique wondered as she poured tea.

"Bellemeade was one of the most prosperous plantations in the low country before this dreadful war," Patrice continued, "now we are just barely holding on to it."

"Patrice dear, I don't think Mademoiselle, ah, Angelique wants to hear about our problems."

"Well by looking at Damian's plantation she wouldn't know other people were having difficulties."

Angelique forced her anger down and answered calmly. "I'm sure everyone has suffered, Patrice. Damian has lost almost all of his stock and most of his crops are being sent to Virginia to help feed the troops."

Patrice had the decency to look embarrassed. "I didn't realize . . ."

"Damian is not the type to talk about what he is doing for the war effort," Angelique answered. "Are you aware that he is one of the few blockade runners who refuses to transport anything but what is needed for the troops? Other blockaders are getting rich bringing in whiskey and other frivolous items."

"Easy, Angelique," Philip laughed. "We are not here to criticize Damian. He has the respect of all the planters for being an honest, hard-working man. I'm sure his principles are above question. May I add, he is very fortunate to have you to champion him."

"It is such a shame you couldn't have been here before the war," Patrice said. "We could have shown you what the South was really like. There was always a Sunday tea or a ball to attend. When Papa was alive he used to have a hunt once a month, and a wonderful breakfast afterward. Oh, it was really something to see," Patrice said, her eyes filling with tears, "but Papa was killed at Bull Run. Now, at least he will be with Mama."

Angelique suddenly felt sorry for Damian's neighbors. They had apparently lost a great deal because of the war. "I lost both my parents several months ago," she said. "I can sincerely say I know how you feel."

For the first time in several minutes Philip joined the conversation. "I had a riding accident just before the war. The doctors didn't know if I would ever walk again. When they asked for volunteers from South Carolina Papa said he would represent our family. He was commissioned a captain in the South Carolina cavalry. He bravely led a charge against the Union, but took a bullet through the neck. He continued to lead his men and turned the Yankees back, but he died shortly afterward from loss of blood. He was honored as a hero."

There was silence in the room. "I just wish it had been me," Philip said, his voice choked with emotion. "Papa was such a good man."

"Your father did what he felt he had to do," Angelique said, reaching out to touch Philip's arm. "He died an honorable death fighting to give you a chance to live the life only he could give you."

"You are very young to be so wise and compassionate," Philip mused, seeing Angelique in a totally different light. Then he laughed. "Look at us. We come to pay a social visit and we're all in tears. God, this war will be the ruination of us all. Come, sister, we should be heading back now. Finish your tea while I say hello to Able." Philip raised Angelique's hand to his lips. "Good day, Angelique. I'm sorry if we've bored you with our sad tales. Give us another chance and we'll try to brighten your spirits instead of burdening you."

"You did not burden me. We have all suffered the loss of our parents and that makes us kindred spirits. I would very much like to visit with you and Patrice and see your Bellemeade."

"Would you come Sunday?" Patrice asked excitedly. "We could have tea, and perhaps you would sit for Philip to paint your portrait. He gets so tired of using me for a model."

"Patrice, you're putting Angelique in an embarrassing position. I'm sure she has better things to do than sit for a struggling artist."

"I have been considering having a portrait done," Angelique mused. "As a gift for a friend."

Philip lifted her chin and studied her facial structure. "I would be honored to try to capture your beauty on canvas. If you would like, Sunday I will make a few sketches and then we'll go on from there."

"Wonderful," Angelique said, excited that she had finally thought of a gift to give Damian. "May I bring Damian's brother and his fiancée?"

"Oh, that sounds wonderful. It will almost be like old times. If Philip can get some sugar I will bake a cake to have with tea."

"I'll see what I can do," Philip smiled warmly at his sister. "Now finish your tea so we can be on our way."

When her brother left, Patrice turned to Angelique. "Philip has been drinking heavily since Papa was killed. He blames himself, yet there was nothing he could do to stop Papa. Today I saw hope in his eyes and I think you're responsible for that. I thank you, Angelique Charbonne."

"Patrice," Angelique hesitated, knowing she couldn't let anyone know how she felt about Damian.

"I want to be a friend to you and your brother, but that is all it can be. I have already made a commitment to someone."

Patrice's lovely face clearly showed her disappointment. "I had hoped you would be the one to take Philip out of Kate Winston's clutches," she said bitterly.

"What is it with this Kate Winston? Does she want every man in Charleston," Angelique exploded.

"Oh yes, I forgot she has her sights on Damian too. She is a tramp, Angelique. She had been Damian's mistress for a long time, but when she realized he wasn't going to marry her, she married an old man who was practically on his death bed. He left her very rich and she thought that would change the way people thought of her. Mama always said blood will tell, and she was so right. Unfortunately Philip doesn't see her faults. She encouraged him to gamble away the little money we had and then she keeps him at her side by doling out enough money for him to get by on. I tell you, if I knew how to use a gun I would shoot her!"

"Oh, no Patrice, don't say that. Philip is a grown man. I'm sure he can take care of himself."

"You don't know Philip very well. He is a dear, sweet man, but he is not very strong."

"Well perhaps his sister and a good friend can make him see the error of his ways."

Patrice smiled, grasping Angelique's hands between her own. "Yes, perhaps we can."

* * *

Philip and Patrice traveled silently past the harvested fields. Patrice was thinking about what she could wear for her company on Sunday. It was getting harder to keep her dresses together with mending. The pink satin she had on was one of her best and even that was beginning to show marks from her needle. She still had the forest green velvet gown she was saving for a special occasion. Perhaps it would be a victory ball and all the young men would come home to Charleston. Then she would have several court her like Mama always said they would. She had been thirteen when her mother died, but even before then her mother had said she could see the beauty that was emerging in her young daughter. She had predicted Patrice would be the most sought after belle in Charleston. But, then Mama had died and two years later the war came and took all the young men away. She had heard Charleston was filled with blockade runners, but Philip wouldn't let her go to the city. He insisted when the war was over she would be surrounded by heroes of the South and could have her pick. She hoped her meager wardrobe lasted until then.

Philip was thinking about his agreement with Kate Winston and wondering how he was going to get out of it. Angelique Charbonne was too nice a person to use. Besides, Damian would never consent to him courting Angelique. Damian above all others knew the extent of Bellemeade's problems. Damian was the one who had loaned him the money and provided the manpower to plant the last crop. He had promised to pay it back as soon as the cotton was picked and sold, but instead he gambled the handsome profit away. Damian had been gentleman enough not to make an issue of the loan, but he wouldn't let it go unpaid forever. What a tangled web we weave when first we practice to deceive, he thought. That was what Kate was doing—deceiving herself, if she thought Damian was going to marry her. She suited Damian in bed and lately it didn't seem he was even interested in that. Philip gritted his teeth. There were times when he thought of choking her to death to put an end to her whoring. He was sick and tired of arriving at her house to find her in bed with some man. What did she call them—her influential friends. Why did he put up with it? He was the only one who loved her, and she was using him to get Damian.

"I liked her very much," Patrice broke into Philip's thoughts.

"I thought you would."

"I think she is in love with Damian."

Philip snapped around to stare at his sister. "Why do you say that?"

"The way she defended him. And then after you left she told me she would enjoy being friends with us, but she let it be known that she was committed to someone."

Why not, he thought. She was beautiful, intelligent and had compassion. Damian would be a fool not to see these qualities. Perhaps Kate realized the same thing and that was why she had been willing to aid him financially if he could win Angelique's attention. He snapped the horses with the whip. Kate Winston was a fool!

"Are you very upset?" Patrice asked sympathetically.

"Upset about what?" he asked impatiently.

"About Angelique being committed."

"No. I just credit it to the luck of the Delacorts," he said bitterly.

"What do you know about the Delacorts, Bessie?" Angelique asked as she sat on the porch swing watching Bessie weave a basket.

"De parents were real good people, but had bad luck. Poor Mrs. Delacort, she died when Patrice was still a child. Then dat poor boy fell off his horse as it jumped a fence. He spent almost a year flat on his back. He's lucky he ever walk again. Then de father went off to fight and ended up a dead hero." Bessie shook her head. "I think Philip tries, but he was very spoiled when he was young. He doan know what it means to work hard. Instead of working and saving his money he drinks and gambles. Dat poor girl knows what hardship means though. Dey had to sell all their slaves when the father died. One old woman stay behind and she ain't much help to de girl. Miss Patrice do her own cooking and sewing, and Ise hear she even does the cleaning. She looks like a frail little thing, but she's strong. One thing I'll say about dat boy, he loves his sister. He protects her like she is gold. I jus wonder what will become of her if he doan stop his squandering. De shame of it is dat de boy is a talented artist, but he wastes his time gambling."

"I wonder if people in the South ever realized the effect this war would have on its people? Not only the soldiers who went off to fight, but the women and children? I haven't met anyone who isn't suffering from the hardships."

"Perhaps dey realize it now, but dey would hear of nothing but a blood purge."

"How do you feel about it, Bessie. I know one of the issues is slavery."

"It is like everything else, child. De circumstances make it right or wrong. De old Master Legare gave his slaves their freedom, but before that he educated most of us. In all his years as a slave owner he only had one slave run away, and he came back. Dat black man went North where he heard black people were treated as equals. No one would give him a job, no one would help him when he was hungry and had no place to sleep. He decided he wasn't so bad off on Mister Legare's plantation. It took him months, but he came back. Now he's married to my daughter, Tally."

"You're talking about Burke?"

"Dat right. I remember when Master Legare bought him at the slave auction. He was only thirteen and had been beaten very badly. He hated all whites and swore he would run away first chance he had. Then he and Damian discovered each other and he forgot all his big plans, and Damian forgot some of

271

his hurt. Dey worked side by side in the fields and then would head for the fishing hole. Burke quickly realized the Legares were different. I doan think he would have ever gone North except he felt he had to experience his freedom. Dat where he learned there is good and bad in North and South. He learned de North uses its women and children in factories jus as if they was slaves. It's goan to take people to change their ways, and perhaps in time they will. Only God knows."

The visit to the Delacort Plantation on Sunday had at first been a shock to Angelique. The large house had shutters closed over most of the windows, giving the place a deserted look. As Bessie had warned, there was only the one black woman and she moved as if in pain. Patrice had shown more concern for her servant than any embarrassment at her obvious impoverishment, and this only served to endear her to Angelique even more. As promised, Patrice served dainty cakes with tea. The elegant china belied the condition of the house and Patrice had beamed proudly when Adam and Lacey had admired it. The afternoon passed quite pleasantly with Adam and Philip discussing the war while he sketched Angelique.

When it was time for them to leave Patrice had tears in her eyes. Angelique was getting into the carriage when she stopped and rushed back up the steps to where the brother and sister stood. "There is to be a dance at Hibernian Hall on Christmas Eve. Why don't you both join us?"

Philip shuffled his feet. "I'm afraid I've already accepted an invitation."

Angelique thought Patrice was going to cry. "Then let Patrice come with us. We can chaperone each other."

"Oh please, Philip. It will be my first dance."

"I don't know, Patrice . . ."

"Adam will be with us and we're hoping Damian will be home by then, and as you said, you will be there," Angelique added, before he could say no.

"I guess there's no harm in her attending."

Patrice gave her brother a quick hug, then turned her attention to Angelique. "I will never forget your kindness," she whispered, giving Angelique a hug that nearly took her breath away.

Philip lay beneath the mirrored canopy watching Kate as she sat at her dressing table brushing her silver blond hair. How long would it be before her sordid life started to show up on her smooth ivory skin? He had already noticed a different look in her eyes.

"Are you making progress with Damian's ward?" she asked over her shoulder.

Philip didn't say anything for a moment, trying to control his anger. They had just finished making love, and here she was thinking about Damian. "I've paid several visits to Enchanteur. Angelique is a charming young lady."

"That's not what I asked, Philip. I asked if you are making progress."

"Angelique tells me she is committed to someone else."

Kate whirled around and faced him. "What do you mean?"

"That is what she said, Kate. She says she values my friendship, but she is already committed to someone."

Kate threw her brush across the room, barely missing Philip's head. "You fool! Can't you guess who she is committed to? She is committed to Damian."

Philip angrily swung his legs off the bed and began to pull his pants on. "Maybe she is, but what the hell do you think I can do about it?"

"I thought I could depend on you, but I should have known you were a coward."

The boot Philip held stopped in mid-air. "Shut up, Kate," he growled.

"You're afraid of Damian."

"You're damned right I'm afraid of him. I've seen his temper in action, but that has nothing to do with this. I have nothing to offer Angelique. She saw Bellemeade. She knows I'm struggling. How did you expect me to turn her head from Damian, who makes more gold from one run than I've made in my life."

"Whose fault is that," Kate screamed. "You could have become a blockade runner."

"I had a plantation to run, Kate," Philip said,

pulling his shirt on.

"Oh, you ran it all right. You ran it right into the ground."

Philip stared at Kate, considering what it would feel like to strangle her. "Love does strange things to people, Kate. I was young and impressionable when I met you. I thought your word was gospel. Everything you wanted I bought for you; that ring on your finger, the fancy carriage you ride in, the monstrosity of a bed you and all your lovers use. When my money started running out you suggested I try gambling so I could still buy you gifts. You even introduced me to my card playing friends, but unfortunately I'm not much of a gambler."

"You're not much of a man either," Kate spat.

Philip ignored her remark. "Give up this obsession to have Damian Legare, Kate. You don't stand a chance. In spite of myself I love you. Marry me and together we can rebuild Bellemeade."

Kate laughed. "Sure, you'll rebuild your precious plantation with my money. Well, I can tell you now, the only way you're going to rebuild Bellemeade is to keep Angelique away from Damian so I can marry him."

Philip's harsh laughter filled the room. "You're never going to have Damian. He's not a fool like I am. He took what you so freely offered and kept his heart intact. I wasn't so lucky. But let me tell you something, sweetheart, you can only lie with so many men before your beauty begins to fade—and if you'll look in that mirror you'll see you're already showing signs of dissipation."

"Get out, you bastard! And don't come back until you're ready to do what I ask."

Philip picked up his jacket to leave, but stopped at the door. "He who covets what belongs to another deservedly loses his own. Think of me when your stream of paid lovers dwindle, my sweet, and remember my words."

Chapter Twenty-one

Cooler weather and gray skies settled over Charleston toward the end of December. The winds stripped the leaves from the oak trees that lined the drive—the drive that Angelique watched every day for some sign of Damian.

"Please dear God, keep him safe," she prayed as she stared out the window while Adam and Lacey played chess behind her.

"Did you see what the latest Northern papers are saying?" Adam asked Lacey. "Gideon Wells, Secretary of the U.S. Navy is sending the new *Ironsides* and four monitors to Charleston. He is also sending 10,000 land troops. The article said that if Fort Sumter falls, so will the Confederacy. The people of Charleston are really something," Adam said proudly. "They insist they are ready. The two new gun boats the women of South Carolina raised money for are manned and ready for action, and land defenses are strategically placed. It seems the people in Charleston have great confidence in General Beauregard."

Lacey concentrated on her game while Adam explained the defenses set up on the various islands around Charleston, but Angelique wasn't missing a word. "What about the blockade, Adam? Are any ships getting through?"

"More Federal ships have been added to the cordon of ships already there and it has cut down on the runners coming in, but if anyone can do it, Damian can."

"I suppose you're right," Angelique answered, but with little conviction to her voice. "The moon has been dark for two nights already. I was sure he would be here by now. Tomorrow is Christmas Eve."

"If Damian said he would be here for Christmas, you can bet he is doing everything possible to make it."

The thought frightened Angelique almost as much as his not coming. Would Damian take a chance and run the blockade if he didn't think he could make it? She remembered hearing him tell Adam about the time they had crossed the dangerous coral reefs in the dark so they could party in Bermuda.

"He's beaten me again, Angelique. You play him this time," Lacey exclaimed, moving away from the table. "You would think he'd be gentleman enough to let me win every now and then."

"Listen!" Angelique exclaimed, almost knocking the chair over as she jumped up. "I hear a rider."

Angelique was gone before anyone had a chance to

move. On the porch she hesitated, then ran down the steps toward the horseman.

"It's Beau! Oh, God, it's Beau," Angelique shrieked, running toward the approaching horse.

Beau leaped from the horse while it was still in motion. He swept Angelique up into his arms, swinging her off her feet while she laughed with delight.

"Oh, how I've missed you, little one. I just kept praying Damian had been able to get you here safely."

"I wrote you. Didn't you get my letter?"

"I sailed here directly from Paris. I must have missed it. But, thank God, you're safe," he said twirling her around again.

"And you're safe," she laughed. "What happened? Tell me everything. Did you have any trouble coming through the blockade?"

"Later, Angelique. We will talk later. Now let me say hello to everyone."

Adam and Beau warmly greeted each other, then Adam introduced Lacey as his fiancée. Beau had met Lacey in Bermuda, but he thought it best not to mention it.

"Where is Damian?" Beau asked.

"He made a run in November and hasn't returned. We are expecting him at any time," Adam answered.

"You didn't see him in Bermuda?" Angelique asked.

"We caught a storm that blew us off course so we came by way of the Bahamas."

"A storm?" Angelique repeated. "Was it a very

bad storm? When was it?"

Beau stared at his sister for a moment. "I'm sure these questions aren't just to satisfy your curiosity, my sweet little sister. Do you have something to tell me?" he grinned.

"Yes, yes," Angelique laughed. "Damian and I are in love!"

"Well, by God, it's about time. I didn't think that rogue would ever admit it. I had hoped you might be the one to tame him," Beau laughed. "You and those violet eyes."

"Damian is not a man to be tamed, Beau," Angelique said defensively.

"Ah, there you are wrong, love. There's no such man living. What did you do to change his mind?"

"Actually, it took Adam and Lacey to make him see the light," Angelique admitted. "But the day before he left he told me he loved me."

"I'm happy for you, sweet. I had always hoped you and Damian would get together."

"I tried to tell him that, but he wouldn't believe me. As a matter of fact, that was part of his reluctance to admit his feelings. He felt he was betraying your faith in him."

"The fool! I told him many times how I felt. Wait until he gets here. I'm going to enjoy giving him a bad time."

Suddenly Beau spotted Bessie on the porch watching them. He took the steps three at a time and smothered her with a bear hug. "Bessie, Bessie, how many times I've thought about your smiling face—

and your fried chicken."

"Go on with you, boy, de chicken de only thing you thought about."

While everyone laughed at the bantering going on between Beau and Bessie, Angelique was silently praying Damian would arrive safe.

The evening flew by with Beau telling funny stories of his blockading experiences. Everyone around the table realized he was forcing the gay mood, dreading the questions he knew would come about France. Finally after dinner, they remained around the table while he explained the events that had taken place after Adam and Damian had helped Angelique escape.

"LaFrancois is dead," he said between gritted teeth. Angelique placed her hand over her brother's. He looked into her eyes, forgetting everyone else in the room. "I finally caught up with him at LeHavre. I wanted to take him back to Paris so he could suffer in prison before they hung him, but he took that opportunity away from me." Beau's voice was filled with emotion. "I had to kill him. I didn't want to . . . I wanted him to suffer as we have suffered."

"Then it is over," Angelique said softly.

"It is over—except for the memories," Beau answered bitterly.

Adam and Lacey had been silent while Beau told his story, but now Adam spoke. "You have to go on with life, Beau. Your need for revenge has kept you going up to this time. Now you need to fulfill the legacy that your parents left. Pick up the pieces of your life. That is what Genevieve and Michel would have wanted you to do."

"I know you're right, Adam, but it is easier said than done. I guess I just need something to take my mind off things."

Those last words gave Angelique an idea. When the conversation turned to the Christmas festivities, Angelique interrupted. "Beau, we are planning to attend a Christmas Eve ball tomorrow night in Charleston. You will join us, won't you?"

Beau laughed. "Leave it to the residents of Charleston not to let the Federals at their door interfere with their social life. Yes, I'd like to join you. It will be a nice change."

Angelique smiled mischievously. "I have a new friend I'd like you to be especially nice to. Her name is Patrice Delacort."

"Delacort." Beau repeated. "That name is familiar."

"They own the adjoining plantation. Perhaps you've met Patrice's brother, Philip."

"Ah, yes, I remember Philip. He was always bragging about being the best horseman in the country. Damian and I were always having to prove him wrong."

"Philip took a fall from his horse several years ago and now walks with a limp. I'm not sure he is still able to ride."

"I'm sorry to hear that, he really was an excellent rider. But, tell me more about this sister. You've piqued my curiosity."

"Oh, Beau, she is lovely. She has silver blond hair and exquisite green eyes, and her complexion is like peaches and cream. But it is her personality you'll like. She is so sweet, so unassuming, yet she can do anything. She sews, cooks . . ."

"Whoa, little one. I'm not planning to marry the girl. I just want to dance with her."

"That's all I want you to do," Angelique assured. "Patrice has never been to a ball. She was fifteen when the war started and never had a chance to enjoy the social amenities of life. She comes from a very good family, but she and Philip have fallen on hard times. You wouldn't believe how hard she has to work for one so young."

"She sounds intriguing," Beau said. "I'll do my best to see she has a pleasant evening."

Angelique had been sure Damian would arrive before the Christmas ball, but now when it came time to go alone she was reluctant.

"What if he comes while we are in the city?" she asked Beau. "He would have no way of knowing we are there."

"Burke is driving the carriage in. He can wait at the docks to see if any blockaders come in," Beau assured her.

"I'm not in a very gala mood," she said reluctantly leaving her vigil at the window.

"What?" Beau pretended to be insulted. "Your brother is home and you're not in a gala mood?"

"I'm sorry, Beau. I didn't mean that. You know how happy I am that you're here."

"I know, little one," Beau said taking her in his arms, "but the night won't be perfect for you until Damian is here."

Hibernian Hall was ablaze with color and gaiety as everyone enjoyed a break from thoughts of war. Mended dresses and dresses made from drapes and quilts were the fashion, but in the candlelight no one cared. Philip, who had joined them on the trip to the city, now made his excuses and disappeared toward the card room. As Beau had promised, he danced the first dance with Patrice, but Angelique needn't have worried about her having partners, for every soldier on leave was at her side as soon as Beau released her.

"I think I'm jealous," Beau said as he joined Angelique. "I had thought she was going to be mine for the entire evening."

"So you do like her," Angelique teased.

"How could I not like her? She is refreshing."

"Then you'd better get back in line for her."

"No. She needs an evening like this. Besides, I'd like to spend the evening with my sister, who I might add, is the most beautiful woman here."

"Even more beautiful than Kate Winston?" Angelique asked as Kate and her partner danced past them.

"Point out this Kate Winston, and I'll tell you,"

Beau said. "I've heard enough about the woman, but I've never met her."

"That is her in the gold satin," Angelique pointed out.

Beau turned and watched the blonde dance past. "So that is the infamous Kate Winston."

"What do you think?" Angelique asked.

Beau turned back to his sister. "She is only beautiful on the surface, my sweet, and any man with an ounce of sense knows that. Now come, let's dance this night away."

Kate Winston had already made inquiries about the dark haired stranger with Angelique, but no one knew any more than he was a French blockade runner. When Kate heard this she was delighted. Angelique had to be in love with the man from the way she looked at him. Luck was on her side. Even with Philip's bungling, she was still going to get rid of Damian's ward.

The evening crept onward. Angelique danced with Adam several times, but she kept most of her dances for Beau, politely turning away other invitations. General Beauregard made a brief visit, shaking hands with everyone before quietly disappearing.

As Angelique and Beau were dancing, there was a commotion at the door. Angelique turned, knowing it was Damian before she saw him. Her heart hammered in her throat like the staccato beat of a drum roll. She saw him across the room speaking to several of the guests. His features were unadorned by his beard and even from this distance his mouth appeared sensual as he smiled at something said to him. He turned and their eyes met, and in the space of that instant the world faded away.

He covered the distance between them without looking right or left. The music continued, but everyone seemed to be mesmerized by the two lovers. Damian bowed before Angelique, a smile touching the corners of his handsome mouth. He twirled her around the floor to the strains of a waltz, holding her close, inhaling the scent of her hair, savoring the feel of her hand in his. Angelique looked up into his eyes. He still had not spoken, but his expression was warm, speculative.

"Angel, Angel," he whispered, pulling her even closer.

"You are aware people are going to know I'm not your ward," she said breathlessly.

"Yes, I know, and we're going to shock them even more by making an announcement," he whispered.

"What kind of an announcement?" Angelique asked hopefully.

Damian stopped dancing. "I have been haunted on this trip by a girl with a way about her that stirs a man's blood to fire. To me you're the morning sun after a stormy day, the fresh breeze off the ocean, the warmth of a fire on a cold winter's night. Oh, Angelique, what I'm trying to say is I love you and I want to marry you—and the hell with what Beau Charbonne thinks."

"You can tell him that in a minute," Angelique laughed as she threw her arms around Damian's neck and kissed him.

Everyone in the room clapped in approval—everyone that is, except Kate Winston. She fought the urge to scratch Angelique's eyes out.

"Looks like you lose, Kate," Philip said at her elbow.

"Who is the Frenchman?" she spat. "I thought . . ."

Philip laughed. "So you thought he was Angelique's new love. That's why you've behaved yourself all evening. Well, my love, that happens to be Beau Charbonne, Angelique's brother."

"This is your fault!" she hissed. "The little tramp must have bought you off with her favors."

"Just because you do your best work on your back doesn't mean everyone does, Kate."

"Ladies and gentlemen, may I have your attention," Damian asked. "I'd like to make an announcement. A very important announcement," he said looking into Angelique's eyes. "There is going to be a wedding at Enchanteur." A cheer went up from the crowd.

"Hold on a minute, brother," Adam said as he and Lacey joined them. "With your permission I'd like to change that announcement."

Damian stared at his brother in disbelief. What the hell was he doing, he wondered.

Lacey moved into Adam's arms as he made the announcement. "There is going to be a double wedding at Enchanteur."

"And you're all invited," Damian shouted over the cheering of the crowd.

A few minutes later Angelique excused herself from the throng of well-wishers and headed for a room set aside for the ladies. She was standing before a full length mirror straightening her hair when Kate Winston walked in. Angelique didn't say anything as she continued to fix her hair.

"If you think you've won, my dear child, you are sadly mistaken."

Angelique's raised eyebrow betrayed amazement. "I didn't realize we were having a contest."

"You know exactly what I mean. Damian and I were planning to be married until you came along."

Angelique took a step forward. "You were planning a wedding, Mrs. Winston. Damian never had any intention of marrying you."

Kate looked smug. "Don't you realize he just told you that? I've known Damian intimately since I was fourteen. He has always hungered after me, even then. Now he is trying to teach me a lesson because I married while he was away."

Angelique fought the conflict that was raging within, but with a smile she tucked her handkerchief in her beaded purse. "Then why didn't he ask you to marry him, Mrs. Winston? I understand you have been widowed for more than a year."

Kate's mind groped for an answer. She hadn't expected this young chit to stand up to her. She tried to think how best to proceed, and decided to change her tactics.

"My dear, I know your parents were killed and Damian is responsible for you, but do you really think it is fair to make him marry you?"

"You have no idea what you are talking about, Mrs. Winston. Damian and I are very much in love. We have been since we were children."

"Oh, child, I am concerned for you. I know all about Damian's voracious sexual appetite, and he gets bored very quickly. Don't be surprised when he starts wandering."

"Thank you for the warning, Mrs. Winston, but I also know all about Damian's voracious sexual appetite, and he won't ever have any need to wander."

White-lipped, Kate walked away from Angelique. "Don't say I didn't warn you."

Angelique was met by Damian as soon as she left the room. "Are you all right, love? You look a little pale."

"I'm fine, but perhaps you'd like to wait here and see how your mistress is," Angelique said walking away from him.

"Angel, wait." Damian grabbed her by the arm and spun her around. "This is not the place to argue," he said pulling her into a room off the ballroom.

"Now explain that last statement," he said angrily.

"I think you're the one who better do some explaining," Angelique snapped back. "Your mistress tells me you're only marrying me to get even with her for marrying Winston."

Angelique hadn't expected Damian's reaction. He started laughing and a moment later she was laughing with him.

"Oh, Angel, do you really think I'd do anything so idiotic? I love you. What do I have to do to prove that?"

"I'm sorry, Damian. That woman has a way of confusing me."

"That is exactly what she wanted to do, love. What you have to remember is you're a fire in my blood, and I love you—only you."

Chapter Twenty-two

It was well into the early hours of Christmas morning when the group returned to Enchanteur after seeing Philip and Patrice off at Bellemeade. They gathered around Bessie's kitchen table and ate leftover cornbread with glasses of cold milk while they discussed the double wedding that would take place in a week.

Damian couldn't take his eyes off Angelique. He felt like a kid, excited beyond anything he had ever felt. Beau's words came to him. *Do you ever get tired of being alone? Don't you sometimes wish you had just one woman waiting for you?* For the first time in his life, he would have someone to love him—someone waiting for him when he came home.

Angelique was keenly aware of Damian. His gaze was warm and possessive, touching her with the intimacy of a caress. She listened to the conversation, but she was remembering the feel of Damian's touch.

She blushed as she saw the look of longing in his eyes, knowing he must be aware of her thoughts.

Lacey was the first to excuse herself and Adam followed a few minutes later, leaving Angelique, Damian and Beau alone.

"Did you have a hard time getting through the blockade?" Beau asked, interrupting the look of longing passing between Angelique and Damian.

"A hell of a time," Damian answered. "We've been lying off the coast for two days. If there hadn't been so much celebrating tonight I'm not sure we would have made it."

"We had the same problem. A fog finally gave us the break we needed."

"It's getting too dangerous for you to run the blockade," Angelique interrupted. "Isn't there some other port you can take supplies? A port that isn't so dangerous?"

"Savannah and Wilmington are having the same problem, love," Damian answered. "Perhaps now that the gunboats are in the harbor they can destroy some of those damned Union ships. Now enough about war. Why don't you go on to bed? You must be exhausted," Damian said hugging her. "I want to talk to Beau for awhile."

Angelique knew Damian was anxious to know about Beau's experience in France, so she reluctantly left the two men with Shadow following on her heels. As she reached the landing Tally was coming from Lacey's room.

"I poured some hot water in the basin for you,

ma'am," the pretty black girl said, "and the fire is built up. Are you ready to get out of dem clothes?"

"You didn't need to stay up for us, Tally."

"Of course I did, ma'am. Mama would skin me alive if I didn't."

Angelique laughed. "Just unfasten me and then go on and get some sleep. I'll be fine."

"Are you sure, ma'am?" Tally asked, hesitant to leave.

"I'm sure. Now go on," Angelique ordered affectionately.

"Thank you, ma'am," Tally bobbed quickly. "Sleep well."

Sleep well, Angelique thought ruefully. I don't think that will be possible with Damian in the next room.

Angelique washed, then slipped into the gossamer sheer gown left lying on the turned down bed. She blew the lamp out before pulling the comforter up under her chin. Staring into the fire she remembered the events of the evening. Everything had been so perfect. She drifted off to sleep remembering Damian's announcement that she was a fire in his blood and he loved her. She smiled in the darkness—he loved her.

Damian and Beau had talked for another hour before Damian had pleaded exhaustion and headed for his bed. But now sleep wouldn't come. He had promised himself he wouldn't go to Angelique again until they were married, particularly with Beau in the house, but now he knew it was either go to her or

293

leave his own house—and he wasn't going to leave. The remembrance of her soft, yielding body had been foremost in his mind since he left Enchanteur over a month ago.

Shadow growled as the door opened, but settled back at the foot of Angelique's bed when he recognized Damian. The room was bathed in the golden glow of the fire, giving Damian enough light to see clearly. He moved toward the bed, gently sitting on the side. Angelique had one slender leg outside the cover and he couldn't resist running a finger along the inside of her thigh.

She opened her eyes and stared into Damian's emerald stare. "I didn't think you were going to come to me," she said, gently touching his cheek.

"I had to come wish you a Merry Christmas," he whispered, kissing the palm of her hand. With slow deliberation he removed the quilt, then began to remove the flimsy gown.

"I stayed awake for awhile waiting for some sound in your room, but I guess I fell asleep."

"Your brother was in a talkative mood and I couldn't very well tell him I wanted to be with you, but I'm glad you were thinking about me coming to you."

"I've thought of nothing else since we got home."

"Since we got home," Damian repeated. "Do you want to know something, my sweet, I have never thought of Enchanteur as home until you came here."

"We will make it a wonderful home and we'll fill it

with our children," Angelique said running her hand over his chest.

"I hadn't thought about that," Damian laughed deeply. "We will have children. Beautiful little girls with black hair and violet eyes."

"And little boys with blond hair and green eyes," Angelique added.

"Oh, Angel, I love you," he declared as he nuzzled her neck. "You have rescued me from the hell I was living in—a hell of my own doing, but still it was hell."

"I know that, love. I guess that is why I persisted."

"Persisted, huh," Damian snorted. "You were certainly enjoying yourself with Adam, and how about Philip? What was he doing with you all tonight? I'm going to have to keep a closer eye on you."

"Promise?" Angelique giggled. "Philip and his sister visited several times while you were away and we became friends. And you know something, I think Beau might just like Patrice a little bit."

"You do, huh, well you won't have time to play the matchmaker there. You're going to be too busy being my wife."

"Your wife," Angelique repeated. "Mrs. Damian Legare. How wonderful that sounds."

"Do you think you'll ever tire of it?"

"No, my love. I will never tire of the name or the man."

"My sweet Angel," Damian whispered before covering her mouth with his.

Damian felt giddy with this new sensation. This

beautiful, loving creature was going to be his wife, his responsibility to love and care for. It made him feel strong and powerful, yet scared at the same time. His first thought would have to be for her—and if there were children . . . "Angelique, are you sure?"

"Damian, I've loved you since I was a child and that love grows every day. Now stop talking and love me," she ordered gently, her eyes dark with desire. "I need you, Damian. Oh how I need you."

In a candlelight ceremony in the poinsettia and pine decorated library of Enchanteur, Angelique and Damian and Lacey and Adam were married with many of their friends from Charleston as witnesses. Angelique, putting memories aside, wore her mother's wedding gown, but this time with no sadness or regrets. Damian wore black pants, a white silk ruffled shirt and a green velvet jacket. Lacey wore an egg-shell white gown of satin while Adam wore a beautiful ruffled shirt that Lacey made from her wedding gown material, under a brown velvet jacket.

After cake and champagne had been served, Damian pulled Angelique aside to the privacy of his study. "I have a wedding gift for you," he said drawing a piece of paper from his green velvet jacket.

"What is it?" Angelique asked, her eyes wide with anticipation.

"It is a deed, my love. A deed to that place in Bermuda you liked so much."

Angelique stared speechless at Damian.

"I thought it would be a nice place to get away to whenever we felt like it."

"I don't know what to say. I have thought about that place so often, but what makes me the happiest is knowing you were thinking about marrying me when you were in Bermuda."

"I'll tell you how much I was thinking about it," he grinned. "There is now a piano in the living room where you suggested, and a . . ."

Angelique interrupted before he finished. "And a bed that sits in front of the French doors where you can see the stars at night and the sun rise in the morning."

"That's right," he laughed. "I had planned for us to honeymoon there, but the blockade has become too dangerous. Someday soon we will enjoy it."

"It doesn't matter where we are as long as we are together."

"My sentiment exactly," Damian said pulling her to him. "What do you say we kick all those people out and retire for the night."

"Damian, they are our guests," Angelique exclaimed, pretending to be shocked by his suggestion, "but perhaps we could yawn a few times and hope they take the hint."

"Good idea," he answered, kissing her quickly on the nose. "Now get out there and start yawning."

"Wait, Damian," Angelique said pulling him back. "I have a gift for you, but now I'm almost afraid to give it to you."

"Why, love?"

"I'm not sure you'll like it."

"Let me be the judge of that."

From behind his desk, Angelique pulled out the portrait Philip Delacort had done, now handsomely framed in gold.

"Oh, Angel, it is beautiful!" Damian said as he picked it up and held it to a better light. The artist had caught her special qualities. Her black hair hung loose, falling over one bare shoulder. Her pink mouth was slightly parted, both sensual and vulnerable, and her violet eyes smiled seductively.

"My God, but the artist captured you. Was it Hastings in Charleston?"

"No, love, it was Philip Delacort."

"Philip?" Damian stared at the painting for several minutes. Walking away from it he studied it from different angles. "The man is in love with you."

Angelique looked shocked. "No, Damian, he is just a friend."

"Angelique, there is no way the man could have captured that look if he wasn't in love with you."

"Damian, whenever I sat for Philip, Lacey or Patrice were with me. Please don't be foolish."

"It is beautiful," he said studying it once more. Her eyes were the deep purple of passion, she looked so inviting, so enticing, and it had been for Philip. "I have a strong urge to kill the bastard the next time I see him. No man sees my wife the way I see her."

"If I had known you would react this way I would never have sat for the painting. I just wanted something special for you."

"Angelique, I have seen portraits done by the experts, but I have never seen an artist capture his subject the way Philip has captured you; your spirit, your passion, everything is there."

"It is there because I wanted it to be there for you, Damian."

"Oh, Angel, I'm sorry. I love it. I really do. You couldn't have given me anything I would cherish more. Forgive my jealousy. I'll have to commend Philip on his talent. I didn't even realize he was an artist."

Many of the guests had already started leaving when Angelique and Damian rejoined the party. In the South before the war guests would have stayed the night, and had breakfast in the morning before leaving, but with the shortage of food, it was a practice temporarily set aside, and the four newlyweds were delighted.

The bedroom was bathed in a soft glow from the fire. The crackling of the pinecones was loud in the stillness. Damian, already in his velvet robe poured them each a brandy.

"Can I help you, love?" he asked as he began undoing the small covered buttons of her gown. "I've poured you a bit of brandy to take the chill off."

"To the contrary, I am burning with fever."

"My sweet wife is all passion and fire," he said as he slid her gown from her shoulders. His lips touched the soft skin at the back of her neck. With deft

299

fingers the undergarments followed in a matter of seconds. One by one he removed the pins from her hair, letting it cascade around pearl-white shoulders.

"Turn around, my beautiful wife," Damian gently ordered. "Let me feast my eyes on your loveliness."

Angelique turned and smiled at her husband. The fire's glow glinted on his fair hair and glowed in the depths of his eyes. "Let me feast my eyes on my handsome husband," she replied, untying his robe and slipping it from his shoulders. A delicious weakness spread through her as she took in the perfectly proportioned body of her husband. Damian moaned as she ran her hand over his chest and down across his flat stomach. "This is the first time I have really seen you, my husband. You are magnificent." Angelique could feel the fever in her body rising.

Damian grasped her buttocks, pulling her against his growing passion. "I'm going to savor every inch of you, my sweet wife—every inch," he emphasized. Damian lowered his head to take her lips. His mouth was warm and firm, parting her lips as he explored and tasted. "My woman, my wife, my love," he whispered as he placed nibbling kisses along her mouth and jawline. His hand moved to cup one firm breast, sending a tingling sensation to the very pit of her stomach. "I want to spend the rest of my life waking up to your lovely face," he swore softly, as he kissed her eyelids. "I want to always know you are here for me," he murmured as he continued his sensuous litany—words that were affecting Angelique as much as his caresses. "All I could think about while I was away was how your eyes deepened to purple velvet with your passion, how your lips taste like the nector of a flower . . ."

Angelique raised her face to Damian's, a smile sparkling in her eyes. "This is a side to my husband I didn't know existed."

"Haven't you heard, love does strange things to people," he answered, while he traced the outline of her lips, now slightly swollen from his kisses. He slipped his arm behind Angelique's knees and easily lifted her into his arms. Gently he laid her on the satin sheets, then laid beside her. Raising on one elbow, he began to quote.

> My love is of a birth as rare
> As 'tis for object, strange and high
> It was begotten by Despair
> Upon Impossibility

"What other surprises do you have in store for me, my husband?"

"You will be amazed," he grinned. His thumb moved against the sensitive point of her breast, while with his other hand he caressed her slender throat.

"I like your face smooth," she whispered hoarsely as she caressed his jawline.

"The morning I left I noticed I had chafed your fair skin with my beard, so I knew it had to go." Damian's gaze traveled over the flushed beauty of Angelique's face. He was purposely slowing the pace, building a web of passion around them. "You're quivering, Angel. Are you cold?"

"No, my husband, on the contrary, my blood is boiling."

Damian's laugh came out like a growl as he took one lovely pink nipple in his mouth. He sucked each peak erect then laid a burning trail down over her flat stomach. Parting her thighs, he explored their softness. Angelique's breathing quickened as he touched her most sensitive area with his warm breath. Her first reaction was to close her legs, but he wouldn't let her.

"It's all right, love. Relax, let me savor the very essence of your being."

Angelique barely heard him, her breathing was so loud in her own ears. Her senses reeled, the pleasure was so intense she felt faint. She cried out as he quickly took her to the peak, every nerve in her body exploding with pleasure.

Still in a daze, she lay with her eyes closed, her skin shining with a fine sheen of perspiration. When she finally opened her eyes she met Damian's warm smile. "I didn't know," she whispered, her eyes wide with discovery.

"I know," he smiled, lifting a strand of her hair and letting it slip through his fingers. "My restraint is near an end," he groaned as he pulled her closer. "I can't get enough of you," he said drawing her beneath him. He pressed deep within her, filling her until she thought they were surely one. She was spinning, dizzy from the tender savagery of his lovemaking. They moved in slow sensual motion, expressing their love in the most beautiful, and most satisfying way possible. Damian lifted her hips to meet his thrusts and a sweet ecstasy flooded over Angelique. She cried out his name as he spilled his seed deep inside her.

They lay silently for a few minutes, their breathing finally slowing. "It is different," he sighed.

Angelique turned her eyes to meet his. "Different? How?"

"It is much more satisfying then a casual mating."

Angelique had to laugh. "I've never been involved in a casual mating, but I agree, this was something very special."

"Yes, very special. A union made against all odds," he whispered, brushing her eyelids with his lips. "And I'll never let you go. When this war is over we'll make Enchanteur the most prosperous plantation in the South. We'll fill it with our children and our grandchildren."

"When will this war be over Damian?"

Damian leaned back, pulling her snugly in his arms. "I don't really know, love, but the end is nowhere in sight. I'm afraid it is going to get much worse for Charleston. The Union sends more ships everyday. They are going to virtually cut us off from the world."

"Will you stop running the blockade?" Angelique asked hopefully.

"I can't, love. The South needs supplies more than ever."

"Oh, Damian, it is so dangerous."

"If I weren't running the blockade, I'd be on some battlefield fighting hand to hand. I prefer taking my chances on the sea. Now, no more talk of war, my sweet wife. Turn over here and love me."

"Damian, you are insatiable."

"Yes, love, I know."

Chapter Twenty-three

Damian's prediction had been correct. On April 7th, the Union fleet steamed slowly up the main channel toward the harbor. The *Weehawken* led eight monitors, plus the new *Ironsides*, and all were sitting low in the water from the weight of their guns. Every wharf and the High Battery were jammed with spectators, as were every rooftop and window that commanded a view of the harbor. After an all day battle, Union Admiral DuPont signaled the order for his ships to withdraw. Charleston's Fort Sumter had defied the attack of the most powerful fleet in naval history. The New York *Herald* described the event as, though almost bloodless, it was one of the North's most discouraging disasters.

Word of what had happened reached the upriver plantations by the morning of April 8th. Adam immediately announced his decision to move into the city where he could work at the hospital and prison.

Angelique understood Adam's decision, but she had been shocked when Lacey decided to join him.

"I have to, Angelique. I've been hiding from reality too long. If I can't do this, then I don't deserve a man like Adam. Medicine is his life and I want to be a part of that life. Adam says the hospitals are desperate for help. They are not equipped with staff to handle the wounded coming in daily. Drugs and medicines are absolutely unobtainable except through the blockade. And, you know better than anyone how seldom the blockaders are getting through."

Yes, she knew better than anyone, Angelique thought. Damian and Beau had left the same night in mid-February and now almost three months later she still hadn't heard anything directly. Adam had obtained a copy of the Baltimore *American* which carried an article about the notorious blockade runner, Damian Legare, and the prizes offered to anyone who captured him and the innovative ship called *Moonlight Dancer*. Several well-laid plans had already been put in motion to capture him.

"Perhaps I could help too," Angelique volunteered, needing something to keep her mind off Damian. "I haven't had any formal training, but Adam taught me a lot on the ship, and a gypsy who spent summers at Chateau Charbonne taught me a great deal about herbal medicines . . ."

"Oh, Angelique," Lacey exclaimed, hugging her friend, "I was hoping you would come. It will be so much easier having a woman friend. Adam has already talked to a lawyer on Calhoun Street who'll rent his beautiful furnished house to us. Adam says it isn't Enchanteur, but it is a lovely house."

Plans were set into motion swiftly and by the first of May they had moved into the lovely three-story house. Bessie wouldn't hear of them going without her and Tally, and Tally's husband, Burke. Bessie's reasoning was that Charleston was filled with riff-raff and they needed someone to protect them. No matter what the reason, Angelique was glad for their company.

The lovely house was built almost upon the sidewalk with its side facing the street, designed to catch the prevailing breezes from the sea. Beautiful heavy wooden doors set in a serpent brick wall provided privacy for its yard and garden, which was already in full bloom.

There was very little evidence of the attack on Charleston. A brave show of keeping up a carefree attitude prevailed as people went about their daily tasks. Angelique was feeling very good about the move until they visited the Battery. The view made her go weak in the knees. The Union ships lying in wait for any fool enough to run the blockade had more than tripled since she had last seen the harbor.

"I know what you're thinking, child," Bessie said, "but you put dem thoughts right outta your head. Dat boy ain't gonna do anything foolish."

"Oh, God, I hope you're right, Bessie. I would die if anything happened to him."

Two weeks later Angelique received her first message from Damian. One of the seamen from *Moonlight*

Dancer had made his way from Savannah to bring messages to some of the crew's families. The seaman assured her Captain Legare was well, but still she sat in the garden, afraid to open his letter. Slowly she broke the seal and read:

My beloved wife,

How I miss your lovely face, your warm, soft voice and the touch of your velvet skin next to mine. If I can't get into Charleston harbor before long, I'm going to have to take on the whole Union fleet to get to you. We've been close enough to see the lights of Charleston, but the blockading fleet is so tight we've had to pull back and head for Savannah. I can't begin to tell you how hard that has been, knowing you are so close, yet so far. I hope and pray on the next dark of the moon, the *Dancer* will be able to slip into Charleston and I will once again be able to hold you in my arms.

Our messenger is waiting to leave but I must give you some instructions to pass on to Adam. Tell him to give all our horses to the army, except for the Arabian stallion and mare, and whatever else he thinks we need. I understand the cavalry is desperate for new mounts. Maybe this will help.

Give my love to all, and stay safe.

Your loving husband

Angelique clasped the letter to her breasts, fear gripped her at the thought of Damian trying to run the blockade. Just this week a blockade runner had attempted to run the gauntlet with a hold full of gunpowder. The ship had been sighted inside the first cordon and blown into a million pieces. Damian would carry the same cargo.

Work on the defenses of the city continued day and night. Pilings were being driven in the shallower parts of the harbor, and the river channels were mined with torpedoes. The drop in blockade runners getting through was being felt by the residents of Charleston. Peanut oil was being used in place of whale oil for lamps, sugar syrup was being extracted from fruits since sugar was nonexistent. Women were spinning and weaving their own cloth, then dying them with bark, roots and berries. When the supply of blankets gave out for the soldiers, women fashioned comforters. When cloth gave out, carpets were stripped from the floor, cut into blanket size and made into blankets. Cooking pots, church bells, and anything else with lead in it was being melted down to make bullets. Church pews and kneelers were used for hospital beds. Everyone sacrificed and suffered great hardships, but it was for their fighting men.

Concentration of purpose and dedication to a cause elevates people. Men are better soldiers when their homeland is being invaded and the lives of their loved ones are at stake. The troops from Charleston were known to be outstanding on the battlefield, not only because they believed in the cause for which they fought, but because they had the unqualified backing of their women.

Angelique witnessed the hardships every day at the hospital. Morphine, quinine, and surgical instruments were desperately needed, but unless a blockade runner came in with these supplies, none was available.

It was best not to become too involved with the patients, but one young soldier had come to mean a great deal to Angelique. She thought it was because he reminded her of Beau. The young man had lost his right arm fighting on James Island, but his spirits seemed to stay high. He talked about his sweetheart, Laura, back in Mississippi. When the war had begun he hadn't been interested in getting too serious at the age of seventeen. But now at the old age of twenty, he knew he wanted to marry Laura and settle down with a family, and Angelique helped him write a letter telling her so.

"Do you see this, ma'am," he said holding up his left hand with a gold band on his little finger. "I bought this off a North Carolina lieutenant who needed a poker stake. Do you think Laura will like it?"

"I'm sure she will, Jeff. She will be very lucky to have a man like you."

His big brown eyes held Angelique's. "Even though I only have one arm?"

"Jeff, there are men here who have lost a lot more than an arm."

"Yeah, you're right, Mrs. Legare. I am lucky."

On Sunday Angelique didn't go to the hospital, and when she returned on Monday she learned that her friend, Jeff, had taken what was called a surgical fever. Angelique sat at his side keeping wet compresses on his head, but nothing seemed to bring the fever down.

Jeff opened his eyes and smiled at her. "I saw Laura last night," he whispered hoarsely. "She was dressed in white and beckoned me to come to her. She looked so happy and peaceful . . . I'm going to her now . . ."

"Shh, sleep now," Angelique encouraged, knowing he was delirious from the high fever.

"You're an angel," were his last words.

Angelique sat motionless for a long time. He couldn't be dead. Just the day before yesterday he had plans to be married. She didn't know how long she had been sitting there before Adam helped her to her feet.

"He's gone, Angelique."

She was struggling for self-control, biting her lip until she tasted blood.

"I'm sorry, Angelique. I know you and the boy had become friends."

"What happened, Adam! On Saturday he seemed fine."

"His arm had been amputated at a field hospital, probably with a dirty knife. Infection spread through his body quickly. There was nothing we could do to stop it."

"I want to write to his girl in Mississippi," Angelique said, determined to let Laura know Jeff's last thoughts.

"I think that would be nice. Also, a young soldier was brought in yesterday who knew Jeff. I think he's from the same town. He wanted to see Jeff, but the fever was too high for him to have visitors."

The boy Adam had spoken of had just heard the news of his friend's death and was taking it very badly. Tears rolled down his face as he stared at Angelique. "I just heard," he said bitterly. "I've been carrying this letter around with me for months, and now he's dead. All this killing . . . what's it going to get us . . . me and Jeff never had no slaves . . ."

Angelique fought back her own tears. "Where can I write to Laura?" she managed to get out.

Suddenly the boy began to laugh. "Laura? Laura's dead. That's what the letter is about. She died of the fever two months ago."

Turning, Angelique ran from the hospital. She began walking toward the house, tears blurring her vision. She thought she heard someone calling her name, but she kept walking, wanting to be far, far away.

"Angelique, Angelique, what is wrong?" Philip Delacort asked, grabbing her by the shoulders.

Angelique collapsed in his arms, sobbing against the rough material of his jacket.

"Come, let me help you into my carriage. I'll take you home and you can tell me what happened."

By the time they reached the house on Calhoun Street Angelique had calmed down and was able to tell Philip what had upset her.

"You shouldn't be in that horrible place. No lady should!"

If Philip had searched all day for the right words to make Angelique go back to the hospital, he couldn't have found any better. Angelique dried her eyes and with a new determination, she calmly poured them tea.

"What brings you into town, Philip?" she asked, handing him the delicate china cup.

"Supplies. I was hoping some blockade runner had gotten through."

"Two got through last month, but the clothing and medical supplies they carried were shipped to Virginia the very same day."

"Yes, and I heard both ships were captured as they left the harbor. Damned poor luck when we need them so badly."

"The talk now is that someone is sending signals to the Union ships when a blockader leaves the harbor."

"Why in the world would anyone in Charleston want to warn the Union? We're all dependent on the ships that slip in."

"Yes, but if someone is tipping off the Union, they probably don't have to worry about doing without things. The Union would supply them with everything they need."

Philip felt a sickening lurch in the pit of his stomach. He stood quickly, almost dropping the china cup. "I've an appointment I almost forgot about. I must be leaving."

Angelique studied his ashen face. "Is there something wrong, Philip?"

He laughed nervously. "Wrong? No, of course not. I just forgot my appointment, that's all."

"I want to thank you again for bringing me home. It helped to talk with a dear friend."

"I'm glad I was there. I just wish you wouldn't go back."

"I have to go back, Philip. I have to do my part for the South."

"But you're not a Southerner, Angelique. You don't have to do anything."

Angelique raised her chin defiantly. "My husband is a Southerner fighting for a cause he believes in. That makes my allegiance to the South just as strong."

"It's a shame not everyone feels the way you do," Philip said as he left.

Angelique watched him climb into his carriage. She went over their conversation, wondering what she had said to make him so nervous.

"Are you finished with tea, ma'am?" Bessie asked.

"Yes, thank you, Bessie. Philip didn't stay long enough for a second cup."

"Don't blame him none. Tea made from raspberry leaves just ain't the same."

"No, it wasn't that. He suddenly got very nervous when we were talking about someone letting the Union know when the blockaders were leaving the harbor."

"Dat's not unusual. Makes me skittish as a mouse caught between two cats to think someone in Charleston would do dat."

"Yes, I suppose you're right. This war has everyone on edge."

"Are you going back to de hospital?" Bessie asked.

The cup and saucer in Angelique's hand rattled. "Yes, I'm going back."

Philip secured his carriage and headed across the street to Kate Winston's house. For the first time he noticed the white clapboard structure was not in disrepair as were other houses on the street. Slowly he stared up at the fourth floor window with the captain's walk that gave a clear view of the harbor and beyond.

Nell, Kate's maid, greeted him warmly and led him into the sitting room. "Can I get you anything, sir?"

"Yes, Nell, I'd love a cup of coffee."

Philip stared out the window overlooking the sea. On this first floor level he could only see a few ships, but he knew you would be able to see for miles from the fourth floor level.

"You really should let me know when you're planning to pay a visit, Philip." It was nearly three in the afternoon, yet Kate was dressed in a gold satin dressing gown, her hair still in disarray.

"Why? Did I interrupt something, my love?" he asked sarcastically. "Were you whoring with one of your new Yankee friends?"

The look of annoyance on Kate's face changed to one of fear. "The usual, darling?" she asked as she moved to pour him a bourbon.

"No. Nell is fixing me a cup of coffee, and I would be willing to bet it's real coffee."

Kate's pallor increased. She poured herself a glass nearly full of brandy. "Where have you been keeping yourself, darling? I've missed you."

Two can play this game, Philip thought bitterly. "If I remember correctly, you didn't ever want to see me again, unless I got rid of Mrs. Damian Legare."

315

"Oh, darling, I was just angry when I said that. You should know me well enough to realize that."

"I know you well enough, Kate. That's why I'm here."

Kate's eyes fled from his knowing look. "Here's Nell with your coffee. Nell, you take care of the upstairs, and I'll pour Philip's coffee. You will stay for the evening, won't you, darling?"

Philip met her aggravated look with a calm and deliberate stare. Why not, he thought. It had been a long time since he had had a woman. Perhaps things would work out for him after all. All he had to do was convince Kate to stop spying for the Union and he would keep her secret. "Is Nell getting rid of the man upstairs?" he asked bluntly.

Kate laughed nervously. "Oh, Philip, I have no secrets from you."

"That's right, Kate, and you would do well to remember that."

Chapter Twenty-four

The days and nights ran into each other as Angelique threw herself into her work at the hospital. There were more and more casualties as the Union forces made advances on Charleston. Adam would often not go home for days at a time. Angelique and Lacey were grateful Bessie had insisted on accompanying them with her family. There were many nights they would drag into the house too exhausted to do more than fall in bed, but Bessie and Tally would be there with a bath and a hot meal.

It was on one of these nights that Angelique woke as Shadow, lying beside her on the bed, growled.

"Bessie?"

Angelique felt the fur bristle on Shadow's back as something moved toward them.

"No, love, it's your husband. Calm that beast down before he goes for my throat."

"Damian," Angelique cried leaping from the bed

317

into his arms. "Oh, my love, are you all right? Did you run the blockade? No, you couldn't have, there is a moon tonight. How did you know we were here?"

"Easy, my love. Let me light the lamp and look at you. Then I'll answer all your questions."

In the golden glow of the lamp Damian savored the beauty of his wife. "You are here waiting for me . . . you're not a dream. There were times I told myself I had imagined you loved me."

"It was not a dream, my husband, although I admit, after five months I was also beginning to think it was a dream."

"You are so beautiful," he said lifting her hair from her shoulders and placing a kiss on her neck.

Shadow, tired of being ignored, was suddenly all over Damian. Angelique laughed as he was knocked off the bed by the dog's exuberance. "My God, what happened to the puppy I left here? This monster must weigh a hundred pounds," Damian managed to say as Shadow licked him all over the face.

"Come, Shadow," Angelique commanded. "Lie." The dog instantly obeyed her command.

"Burke is drawing me a bath. Will you come sit with me while I scrub this salt grime off?"

While Damian scrubbed, Angelique sat on a stool and shot questions at him. "But how did you get through tonight? There is almost a full moon."

"We didn't wait until dark. We came in at dusk."

"At dusk?" Angelique asked, "but how?"

"I lost count of how many times we tried to run in at night, and each time found them waiting for us.

Last night we took a hit and lost a boiler so we decided to make a run for it. We slipped in between dusk and moonlight when they weren't expecting us."

"Oh, Damian, if I had known you were taking such a chance . . . The papers are always carrying stories about the Union's plans to capture you."

"Don't think about it. I'm here safe and sound now. Your brother gave me a letter for you and sends his love. He hopes to make a run in the next month."

"Where did you see him?"

"He arrived in Bermuda as we were preparing to sail. He had been back to Crozon to take care of some legal matters. By the way, he also sent a letter to Patrice Delacort. Have you been playing cupid while I've been gone?"

"No," Angelique laughed, "I've been far too busy to even think of it, but I'm glad Beau wrote to her. Perhaps Sunday we can drive out to Bellemeade and give it to her."

"I think we might be able to manage that. I'd like to spend a few days at Enchanteur while I'm here. Now come and scrub my back. You're driving me crazy sitting there so innocently in your nightgown. If I weren't so dirty . . ."

"My thoughts are far from innocent," she grinned, taking the cloth from his hand. "Now tell me, how did you find us here on Calhoun Street?"

"When I stopped at Trenholm's to arrange for the ship to be unloaded and repaired he told me you were renting the Gregory house. At first I was delighted to find you so near, but now I'm furious to know you're in the city with the Yankees so near. I intend to take you to task about it—but not tonight."

"Duck," Angelique ordered, pushing him under the water after she had shampooed his curly hair.

Damian came up sputtering. "Are you trying to drown me, lady?" he laughed. "I would have thought you'd be glad to see your long, lost husband."

"Oh, Damian, you have no idea how much I've missed you," Angelique admitted, tears glistening in her violet eyes. "I was planning to go to sea to find you if you didn't show up soon."

Damian stepped from the brass tub and wrapped a towel around his bronze torso. "Would you have done that?"

"You know I would have. I've waited long enough to call you my own, Damian Legare, and I'm not about to give you up for any war—or any woman."

Damian wrapped her in his arms and led her back toward their room. "It will never be another woman, Angelique. You needn't ever fear that. I am a one-woman man."

Angelique had to laugh. "After having affairs with practically every woman on this green earth, you can stand there and tell me you're a one-woman man?"

Damian grinned sheepishly. "I was looking for the perfect one, love, and now that I've found you I need no other."

"The perfect woman . . . uhh," Angelique murmured, undoing the towel from Damian's waist. "That sounds like a very hard title to live up to."

Damian slipped her gown over her head, then pulled her hard against him, wrapping his powerful arms around her back. "Just follow my instructions to the letter, my little one, and you will always be the perfect wife."

"And what might those instructions be, my husband?"

"To love and cherish me until my dying day," Damian whispered before seeking her mouth.

His touch sent her blood dashing through her veins like wildfire, as his kiss deepened, tasting, exploring. "Oh, Angel, how I've missed you," he whispered against her temple. "At night I would lie in my bunk and remember how your body molded itself to mine." He growled, low in his throat, his long denied hunger for her body surged through him like a raging river. "I want to hold you just like this for the rest of my life."

Angelique ran her hands over his back and down to clasp his buttocks. "The prim and proper matrons of Charleston might not approve, but as I've said before, I've never cared what people thought."

"Shameless wanton," Damian murmured with a deep throated chuckle.

Angelique moaned impatiently, her response heightened by their long separation. She could feel his readiness, straining and throbbing against her stomach.

Damian took her mouth in a possessive kiss as he lifted her off the floor. Gently laying her on the bed he dropped beside her, partially covering her body with his own.

"I hope you aren't tired."

"Not any longer."

"I'm going to make love to you until the sun rises, and then . . ."

"And then what?" she asked, her eyes smoldering purple with passion.

"And then I'm going to keep you here until the sun sets."

"What will you do for food?" she asked provocatively.

"Who needs food when I have the nectar of the gods." His mouth and tongue moved slowly over her body, touching every sensitive part of her until she begged with wild abandon, whispering his name over and over until he entered her.

The night was an unforgettable sensuous experience as they loved and taught each other, arousing desires so powerfully awesome they defied description. On that warm spring night they existed only for each other. The horrors of war and death were another time—another world.

They were thrown back into the real world all too soon the next morning. Angelique left bright and early for the hospital while Damian headed for the dock to see about his damaged ship. A heavy shot had entered the starboard side, passed through the condenser and exploded against the port side, blowing a five foot hole in the hull. By some miracle it hadn't exploded the cargo of gunpowder. Damian hadn't told Angelique that they had no choice in running the blockade in daylight. It was either that or sink within sight of Charleston. Several of the seamen had been scalded when the condenser had been hit and they had needed immediate attention. Lady Luck had deserted them for the past month, Damian thought, but she must have returned when they made their run in. That, or the Union was preoccupied with bigger things.

Dinner that night was a joyous homecoming celebration. Foods that had been missing from their diet for months now appeared on the table, thanks to Damian. Even when his cargo consisted of ammunition and gun powder, he managed a few items for Bessie's kitchen.

"Tea. Real tea with real sugar," Angelique exclaimed, savoring her second cup. "Do you know we've been making tea from dried raspberry leaves?"

"Angelique misses the tea," Lacey said, "but I have missed coffee. I had a cup made from peanuts and it was terrible. Bessie makes coffee from ground okra seeds and it really isn't too bad."

"Well, there will be a real cup of coffee for you in the morning," Damian announced, "and some French brandy to top our dinner off now, compliments of Beau Charbonne."

Damian and Adam left the women so they could discuss the war in private. Adam explained the problems at the hospital. "Drugs and most medicines are absolutely unobtainable except from the few ships that make it through. We need morphine, quinine, surgical instruments, anything and everything. Angelique has shown some of the women how to obtain substitutes from flowers and wood plants. That has been a godsend. She told me she learned about herbal medicines from a gypsy who used to live on their property in the summer."

"I remember her. Beau and I thought she was crazy. Who would ever have thought Angelique would put her knowledge to good use."

"Angelique is an incredible woman. I am so grateful to her for helping Lacey get back into medicine, but more than that, for what she has done to help the soldiers. They all call her their angel of mercy."

"I never meant for her to get involved in this damned war. If I had known how bad things were here I would have left her in Bermuda—I would have left you *all* in Bermuda."

Adam placed his arm around Damian's shoulder, knowing the weight of responsibility his brother felt. "We are all adults, Damian. We are doing what we have to do. The hospital is filled with men who not only need medical help, but need a tender touch or a kind word to keep them sane. Lacey and I can provide the medical help, but Angelique provides that tenderness they all need."

Damian didn't want to think of Angelique being submitted to the horrors of a war-time hospital. The next day after leaving the docks, he decided to go by the hospital and see it for himself.

Several Army ambulances were lined up outside the doors of the hospital. Damian questioned one of the drivers and found the Yankees had waged a battle for Morris Island. The Confederates had held them back, but not without tremendous casualties.

Stretchers lined the hallway while Adam and another doctor examined each patient, determining who could wait a few hours and who needed immediate attention. Damian caught a glimpse of Angelique, her beige dress and white apron already stained crimson with blood as she knelt beside a wounded soldier.

The moans and cries of agony tore at Damian. He could see now why Adam said they were all needed. He, himself had seriously considered staying in Charleston and giving up blockade running, but after seeing this scene he realized he couldn't quit. As long as this war continued he would make every effort to bring in supplies.

That evening Damian asked Bessie if she would just fix Angelique a light meal to have in their room. "I can see to her needs tonight. Adam and Lacey are going to be exhausted and will need your help."

"Nuther bad day?" Bessie asked.

"Yes, a very bad one," Damian answered. "Have there been many, Bessie?"

"Too many. I feared for de health of de ladies many times. They doan want to eat when they come home all tired and sick at heart, but I always makes dem something. I jus wish it would end and we could get back to normal."

"Normal? I'm not sure I remember what normal is. It sure as hell isn't the way the South is living now," Damian said angrily.

Angelique and Lacey arrived home just before dark without Adam. He was still performing surgery, but had insisted they wouldn't be any good to anyone if they didn't get some rest. Bessie led Lacey to the kitchen for a cup of real coffee while Damian led Angelique to their room where Tally was just finishing filling the brass tub with steaming water.

"Wait just a minute and I'll give you these clothes," Damian said stripping the stained garments from Angelique. Any other time she would have objected to being treated like she was helpless, but she was too tired to protest. Shadow sat beside the bed with his chin resting on the mattress. He whimpered as Damian removed Angelique's shoes and stockings. "It's all right, boy, she'll be fine as soon as she rests," Damian said giving the big dog a reassuring pat.

"I should be hung for bringing you to Charleston," he swore as he lowered Angelique into the steaming water. "I should have known you wouldn't stay where you'd be safe and away from the atrocities of this war."

"Would you really want a wife who would stay

hidden safely away while people needed help?"

"No, I suppose not," he answered as he gently wiped her face. "Just lie your head back on the edge of the tub and let me take care of you." After Angelique was washed and shampooed to Damian's satisfaction, he lifted her from the tub and rubbed her briskly with a towel. "Now lie face down on the bed and let me massage some of those aches away."

"I'm sorry, Damian," Angelique said as Damian massaged her shoulders.

"Sorry for what, love?"

"This is only your third night here and we should be making love instead of you having to take care of me."

Damian smacked her playfully on the derriere. "I'm learning that loving someone doesn't just mean making love to them."

Angelique moaned in agreement as Damian kneaded her lower back. "What about Lacey?"

"I don't think Adam would like me doing this to Lacey."

"I don't mean that, you fool," Angelique laughed. "I mean is she having to eat by herself?"

"By now Bessie has seen that she has had a hot bath and is tucked in bed where she will be served a hot meal."

"Did you arrange all this?"

"Of course, I have to take care of my women."

"Careful, Damian Legare, or I'll somehow find the strength to box your ears."

"Correction. I have to take care of my family. I'll

also see that Adam is taken care of when he comes home."

Angelique rolled over and faced Damian. "I doubt if we'll see him for a few days. He is a very dedicated doctor, Damian. It breaks his heart to lose a patient. The other doctors at the hospital have great respect for him."

"I thought he'd be a good doctor. I guess we could say Colette did something good by taking Adam with her."

"Now, Damian, remember, you promised not to be so bitter. If we have children you don't want them to hate their only living grandparent."

"You're incredible," he said kissing her nose before he covered her.

"No, you're the one who is incredible. I feel better already. Perhaps we could . . ."

"No, my little one, tonight you're going to rest. If you'd like I'll read some poetry to you while you eat."

"My word, will wonders never cease! Not only can he read, but he can read poetry."

"Don't push your luck, you little minx. I'm liable to make you pay for those insults."

A knock at the door interrupted their banter. Bessie entered with two bowls of clam chowder and a loaf of warm bread. "I thought you could both use some nourishment. Dis will get you started. I'll bring you some of dat beef from last night with some rice, but I'll keep it hot till you're ready."

Angelique ate the soup and bread with a hearty appetite, but before Bessie returned with the rest of the meal, she was sound asleep. Damian lowered the lamp but remained sitting on the side of the bed thinking about his life. This beautiful woman had changed him from a bitter, tormented man to a contented one. At one time he had thought only fools fell in love, but he had been wrong. This woman made his life worthwhile. She gave him a reason to want to live. Some day, God willing, this war would be over and they would be able to start a family and lead a normal life—some day.

Chapter Twenty-five

The oppressive heat seemed to permeate everything from the cobblestone street to the walled gardens. The leaves on the trees drooped and the flowers wilted on their stems. Shutters on the houses were closed to keep out the sun, and the piazzas behind the walls were deserted. Before the war you wouldn't have found people in the city in July and August, but now they stayed, determined to protect their homes any way they could.

Angelique, Lacey and Damian walked slowly down Meeting Street toward Mrs. Roberts' house.

Angelique touched her handkerchief to her damp neck. "I think I am wet clear through," she sighed. "How much longer will this terrible heat last?"

"Probably until the end of August," Damian answered.

"Another month?" Angelique exclaimed.

"You wouldn't feel it nearly as badly if you'd

return to Enchanteur as I asked."

"I wouldn't be of help to anyone there," she snapped.

Damian left them in front of Mrs. Roberts' house while he went to the hotel for news from Virginia. He arranged to meet them in thirty minutes.

Mrs. Roberts was a widow from one of the founding families of Charleston. She was eighty-seven years old and not in very good health, but she would not leave her house with its family antiques and treasures.

"No Yankee is going to chase me out of my home," she declared to the two women. "My ancestors fought the British to protect this house. Afterward they patched the holes and started life over. That's what we'll do again, as soon as we send those Yankees home."

Angelique poured tea for Mrs. Roberts while Lacey checked the pantry to be sure there was enough food. Only one servant remained, and Lacey was afraid she wasn't feeding Mrs. Roberts properly.

"A Northern paper says the people in Charleston deserve to be exterminated, but even if we are, this city will never die," Mrs. Roberts exclaimed.

"I think you're right," Angelique agreed. "I've never seen people with such determination."

It wasn't long before Mrs. Roberts was dozing in her rocking chair, tired out from having company. After leaving instructions with her servant, Angelique and Lacey returned to the steaming street.

"Let's see if we can find Damian and get him to

buy us a lemon drink," Angelique suggested as they headed toward the Charleston Hotel. As they rounded the corner they saw Damian leaning against a store post talking to Kate.

"She's cornered him again," Lacey said disgustedly. "Will that woman never give up?"

"Damian doesn't look like he's trying to get away," Angelique answered angrily when she saw her husband smile at Kate. Both women stopped dead in their tracks as Damian offered Kate his arm and walked across the street.

"That bastard!" Angelique hissed.

"Now, Angelique, there has to be an explanation. Damian wouldn't do anything to hurt you."

"It's called animal lust," Angelique spat. "I'm going home. Are you coming?"

"Why don't we wait to see if Damian is coming right back. He'll wonder what happened to us if we're not here."

"You're going to have a long wait," Angelique said turning on her heels.

Angelique hadn't been at the house more than twenty minutes before Lacey and Damian arrived, but her tension and anger had already built itself to a fevered pitch.

Damian strode into the room, a concerned look on his face. "Honey, are you all right? Lacey said you weren't feeling well."

"Lacey lied to you. I feel just fine."

"Then why didn't you wait for me?"

"It looked to me like you were going to be busy for

the afternoon."

"Angelique, what are you talking about?"

"I'm talking about you and Kate! I saw you sashaying down the street with her. I thought I could trust you. You said you loved me." By now the tears were beginning to flow.

"Angelique, Kate was being harassed by some soldiers in town. She asked me if I would escort her past them. That's all there was to it. I'm sorry if what you saw upset you." Damian moved to take her in his arms.

"Stay away from me!" she screamed. "I won't have you touching me after you've been fondling her."

"My God, woman, you are beyond words. I told you what happened. Kate has been a friend for a long time and I couldn't very well refuse her request to walk her across a street. You should certainly have a little trust in me."

"Trust? How can I trust you when you've had women in every port? Even your own sister-in-law is one of your ex-lovers."

"That's enough, Angelique," Damian ordered between gritted teeth.

"No. It's not enough. Every place I go I hear about you and Kate, or you and some other woman. I'm sick of it," Angelique screamed, near hysteria.

Damian forced himself to remain calm. "I realize the heat is getting to you, but if you'll stop and think about what you're accusing, you'll realize how stupid your accusation is."

"Oh, so now I'm stupid?"

"This argument has become absurd," Damian said heading for the door. "I'll be at my ship if you decide to come to your senses."

"Oh, I've already done that," Angelique said sarcastically.

Damian stared at her for a long moment. "This just confirms my belief that you should be away from here, Angelique. The pressures are getting to you."

"I just bet you'd love to have me away from here. Then you could carry on with Kate whenever you wanted."

"Jesus, woman," Damian hissed. In two steps he crossed the room and grabbed her by the shoulders. "I love you! Only you! Why can't I make you believe that?"

"Stay away from that whore and maybe I'll believe you."

Damian dropped his hands. "Don't tell me who I can and can't see, Angelique. Kate and I have been friends for a long time—and friends is all it is now. I'm going to my ship now. Send for me when you calm down."

Angelique collapsed on the bed in a fit of tears. Damian was right, she was being irrational. His story was plausible. There hadn't been time for him to do anything. What was the matter with her? Lately everything upset her . . . she was always on edge, always on the verge of tears. It had to be because she knew Damian would be leaving her to run the blockade again.

334

Damian headed for his ship, unaware Kate's servant watched him leave the house. By the time he reached the docks his anger had already dissolved. Angelique had been pushing herself too hard lately and was probably tired. The heat didn't help things either, he told himself. He just wished he could get her away from the city.

Lacey was concerned when she heard Damian leave, slamming doors behind him. "Are you all right?" she asked.

"Oh, Lacey, I made such a fool of myself. I don't know what is wrong with me. The hateful words just tumbled out. Lately I've been so tired and irritable, and Damian has been so patient with me. Even today he didn't get angry. He just let me go on ranting and raving."

Lacey sat on the side of the bed. "When was the last time you had your monthly cycle?"

"I don't know. Things have been so hectic I haven't even thought about it. But it couldn't have been very long ago. Let's see, it was when . . . Oh, God, I can only remember one time since we've been working at the hospital. That could mean I'm pregnant."

"Yes," Lacey beamed. "Isn't that wonderful?"

Angelique was silent for a moment. "I'm going to have Damian's child," she smiled. "That could account for the nausea and tears . . . Oh, Lacey, Damian and I are going to have a child," she squealed, grabbing Lacey's hands. "I've got to find Damian and tell him."

"Are you sure you don't want to wait until he comes back? It is still very hot out there."

"No, I owe him an apology. After the way I acted he may not come back before he sails tonight, and I wouldn't blame him. I'm going to freshen up and change into one of my prettiest dresses."

"Do you want me to go with you?"

"Thank you, Lacey, but I'll be fine."

Lacey hugged Angelique again. "I envy you, Angelique. I had hoped Adam and I would start our family right away, but Adam wants to wait until after the war."

An expression of fear came over Angelique's face. "Suppose Damian doesn't want a child now? Oh, Lacey, what will I do if he doesn't want this baby?"

"Damian had as much to do with the child as you, sweet. Believe me, he'll be happy."

"Yes, I think you're right," Angelique smiled. "I think he'll be very happy."

It was all Angelique could do to keep from running to the ship. As she rounded the corner she saw it. She went over in her mind how she would tell him, all the while a smile covering her face. She stopped when she saw a flash of color on board the gray ship. She clenched her fist to her side as she saw Kate Winston at the gangplank. Her first reaction was to flee the scene, but instead she walked forward, reaching the precarious gangplank the same time Kate began to disembark. She would kill them both, she swore to herself.

"Oh, my dear, I'm sorry you had to find me here," Kate said as she moved cautiously forward, "but it was bound to happen sooner or later. You may have Damian's name, my dear, but I am the one he comes to for . . ."

Before Kate had a chance to finish Angelique gave her a shove. Kate screamed as she toppled backward into the muddy water. The pink silk dress with white lace overlay billowed on top of the water.

"Oops," Angelique said. "Woman overboard." Angelique paid little attention to the cursing woman as she made her way past the men who were laughing at Kate. She heard Damian before she saw him.

"Why did you do that?"

Angelique turned on him, too angry to notice he had grease up to his elbows. "I came here to apologize, but I should have known better. Your whore told me all I needed to know."

"I didn't even know she was aboard," Damian said, "and how many times have I told you never to pay any attention to what Kate says."

"That's very convenient, isn't it Damian. I've always believed that before, but I'm learning. When you return to Charleston I won't be here," she said storming off the ship.

"Damn! What a hellion." Damian said watching his wife practically run up the hill. What was he going to do with her? They couldn't continue this constant battling. And what in the hell did Kate think she was doing? Women! Bah!

If Damian had had any idea how dangerous Kate Winston really was, he wouldn't have made light of the situation. Angelique had been a rival to her before this incident, but now she was her mortal enemy.

Damian sailed that night, hoping his absence would give Angelique a chance to sort out her feelings. He was afraid their relationship was going to be damaged if they continued arguing. When he returned to Charleston he would make it a point to avoid Kate Winston at all cost.

Angelique was spending another sleepless night wishing she hadn't let Damian leave the way he had. She was going to end up losing him if she didn't stop acting so foolish. She turned over and stared at the wall. Is acting like a fool what pregnancy does to you? Adam had assured her it wasn't just the pregnancy, but a combination of her tiredness and the pressures. She guessed he was right. She was usually tired to the bone, and knew she was going to have to start taking better care of herself. "Oh, Damian, why did I say those terrible things? It all seemed so clear at the time, but now that I've had time to think about it I know she was lying to me again. Please come home to me. I swear I'll never mistrust you again."

Damian's run to Bermuda was uneventful until they were a few miles off the island. A waiting Union ship gave chase, but *Moonlight Dancer* scooted into the harbor safely. The usual procedure was to stay in port for several days so the crew could have a rest, but this trip Damian requested his crew to be back on board the next day, and no one protested.

He had been angry and hurt when he left Charleston, but now all he could think about was Angelique. He shouldn't have left without straightening things out. It wasn't any wonder she was short-tempered. She had been under a lot of pressure the past year. He cursed himself for having taken her to Charleston. He should have left her safely on the island, but his selfishness to have her with him blinded his good sense. When he got back to Charleston he would make her see she was the only woman for him.

Damian smiled to himself. "Damn little vixen. Who would ever have thought some woman would have me talking to myself."

On August 21, 1863 Union General Gillmore sent a communication to Confederate General Beauregard demanding the immediate evacuation of Morris Island and Fort Sumter. In the demand Gillmore said if they refused compliance with this demand, or should he receive no reply within four hours after it was delivered into the hands of the subordinate at Fort Wagner, he would open fire on the city of Charleston from batteries already established within easy and effective range of the heart of the city.

General Gillmore must have known when he sent the demand that it would be almost impossible to receive a reply within the stipulated four hours. This involved sending the note from Fort Wagner to Cummings Point, finding a boat to take it across the harbor, getting it to General Beauregard's headquarters—with the possibility he might not be there—and then reversing the entire route.

It so happened that General Beauregard was away inspecting fortifications when the demand arrived. Before he returned, General Gillmore opened fire on the city with his 200-pounder Parrott rifle gun.

The citizens of Charleston were unaware what was going on and life moved on as usual. Angelique and Lacey moved slowly down Church Street returning from their day at the hospital. It was much too hot to hurry, even though it looked like rain was coming.

"I would give anything for an ear of buttered corn," Angelique said out of the blue.

Lacey laughed. "I've always heard pregnant women crave strange things. Do you know corn is selling for two-hundred and twenty-five dollars a bushel. Isn't that the most incredible thing you've ever heard?"

"I think I miss a good cup of coffee most. I hope Damian is able to bring some back with him."

"I just hope he comes back. I wouldn't blame him if he didn't."

"Now you know he will be back. He loves you, sweet. When he returns the first thing you have to do is tell him about the baby. It would be a terrible shock to him if he arrived here one day and you were out to here," Lacey held her arms out wide.

Angelique laughed until she was holding her sides. "Oh, Lacey, let's sit for just a minute," Angelique suggested, pulling her friend along toward the empty park bench in the shade of an oak tree.

A tearing, crashing sound suddenly filled the air. "Yankees," someone screamed, sending the people on the street scattering. Angelique stood glued to the spot. A cannonball had plowed a furrow in the street where they had been walking. If she hadn't wanted to rest . . .

The sound of a cannon firing in the distance brought her back to the present. She grabbed Lacey's hand and yanked. "Come on, we've got to get out of here!" No sooner had she said the words then another cannonball hit the oak tree, splintering it all over the street. By now the bells of St. Michael's were ringing, sounding the alarm, and Angelique and Lacey had to dodge the people who swarmed out in the street. They left a wake of panic behind, neither saying anything until they reached the house. Angelique leaned her forehead on the marble column, her breathing coming in painful gasps. Tally besieged them with questions as the sound of cannon fire still filled the air.

"The Yankees are shelling the city," Angelique managed to get out. "We were right there . . . cannonballs were dropping out of the sky."

"Do we need to leave here?" Tally asked, her eyes wide with fright.

"I don't know, but I think we'd better wait until Adam gets here. It seemed like they were only shell-

341

ing around St. Michaels."

"Come inside," Bessie urged, "we doan want no Yankees to see you."

Angelique and Lacey were still answering questions when Damian came running into the house, his face white with fear for the safety of his wife. Angelique ran into his arms and held to him for dear life.

"Are you all right?" Angelique just shook her head.

"We're all right, Damian," Lacey said, "but we were right there. The cannonball fell where we had been standing. If Angelique hadn't decided she wanted to sit for a moment . . ." Lacey shuddered.

"Christ, I knew it was too dangerous for you all to be here. We could see the smoke and fire when we were still out at sea. I don't mind telling you, it scared the hell out of me."

"I'm so glad you're home safe," Angelique said, still clinging to him, "but how did you get here in the daylight?"

"The bombing of the city had the full attention of the blockading fleet, so we were able to slip into the harbor nearly unnoticed."

"Nearly unnoticed?" Angelique asked, catching his choice of words.

Damian grinned sheepishly. "One of the Union ships got a shot off and hit us broadside. *Moonlight Dancer* has a nasty hole in her side."

"Oh, Damian, you could have all been killed."

"I was so worried about you I would have run the blockade even if the Yankees hadn't been preoccupied."

"Listen," Lacey said, "it has stopped."

Alone in their room, Damian clung to Angelique. "I'm sorry, love. I never should have left here without straightening things out. I've been going out of my mind thinking about that day."

"It was my fault, Damian. I thought about it afterward, and you weren't exactly in any shape to have been in bed with that woman." She giggled. "You had grease up to your elbows."

"I told you at the time, I didn't even know she was aboard."

"You'll have to forgive me. Pregnant women sometime do strange things."

"You're going to have to learn to control that . . . pregnant women? What did you say, Angel?"

"I'm going to have your baby, Damian."

"Damn!" Damian shouted, twirling Angelique around. Suddenly he stopped, placing her gently on her feet. "Are you all right? I didn't hurt you, did I?"

Angelique laughed. "You really are happy?"

"Of course I'm happy. My beautiful wife is going to have my child," he said in wonderment. "I'll be the best damned father there has ever been."

"I never doubted that for a minute," Angelique said, kissing him.

Adam came home later that evening with the news that a few people had been injured by flying debris, but miraculously no one had been killed. The biggest danger had been the fires. Everyone now knew of Gillmore's demand, and of the letter General Beauregard sent back stating that "Among nations not barbarous the usage of war prescribes that when a city is about to be attacked, timely notice shall be given by the attacking commander, in order that noncombatants may have an opportunity for withdrawing beyond its limits . . . It would appear that despairing of reducing these works, you now resort to the novel measure of turning your guns against the old men, the women and children, and the hospitals of a sleeping city, an act of inexcusable barbarity . . ."

Gillmore granted a twenty-four respite. Many people who had means left the city, but a great many stayed, moving uptown out of the range of the shells.

"Well, we're going to have a celebration," Damian announced.

"A celebration?" Adam asked. "This seems like a hell of a time to have a celebration."

"If you had found out you were going to be a father, wouldn't you want to celebrate?"

"Oh, that."

Damian's face darkened. "Oh, that. What the hell is that supposed to mean?"

Adam laughed. "I'm sorry, Damian. We've known abut the baby for several weeks. I forgot that you didn't know."

"Damn it! It's a fine thing when the father is the last to know."

Angelique stared at her husband. Only minutes before he had been the happiest she had ever seen him, and now the arguing was going to start all over.

"But, I have no one to blame but myself. So I still say we're going to have a celebration."

The celebration had been a warm family affair, with many toasts to the loving couple. Damian beamed with pride as they talked about the coming event. Then the conversation turned to the safety of the women.

Damian was adamant about the women returning to Enchanteur, but neither one of them would agree.

"You are the most stubborn, irritating woman I have ever met," Damian said angrily. "You're carrying my child and still you won't protect yourself."

"I could be at Enchanteur by myself and encounter Union troops bent on plundering and looting. No, I won't leave here. This is where I'm needed."

"What am I going to do with her," Damian asked his brother.

"Don't ask me," Adam laughed. "I haven't been any more successful getting Lacey to return to Enchanteur."

That evening they made slow, sweet love into the early hours of the morning. Angelique fell asleep knowing that no other woman had ever been the recipient of Damian's devotion as she was.

Stories of Damian's run into Charleston, and exaggerated tales of the damage he sustained, reached

Beau as soon as he arrived in Bermuda. Everyone was talking about Charleston's hardships and how the Union were adding ships daily to the blockade, making it almost impossible to enter the harbor, and how the city was being bombarded day and night.

Beau had brought medical supplies and clothing to Bermuda with the intention of leaving his cargo for one of the blockade runners to carry on to one of the Confederate ports, while he stocked up with cotton for his return to Europe. But now all that was changed. He was determined to go on to Charleston so he could find out for himself what was happening with Angelique and Damian.

After a twenty-four hour respite, the 200-pounder Parrott gun, nicknamed *Swamp Angel* by the soldiers who fired it, again began lobbing shells into the city relentlessly, day and night. At first the people of Charleston had been frightened, but now the shelling only caused scorn and indignation. The Union now used shells of Greek fire, which in theory were to make Charleston a raging inferno, but fortunately, most of the shells were defective. When the Union gunners saw flames from their handiwork, they would increase their rate of fire so the firefighters couldn't put the flames out, but in spite of this, the firemen worked uninterruptedly, keeping the fires under control.

Damian stood on the deck of his ship surveying the work. The repairs on *Moonlight Dancer* were finally finished and she would be stocked with cotton and ready to sail by the next dark of the moon. But Damian was torn between his restless mood to get back into action, and his need to keep Angelique safe. Turning an unlit cheroot in his hand he stared out toward sea. The wind was rising and a heavy bank of clouds was rolling in. He moved to the rail to peer into the grayness. If the ship was ready this would be a perfect evening to run the blockade. Hopefully there were one or two ships out there waiting for an opportunity like this.

He needed a distraction from his forced idleness. Maybe tonight he'd go with his crew to O'Brien's and have a few drinks. He sure as hell didn't feel like going home and arguing with Angelique about her leaving the city again. Lacey was Adam's problem, but he was considering kidnapping his own wife and taking her to the island. Damn her for the spirited, stubborn woman she was. Then he smiled. And what a woman she was. If their children were anything like Angelique he was going to have his hands full.

O'Brien's was a hangout for the hardy, adventurous breed who ran the blockade. It was where the rumors were gathered and passed, and where each blockader told his tale of high adventure. Damian used to frequent the place often, but lately he had been occupied with his beautiful wife. He ordered a drink and joined in the conversation. Everyone was talking about the shelling of the city and the danger to the people. This wasn't what he wanted to hear.

He wanted to get his mind off the danger Angelique was in, not be reminded of it.

"Has anyone heard anything about Tom Taylor?" Damian asked. Someone replied that he had a swift new ship he was trying out. In another few minutes everyone was telling tales about the English blockade runner. Damian sat back and enjoyed his drink as he listened.

"Blockade runner just slipped in," a seaman stuck his head in the door and announced. "It looks just like your *Moonlight Dancer*, Cap'n."

"Beau!" Damian knocked his chair over backward as he leapt to his feet. "Pack your bags, my sweet Angel, you're going home."

Chapter Twenty-six

Beau's ship had barely lowered the gangplank before Damian was aboard. "I have never been so glad to see anyone," he said embracing his brother-in-law.

"What's wrong? Is Angelique already driving you crazy?"

"No, no, nothing like that, but her stubbornness is driving me to distraction. I have got to get her away from Charleston. The city is being shelled day and night."

"Yes, I had heard, but surely she isn't affected by that at Enchanteur."

"Damn it, that's the problem. She isn't at Enchanteur. When I was on my last run she and Lacey moved into the city with Adam so they could all work at the hospital, but now that she is expecting our child I want her away from here."

"A child?" Beau asked, his face lighting up.

CASEY STUART

"Angelique is pregnant?"

"Yes, I'm sorry, Beau, I should have told you that first. I tell you, Beau, this whole thing has me going crazy. I can't think straight."

Beau laughed uproariously. "I never saw you like this."

"This is serious, Beau. This damned place is a powder keg waiting to go up. Most of the houses on the lower part of town have already been destroyed by the fire bombs the Yankees drop into town daily."

"I'm sorry, Damian. I see your point, but why didn't you just take her to Bermuda?"

"I couldn't chance having her aboard *Moonlight Dancer*. The prize on my head makes me too tempting a target. Besides, she is so involved in her hospital work she probably wouldn't have gone anyway. We've got to come up with something that will make her leave."

Beau paced for a moment. "Angelique is not stupid. It's going to have to be . . . I think I have it. We could tell her there are legal matters that have to be taken care of by both of us or we'll lose the chateau."

"Do you think she'll believe that?"

"Who knows, but it's the best I can come up with."

"I wish there were some way to involve Lacey and Adam in the plan and get them away from here too."

"It's really as bad as I've heard," Beau sighed.

"Yes, and it's going to get much worse," Damian warned. "When can you sail?"

"For God's sake, Damian, I just got here. You haven't even given me a chance to get off my ship."

"I'm sorry, Beau. I'm just anxious to have Angelique safe."

Angelique believed Beau's story and reluctantly agreed to make the return trip with him. Damian had suggested Lacey accompany her, hoping to get both women away from the city, but Lacey declined, wanting to stay with Adam.

"Perhaps Patrice Delacort would like to make the trip with me," Angelique suggested.

Beau and Damian looked at each other, wondering how they were going to work around this hitch in their plan, since they didn't plan to return to Charleston until the war was over.

"I'll talk to Philip," Damian said when he and Beau were alone. "I have a feeling he might be happy to have his sister away from here."

"I'd be glad to see her away from here," Beau said.

Damian stared at his friend. "Are you serious about the girl?"

"I didn't say that, but she is such a sweet innocent. I'd hate to see anything happen to her. Besides, in normal times she would have had the opportunity to see Europe. This way she'll have that chance."

"Did you send the explanation to your solicitor so he'd know to have papers drawn up to look convincing?"

"Yes, it went on the *Banshee* last night. Tom Taylor promised to deliver them personally."

"I hope she never finds out what I've done," Damian admitted.

"What we've done, *mon ami*, but it is for her own good. Knowing Angelique, she would continue to work at the hospital until she was ready to give birth."

In the flurry of activity of getting ready, Damian hadn't had time to think about Angelique leaving until the night before he was to sail. Now a web of fear wove itself around him and he voiced his feelings to Beau.

"I won't be carrying any cargo," Beau assured him. "I'm going to fly the flag of France and if we should be stopped I'll claim *Mouette* is a passenger vessel."

"They will never believe that sleek ship is not a blockade runner."

"Damian, you're going to have to decide if you want Angelique to stay here where the Yankees are getting closer everyday, or if you want her to run the blockade to safety."

"I've already made my decision. She sails with you the night after I sail. Wait, maybe I should sail at the same time and act as a decoy."

"For God's sake, *mon ami*, that doesn't make any sense. You'll spend the rest of the war in prison.

Please, just let me do my job as I've always done it, and you stick to your plan of leaving the night before us."

Damian headed for his room, still uneasy, but he knew he'd also feel uneasy if Angelique were staying in Charleston. It was a time of uneasiness—there was nothing he could do to change that.

The sight that met his eyes when he opened the door took his breath away. Angelique was sitting up in bed, the sheet barely covering her breasts, and her black hair hung loose, cascading over her ivory shoulders.

"I wondered if you were coming to bed tonight, my husband."

"I'm sorry, love. Beau and I had some last minute business to take care of."

"You and I have some business to take care of," Angelique replied, letting the sheet slip a little.

"I thought you would need your sleep tonight," he said, a twinkle in his green eyes as he began to undress.

"I can sleep anytime. Besides, by the time you see me next I could be fat and ugly."

"Never! You may blossom with my child, but you will never be fat and ugly." Damian was slipping out of his clothes as he talked.

"I'm glad you feel that way. I want to always be beautiful in your eyes."

"You will be beautiful to me when you're ninety-five," Damian pledged as he gathered Angelique in his arms.

Laughter burst from Angelique. "You don't have to go that far."

"But it's true. You grow more beautiful in my eyes every day. Why should it ever stop?"

Angelique stroked his golden curls, her heart filled with love for this man. "How long will we be apart?" she asked, forgetting the lighthearted banter of a moment ago.

"It won't be long. When you return from Crozon I'll be waiting in Bermuda for you. We'll have some time together in our home there."

"Are you still planning to sail tomorrow night?"

"Yes, *Moonlight Dancer* will be loaded with cotton while *Mouette* will be free of cargo. You'll make much better time that way."

As Damian talked his hand made patterns down the small of her back, spreading his fingers over the swell of her hips.

"I wish I were sailing with you."

"I wish it were possible, love, but it is far too dangerous."

Damian placed his fingers along the tender line of her jaw, raising himself to meet her lips. He gently pulled her downward to lie beside him, her breasts against his chest. Their kiss deepened, becoming more passionate. His arm tightened, crushing her to him as if the pain could make them forget the parting that was to come.

The urgent need to be a part of him touched Angelique and she drew a breath with a sound of distress. "Love me, Damian. Please always love me."

"Love you, my sweet Angel? I can't find the words to tell you of my love. I don't know how I ever lived without you. You are a part of me, as important as breathing. I want to bind you to me. Come war or hell, I will never let you go."

Damian's hand cupped the firm mound of her breast, sending shivers down her spine. "Your breasts are full and ripe from our child," he whispered, kissing first one then the other.

Angelique took his hand and laid it on her stomach. "Our babe is growing within me. Can you tell?"

Damian gently caressed her stomach. "Ah, yes, you are rounded where you were flat."

"I believe our child will be a son," Angelique said.

"Son or daughter, it doesn't matter. Just as long as you and it are healthy."

They felt closer than they ever had. The intimacy of the moment left them both trembling with desire. Spreading his hands on each side of her head he raised himself above her, moving against her slowly, but not entering.

"You will not hurt me, love. The babe is well protected."

Damian slowly entered her, fusing her to him, plunging deeper and deeper within her. She clung to him, raising her hips to match his moves. Tomorrow they would be separated, but for tonight they were one—alone in their world—indestructible and immortal.

Nell undid the buttons of her mistress's dress, then helped her slip into a sheer nightgown of shimmering blue. Kate ignored her idle chatter until she heard Mrs. Legare's name mentioned. She turned abruptly on the girl, causing her to jump in fear.

"What did you say?"

"Bout what, ma'am?"

"About Angelique Legare, you fool!"

"I said, wasn't Miss Patrice lucky to be going to Europe with Mrs. Legare?"

"What are you talking about? When are they going to Europe?"

"Why tomorrow night, ma'am," Nell said getting her facts mixed up. "Dat right, dey gonna sail with Mrs. Legare's brother."

"I haven't heard anything about this. Are you sure?"

"Yes, ma'am. Miss Patrice's lady, Maude, told me how they was packing for her trip. She told me all about Miss Patrice gonna be Mrs. Legare's companion."

"And Damian is not going?"

"No, ma'am. Jus her brother."

Kate Winston went to bed with a plan forming in her devious mind. She had sworn to have Damian at any cost, and this was her chance.

* * *

Damian and Angelique stood on the deck of *Moonlight Dancer*, neither saying anything, but clinging to each other. Shadow sat close by, confused by the tension he felt between his mistress and master. There was a stiff breeze blowing, lifting Angelique's ebony hair about her shoulders and molding her cloak to her body. It had been dark for several hours, but Damian waited until he felt the opportunity was perfect.

"I can't bear these farewells, Damian. When will it end? Why can't we just have a home where you work and come into dinner every night and wake up beside me each morning?"

"We will one day, love. I promise." Damian adjusted her cloak around her shoulders. "You must take care of yourself."

"I will," she answered, the weariness evident in her voice. She pressed her body closer. Time was fleeting and she wished she could hold fast to it.

"It's time, love," Damian said softly.

"All right," she answered, never taking her eyes from her husband's.

"I love you, Angel. Don't ever forget that."

"Oh, Damian," she sobbed, throwing her arms around his neck. "I don't want you to go. I don't want to be away from you. I have this terrible feeling we are saying goodbye."

"Now you know better than that, love. I'm not going to let you out of my sight for long. Besides, you're sailing behind me tomorrow night, so you wouldn't be here even if I stayed."

"You promise you'll be in Bermuda when I get there? Swear to me, Damian. Swear we'll be together in Bermuda."

"I swear to you, my love. Nothing on this earth can keep me away from you."

"Angelique, you must let Damian leave now," Beau encouraged. "He should catch this mist before it disappears."

Kate Winston paced the narrow captain's walk on her fourth floor level, waiting for her driver to send the prearranged signal when Beau Charbonne's ship left its mooring. She still thought it was Beau's ship with Angelique aboard getting ready to sail. Nervously she rechecked the copper lantern she would use to signal her Union friend. Everything had to go just right. This was her last opportunity to have Angelique out of the way so Damian could come back to her. Captain Drummond had assured her after Angelique spent the rest of the war in prison, Damian wouldn't want her. As for her brother, he would be hung as a spy, along with Damian Legare, if his trap went off as planned. Kate smiled to herself. Drummond was going to have to be satisfied with Beau and Angelique Charbonne, because there was only one trap Damian was going to fall into, and that was hers.

* * *

Damian peered into the blackness, counting on the storm that was brewing to screen his vessel as they slipped through the blockade. It was well after midnight and no object could be distinguished at twenty yards. The conditions were perfect. The sea was foaming and lapping noisily, and a light mist had settled over the water giving them perfect cover. They cleared the bar, and passed the first fleet without discovery. The pitching sea drowned out the noise of *Moonlight Dancer's* propellers, and she slipped through the mists like a ghost ship.

Aboard the Union ship, *Merriam*, Captain Drummond played poker while waiting for word that the signal had been sighted. He glanced at his watch, wondering if Kate could have been mistaken. He'd have her pretty ass if she was wrong. Kate wanted Damian Legare's wife out of the way, but he planned to have Damian Legare. He needed this prize to keep his commission and his ship. Capturing Legare would show the stuffed shirt admirals that you didn't have to go by the book to be successful. He smiled to himself. He'd never gone by the book in his whole life and he didn't intend to start now.

"Captain, the signal was just sighted."

Drummond went on deck and took the glasses from his young lieutenant. He could just barely make out the dark outline of a vessel coming toward them.

* * *
359

Damian had seen the light signal too late. A shot was fired across the bow before he had a chance to change course.

Captain Drummond was informed that the ship they had captured was *Moonlight Dancer*, captained by Damian Legare. Drummond couldn't believe his luck. He smiled to himself. "Put a longboat over and get a message to Mrs. Winston," he ordered his lieutenant. "Just say, thanks for your help. We have captured Damian Legare."

Chapter Twenty-seven

Adam paced the dining room while Beau pored over the maps and charts spread out on the table. "I really thought they'd taken him to Hampton, but Steele said no. We know he isn't at Point Lookout. Damn!" Beau exclaimed throwing the maps across the table. "This guessing isn't doing any good. We're wasting too much time. We've got to find out where they've taken him."

"Well, the damned Union officials aren't about to tell us anything," Adam said angrily. "It's been a waste of precious time trying to get them to."

"I know, Adam. It was a long shot, but the alternative was to visit all the prisons on the coast in hopes of finding him. Think how time-consuming that is going to be."

"I feel so damned useless," Adam said running his hand through his hair. "What scares the hell out of me is the talk that Damian would be hung if captured. For all we know he could already have been hung."

"I know, and unfortunately Angelique has heard the same stories. I'm worried about her, Adam. She has been through so much in the last year. I don't know how much more she can take."

Kate Winston lounged back against the pillows of her bed watching Ely Drummond dress. What a cold fish, she thought. His only thought was in his own pleasure. Damian was the only man she'd ever known who cared about her satisfaction, and he was in prison because of her.

"When can you arrange to have Damian released to me," she asked.

Drummond stopped tucking his shirt in his pants and stared at her. Then he began to laugh. "Oh, Kate, I thought you were a smart woman."

"What is that supposed to mean?" she asked angrily.

"Your precious Damian Legare is going to rot in prison—if he isn't hung first."

"No! You promised you would release him to me after he had spent a few months in prison."

"My dear Kate, I would lie to my mother to get what I want. Damian Legare, the great savior of Charleston," he laughed as he pulled his boots on. "Do you know what's so ironic, Kate? Legare is now a prisoner on Morris Island and the good people of Charleston are dropping cannonballs in his lap."

"You bastard," Kate hissed as she leapt off the bed

and began beating at his chest.

Drummond captured her wrists and shoved her back on the bed. "Mind your manners, Kate, or you'll find yourself in prison. Your usefulness to the Union could come to an abrupt ending if I decided to tell Anderson you're also spying for the Confederacy."

"That's a lie" Kate hissed.

"Of course it is, but who but you and I would know that. Now be a good girl and have your maid prepare a nice dinner for us this evening. I'm going to slip back to the ship for awhile, but I shall return."

"I can hardly wait," Kate said sarcastically.

Drummond grabbed her by the hair and twisted her head around to bring her face within inches of his. "Do you know what they do to spies, Kate? You'll hang. They will put a rope around this lovely neck and stretch it. Your eyes will bulge out and you'll gasp in pain until all your oxygen is gone. It's a hell of a way to go, my lovely Kate."

"I'm sorry, Eli. You know I want you to come back to me. I haven't had a real man like you in a long time."

Eli laughed as he pushed her away from him. "Not since your precious Damian Legare, eh."

Damian sat outside the small makeshift tent he shared with three other officers. He had spent the last three nights in stocks for his part in an escape attempt and hadn't been given anything to eat while confined. Now he anxiously waited for his ration of crackers that were filled with bugs, worms and cobwebs, that he had previously been unable to eat. He was sure his stomach was touching his backbone as the pangs of hunger gnawed at him. He tried to concentrate on the sound of the sea, but the grumbling of his stomach was louder.

"These damned Yankees are trying to starve us to death, Captain," one of the officers said.

"It does seem that way," Damian answered, trying not to think about his hunger.

"Sometimes I lie at night and think about my wife's cooking," the officer continued. "God, that woman can cook." The officer laughed and shook his head while remembering, and the other officers hung on his every word. "She's already starting teaching my little daughter how to bake. When I was home last my baby baked me sugar cookies." Tears welled up in the officer's eyes, and he rubbed the back of his hand across his face. "Can you imagine that. She's only seven years old and her mother has already taught her to bake cookies."

"Are you married, Captain Legare?" one of the other officers asked when his friend fell silent.

"Yes. My wife is expecting our first child."

"Hey, that's wonderful, Captain. Hope you are out of here soon."

"I will be." Damian answered, already planning his next escape. He was too close to Angel and Charleston not to try again.

Adam was examining a patient when the nurse gave him the message that Kate Winston was waiting to see him. He washed his hands and changed into a clean hospital jacket before joining her.

"Hello Mrs. Winston. What brings you here?"

Kate stared at him for a long moment, realizing for the first time how much he looked like Damian even though his coloring was different.

"I . . . I have news to give you," she stammered. "I have learned where Damian is being held."

Adam was across the room in a flash. He grabbed her by the shoulders and practically shook her. "You know where Damian is? For God's sake woman, where?"

"Morris Island. The Union has imprisoned 600 Confederate officers on the island in the hope that their presence would force the cannoneers in Charleston to stop the rain of shells on the island."

"How did you learn this?" Adam asked, reluctant to believe her information.

Tears came to Kate's eyes. "Please, don't ask questions. Just believe what I tell you. Damian is being held there, but for how long I don't know. You must do something quickly to help him."

Adam paced the room in silence while Kate watched him. "I need to talk to Beau Charbonne," he finally said. "Together we'll come up with some plan."

As Adam walked Kate to her waiting carriage he said. "I don't know how you got your information, Kate, but I am grateful."

"Just save Damian," was all she said as she climbed into her carriage.

* * *

The wind was blowing the sand, turning the grains into needles that pricked the skin. Damian and several other officers huddled in the tent trying to stay warm. When Damian had been captured he was dressed in light clothing that now did nothing to keep him warm. The residents of Charleston had sent blankets over for the prisoners, but there weren't enough to go around after the Union guards took their share.

He had to escape soon, he thought. He was slowly starving to death and would be too weak to escape before long. He closed his eyes and thought about Angelique. It had been almost three months. By now she would be showing her pregnancy. She would be beautiful carrying his child. Damian shook his head in despair. There was no way they were going to keep him on this island. Somehow he would get to Angelique.

"All right, you Rebel scum, out of there," one of the guards shouted, shaking the flimsy tent.

Damian stiffly crawled from the tent, stretching his tall frame. "What's this all about?"

"You boys are going for a physical exam," he laughed, poking his rifle in Damian's back.

"What's the matter, Yank, are they afraid we're not suffering enough?"

"Don't smart mouth me, Reb, just do as you're told or you'll answer to me later. You know what that means, don't you?" he grinned a toothless grin.

* * *

With a few connections and a substantial bribe, Adam had been granted permission to make a medical tour of the stockade on Morris Island. The plan was for him to find out for sure if Damian was on the island and to inform him of the time and place he was to meet them. Most escape attempts had been made through the swamps toward Charleston, but Adam and Beau planned to bring a longboat into the ocean side of the island where only a few guards were stationed.

Adam had been on the island since dawn and still hadn't seen any sign of Damian or his crew. He was involved in writing his findings to the Union Officials about the food and water on the island when the last group of officers were brought into the hospital tent. Adam looked up and met the eyes of his brother. There was the slightest hint of a smile in Damian's eyes, but neither said anything.

As Adam examined the officer in front of Damian he couldn't keep his eyes off his brother. Damian had probably lost more than twenty pounds in the months he had been imprisoned. His eyes were dull and listless and his lips were cracked and split from lack of water. When Adam finished examining the officer he motioned for Damian to come forward.

"Are you all right?" he whispered.

"I'm better now. Can you get me out of this place?"

The guard moved toward them. "Why does this man look so emaciated?" Adam asked.

"The man is a trouble maker. He's tried to escape

twice so he's kept in confinement most of the time."

"Stay out of confinement, Captain," Adam warned when the guard moved away. "Tomorrow—midnight," he whispered.

As the guard moved back toward them Adam continued his examination. "This man needs some decent food," he said as the guard passed near.

"We all need decent food," another soldier chimed in. "They only feed us when they feel like it and the food is infested with bugs and worms."

"Bah," the guard spat, moving away again.

"Bring your crew to ocean side of island, below the line of trees," Adam said examining Damian's ears.

"Only officers here," Damian whispered.

"Come on, Doc, it's time to move on to the next man," the guard ordered. "We're gonna be here all day this way."

"Don't fail me, brother," Damian whispered as he moved on past Adam.

"You are not going without me!" Angelique insisted. "Damian may need my help."

"That is exactly why I'm going along," Adam interjected.

"You said there was a chance you wouldn't be able to come back to Charleston. That would mean I wouldn't see Damian for . . . for who knows how long."

"Angelique, there is the distinct possibility that our plan won't work at all and we could all be captured," Beau warned. "Damian would go crazy if you were harmed in any way, not to mention the fact that he would probably kill me."

"I will take my chances with the rest of you," Angelique said.

"No! Absolutely not, Angelique. I will not give in to you this time. This is entirely too dangerous, even if you weren't pregnant. You will have to abide by my decision this time."

"We shall see," Angelique said before storming from the room.

"Has she always been this stubborn?" Adam asked, admiration in his voice.

"Always," Beau said. "But this time I'm really worried about her. I'm afraid anything I say or do will send her over the edge. This past year has been a living hell for the both of us, and now on top of that she has to live with this.

"I have to admit I don't like the way she has so calmly handled this whole thing. I thought at first she might be in shock, but there are no other signs of it, other than the headaches, but she said the powders I gave her helped."

"She didn't say anything to me about headaches, but then everyone has been in such a turmoil. I suppose the only thing we can do is watch her very closely. Hopefully when she and Damian are reunited everything will be fine."

A storm had been brewing all day. Now as Beau prepared to run the blockade it was coming strong and furious, but there was no way they could delay or change plans since there wasn't any way to let Damian know.

Angelique had boarded the *La Mouette* unobserved while Beau was seeing to last minute details. She slipped down the hatch and into the cabin prepared for Damian. She ran her hand over the heavy black covers that had been secured over the portholes. Adam had said it was just a precaution in case Damian needed some medical attention; he would be able to use light. He had assured her Damian was only undernourished but she hadn't been able to get him to talk about his visit to the prison. Angelique sat on the edge of the bunk, staring off into space. She wondered if Damian would be angry with her for coming. Didn't any of them understand what she had been going through? She had thought he was dead, but now he would be with her when their child was born. He would be there for her when she needed him, just as she would be with him tonight.

The wind filled the black sails, moving them swiftly and silently past Fort Sumter, through the blockading fleet, and around the tip of Morris Island. In the blackness of the storm Beau anchored *La Mouette* and launched two longboats into the rough churning seas. The crew stood by alert and tense, knowing it was going to be a long night.

Angelique slipped up on deck and stood silently looking out into the blackness of the night. Spray from the sea soon had her cloak and hair drenched, but she continued to cling to the railing. She knew it was too soon for the boats to return, yet she was unable to take her eyes off the black sea where they had disappeared.

"I really should wring your neck, Angelique," Beau said from behind her. "The danger of this trip has been doubled with the storm, and still you endanger yourself and your child with your stubbornness."

"I had to be here," she said still looking out at the sea.

"I pray God you don't regret your foolishness," Beau spat as he turned back to his duties.

"You should go below," Adam encouraged. "You won't do that child any good if you catch pneumonia."

"I have to be here when he comes, Adam. Why can't anyone understand that?"

Adam wrapped his arm around her shoulder. "I understand. I'll stay with you."

At least thirty minutes had gone by and there was still no sign of the boats. Angelique peered into the blackness, then suddenly stiffened as the sound of gunshots echoed over the roar of the sea.

"Oh God, no," she cried, leaning against Adam.

"Quiet," he ordered. "Your voice may carry over the water."

Everyone on board waited and listened. Thunder began to rumble and lightning lit the sky. Beau was beginning to suspect that this wasn't merely a storm, but a hurricane that could spread for hundreds of miles. He waited and prayed, counting the minutes in his own mind.

The sound of the longboats hitting against the side of *La Mouette* was heard before anyone saw the boats. Angelique started to run toward the railing, but Adam held her back.

"We have to give them a chance to get aboard, then we will see to him." One by one the men were helped aboard, climbing the rope ladder that had been thrown over the side.

Angelique began to feel weak in the knees. Where was Damian? Why hadn't he boarded? Then all her fears were answered as she watched them carefully lift an unconscious man to the deck. In the darkness she couldn't see who it was, yet she knew, she felt it. She broke from Adam's grip and ran toward Damian.

"Angelique, lead the way to the cabin," Adam ordered, afraid she was going into shock as she stared down at Damian.

Angelique stood frozen for a second, then turned and headed for the cabin. The only light on the ship was in this enclosed cabin which Adam had prepared for just such an emergency. Angelique watched silently as Damian's officer tenderly lowered Damian onto the table in the center of the cabin. Damian's face and hair were covered with blood from a wound at his temple, and his left arm hung slack from his side. What was left of his once white shirt was now covered with blood.

"What happened Lieutenant Maxwell?" Adam asked as he began to cut away the shirt.

"Two guards discoverd us as the boats hit the beach," the officer said. "Captain Legare insisted we go on. He had a knife he had kept hidden and quickly overcame both guards, but before he made it to the boats another guard appeared and began shooting at him. I saw him spin and fall to one knee when the shot creased his head, but he got up and staggered toward us, until another shot hit him. Lansing and I had already jumped out of the boat to help him, but we were too late. All we could do was drag him into the boat." The officer had tears running down his face. "Please Doc, you've got to help him. He saved all our lives back there."

"I'm going to do my best. You go on and get something to eat. I'll let you know when he's conscious."

While Adam prepared his instruments, Angelique bathed Damian's face. The bullet had just grazed his temple, leaving a red, ugly gash along the hairline. She ran her finger over the hollow lines of his cheeks, and over his cracked lips. He was pale and dirty and soaked to the skin.

The gimbal light danced wildly overhead as the storm grew in intensity.

"Is he going to live, Adam?" Angelique asked hoarsely.

"I can remove the bullet from his shoulder and it should heal all right, and I think with rest his head wound will also heal fine, but he's lost a lot of blood and in his weakened condition that isn't good."

"What can we do?" Angelique whispered.

"Let's start with one thing at a time. First, let's get him out of these wet clothes. Then I'll start by removing the bullet from his shoulder." Adam looked at Angelique's pale face. "I'll need help, Angelique. If you're not up to it tell me and I'll ask one of the men."

"No. I'm fine, Adam. I'll help with whatever needs to be done. That's why I'm here."

The blockading fleet had moved into place blocking the channel back to Charleston as soon as the guards on Morris Island had signaled an escape. They had no place to head except Bermuda. There was no danger of Union ships following them—they weren't fool enough to be out in this storm.

The hull of *La Mouette* strained as the wind increased its fury. Beau gripped the wheel as he was pelted with the stinging blast of cold rain. The entire hull moaned under the assault of the wind and the wild water that surged over the decks. Thunder rumbled and a bolt of fire slammed into the white-capped breast of the ocean just ahead of them. Beau met the raging sea by quartering into it, receiving the force of the crest on the windward bow, then straightening course and taking advantage of the momentary calm that follows a heavy sea.

Adam was finding it almost impossible to keep a steady hand as he attempted to remove the bullet from Damian's shoulder. He had tied Damian to the table in an effort to keep him from falling as the ship pitched and rolled. He was grateful Damian remained unconscious since he had no chloroform.

Angelique's nerves were drawn beyond endurance as she watched Adam probe for the bullet embedded in his brother's shoulder. It was cold and damp in the cabin, yet there was a fine bead of perspiration on his forehead. The ship suddenly felt as if it dropped off the side of a mountain, throwing both of them across the cabin.

"Are we going to make it, Adam?" Angelique asked as Adam helped her back to the table.

"I've heard stories that Beau is second only to Damian Legare in his expertise as a captain." Adam forced a laugh, hoping to ease Angelique's fears, but he was concerned himself. They hadn't bargained on this storm. Again he began to probe and the ship pitched again. "Christ!" Adam swore, but the blasphemy was censored on his lips by the storm.

Damian opened his eyes and weakly smiled at Angelique. Then suddenly he bolted upward, but the ropes held him. "Angel. What are you doing here . . . Why . . . God damn it, Adam," he swore as Adam forced him back.

"I had to be here when they came for you."

"The danger . . ."

"We'll face the danger together," Angelique cut him off.

"God, I love you, woman."

Tears came to Angelique's eyes. "And I love you,

darling."

Damian screamed out as Adam hit the hard metal imbedded in his flesh.

"Hang on, Damian. It won't be long now."

The storm had unleashed its full fury on them. It was as if the whole world had turned to wind and water. They had been at sea three hours, but it seemed like a lifetime to Beau. The wind was taking the top off the sea in thick sheets and lifting it over the ship. Desperately he wished Angelique wasn't aboard. *La Mouette* was built better than most blockade runners, but even she hadn't been designed to take such punishment. Every man who could be spared was bailing water, but he knew it was useless. He checked the compass, no longer certain of their direction, but it jerked erratically. How close to land were they, he wondered. Each time the ship was lifted on the crest of a twenty-foot wave, the steerage and power were lost so they couldn't have gone too far.

The hull of the sleek *La Mouette* strained and shuddered as one of the twin-screw engines quit. Beau knew the time had come to start preparing for the worst. "Start sending on SOS," he ordered his firstmate. "I'm gong to head her toward land and try to beach her. Inform Doctor Legare of our situation," Beau said to another of his officers.

Beau struggled with the wheel, his efforts made even more difficult by the one engine failing. He was heading for what he thought was land, but they had been tossed about and he wasn't sure which direction they were heading. "If only Angelique wasn't on board," he cursed over and over.

Above the howl of the wind Adam could hear Beau's voice cracking out orders to his crew. He knew very little about ships, but he knew this one was suddenly moving differently under them. He took another gulp of quinine, willing his stomach to settle while he helped Angelique get Damian into dry clothes.

The door suddenly flew open and one of Beau's officers stumbled in. "Captain says to tell you things are bad. He's heading toward land, but . . ."

The wail of the wind suddenly seemed mild in comparison to the sickening sound of metal ripping apart.

"We better get Captain Legare up on deck," the officer warned. "The ship is breaking up."

Beau felt icy despair clutch and squeeze his guts. The sound of the signal light flashing an SOS to anyone drummed in his brain. Still he fought the wheel, praying they were close to land.

As the officer opened the hatch the wind ripped it from his hands and spun it into the air. He turned and put an arm under Damian's shoulder while Adam supported the other side. Then he turned and gave Angelique a hand. The salt water ripped at her face as abrasively as ground glass. She clung to the rail, desperately trying to resist the wind that threatened to lift her from the deck.

"Get in the boats!" Beau yelled over the screaming wind.

Angelique turned and looked at her brother. He clung to the wheel like a specter, his eyes dark and wild. His hair was plastered to his head and his shirt flapped around him in tatters.

"Hurry, Angelique," he shouted.

Turning back to the railing, she found Adam and two other officers were already in the boat, struggling against the wind to take Damian's unconscious form from the men on board *La Mouette*. "Hurry Mrs. Legare," one of the seaman ordered.

The longboat swung back and forth on its ropes, smashing against the side of the ship. "Hurry, it's going to be broken up if we don't get her in," someone shouted. Angelique was between the boat and the ship when the rope snapped, dropping the longboat heavily to the churning water below. She was left dangling precariously by only a rope, watching in numb horror as the boat beneath her disappeared into the blackness.

She was pulled back to the deck, cold, wet and in shock. Clinging to the railing with every ounce of strength she had, another wave washed over her. She watched numbly as the two seamen who were lowering the boats disappeared into the sea.

In a matter of minutes another boat was lowered and this time she was in it with several others before it broke its lines and was set adrift on the white-churning sea.

The movement of the boat was a nightmare of

coordinated movement. Each whim of the sea and wind tossed them around. The waves were up to twenty-feet high and the little boat swooped up over them and dropped heavily into the troughs, then spun around in circles. Angelique started vomiting. She clutched the side of the boat as she hung her head over the side. Despair cramped her stomach and she cried out in protest against this cruelty of fate. A hand smoothed her hair back from her face and turned her into a strong shoulder. She looked up into the brown eyes of Lieutenant Maxwell, the officer who had carried Damian from the island.

"I'm not going to die," she sobbed, clinging to him. "I won't die."

"I won't let you die, Mrs. Legare. Everything will be all right," he assured. "Just hold on to me."

Chapter Twenty-eight

"Are you hungry?"

Damian opened his eyes, staring uncomprehendingly at the black woman who had raised him. He bolted upright, moving too suddenly. "My God," he moaned as he clutched his head. "Have I been dreaming?"

"No dream," Bessie said, waiting to spoon soup in his mouth. "Master Adam brought you here three days ago. You've been outa your head ever since. De fever finally broke last night."

"Angelique? Where is Angelique?"

Bessie shook her head, unable to look him in the face.

"Bessie," Damian shouted. "Where is Angelique?"

"Doan know," she answered, tears filling her eyes. "Dey got people searching the coastline below Charleston where you came in."

"Oh God," he moaned falling back on the bed. "It can't be. Oh God, it can't be," he moaned as he remembered the storm.

Adam and Beau, with the crew of several blockade runners, searched the long expanse of coast, starting at dawn every morning and not stopping to rest until it was too dark to search. Seven men out of the crew of forty were still unaccounted for. Among those was Lieutenant Joshua Maxwell, the American officer who had signed on with Beau in France, and who had become Damian's right-hand man aboard *Moonlight Dancer*, and crewman Tibbs. Eleven bodies had already been found along this Carolina coastline. Three of Damian's officers had been among the bodies found.

The day after Damian's fever broke he joined in the search. "She's alive, Adam. I can feel it," he insisted when the searchers started drifting away. "You've only accounted for four boats. That means one is still out there or has found a safe haven. We have to keep looking."

"Damian, it has been six days. I don't know if Angelique could survive that on the sea," Adam gently told his brother.

"No. You're wrong. She's alive. I know she is," Damian insisted, his voice breaking, as he clutched himself in a spasm of chills.

"Look at you, Damian. You're feverish again. You shouldn't be out here so soon. What good is it going to do for you to kill yourself?"

"I just need some rest," Damian said clutching the blanket around him as he took a long gulp from a bottle of rum. "I won't give up, Adam. She's alive."

Beau sat staring into the fire, drowning in his own grief. "If anyone had to die, why not me?" he said. "Why Angelique and her unborn child?"

"I can't answer that, Beau, but I do know life has to go on. Nothing has changed the fact that a war is still going on, and Charleston is in grave danger. It gets worse everyday."

Damian tilted the rum bottle to his mouth and drained the contents. "To hell with this war. I don't want anything to do with it. This stinking war took my wife and child from me," he shouted, throwing the bottle into the fire. "They can all go to hell. Every damned Yankee and Rebel can go to hell!" Damian's shoulders began to shake uncontrollably as his body was wracked with sobs. "Why, oh God, why?"

Angelique and Joshua Maxwell were picked up by a boat on their third day out. Seaman Tibbs had been washed overboard during the storm. He was probably the lucky one. The rescue boat was owned by a Cuban fisherman and mercenary, named Di-Salvo, who saw an opportunity to make some easy gold by selling his two passengers into slavery on one of the sugar-growing islands.

Unaware of this, Angelique and Joshua were makng the best of being on the smelly boat, with only ish to eat. After thinking they were going to drown, this seemed like luxury. The two of them sat at a wooden table in the captain's cabin and ate a meal of fish soup and crackers with ravenous appetites.

"Do you think the rest of them made it all right?" Angelique asked her companion of the last few days.

"I'm sure of it," Joshua said between bites. "We made it, didn't we?"

Angelique looked across the table at her companion. "I wouldn't have made it without you, Joshua. I would have died out there and I know it. I would have gone over the side just like Tibbs." Angelique shuddered, remembering the screams of the man as he was washed out of the boat by a monster wave and swept away from them in the blink of an eye. The only thing that had kept her in the boat was Joshua's weight holding her.

"Don't think about it, Angelique. It's over now. As soon as we get to Havana I'll arrange for a ship to take us back to Charleston. Then you can let your husband and servants take care of you. Every woman expecting a child should be pampered."

"Damian may need my care," Angelique said, remembering the last time she had seen him.

"Yes, but Damian's a strong man. He's probably up and about already. If I know him, he has everyone in Charleston out looking for us."

Angelique smiled. "You're probably right."

"I know if you were my wife I'd never stop looking for you."

Angelique looked at Joshua in surprise. "Wh
that's very nice of you, Joshua."

"I mean it, Angelique. Damian is a very lucky
man."

"I'm also a very lucky woman, Joshua."

"Ah, you are both looking better," the captain said
as he stepped into his cabin. "I thought you would be
pretty once the salt water was washed off you," he
said to Angelique, as his eyes undressed her.

Angelique knew she should be grateful to the man,
but she didn't like him. His black eyes made her
shrink instinctively whenever he looked at her. She
was glad for the protection of Joshua Maxwell as the
captain sat down across from her.

"I see the oil has helped your mouth," he said,
reaching across the table and running his rough,
dirty finger along the outline of her lips.

Angelique pulled back and instinctively wiped her
hand across her mouth.

"Captain, we are grateful for your aid, but I must
warn you to keep your hands off Mrs. Legare,"
Joshua protested, anger gleaming in his eyes.

DiSalvo laughed, his eyes still lingering on Angelique. "You're going to have a hell of a time, protecting her where you're going."

"What is that supposed to mean?" Joshua asked
angrily.

"Ah, you will see, gringo."

"Don't play games with me, DiSalvo. You don't
want trouble with my government."

"Your government?" the Cuban laughed. "The

384

Confederate States of America? They have their own problems. What are they going to care about two people lost at sea?"

"Is it money you want, DiSalvo?"

"That's part of it. I also want the lady."

"You touch the lady and there won't be any money," Joshua warned. "The lady is from a very rich family in France. They will pay for her safe delivery."

Again DiSalvo laughed. "I'm going to have the lady until I'm tired of her, then I'll sell her. I don't need any money from her family. You both will bring a very nice price. The sugar planters are always looking for a good strong arm," he said looking at Joshua, "and for a pretty piece like Mrs. Legare."

Joshua's grip on Angelique's hand tightened until she thought her bones would break. Her blood was pounding in her ears as she stared across the table at the captain who had saved them from the sea. Joshua stood up suddenly, knocking his chair over backward. "You'll touch her over my dead body, you bastard."

"Done," DiSalvo said as he slowly stood up and pulled a long double-edged knife. "But you'll die slaving on one of my islands, *mi amigo*—not the easy swift death of my knife."

Angelique, mindless with terror and revulsion, shoved the table between the two men. "No, please no, DiSalvo. My husband and brother will pay you well for saving us. Please stop this madness," she shrieked.

"Get out of here, Angelique," Joshua shouted, as he circled the table. "Try to get away . . . into a boat . . . anything."

"Oh, God, please," Angelique began to sob.

"Stay, my pretty little pigeon. Watch me geld your brave but foolish friend." DiSalvo grinned demonically.

Angelique shrieked as DiSalvo swiped the knife across Joshua's chest, leaving a long red gash. When Joshua tried to stop the next swipe, the blade cut across his hand, opening the palm from end to end.

"This is like the cat playing with the mouse, no?" DiSalvo grinned, opening another gash down Joshua's stomach. "You are defenseless, *amigo*. How you think you gonna stop DiSalvo?"

Joshua kicked his demented torturer in the groin, and as DiSalvo doubled up in pain, he grabbed Angelique by the hand and shoved her before him out the cabin door. "Run, love, for God's sake, run . . ."

The words froze in his throat. Angelique turned, trying to get him to follow her, but he stared at her with cold, vacant eyes, then fell before her like a toppled tree. The silver double-bladed knife was embedded between his shoulder blades.

"God damned bastard," DiSalvo swore, still holding his groin as he struggled to his knee. "That bastard just cost me a lot of money with that stupid trick."

Angelique closed her eyes and covered her ears, trying to block out the terrible screaming that filled the room. Why wouldn't it stop? It was going to drive her insane. Everything was red . . . blood red. "Shut up, bitch!" DiSalvo shouted, slapping Angelique across the face.

"*Diable . . . diable . . .*" she shrieked, her mind retreating from this new living nightmare. DiSalvo balled his fist and hit her hard in the face, splitting the skin on her cheekbone. Still she screamed, her hands drawn up like claws.

"Crazy *gringa*," DiSalvo snarled shoving her away from him. He left her cringing against the wall, still mumbling the Spanish word for devil, while he pulled his knife from Joshua's back. After wiping the blood off on his pants leg he tossed it onto the table where the remains of their meal still sat.

"Get on the bed, *puta*. Killing always makes me horny."

Angelique's pupils were dilated as she moved silently from her corner. DiSalvo had his back to her, his head over a copper basin as he splashed water over his face and head. She picked up the shining silver knife and with the strength of a person demented she plunged the cold steel to its hilt in the Cuban's back.

"Agh . . ." he screamed, clawing at his back, trying to reach the knife. His efforts were useless and he stared at Angelique, his eyes filled with hate and pain. "*Bruja . . . bruja*," he hissed before falling at her feet.

One of the seamen came running to the cabin. "*Madre de Dios*," he muttered, crossing himself.

"*Diable, diable*," Angelique chanted, rocking back

387

and forth as she sat next to Joshua Maxwell's mutilated body.

By now the doorway was filled with the crew, but none would come into the cabin. "*Demente*," one of them whispered and backed away, closing and locking the door behind him. "We should throw her overboard. She is *diablo's* pawn," he encouraged his fellow seamen.

"Then we will be blamed for those dead men," a younger man said. "The island is only hours away. We will take her there," another insisted.

"What if her spirit comes through the door and gets the rest of us?" a frightened seaman asked.

"We don't know what happened down there," the young man said. The *capitan* was an evil man. Perhaps she did us a favor."

"*Si*," the men mumbled as they moved away, but they didn't believe for a minute that Angelique wasn't the devil's pawn.

"As always, Simon, I hate to see you go. Your once a year visit is not enough," Carlos Sola said. "The students will talk about your lecture for months. I don't know why you won't stay here and teach."

"It is kind of you to offer, Carlos, but Bermuda is my home now."

"But why, Simon? You and Rosita loved it here in the islands."

"True, Carlos, and I guess that is what keeps me

coming back at least once a year, even though I'm getting too old for all this traveling, but Rosita is buried in Bermuda and that is where I will stay now."

A young fisherman ran past them on the docks, almost knocking the two men over. "I'm sorry, Simon. I don't know what gets into them sometimes." Before the young man had a chance to finish, the fisherman was running back toward the end of the fishing dock with another man in tow.

"What is all the commotion?" Simon Maclean asked. "It looks like they are around my yacht."

Carlos held a hand up to his eyes to shadow the sun, but he couldn't tell what was taking place at the end of the dock. "Shall we go see? My curiosity is piqued."

The captain of Doctor Maclean's yacht was standing on the dock staring down at the small, dilapidated fishing boat.

"What is going on, Andrew?"

"I'm not sure, doctor, but they're babbling something about a devil woman being on board and killing two men. No one will go into the cabin."

"They are only ignorant fishermen, Simon," Carlos explained. "They can be very superstitious."

"Let's see about this," Simon said, as he dropped down on the boat. "Where is this devil woman?" he asked one of the men. After blessing himself the fishermen pointed toward Capitan DiSalvo's cabin.

Simon slowly unlocked the door and pushed it open. The door stopped against Joshua Maxwell's body. "Jesus," Simon Maclean exclaimed as he looked around the cabin. There were two dead men on the floor, but in the evening light he couldn't see very well. He knelt beside the Cuban and felt for a pulse. Moving cautiously around the cabin he thought he could hear someone breathing. "Who is there?"

"Do you see anything, sir?" Andrew asked.

"More than I bargained for. But I don't see a girl. Put a match to that lantern."

The cabin was flooded with a silvery white light and immediately they saw her sitting cross-legged against the wall.

Simon Maclean moved hesitantly near the girl and lifted her chin. The skin over her cheek bone hung open and her face was covered with blood.

"*Diable*," she hissed.

"No, I'm not the devil, but I do believe you've seen him," the doctor said as he looked into Angelique's horror-filled eyes.

"*Diable*, she repeated, rocking back and forward.

Doctor Maclean spoke to Angelique in French, but still she didn't respond with anything but the one word.

"This man over here is a lieutenant in the Navy of the Confederate States of America," Andrew said going through Joshua's pockets. "His name is Joshua Maxwell."

"Joshua," Angelique mumbled.

"Sweet Mary," Andrew exclaimed. "Doctor, this man has knife wounds all over his body. It looks like someone was trying to cut him into ribbons."

Doctor Maclean knelt beside the American. "This isn't the work of a woman. I'd venture a guess that the Cuban probably did this before the woman killed him."

"Aye, but I'd wager they won't believe that on the island, sir. They will put her in prison and throw away the key."

Doctor Maclean looked around them. Angelique was still rocking back and forward mumbling. "It's almost dark. If I can cause a panic up on deck do you think you can get her on board the ship?"

"I'll do my best, sir. But will she let me move her?"

Again Doctor Maclean knelt in front of Angelique. He lifted her chin to look in her eyes. "It will be all right, lass. You do as Andrew tells you. Do you understand?"

"*Diable*," Angelique whispered.

"I know, lass. I know."

"She is using the French word for devil," Andrew pondered. "Have you tried speaking to her in French?"

"Yes, but nothing gets a respone. She's in shock, Andrew. I'm sure of it."

The deck of the fishing boat cleared when Doctor Maclean confirmed that he also thought the woman was a devil. The ignorant men fled from the boat in a panic, enabling Andrew to carry Angelique to the doctor's yacht.

"You may be able to fool those ignorant peasants, Simon, but I'm not falling for that story about a devil woman," Carlos protested. "What's going on here?"

"I'm sorry, Carlos, but I'm taking the girl with me. She needs my help."

"Simon, there are two dead men in that cabin. You said so yourself."

"She may have killed the captain in self-defense, but I'm sure she didn't kill the other man, Carlos. You know as well as I do that those people aren't going to give her a chance. Even if she could defend herself they wouldn't listen. But she can't defend herself, Carlos, She's in shock."

"*Dios*," the Cuban swore, running his hand through his hair. "Go ahead and get your ship out of here," he finally said. "And Simon, be careful. She could be dangerous."

"I don't think so, Carlos. I think she just needs help. The doctor jumped to the deck of his sailing ship as if he had springs in his feet. "*Despedirse, mi amigo*," the Scotsman saluted.

"She just may be a devil-woman, my foolish friend," Carlos pondered as he watched the sleek sailing ship catch the evening wind. "In the twenty-five years I've known you I've never seen you act so strangely."

Havana, Cuba was the first place Simon Maclean

had practiced medicine after graduating from the University of Edinburgh in 1839. It had been on that lovely island that he had met and married Rosita Sola, Carlos's cousin. For fifteen of those years they had lived in Bermuda, building a dream house overlooking the sea. For twenty years Rosita had made his life happy, but then she was taken from him during a yellow fever outbreak on the island in 1859. He had been a lost man ever since, alone with no children and no family. If it hadn't been for the love and care of his Scottish housekeeper, Caitlin, and her husband, Andrew, he would surely have gone crazy. His yearly visit to Havana was a sort of pilgrimage, bringing back memories of his beloved, while he lectured at the university. But he had never encountered anything like this before.

Simon had prepared a double dose of laudanum, a strong blend of opium and alcohol, to give to Angelique. But now, after examining her he changed his mind. "So you are with child," he said, gently touching her stomach. "Six or more months I'd imagine." She returned his stare, her violet eyes still wide with fear. "Was the American your husband, lass? I know what it is like to see a loved one die and not be able to do anything about it. Don't you worry. I'm going to take care of you and your bairn," he smiled. "You will like Bermuda. It is warm, with the smell of flowers always in the air. My Rosita loved it. She liked looking out over the sea. We never had any children, but I always thought it would be a wonderful place to raise little ones. I have a housekeeper named Caitlin who will just adore you. She likes to mother things."

Angelique finally gave in to the soothing, hypnotic drone of Simon's voice, just as he had hoped she would. "We'll have to try to make you forget without the use of sedatives, lass. We don't want anything to harm the bairn now, do we?"

Chapter Twenty-nine

Damian braced his hand against the rail of the *Sorceress* and automatically scanned the coastline. They were in Charleston harbor after searching the entire Southern coastline for the past six months, and finding nothing. No washed-up bodies—no ship-wrecked survivors—nothing. Now Beau was preparing to return to France on a ship scheduled to run the blockade that night.

"What will you do now, Damian?" Beau asked, throwing his gear on the dock.

"I don't know It's spring. I guess I should go home and see that the fields are planted."

"Why don't you come with me. My men are finishing a new ship. You can supervise the finishing touches and then captain her."

Damian stared at his friend, then slowly a smile came over his face. "What did I ever do to deserve a friend like you?"

"We are family," Beau said.

"Yes, we are family," Damian said sadly.

"Can you be ready to sail tonight?"

"I can't go, Beau. Not yet, anyway. I have to put things in order here and in Bermuda. Perhaps later I will join you. Right now I just don't know what I'm going to do."

"Don't stay here, Damian. The Yankees are too near, and too anxious to have your head since the Northern papers reported that you had made fools of them."

Damian stared out toward the blockading fleet. "If only they knew how dearly I paid for that escape—a wife and a child."

"Damian, you can't keep thinking about it. Angelique wouldn't want you to go on mourning her. She'd want you to go on with your life."

"I will mourn her for the rest of my life, *mon ami*, but I am going to try to put these ghosts to rest. It just has to be in my own way—and in my own time."

The sun was setting as Damian made his way through the rubble that was once the lower part of the city. Everything as far as he could see was either in ruin or deserted. He stopped in front of the hotel where he had stayed with Angelique that first night he had brought her to Charleston. The second floor window of her room was boarded up, as were all the windows, yet if he tried, he could almost hear the clinking of china and crystal coming from the empty dining room. He looked around in disbelief. The city that had withstood Indians, fires, and the British, was now being destroyed by Americans—the very same people who had stood side by side with South Carolinians against the British. Together they had fought for their independence and now they were going to annihilate each other.

Later that evening Damian sat with Lacey and Adam on the front porch of the townhouse on Calhoun Street.

"It is only a matter of time," Adam predicted. "They are hurling more than a thousand shells a month into the city. As you saw, the whole lower part of the city has been destroyed."

"I saw," Damian answered, staring out into the darkness.

"The last time I walked down there, I felt as if I was going from life to death," Lacey said. "The streets are overgrown with weeds and there were glass and bricks everywhere."

"Is it necessary for you both to stay here?" Damian asked. "Wouldn't it be safer at Enchanteur?"

"It would probably be safer," Lacey answered, "but we are needed here."

Damian shook his head. "Somehow I knew you would say that. Damn, I curse the day I got you both involved in this war."

"Damian, we could leave any time we wanted to," Adam reminded. "We stay because it is something we have to do. Our soldiers are fighting without food and shoes to wear, but they are fighting. How could we let them down. We don't have much to work with. Our medical supplies are about depleted, but we stay and do what we can for them."

"I hope in the next few months you won't regret that decision," Damian said as he stood up and stretched. "I'm leaving for Enchanteur in the morning so I guess I'd better get some sleep."

"Will you be staying there long?" Lacey asked.

"I don't know. I had planned to go home and try to forget the war . . . and . . . and the last few months, but seeing what has happened to this city makes me so damned mad I can't see straight. I don't know how long the *Sorceress* can last as a blockade runner, but maybe in a month or so I can make at least one or two more runs and bring back some medicine and shoes."

"It is too dangerous for him to return to blockade running, Adam," Lacey expressed her concern. "Every week the Northern papers are begging for his head."

Adam wrapped his arms around his wife. "I'll tell you something, love, I think the danger he faces as a blockade runner is far desirable to his losing his sanity sitting around alone at Enchanteur and mourning Angelique. She is the only person he has ever truly loved and he is taking her death very hard."

"I know," Lacey said looking up at her husband. "Did you see the look in his eyes when he first got here. I wanted to cry for him. There must be something we can do to help him."

"Time is the only thing that will ease his pain, love. Time and staying busy."

Damian's bleakness increased each day he stayed at Enchanteur. He'd work from sunup to sundown in the fields with his laborers, but then he spent every evening drinking himself to unconsciousness while sitting in front of Angelique's portrait. He wouldn't allow anyone in the room except for Shadow, who faithfully stayed at his side. When Damian had decided that life wasn't worth living, the memory of Angelique's violet eyes reminded him that there was still the smallest chance that she was alive.

After a week of trying to destroy his anguished memories, he finally decided he had to get hold of his life. In the middle of the night he decided he couldn't stay at Enchanteur any longer. Tom Steele was waiting for his orders and it was time to give them. With one last glance at Angelique's portrait, he removed it from above the mantel. With Able's help he buried most of the family heirlooms and paintings which his parents had brought over from Europe.

"What about dat one?" Able asked, pointing to Angelique's portrait.

"That one will go with me." *To a safe haven, or the bottom of the sea, but it would go with him.*

* * *

Damian's servants congregated at the front of the house, waiting for him to tell them what to do. "I don't think you have anything to worry about," Damian said as he shook hands with each of them. "There are papers in the library and in Mr. Lassiter's law office proving that you were given your freedom when my father died. Able knows to go to my brother Adam if you need anything, or have any problems."

Nobody said a word as Damian mounted his horse. He smiled down at them. "I'm depending on you. Be sure you get a good crop so you will have something to live on. I don't know when, or if, I'll be back."

Damian's voice was choked with emotion as he looked at the faces he had known since he was a boy. "God bless you, and keep you safe."

Hours later, when Damian arrived at the wharf in Charleston, Shadow was with him. The dog had run behind him all the way from Enchanteur.

"So you're signing on to sail with me, boy? All right. Come aboard. I guess it's you and me now."

The *Sorceress* made an uneventful run to Bermuda, encountering only one Yankee cruiser. It was going to take two days to load the ship with clothing and medical supplies, so most of the crew took the opportunity to enjoy a few days on the island. As Tom Steele was getting ready to go ashore he realized Damian was still in his cabin. He had known the captain for a long time. They had been together through good and bad times, but Steele was really worried about his friend this time. Damian moved as if in a fog—acting, but not reacting. Nothing seemed to matter to him. He seemed bent on a path of self-destruction. When they had encountered the Union cruiser Damian had stood on the bow, idly watching the ship, as if daring it to take him. Luck had been with them, and for some unknown reason the cruiser had decided not to chase them.

Steele headed toward Damian's cabin, determined to get his friend to join him for a drink. "How about going ashore for a drink?" he asked, when Damian opened the door.

"No, I don't think so, but thanks anyway."

"Well, if you won't go ashore with me, how about offering me a drink here."

"Sure. Come on in."

While Damian poured them both a drink Steele took one of the chairs from the table. "I really think we need to talk, Captain."

Throwing Steele an impatient glance, Damian sat across the table from him. "Why aren't you ashore enjoying some female's favors?" Damian asked.

"Why aren't you?" Steele asked. "I remembered a time you were very popular on this island. Wow, I remember you with that redhead who ended up being your sister-in-law."

Damian glared at him with undisguised venom. For a moment Steele thought he was going to get the reaction he had hoped for. "You bastard," Damian hissed.

401

"Come on, man, you want to fight?" Steele prompted. "Come on, hit me! At least I'd know you were still alive."

"What in the hell are you trying to do, Steele?"

"I'm trying to make you come alive, friend. Do you think Angelique would want you closing yourself off from your friends?"

"It's none of your business what I do, Steele!"

"That's where you're wrong, Damian. You and I have been friends for too long for me not to care what you do to yourself."

The expression on Damian's face changed. He turned his back to Tom, pouring them both another drink. "I appreciate your friendship more than I can ever tell you, but it's going to take me awhile to get over losing Angelique. Adam assures me that in time the pain will ease." Damian downed his drink. "I just hope he's right. Now go on and have a good time. I'm fine."

"All right, Damian. Maybe tomorrow night you'll feel like going ashore."

"Yeah, maybe tomorrow night," Damian murmured as Steele left his cabin.

Between June and October Damian made four successful runs, and one not so successful one. On October 13th the *Sorceress* was returning to Charleston from Bermuda, loaded with medical supplies and clothing. They swept swiftly past the blockading fleet and were almost to the sandbar when they were fired upon. Damian felt the adrenaline surge for the first time in a long while. He cracked out orders as the Federals let loose a broadside that hit the stern of the ship. The *Sorceress* was a sailing ship and had no means of increasing speed unless they caught the wind, but this night luck deserted them. The wind suddenly died. The *Sorceress* dug her bow into the bar and without the wind and strong tide, she quickly broached to. The Union ship was sending up rockets as it closed in on them for the kill. They were only a hundred yards from shore so Damian ordered his crew over the side in the longboats. Now only he and Tom Steele waited.

"You should have gone with them, Damian. They will hang you this time," Steele warned.

"A captain doesn't leave his ship until he has to. Besides, I haven't given up yet." Damian piled rags, trash and rope in a heap on the deck, then lit a match to the pile and stood back.

"Now let's see if our friends still want the ship."

A young lieutenant with five seaman boarded, brandishing guns. They were totally taken back when they found only two men aboard. "Where is your crew?" the officer asked angrily.

"They jumped ship when one of your shells set us on fire. I guess they preferred drowning to being blown sky-high."

"Blown sky-high? What are you talking about?"

"We're loaded with gunpowder," Damian answered.

The Union sailors panicked, making a mad rush

for their launch, as the lieutenant shouted orders for their ship to get ready to get out of there.

"Maybe lady luck hasn't deserted us," Damian commented as the wind picked up as suddenly as it had died. The grating sound of the hull sliding across the bar was like music to their ears. "We'd better get the fire out. I think we just might make it."

"Those blue devils are going to be mad as hell when they realized you lied," Steele laughed.

Steele was right. As soon as the Union officer realized he had been duped he opened fire on the *Sorceress* again. Shells whizzed overhead, bringing the masts crashing down around them.

"Come on, baby, you can make it," Damian whispered to his ship as she slowly moved into the harbor.

When they were in range of the fort, the Confederates opened fire on the Union ship, forcing it back to sea. The *Sorceress* limped into port, listing badly, but still afloat.

Tom Steele slapped Damian on the back. "You did it, Captain. You outfoxed those damned Yankees."

Damian smiled. "It felt good." Then he laughed out loud. "It felt damned good!"

Damian lost track of time while he was in Charleston. He had been staying with Adam and Lacey since October so he could oversee the work on his ship, but there had been many interruptions. The end of October saw a yellow fever epidemic, probably brought in by one of the blockade runners. Damian lost two friends, Able, the black man who had been like a father to him, and Philip Delacort, his neighbor. November brought the news of Sherman's march to Atlanta, and December brought even more devastating news that Savannah had fallen and Sherman was on his way to Charleston.

The morale of the Confederacy was at an all time low. The year had seen the dashing, heroic Jeb Stuart killed, the Confederates routed from Tennessee and now Atlanta and Savannah in the hands of the Yankees. Even though the people of Charleston hated to admit it, they knew it was the beginning of the end.

Damian spent most of his evening home with Adam and Lacey. He was happy they had found love together, yet there were times when he had to excuse himself, the pain was so intense when he saw them touch or look at each other with love shining in their eyes. On those occasions he would lie sleepless in his bed, remembering his beautiful wife, and how she had looked that last night they had lain in this bed and made love. He remembered touching her stomach and feeling the beginning of their child growing within her. Adam had said time would ease the pain, but he was wrong. If anything, he thought of her more with each passing day.

One evening in late January, Damian and Adam

were summoned to General Hardee's headquarters. They waited tensely in his office for nearly thirty minutes before he finally appeared.

"I'm sorry to keep you waiting, gentlemen, but I've been involved in meetings all day. Would you care for a drink?"

"To be honest, General, we'd really like to know why you asked us here," Damian admitted.

"Please, sit down, gentlemen," he said pouring each of them a drink before he sat at his desk. "I'm told the name Legare has been an honorable one for quite some time, but you two have certainly brought honor to it during this time of trial." The general raised his glass in toast and then took a long drink.

Damian and Adam looked at each other, both wondering if that was all he had to say when he spoke again.

"But that is not why I asked you here, gentlemen. General Beauregard informed us today that the city is to be evacuated. In another few weeks there won't be a chance of you sailing out of here. To be honest, I'm not sure what your chances are right now, but General Beauregard wanted me to advise you and your family to leave within the next few days. We don't expect the Union Army to show the people of Charleston any mercy, particularly the Legare family."

Damian let out a long breath. "I knew this was coming, but damn, it is hard to accept."

"The people of Charleston need never be ashamed of having to finally give in," the general continued.

"Their spirit and determination against such odds has been magnificent. In all of history there has never been a city that withstood a siege for so long, and still kept its spirit." Hardee stood and walked toward the windows behind his desk. "I just hope in years to come there will once again be a city of grace and charm on this same spot."

Hardee turned and faced the two silent men. He raised his glass again. "To Charleston, gentlemen. May she survive."

"To Charleston," they repeated.

Chapter Thirty

"What is going on?" Lacey asked as she walked into the room where Damian and Adam were talking. "First you have a secret meeting with some high-ranking general, and now you're cloistered in here."

Adam stood up and hugged his wife. "We're making plans, love. We're going to be leaving Charleston soon."

Lacey sank down into a chair. "Is Charleston . . . is Sherman . . ." She couldn't seem to get a complete sentence out.

Adam sat on the arm of her chair. "Charleston is to be evacuated soon. It is believed Sherman is on his way here."

"But what will happen to the men at the hospital?"

"They will be the first to be evacuated, starting tomorrow. Damian has agreed to wait until the next day to sail so we can be sure everything goes smoothly at the hospital."

"But I have to . . ."

Adam placed a finger on Lacey's lips. "Love, we can't wait any longer than that or we'll lose our chance while there's no moon."

Lacey looked at Damian. "What about Enchanteur?"

"I took care of everything I could months ago. There is nothing else I can do."

Tears ran down her cheeks. "Oh, God, what will we do? Where will we go, Adam?"

"We'll talk about that upstairs, love. Right now I think we should tell Damian our news."

The drink in Damian's hand splashed over the side, as he waited, knowing what their announcement would be.

"Lacey is with child, Damian. She is in her third month."

Damian swallowed hard. "That's wonderful," he managed to force out, but all he could think about was Angelique and his unborn child. A year ago they had sat in this very room making their own announcement.

Lacey moved to stand beside Damian. "I know this is hard for you, Damian. We dreaded telling you and bringing you more pain, but you would have guessed soon enough."

"I'm happy for you," Damian smiled. "Someone is going to have to carry on the Legare name. I think I'm going to turn in now. You and Adam must have a lot to talk about." Damian started to leave the room, but he turned back and hugged his brother. "I'm happy for you, Adam. I truly am."

Everyone who worked for Damian had been invited to go with him, if they wanted. At breakfast Bessie announced she wouldn't be going. Her place was at Enchanteur, she told them, and nothing Damian or Adam could say would change her mind. She wanted Tally and Burke to go with Damian, but she would stay behind.

"What about Patrice?" Lacey asked. "Beau invited her to visit him in Europe. Perhaps this would be a good time. She has been staying with the Wainwright sisters ever since Philip died, but I know she is anxious to be away from those two old ladies."

"By all means, invite her, but be sure to tell her what the dangers are."

"I will, Damian. I'm going to go write a message to her now," Lacey said, excited that another woman would be going with them.

"What about Kate?" Adam asked when he and Damian were alone. "You know she was the one who told us where you were."

"Yes, I know, and it seemed strange to me that she knew where I was being held."

"Since Philip died she seems to have changed," Adam continued. "She has even been helping Patrice financially."

"Saint Kate," Damian mumbled. "Ask her if you want, but keep her out of my sight."

Much to Adam's surprise, Kate turned down the

ffer to sail with them. He didn't know that she was becoming very rich with her spying and had been promised her pick of whatever land she wanted around Charleston when the Union Army took over. She wanted Enchanteur.

They waited hours in the dark for just the right moment to sail. Lacey, Patrice, and Tally huddled in the darkness, all silently praying for a safe trip, but also that the nerve-wracking waiting would hurry and come to an end.

Damian paced aimlessly, waiting for the wind, with Shadow following on his heels. The night was cold and brisk, and unfortunately very clear, but if they didn't sail tonight they would have to wait weeks before the moon was right.

Damian smiled to himself in the darkness. He remembered a time he had argued with Beau about the merits of sail against the steam engine. What he wouldn't give now to have *Moonlight Dancer*. They would have been on their way long ago. The last he had heard, the sleek ship had been sighted off the coast of Virginia, being used as a Union flagship.

"Do you think we'll get away tonight?" Adam asked from behind him.

"I'm counting on it," Damian answered.

"Damian, there is something I've been wanting to talk to you about."

Damian turned and faced his brother in the darkness. "Go on."

411

"Lacey and I are going to go on to Europe as soon as we can book passage from Bermuda."

"Why?" Damian asked. "I have a large house. There would be plenty of room."

"I know, Damian, and believe me, Lacey and I appreciate your offer, but it is time Lacey meets the duchess. This will be Mother's first grandchild. Maybe it will mellow her."

"I understand, Adam. Angelique said she thought it was time I made peace with Mother. She reminded me that she would be the only grandparent our child would have."

"Why don't you go with us to Europe?"

"No. Not yet. Maybe I'll join you there later. I need time to work things out, Adam."

Suddenly a grin replaced the look of tenseness on Damian's face. "Do you feel that?"

"What?" Adam asked.

"The wind, little brother. The wind is up."

The first line of blockading ships was spread close enough to shore, just out of the reach of the Confederate batteries. They moved silently past these shadowy hulks, and on toward the second line, passing the admiral's flagship close to hear voices and laughter coming from the ship. From here Damian slipped through a hole in the patrolling ships and headed out to sea.

Tom Steele stood beside him, peering into the inky blackness with eyes like a cat. "I think we are through the last of them," he whispered.

"I hope you're right. It sounded like those Yankees were celebrating something."

"Just so they aren't celebrating the recapture of Damian Legare," Tom laughed.

"How many times have we done this, Tom?"

"God, I don't know. At least twenty-five round trips, I'd have to guess. You know, it's strange, but I have mixed emotions about this being our last run."

"I feel the same way, Tom," Damian admitted. "Do you have any idea what you'll do now?"

"I've thought of little else since you told me Charleston was going to be evacuated. I'm sure that will be the end for the South, so since the Union has never identified me as one of your crew, I thought I'd make my way home to Baltimore and see what I can do to help convince the politicians to be fair to the Southern states."

Damian laughed. "I had forgotten your father was one of Lincoln's cabinet members. Let me see, if I remember, you also have a brother fighting for the Union . . ."

"Two brothers," Tom corrected.

"Right, two brothers. And your family thinks you are in Europe studying . . . what the hell were you studying?"

"Don't laugh now," Steele warned, "but I am supposed to be studying art."

"Art?" Damian repeated unbelievably. He stifled his laughter. "How are you going to explain those callused, leather tanned hands?"

"I don't know. I'll think of something. How about

you, Damian? What are you going to do?"

"I'm going to stay in Bermuda for awhile. I don't know for sure what I'll do, or if I'll do anything."

Tom Steele regarded Damian, thinking what a shame it was he had a price on his head. A man with his intelligence and ability to deal with people could be a great help to the South right now. Instead he was going to have to flee the home he loved—because he had chosen to help the South without assuming a false name.

Damian was also lost in thought, but his were more personal. He was wondering how he was going to live in the house he had bought as a wedding present for Angelique without going crazy.

With clear weather and stiff breezes, the *Sorceress* arrived safely off Saint George's harbor a few nights later. They anchored off shore until dawn so they wouldn't hang up on the murderous assortment of reefs that surrounded the island. Bright and early the next morning they moved into the harbor.

Lacey stood on the deck, a look of apprehension on her lovely face.

"What's wrong, honey?" Adam asked.

"Oh, Adam, I don't want to be an embarrassment to you," she said with tears in her eyes. "The people on the island will remember what I used to do, so I'm just going to stay aboard the ship."

Adam pulled her into his arms. "Love, you could never be an embarrassment to me. I know everything about you, and I have only respect and admiration for you."

"I'm so lucky to have you," Lacey said hugging her husband.

"I'm so lucky to have you, sweet, and I'm going to do everything in my power to make your life a little easier from now on. I know these last four years have been hell for you."

"It has been hell for everyone, Adam, and it was all for nothing."

"No, I wouldn't say that. The Southern people did what they had to do, love. If you asked Damian, I'm sure he'd tell you he'd do it all over again if he had too, and he has lost more than any of us."

"I never imagined it would look like this," Patrice said, joining them at the rail. "There must be a hundred ships in the harbor."

"It looks like Saint Georges has become a harbor of refuge for the blockaders who suddenly find they can't get into other ports. I imagine with the war so near an end, things will change quickly," Adam said.

Damian suggested the group stay at the hotel until he could get the house in order. He had been to the island three times since Angelique had disappeared, but each time he had avoided the house and its memories. The last time he had been in the house was to move the piano and other furnishings in to surprise Angelique for their wedding trip. But they had never made it back to the island together. Going to the empty house now was going to be one of the hardest things he had ever done.

Shadow whined as they walked up the palm tree lined drive. "Do you remember this place, boy? The last time you were here you played on that lawn right over there with Angelique." Damian stared out over the weed-grown lawn. "God, I remember it—and everything else about her."

Damian stared at the deserted pink house. The shrubbery needed trimming, but the house looked to be in pretty good shape, considering it had been deserted so often.

The stale, musty odor hit Damian as he opened the door. He stepped just inside and stared around the dark house. "I guess I should have had someone airing the house," he said to the dog." The first thing I'm going to do is open the shutters," he murmured, as he stepped back out into the bright sunshine. "You know, boy, I've never cleaned a house before, but I guess there is always a first time."

After opening all the lower shutters, Damian sat on the lawn with a cool drink of water from the well. He was engrossed in thoughts of what needed to be done to the house when Shadow started barking a greeting to Tally and Burke as they came up the drive loaded down with cleaning supplies.

"We thought you might need some help, sir," Burke said.

"You don't know how right you are," Damian laughed.

The house looked better once all the shutters were nailed back and the windows were opened. The sunlight streamed in across the white stucco walls and dark wood floors. The fragrance of ever-blooming flowers quickly chased the stale, musty odor from the interior.

Damian wandered through the rooms, uncovering pieces of furniture as he went. He ran his hand across the keys of the piano he had brought to the island from Europe for Angelique, but she had never had the chance to see it. Slowly he closed the cover over the keys and moved on to uncover another piece of furniture. Each piece brought more memories. This was to be their retreat—where they would come for holidays when the planting season was over at Enchanteur.

It was strange, he had dreaded coming back to this house, but somehow it made him feel closer to Angelique.

"Excuse me, sir," Tally interrupted his thoughts. "Mama packed linens and china on board de ship. Can I send Burke to fetch dem?"

"Yes, of course, Tally. Tell him to rent a wagon from Mr. Smithson and put it on my account. I want all of my things taken off the ship and brought here. Also tell him if Tom Steele is there, I'd like to see him as soon as possible."

In a few hours time the house was beginning to shine. Damian, his shirt sleeves rolled to his biceps, washed windows for the first time in his life. He smiled as the gray film disappeared, giving him a beautiful view of Saint George's Harbor. From the back windows he could see Tally hanging curtains on the line to catch the breeze. He wished she and Burke could stay with him, but he had already decided Lacey and Adam would need their help more. He would have to talk to them soon about going on to Europe.

From the balcony of his bedroom Damian could see the large white house that belonged to his nearest neighbor. Even from this distance he could tell the gardens and grounds were well kept. He remembered Bourne mentioning who lived there, but for the life of him, he couldn't remember now who it was. At the sound of wheels crunching on the shell drive, Damian headed back downstairs to help unload the wagon. He laughed when he saw Adam and Tom Steele sitting on top of the many crates that filled the wagon.

"Adam, I gave you more credit than to come here this afternoon," Damian laughed. "I guess you know Tally is going to put you to work."

"I had planned to come as soon as the ladies were settled," Adam explained, "but I realized I didn't know where your house was, so I had to go to the ship to find out from Tom. That's where I met Burke."

"Well, I'm glad you're here. I think we'll be ready for Lacey and Patrice by this evening."

Adam jumped down from his perch on the wagon. "That's what I wanted to talk to you about, Damian. There is an English man-of-war leaving in the morning for Liverpool. They will give us passage if we vant it."

"Tomorrow morning? I didn't think about you leaving that soon."

"I know, Damian, but the longer we wait the harder it will be on Lacey."

"Of course. I hadn't thought about that."

"Since we had planned to have dinner at the hotel tonight, I thought it made more sense for us just to stay there."

"Have you already booked passage?" Damian asked.

"No, I told the captain I'd be by later."

"Good, because you and I need to talk to Tally and Burke about going with you."

"To Europe?" Tally squealed excitedly before remembering her mama's instructions to take care of Damian. "But, sir, you need us."

"I need very little, Tally. I can get someone on the island to come clean and cook for me. Lacey is the one who will need your help; the choice is up to you and Burke."

"Is it the money, sir?" Burke asked. "Because if it is, Tally and I can work for other people too."

"Thank you, Burke. That means a great deal to me, but it isn't the money. I've done very well these past few years."

"Then we will go to Europe," Burke announced proudly.

Listening to the laughter and happy talk at dinner made Damian wonder if he was making a mistake

staying alone on the island. Even at Enchanteur h[e]
had Bessie or Tally with him. He had to stay, he tol[d]
himself. It didn't make any difference where he wa[s]
or who he was with. Angelique's memory would be
with him. This was his home now and he was going
to make the best of it. Maybe he would eventually go
back to Charleston. He just didn't know. He had
given the *Sorceress* to Tom Steele earlier that afternoon, so any traveling he did would be on someone's
else ship. He looked across the table at Adam and
Lacey. Adam had his arm around his wife, hanging
on every word she said. It made him ache inside for
the touch of Angelique's hand or a look from her
violet eyes telling him she wanted him as much as he
wanted her. All those years he had wasted, telling
himself he didn't need anyone, and now he was lost
without his wife. Life meant nothing to him without
her.

A bird chirping in the tree next to the balcony
caused Damian to stir. He listened to the other
sounds around him, and realized it was the first time
he had noticed them. It had been three days since
Adam and the others had left, and he had done little
other than sit in front of Angelique's portrait and
drink himself into a stupor.

As he swung his feet off the bed Shadow jumped
up from his spot on the floor. "Have I been feeding
you, boy? God, I can't remember," Damian said
rubbing his head. "I can't go on like this or I'm
going to go stark raving mad. All I remember is

hearing Angelique playing the piano all night."

Shadow tilted his head to the side, listening to everything Damian was saying. "Look at me. I'm still in the same clothes I had on three days ago." Damian stood up and stretched. "It's time I pulled myself together, isn't it boy? Today I'm going to see John Bourne and find out what is happening with the war, and then I'm going to hire us a housekeeper."

After shaving and washing, Damian dressed in denim pants and a white cotton shirt, and headed for the kitchen. He found the cupboards amply stocked with food. "Bless you, Tally and Burke," he said as he made a pot of coffee. While he waited for his coffee he fixed Shadow a bowl of salt pork. "There is one thing to say for being in the islands, boy. There won't be a shortage of food. All we have to do is find someone to cook it for us."

John Bourne didn't have any news of the war, but he did have a suggestion for a housekeeper.

"I understand you gave your ship to your first-mate," Bourne said.

"Yes, he wanted to return to Baltimore and try to help the South from there. Besides I finally have to admit the *Sorceress* was outdated."

"I'm not surprised you feel that way after that beauty you were running. What was her name?"

"*Moonlight Dancer*," Damian answered, remembering when Angelique named the ship.

"Yes, I like that. I think Tom Steele must have

renamed the *Sorceress* after a girlfriend."

"We both agreed he should change the name, but he never told me what he had changed it to," Damian said.

"Angelique," Bourne answered, unaware of the effect the name had on Damian. *Thank you, Tom*, Damian thought silently.

"Well, if I'm going to see about a housekeeper, I better get moving," Damian said anxious to leave. "By the way, who did you tell me was my neighbor in the big white house?"

"Simon Maclean," John answered. "Doctor Simon Maclean."

Chapter Thirty-one

The housekeeper Bourne had suggested was a middle-aged English lady who had been widowed a few months before. After talking with her, Damian was sure she would suit his needs. She would cook his meals and clean his house, but she would live at her own home not far from him.

After hiring the housekeeper Damian headed for the hotel to have a drink with some of the other blockade runners who found themselves out of work. As Damian entered the front door of the hotel, Shadow headed for the kitchen door, where the last couple of nights his nose had led him for a nice handout.

Damian listened to his friends discussing the war, but he remained silent. The main topic of conversation seemed to be whether or not the South would surrender.

"Our soldiers are starving, and most of them don't

even have shoes to wear. How can you expect them to continue fighting?" one officer asked. "Sherman has been pitiless with his devastation of the deep South, while Sheridan is destroying the Shenandoah Valley, the breadbasket of Lee's army. No sir, I don't see how they can go on."

"But we won at Manassas, Antietam, and Chancellorsville," another chimed in. "And we have the best soldiers and cavalry. How can you talk about surrender. We could still win this war."

For the first time Damian spoke. "You can't win war with memories of past victories, my friend, and you can't expect our men to continue fighting when they are starving. Lee's army is existing on parched corn. They are fighting on nothing but pride. They have forgotten the ideologies long ago raged upon by politicians, fanatics and the press. Now they are fighting as fighters, with individual reputations in the balance. Pride is keeping them moving and fighting. They believe their homeland injured, so personal self-respect is at stake. They will continue to fight with their last breath—until Lee tells them to stop. And gentlemen," Damian said as he stood up and threw a coin on the table, "that time is near."

The next few days passed slowly for Damian, even though he worked from sunup to sundown putting his home in order. He trimmed and transplanted shrubs, weeded flower gardens, and cut down trees that were blocking his view of the harbor.

He would have been fine if he didn't have to face the evenings. As soon as he drifted off at night he would be awakened by the sound of piano music. From then until dawn he would lie listening to the haunting melodies, convinced it was Angelique's spirit playing for him.

Standing at the piano one morning, Damian wondered if he was going crazy. Last night he was sure the music he heard had been the piece Angelique had played for him at Chateau Charbonne. "Are you here, Angelique?" he whispered, running a finger over the ivory keys.

"Good morning, sir. Are you ready for breakfast?" the housekeeper asked.

"Yes, thank you, Emily," Damian said following her into the kitchen. "Have you seen Shadow? He hasn't been around all night."

"No, sir, I haven't. He's usually here to greet me, wanting his breakfast first thing," she laughed.

"This is the second night he has disappeared," Damian mused.

"Perhaps he has a girl friend," Emily suggested.

"You're probably right," Damian agreed as he poured a cup of coffee. "I'm going to put a fresh coat of paint on the house today. I noticed yesterday that it is peeling in places."

"That will be lovely, sir. This poor house has been neglected for too long. Everyone on the island is already talking about how you are fixing the place up. Why just yesterday I heard two mothers talking about you being quite a catch for their daughters."

Damian looked up angrily. "I'd appreciate it if you would pass the word around that I am already married, Emily."

"I'm sorry, sir. I didn't know."

"My wife . . ." Damian couldn't say the words. "Just tell them I'm married," he said as he left the kitchen.

Taking a moment's break from painting the trim on the roof, Damian looked around. From the rooftop he could see a long way in both directions. Toward the harbor he could see the ships anchored, and to his left he could see his neighbor's estate. The large white house was impressive with its black wrought iron balconies. Damian started to resume his painting when he spotted Shadow. The dog was romping around his neighbor's yard, apparently entertaining a small child who played nearby.

"Well that rascal. I wonder what he thinks he's doing? I suppose this afternoon I'd better meet my neighbor and apologize for my dog taking over his yard."

Late that afternoon, after cleaning up and changing clothes, Damian walked down the beach and up the wide expanse of lawn toward the white house. He could see several people on the veranda and hoped they didn't mind him just walking in on them. A white-haired man sat at a chessboard across from a heavyset woman. Neither seemed to notice him until Shadow bounded toward him in greeting.

The man stood up and smiled. "Please excuse the intrusion," Damian apologized. "My name is Danian Legare. I live next door."

"Ah, Captain Legare, it's good to finally meet you. I've been meaning to come over and introduce myself," the man said offering his hand. "I'm Simon Maclean, and this is my friend and housekeeper, Caitlin McGregor."

" 'Tis nice to meet you, sir. Please come sit down. I hope ye dinna come to complain about the piano playing."

"The piano playing?" Damian asked puzzled.

"Caitlin, why don't you fix Captain Legare a tall drink," the doctor suggested.

"What did she mean about piano playing?" Damian asked as the housekeeper disappeared.

"My daughter doesn't sleep well at night and often plays the piano long into the night. Caitlin was afraid it might be disturbing you."

Damian didn't say anything. "Is something wrong, Captain?"

"No. No, nothing at all. As a matter of fact, I came here to apologize to you for my dog taking over your household."

"Oh, it's your dog. We wondered where he had come from. My grandson loves him. Ah, speaking of my grandson," Simon Maclean said, his face lighting up as Caitlin joined them holding a young child in her arms. "Captain Legare, meet Joshua."

The little boy let out a squeal and held his arms out for Damian to take him. "I hear you like my dog," Damian said as he studied the boy. The child had black hair and green eyes, a striking combination that held Damian's rapt attention. "He's a beautiful child," Damian said raising Joshua above his head.

"His mother is very beautiful," Caitlin said.

"Do you play chess, Captain?" the doctor asked.

"Please, call me Damian. Yes, I play, but it's been a very long time since I have."

"It doesn't matter how rusty you are," Simon laughed. "Just having someone new to play with will be a challenge. Can you stay and have a game now," Simon asked.

"I would enjoy that," Damian answered.

"Come, lad," Caitlin said taking the child from Damian. "I baked some cookies while you were napping."

"Bye," Joshua waved, his green eyes sparkling.

"Bye, Joshua," Damian smiled. "I'll see you later."

Reaching into his jacket, Damian withdrew a long, black cheroot and slowly lit it. He lay back on the sand, studying the stars overhead. His evening with Simon Maclean had been enjoyable. Caitlin and her husband Andrew had joined them on the veranda after the chess game, and he had enjoyed listening to their light-hearted banter. When Andrew started telling jokes he had heard at one of the local bars, Caitlin scolded him for his lack of manners in front of company. They had all had a good laugh at that.

Damian thought of the boy, Joshua. What a delight the child was. "I can see why you spend so much time there, boy," Damian said scratching the dog between the ears. Suddenly the sound of music drifted down from the house. It's strange, Damian thought. I should be relieved to know it was Maclean's daughter who played every night, but somehow he felt cheated. He wanted it to be Angelique's spirit. "You really are crazy, Legare," he said aloud. "Come on, Shadow. Let's go see what Emily left us to eat."

Damian found himself spending a good deal of time on his bedroom balcony where he could observe Joshua with Caitlin. He wondered briefly if there was something wrong with the boy's mother. He hadn't seen any sign of her. She certainly didn't seem to spend much time with the child. At least the child had his grandfather, Damian thought.

Shadow continued his disappearing act every day, but Damian stopped worrying about him. Damian couldn't blame the dog for wanting to be around the child. He often found himself thinking about the green eyed boy.

Damian offered to help John Bourne inventory the warehouses that were still stocked with supplies for the Confederate army. Only one ship had gotten through the blockade in the past two weeks and her captain had reported that he wasn't going to try it

again. Many of the blockade runners who were in it
for the money had already left the island. Others
stayed to spend their hard earned money gambling
and on whores. The war had brought a lot of money
to the island, but it had brought a lot of undesirables
with it.

Damian had many invitations from families on the
island, but he refused them all. He was ending up in
a prison of self-created loneliness, but he had no
desire to do anything about it. He occasionally had
dinner with John Bourne after they worked, and he
had played chess with Simon Maclean one rainy
afternoon, but other than that he chose to be alone.
It wasn't until Caitlin McGregor insisted he come to
dinner one Sunday afternoon that all this changed.

Damian stood looking out the window of Simon
Maclean's living room while the doctor poured them
a drink. In the distance he could see a woman
coming from the beach carrying a baby. "Is that
Joshua's mother?" he asked.

Simon looked in the direction Damian was staring.
"Ah, yes that is Chantel. She doesn't socialize much,
but I believe she will be joining us for dinner this
evening."

Damian continued to watch as the woman came
closer. The hair began to bristle on his neck and the
drink in his hand spilled over the side. "Angel . . .

430

Oh God, Angel."

Simon Maclean looked at Damian strangely, then looked back toward Joshua and his mother. "Ah, yes she does look like an angel doesn't she?"

"No, no you don't understand. That is my wife, Angel," Damian said as he sat his drink down and started for the door.

"No! Wait!" The panic in Simon Maclean's voice stopped him in his tracks. He turned and stared at the doctor. "We have to talk first," Simon demanded.

"How can you expect me to talk when my wife is here. For almost two years I thought she was dead."

"She might as well have been," Simon said.

Damian moved back toward the doctor. "What in the hell are you talking about?"

"Let me just tell you this before Chantel and Joshua get here. If you blurt out you are her husband, you could lose her for good. I have been treating Chantel for shock, and she is still walking a very fine line. I beg you, do as I say now, and I will explain everything."

Damian didn't know if he could contain himself, but as he heard Joshua's voice he turned and faced the doorway. Angelique appeared, wearing a white caftan that flowed loosely around her bare feet. One side of her long black hair was held back with a vivid orange hibiscus, while the other side hung across her right cheek. She showed no sign of recognizing him.

Simon's voice was shaky as he introduced Damian to Chantel. Damian couldn't help but notice the fear in the man's eyes. He seemed to grow old right before his eyes. Damian stared at him for a moment, then turned and offered his hand to Chantel.

Angelique had the look of a frightened doe, and Damian, torn with the desire to take her in his arms, knew what Simon had said must be true. "It's very nice to meet you, Chantel. I've enjoyed visiting with Joshua." As Damian said the boy's name he realized Joshua was his son. It hit him like a ton of bricks. He stared at the child, now seeing his own green eyes and Angelique's black hair. "Joshua," he said holding his arms out to the child. "May I hold him?"

Chantel still hadn't spoken, but she smiled at Damian as she let him take Joshua from her arms.

"You are a fine boy, Joshua," Damian smiled at the child. "One of these days you will have to go sailing with me."

"No!" Chantel screamed, grabbing her son back.

Damian touched her hand. "It's all right, Ange . . . Chantel. If you don't want him to go sailing, that's fine."

Angelique hugged the child to her breast, turning away from Damian and Simon. "He is too young," she said, tears glistening in her violet eyes.

"Yes, he is too young," Damian agreed, smiling at her and the boy. "Perhaps I could just come here and visit with you and Joshua."

"Damian," Simon's voice had a warning note to it, but Angelique was smiling at Damian and he was oblivious to everything and everyone.

"Yes, that would be nice," Angelique said.

"Chantel, why don't you let Caitlin put Joshua

432

down for a nap now. You must get ready for dinner since we have a guest tonight."

"Yes, I will," she said. "It is nice to have you here," she smiled at Damian.

When Angelique left the room, Damian sank into a chair, his head in his hands.

"I'm sorry, Damian. I appreciate your not saying anything."

"My God, do you think I'd do anything to harm Angelique? She is my wife and I love her."

"I know this has been a shock to you."

"That's an understatement, Simon. In the last five minutes I found my wife and son living right next door to me." Damian shook his head, still unable to believe what was happening. "Somehow I knew she was alive, but I never imagined . . ." Damian looked up at the man who had become his friend. "You told me she was your daughter . . ."

"Yes, there is much I have to explain," Simon said, sitting across from Damian. "First, let me explain her condition. She has amnesia brought on by shock. *She doesn't want to remember!* That is why I warned you not to try to make her remember you. When I found her she was on a Cuban fishing boat, in a cabin with two dead men."

Damian closed his eyes for a long moment, then took a deep breath as Simon continued. "I had thought the American with her was her husband. His name was Joshua Maxwell."

"Joshua was my first-mate," Damian explained. "You said he was dead?"

"Yes. As far as Andrew and I could figure, the Cuban had fought Maxwell. I don't know what the fight was over, but the American must have put up a valiant effort. The poor man was sliced to ribbons before he finally took a blade between his shoulders." Simon shook his head, remembering the sight. "The cabin was covered with blood. It was an incredible sight, one no man should have to witness, much less a pregnant woman. As I said, I thought Chantel had witnessed her husband's death, and then had killed the Cuban. But the Cubans were ready to hang her. Andrew slipped her aboard my ship when they were going for the authorities."

"Angelique killed him?" Damian asked incredulously.

"It had to have been her. The Cuban was stabbed in the back. When I found Chantel she was huddled in a corner mumbling the French word *diable*, and for almost a year we couldn't get her to say anything else."

The two men were silent for a few moments. "Damian, I don't know what happened on that fishing boat, but it had to have been bad for Chantel to just withdraw from life like she did. Perhaps the American caught the Cuban raping her. I just don't know, and I'm not sure we'll ever know."

"Angelique lost her mother and father to a terrorist in Paris several years ago. A terrorist who just happened to be her fiancé. It was a terrible time for her. When it all happened she even thought her brother had died with her parents, but he showed up n time to stop her wedding to the maniac. It wasn't ong after that, that we were married. Being a block- de runner, I had to leave Angelique in Charleston where she was caught right smack in the middle of the war. She even worked at the hospital, dealing with horror every day. Then a year ago I was captured and sent to a Union prison. Angelique's brother, my brother and Angelique rescued me. Everything would probably have gone all right, but then we were caught in a storm and the ship broke apart. That's when we were separated."

"My God, it's no wonder she is trying to forget what has happened to her. Most people don't have to handle that much stress their whole lifetime. Chantel had it all in one short period."

"If I could change things for her I would," Damian said agonizing over what had happened to his wife. "All I can do is try to make things better for her now."

Simon Maclean didn't say anything as he paced the room.

"Why do you call her Chantel?" Damian asked.

"It was Caitlin's idea. As I said, the only word she would say was, *diable*, and since that was French, Caitlin surmised she must be from France and should have a French name."

"Caitlin wasn't far from right. Angelique is from Brittany. Her name is Charbonne."

"We named our son Joshua, because we thought the American was his father. Andrew found identification on him, but we found nothing on Chantel."

435

"I'm proud to have my son named for him. Joshua gave his life trying to protect Angelique, and just before the shipwreck, he had saved my own life."

"So, now you see why you must not try to jar her memory. It would be better if you never saw her again."

Damian stared at Simon, not believing what he was hearing. It was as if Simon Maclean hadn't heard a thing he had said. "You're out of your mind if you think I'm just going to walk away from here. I've found my wife after years of searching, and I'm not about to walk away. If I have to go along with this new identity, then I will, but you better damn well be prepared for me eventually taking my family home."

"You're going to send her over the edge, you fool!" Simon shouted.

Caitlin appeared in the doorway, alarmed by the shouting that was coming from the room. "Sir, what is wrong?"

"You better come in here, Caitlin. This is going to concern everyone here." Caitlin moved into the room, looking from one to the other. "Captain Legare is Chantel's husband," Simon blurted out.

Caitlin's hand went to her mouth. "Holy Mother of God, 'tis a miracle," she gasped.

"It's no such thing," Simon said angrily. "You've seen what Chantel has been through. Do you want her to go back to the way she was?"

"No, sir, but if he's her husband . . ."

"Chantel didn't recognize him. He's a stranger to

her."

Caitlin looked at Damian, sympathy in her eyes. "I'm sorry Damian. She is just a bairn."

"A bairn?" Damian repeated.

"Yes, Captain," Simon interrupted. "Caitlin is telling you that Chantel is a child. She has no meaning of the word wife. In the two years she has been with us she has never questioned who Joshua's father was or where he was. She lives in her own safe world, and I will not allow you to change that."

"You're going to have one hell of a time keeping me away from here, Maclean. I'll abide by your request not to tell Angelique who she is, but now that I've found her and Joshua I'm going to be here day and night. Whether it's Angelique or Chantel, I'm going to win her back."

Caitlin looked at Simon, waiting for him to agree, but instead he slammed his glass down on the table and left the room with a snort.

"Be patient, Damian. He is a good man. This has just been a shock to him. He loves Chantel and Joshua, and now he is afraid of losing them."

Damian began pacing. "Am I doing the right thing, Caitlin?" He turned around and faced her. "Forget you are Doctor Maclean's friend. Tell me honestly, if you think I will harm Angelique by staying."

"Only God knows that, lad. But I will say this, there is the child to consider. It is one thing to give up your wife because she is ill, but the child is a healthy one. It won't be long before he will have the need of a father."

"Thank you, Caitlin. You've given me the answer I needed. Come hell or high water, Simon Maclean is going to find me on his doorstep every day until Angelique is ready to come home with me. I want my son more than I can tell you, but I want his mother just as much." Damian smiled at the housekeeper. "Now, if you don't mind, will you remind Doctor Maclean that I was invited to dinner."

"Good for you, boy," Caitlin said as she headed for the door. "Stick to your guns, now," she whispered, as she slipped out.

Chapter Thirty-two

Simon Maclean hovered over Angelique like a mother hen, hardly giving Damian a chance to talk with her. Shortly after the meal was over she excused herself, leaving Damian alone with the doctor.

"Do you see what I mean?" Simon asked. "Chantel is not the woman you were married to. Give up this foolish idea of having her back."

Damian was confused by the whole situation, but he wasn't about to give up. "I'm sorry, Simon, but it involves a whole lot more than just having Angelique back. It involves *my* son." Damian set his glass of wine on the table and got up to leave. "Simon, I'd really appreciate it if you wouldn't stand in my way. This is going to be hard enough without having to fight you every step of the way."

"Chantel is like a daughter to me. I won't stand by and see you hurt her."

Damian was losing his patience. "Why in hell do

you think I'm going to hurt her? I love the woman, and I want a chance to love the boy."

"If you love her you will leave the island. Let her live in peace."

"Let her live in peace with you?" Damian stared at the doctor for a long moment. "Are you in love with her, Simon. Is that what this is all about?"

The man's face turned beet red. "Don't be a fool, man. I told you she is like my daughter."

"I know what you told me. But I think I'm beginning to see the light—and I warn you, Simon Maclean, if I find out that you've touched my wife I swear I'll kill you."

"You're a bigger fool than I thought. Get out of my house and don't come back."

"I'll be back in the morning, Simon. If you don't want to see Angelique hurt then don't try to stop me from seeing her."

Damian sat alone on his balcony staring toward the big, white house. A sad haunting melody drifted on the air, making him feel more alone than ever. He should be happy, he told himself. He had found his wife and son. But had he really found Angelique, he wondered. His wife was warm and loving. This woman in Angelique's body was a stranger to him. A cold and distant stranger.

Shadow nudged Damian's leg wanting attention. "So it wasn't just the child, boy," he said patting the big dog. "Why didn't you tell me you had found

Angelique? No matter. Let's just hope we have Angelique and Joshua home before long." Damian's attention went back to the house. The piano playing had stopped and there was only one room on the upper floor with a lamp lit. That must be her room, he thought. God, how he would like to have her in his arms tonight.

"Angel, Angel, now that I've found you will I ever be able to make you mine again?"

In the morning when Damian arrived at the Maclean house he was met by Caitlin, a sheepish look upon her broad face.

"I'm sorry as can be, sir, but the doctor took Chantel with him to the clinic. She often helps out there, you know."

"No, I didn't know," he said angrily. "Damn the man! He knew I was coming to see Angelique this morning. Where is his clinic?" he demanded.

"Oh no, sir, you don't want to be going there. I agree, it wasn't fair of him to take her this morning, but don't be losing your temper and hurting poor Chantel. She has no idea what is going on. They will be coming home in an hour for the mid-day meal. Wait here and then you can see her. If you like you can play with Joshua until then."

Damian stared at the housekeeper for a moment and then began to laugh. "I like having you on my side, Caitlin. Thank you."

"Now, sir, it's not sides we're on. I just know

Chantel should be with her husband. If you are given half a chance you may be able to bring her around."

"That's all I'm asking, Caitlin. I wouldn't hurt her for the world, but I can't seem to make Simon believe that. He tells me he thinks of her as a daughter, but I think it's more than that." Caitlin didn't say anything. "Is Simon in love with her, Caitlin?"

"Aye. He loves her, but it is different from the love you have for her. The doctor lost his own wife to the fever a few years ago and he was a very lonesome man. Then when Chantel came into his life it was as if he was able to roll back the years. He seemed young and energetic again—someone needed him. And believe me, young man, Chantel did need him. I never saw a poorer sight in all my life. She was like a wounded animal, afraid of everything and everyone. It has just been in the last five or six months that she has been as she is now."

"You said she doesn't sleep well at night. Do you know why?"

"Aye, it is dreams. She is afraid to go to sleep at night because of them. She doesn't seem to have them when she sleeps during the day."

"And it's been like that since Simon found her?"

"Aye. Have you heard her playing the piano at night? She plays beautifully."

"Yes I know. There was a time her teacher wanted her to travel giving concerts all over Europe, but her father wouldn't allow it."

"She seems to have many talents. Several times

hen Simon has been away she took care of his atients. She works as efficiently as the doctor."

"Yes, Caitlin, my wife is an unusual woman, and omehow I've got to make her part of my life again."

Damian was on the floor playing with Joshua when Simon and Angelique came in. He didn't miss the look Simon gave him when Angelique joined them on the floor. She leaned her back against the chair watching them play.

"You like children, Captain Legare?"

"Yes, I like children very much, and remember the name is Damian."

"Damian," she smiled. "Caitlin says Joshua should be taking some steps by now, but he is still crawling."

"All right, Joshua, let's see what you can do." Damian stood the child up, holding him under the armpits. "Ange . . . Chantel, hold your hands out to him."

Joshua bounced up and down on his chubby little legs, thinking this was a wonderful new game. "Mama," he said.

"That's right, Joshua. You're going to walk to Mama. Tell him to come to you, Mama."

"Walk to me, Joshua," Angelique encouraged, holding her hands out to her son.

Caitlin laughed as she watched him trying to get the baby to move his feet. "He is lazy. He would much rather be carried around."

Simon pretended to be reading a paper, but he was watching, feeling a twinge of jealousy as Chantel laughed at something Damian said.

"Now, Joshua I'm going to let you go. Walk to Mama."

Joshua took one step then swayed back and forth. "Easy, Joshua. Go to Mama." Damian knelt right behind the child, ready to catch him if he fell. Joshua took one more step, then another, delighted with all the attention he was getting. Another step and he was in his mother's arms.

"Oh, that is wonderful," Angelique exclaimed. "Thank you, Damian. You are a very good teacher."

"That is nice that you got to see Joshua take his first step," Caitlin said, with tears in her eyes. "He is growing so fast."

"Are you going to fix me something to eat, Caitlin?" Simon growled. "I don't have all day." After Caitlin hurried from the room Simon turned on Damian. "I suppose I'm feeding you again, Captain."

"No, Simon, I wouldn't think of imposing on your hospitality. As a matter of fact, I came to take Ange . . . Chantel and Joshua down to my place. My housekeeper has prepared a picnic for us."

"No! It is out of the question."

"Simon, I would like to go," Angelique said, not understanding the anger in his voice.

"I need you to go back to the clinic with me."

"But, we only had three patients all morning."

"I don't like you going away like this, Chantel."

"I will have them back in a few hours," Damian said picking the child up, determined to leave before Simon convinced Angelique not to go. "Do you need to take anything special for Joshua?" he asked.

"Yes, let me take him now. We'll be just a few minutes." She looked back at Simon. "We will be fine, Simon. I'll see you when you return from the clinic."

"I'll not tolerate this, Legare," Simon said when they were alone. "If you think you can come in here and start ordering Chantel around . . ."

"It seemed to me you were the one ordering her around. All I did was invite her to have a picnic with me. Why don't you just back off a little, Simon. I don't want to fight with you. All I'm asking is that you give me a chance to win my wife back."

"How do I even know she is your wife. You could be telling me that story just to get at Chantel."

"For God's sake, Simon, you're acting like a jealous fool. You know she's my wife. Do you think you can keep her closed away from the world for the rest of her life."

"Seeing the house could bring back memories. I'm warning you . . ." Simon started, but cut his words off as Angelique came back into the room.

"Are you ready?" Damian asked, taking Joshua from her arms.

"Yes, we're ready," she answered, looking from one to the other men. "Were you arguing?"

Simon turned his back to her, leaving Damian to

explain. "No, we were just discussing a chess game."

"The house isn't as big as Simon's, but I think it's nice," Damian said as he guided her through the rooms. He closely watched her face to see if there was any glimmer of recognition, but she didn't even say anything about the portrait . . .

"It is a beautiful house, Damian. I particularly like the room with the piano."

"Yes, I thought you would like that room. Perhaps you would play for me a little later."

"Perhaps," she smiled.

"I thought we'd picnic on the lawn. That way Joshua and Shadow can play."

"You have thought of everything, Damian."

Not quite, he thought, I haven't figured out how to bring you back to me. "Come along, Joshua, my lad. I do hope you can handle a chicken leg or two."

"Oh, Damian," Angelique laughed, "you haven't thought of everything after all. Joshua can't eat a chicken leg."

"Nonsense. I'll pick the meat off it for him."

Emily had spread a cloth and set out a picnic basket for them, filled to the brim with chicken, cheese, fruit, and a bottle of wine.

"It looks like Emily thought of everything," Damian said pleased.

"Emily is your housekeeper?"

"Yes. She's only been with me a couple of weeks,

out she is wonderful."

"I thought I heard Caitlin say you were married."

Damian hesitated. "I lost my wife."

Angelique studied her hands. "I too lost someone."

Damian held his breath. "Do you want to talk about it?"

"It was Joshua's father, but I don't really remember anything about it. I think he was killed in the war. You know, America's war."

"Yes, I know the war. Did he fight for the South or the North?"

Angelique looked toward the ships in the harbor. "Please don't think I'm crazy, Damian, but I don't know. Simon says I am blocking out what I don't want to remember."

"What about the things you do want to remember?"

Angelique looked at him, her violet eyes filled with tears. "I remember nothing, Damian."

Damian was ready to pursue the subject, but Joshua took that moment to pull himself up on his leg. "Well, what do we have here? Are you wanting to play, my little friend?" Damian laid flat and lifted Joshua above his head. The child squealed excitedly, bringing Shadow bouncing into the act. Angelique laughed, scurrying to get away from the three of them, but Damian grabbed her by the wrist and pulled her into the fracas.

"No, no," she laughed as Shadow licked her all over the face. "Please, Damian," she gasped, but instead of helping her Damian began to tickle her until she couldn't catch her breath.

Joshua, anxious to have Damian's attention back, grabbed a handful of his hair. "Eee-ouch," Damian screamed as Joshua gave a yank.

Angelique took the opportunity to escape. She stood at Damian's feet, holding her sides as she bent over laughing. "Thank you, son. You saved your mother."

Moments later Joshua crawled across the lawn to play with Shadow, leaving Damian and Angelique alone. "It is so strange," Angelique said, as she sipped a glass of wine. "I feel as if I've known you all my life. I can't believe we're carrying on like this and it's the first time we've been together."

"Perhaps we knew each other in another life."

"I guess that's one explanation."

Damian wanted to tell her, but he didn't dare, remembering what Simon had said. "Do you want to eat yet?"

"No, not yet. Tell me a little about yourself, Damian? Where are you from?"

"I'm from Charleston, South Carolina," he answered, watching her face. "Have you ever been there?"

"Charleston, South Carolina. No, I don't think so. That is where most of the blockade runners go, isn't it?"

"Yes," he answered hopefully. "How did you know that."

"Simon treats a lot of them, and I remember hearing them talk about Charleston. What made you come to Bermuda?"

Damian leaned back, resting on his elbow. "The beautiful lady that I lost, she found this house and loved it, so I bought it for her. Now I live in it alone, praying that she comes back to me."

"Oh, Damian, that is so sad. What happened to her?"

"The war took her away from me."

Joshua tugged Damian's pants leg. "See," he said, pointing to Shadow. "See," he repeated. Damian leaned up and swept Joshua into his arms.

"That's a dog. Say dog," Damian encouraged. Joshua hooked a finger in the side of Damian's mouth. "Dog," he repeated in barely understandable gibberish.

"Listen to him," Damian said astounded. "Did you hear him say dog? This is the smartest child I have ever seen."

Angelique laughed. "Mama and Cat, for Caitlin, are the only things he has said before now."

Damian smiled, thinking of something he would teach the boy when they were alone. For now he concentrated on other words. "Say Shadow. That's Shadow," he said pointing to the dog.

"Dog," Joshua said.

Damian laughed. "You're right, Joshua, that is a dog. I'm expecting too much."

Joshua laid his dark head on Damian's chest and closed his eyes. "He likes you very much, Damian. I am glad we have you nearby."

"I'm glad too, Angel."

"Angel?" she said puzzled.

"I hope you don't mind my calling you that. It's just an affectionate term."

"Angel," she repeated. "I like it. Here, let me lay Joshua down on the blanket and then we can eat. I am suddenly famished."

Looking at her thin frame Damian was glad to hear that. She had lost a lot of weight, but he knew how quickly it could be put back on from his experience in prison.

"First some chicken," he said offering her a piece. "Here, let me break you off a piece of bread. Emily bakes great bread. If we're lucky she put some of her cookies in too."

After eating, Angelique kicked her shoes off and leaned back on her elbows next to Damian. "This has been so pleasant. I haven't done anything like this in so long."

"When was the last time."

"I don't remember, but I enjoy it so much, I know I must have done it before."

"We'll do it every day if you'd like." At her surprised look, Damian added, "It's good for Joshua to be out here like this."

Angelique studied her son lying beside them. "Yes, I know it is. I don't usually spend any time with him during the day."

"Why is that, Angel?"

"I don't sleep very well at night. Most days I have to lie down in the afternoon because that is the only time I seem to sleep well."

"You seem fine this afternoon."

"I am tired, but I'm enjoying myself too much to go home."

Damian cringed at her words. Why couldn't he tell her this was her home. This was where she belonged. If she stayed with him he'd hold her during the night and never let her have another bad dream.

"Lie back and close your eyes. Rest here and I'll watch over you."

Angelique did as he suggested. In just a few minutes her breathing was soft and even as she slept beside his son. His son—Damian touched a lock of the child's black hair. What a fine boy he was. He looked very much like his mother, but he definitely had the Legare green eyes. He felt happier than he had in a long time with them lying beside him. But it wasn't perfect yet. Not until she stayed with him. Not until they were a family.

He turned on his side and watched them sleep. Maybe he should let Beau know she was alive, he thought. No, it would be better to wait until things were normal again. He studied his wife's face. The scar that Angelique tried to hide with her hair stood out vividly in the sunlight. God, what she must have been through, he thought in anguish. Angel, Angel, if only I had been able to protect you.

He turned on his back, putting his hands under his head as he stared up at the sky. "Lord, I know I've never prayed before, but I hope you'll listen to me now. Let her get well. Let her love me again so we can be a family."

* * *

Joshua woke first. He was delighted to find Damian at his side ready and willing to play. Eager to talk to his new friend, he released a whole tirade of chatter.

"I didn't understand a word you said, boy. Come here," he said picking the child up and sitting him on his stomach. "Let's try a new word." He glanced sideways to make sure Angelique was still asleep. "Say daddy."

Joshua giggled and pointed to Shadow sleeping a few feet away. "No, that's a dog. Say daddy," Damian repeated patiently. "Daddy."

"Dada," Joshua squealed. "Dada, dada, dada."

Damian laughed. "Shh, don't get carried away, son. We don't want to wake your mother up."

They had gotten a late start on the day, and now the sun was setting like a ball of red fire over the sea. Angelique opened her eyes and stretched.

"How long did I sleep."

"An hour and a half, maybe two," Damian said.

"Has Joshua been awake long," she asked as she straightened her skirt.

"No, not too long. He just finished eating some chicken and bread."

Angelique giggled. "You didn't give him a leg?"

"No. Together we picked it off the bone."

"Oh, he must have loved that. Here, let me see you, Joshua. My heavens, you don't have it all over you. How did you ever keep him so clean," she asked Damian.

Damian laughed and showed her his shirttail where he had been wiping Joshua's mouth. "Oh, you must let me take that home and have Caitlin wash it for you."

"No, that isn't necessary. Emily will do that. How about another glass of wine. We still have plenty left."

"Yes, that would be nice. I am thirsty."

Their pleasant afternoon was suddenly interrupted by Simon's booming voice. "Where are you, Chantel?"

"I guess it is later than I thought," Angelique said. "We must go now."

Damian stood up and offered her a hand, pulling her to her feet.

"Tomorrow? Remember, it is good for Joshua."

"Yes, until tomorrow," she smiled.

Her smile disappeared as Simon found them, his temper in a fury. "I should have known better than to trust you, Legare. You're a lying low-life . . ."

"Simon," Angelique reprimanded. "You have no reason to talk to Damian like that."

"You have been with this man for four hours . . ."

"I didn't know I had a time limit. Besides, I fell asleep and Damian has been playing with Joshua. We just lost track of time."

"I don't care. I don't want you around any more, Legare. Just stay out of our life."

Damian turned his back to Simon. "Until tomorrow, Angel."

"Yes, I shall look forward to it."

Damian turned his attention to the bundle of energy in Angelique's arms. "Bye, Joshua."

"Bye," Joshua squealed, holding his arms out to Damian. "Bye, dada."

"No, no, Joshua," Angelique laughed embarrassed.

"You bastard!" Simon swore. "I warned you," he said moving toward Damian.

"My God, Simon what is wrong with you?" Angelique asked, her eyes wide with shock.

Ignoring her, Simon shoved Damian. "Don't do anything foolish, Maclean. I'm not going to fight a man your age."

"My age! Why you young whelp, I can whip you with one hand tied behind my back." Simon swung at Damian, but missed as Damian side-stopped his fist.

"Go home, Simon. I'm not going to fight you."

"You're not to see her again. Do you understand me, Legare?"

"Don't threaten me, Simon. The courts would be on my side and you know it."

Simon fell silent as Damian turned to Angelique. "I'm sorry, Angel. Don't be afraid. Everything will be all right. You go on with Simon and I'll see you tomorrow."

Angelique looked back over her shoulder as Simon led her away. The look of bewilderment on her face pulled at his heart. Maybe he was moving too fast. But, damnit, he had to, he told himself. Simon Maclean was going to do everything in his power to keep them apart. For all he knew the man was lying to him about it being dangerous for Angelique to remember her past.

Angelique sat patiently listening to Simon's lecture about the evil Damian Legare. She couldn't understand why he was so adamant about her seeing Damian. He seemed like such a nice man.

"Simon, I'm a woman. I've been married and I have a child. What is wrong with my enjoying Damian's company? I like him."

Caitlin listened, shaking her head as Simon continued his tirade.

"I never thought you'd be ungrateful for the things I've done for you," Simon said.

"Ungrateful? How can you say that?"

"I've given you and Joshua the clothes you wear, the food you eat, and a roof over your heads. All I ask in return is that you abide by my decision for you not to see Damian Legare again."

Tears came to Angelique's eyes. "Are you asking me to live here as your ward for the rest of my life. Do I just close myself and Joshua off from the rest of the world. Is that what you're asking, Simon?"

"Damnit, you were happy here until Legare showed up."

"I have been happy here, Simon. You've been good to Joshua and me, but that doesn't mean I don't ever want to have a life of my own again. I want to remember who I am and what Joshua's

father was like. I may even want to remarry som
day."

"If it's marriage you want, I'll marry you. I ca
make you happy."

Caitlin had sat quietly as long as she could. "Simon, don't be foolish. You're old enough to be
Chantel's father. Besides, aren't you forgetting something very important?"

"Just stay out of this, Caitlin. Chantel, I'm supposed to go to Cuba in a couple of weeks. Go with
me and we'll be married there. It's a beautiful place.
If you like it—we could even live there."

Angelique was developing a terrible headache. "I
don't love you, Simon. Not the way you want me to."

"You can learn, Chantel. I'm a rich man. I'll
provide for Joshua. I'll see that he goes to the best
schools in Europe."

"Please stop!" Angelique screamed. "Please no
more tonight. I can't think straight."

"Leave the bairn alone now, Simon Maclean. It
isn't good to upset her and you very well know it."
Caitlin led Angelique to the door.

"Wait. Chantel, I have to leave very early in the
morning to go to the other end of the island to give
inoculations. I won't be back until the next day. I
want your promise that you won't see Damian Legare
while I'm gone."

Angelique looked defeated. "I won't go out of my
way to see him, Simon. That is all I will promise."

"All right. But will you also think about what I've
said. You and Joshua would have a good life."

"Yes, I'll think about it."

"What am I going to do, Caitlin. I don't want to marry Simon. I love him like a father."

"I know, child. Don't you worry about a thing. Caitlin will take care of everything," she said slipping a soft cotton nightgown over Angelique's head. "Simon is just afraid of losing you and the boy. It's the only way he can think of to keep you."

"I don't understand why he doesn't like Damian. I thought they were friends. Didn't they used to play chess together?"

"Aye, but that was before Damian took an interest in you."

"He is a nice man, Caitlin. I really like him."

"I know, Chantel, I like him too. He seems like a fine lad."

Angelique sat on the bed, her legs crossed under her in little girl fashion. "Simon says he is a womanizer, but he isn't. I spent the whole day with him and he never touched me. He was wonderful. He loves Joshua, Caitlin, and he is so good with him. Do you know Joshua called him dada when we were leaving."

"He sounds like a man who respects you. Come now, why don't you get in bed and try to sleep a bit."

"No. I can't sleep now. Please, stay and talk with me, Caitlin. Tell me what I should do. I don't want to hurt Simon."

Caitlin stirred her tea, clicking the spoon against the cup over and over until her husband, Andrew, finally looked up. "Caitlin, what is bothering you?"

"It's Simon. I think he has gone daft. He is pretending Damian Legare doesn't exist. He has forbidden Angelique to see him, and now the poor man is even talking about marrying Chantel himself. How can he marry her when she has a husband?" Caitlin clucked her tongue. "I don't know what is the matter with him, Andrew, but we have to help him before he loses Chantel and the child."

"You mean help him to marry Chantel?" Andrew asked, disbelieving.

"Heavens no. I mean get Chantel back with her husband. At least that way Simon would have them living right next door. Joshua thinks of Simon as his grandfather and that is the way it should be. Can you imagine that old fool wanting Chantel to marry him."

"Caitlin, be careful. I can tell you're scheming. If Simon finds out we'll be in bad trouble."

"I'm only thinking of him, Andrew. I love that man and I've got to make him see he is making a terrible mistake. Besides, my character is reasonably virtuous and untainted." She shoved at her husband. "And that is more than I can say for the likes of you. Now I need your help. You must try to delay returning home by at least an extra day. Will you do that?"

Andrew moaned. "I should have known it would be something like this. What am I supposed to do, shoot the horse."

"Nothing quite that drastic, Andrew, but maybe the horse could go lame."

Andrew laughed. "Ye make it sound so easy." He

stuffed his pipe with sweet-smelling tobacco. "Oh, Caitlin, why do I let you get me into these wicked situations? You are the undoing of me, you know that don't you?" Caitlin gave him a peck on the cheek. "All right, I'll think of something."

"I'm depending on you, Andrew."

"You're a wicked woman, Caitlin McGregor," he said giving her a bear hug. "I guess that's why I love you so."

"Go on with you," she laughed. I've got work to do."

"You've got scheming to do," Andrew corrected. "Just don't get caught."

Chapter Thirty-three

Caitlin came bustling into Angelique's room, whistling as she drew the drapes back. "Come along, lass, it's too pretty a morning to be sleeping. I expect we will be having company before too long and you want to be looking your best."

"Company?" Angelique asked, rubbing her eyes. "What are you talking about?"

"Why Captain Legare, of course. He said he'd be here for you today."

"I'm not going to see him," Angelique announced, turning her back to the housekeeper.

"Not see him? Has everyone in this house gone daft? Of course you are going to see him. Now get up and bathe. I suggest you put on your lavender muslin."

"Caitlin, I have made up my mind to marry Simon."

Caitlin stopped in her tracks. "Oh no, girl, you

don't mean that. You would never be happy being his wife. He has been like a father to you. How can you possibly think of him as a husband."

"I can't, Caitlin, but as he reminded me, I owe him too much to refuse his request."

"When he sees that Captain Legare isn't going to put up with any foolishness, he will come to his senses. You know, the captain is very serious about you, Chantel."

"Serious? Caitlin, wherever did you get that idea? We are just friends."

"I have talked with the captain, Chantel, and I know he is serious about you. He just doesn't want to scare you off by telling you just yet."

Angelique smiled. "I would like to see him today, but Simon is going to be very angry."

"Simon won't be home until day after tomorrow. That will give you time to get to know Captain Legare better. Then when Simon returns you can make your decision. Now doesn't that make more sense than refusing to see him?

Damian found Angelique seated on a wrought iron bench in the garden. She didn't hear him approach and for a long moment he watched her as she was engrossed in watching a yellow bird upon a flower. She was wearing a gown of lavender and her hair was pulled back on one side and held with a lavender hibiscus blossom.

He said her name softly and with a start of surprise she turned around. As soon as she met his eyes she knew Caitlin had spoken to him about Simon.

He sat on the bench next to her. "I'm sorry to have caused you so much trouble."

"Simon has not been himself for the last couple of days. He is really a wonderful man."

"I'm sure of that. I want you to know that whatever happens, I'm here for you."

Angelique stared into his eyes. "As a friend?"

"As anything you want," Damian said taking her hand. He hesitated! afraid to say more for fear he'd frighten her. He had no intention of causing her more problems.

"Caitlin suggests we leave Joshua with her until later this afternoon. Is that agreeable with you?"

"That will be fine. What will we do today?"

"What do you want to do?"

Angelique smiled. "I would really like to go into town and see Shinbone Alley."

"Angelique," Damian laughed. "Why in the world would you want to go there?"

"Because I've never seen it, and I hear people talking about it."

"That's a good enough reason. All right, first Shinbone Alley, and then what?"

"I'd like to walk on the beach."

Damian kissed her hand. "You're easy to please. Come on then, let's not waste any time. On to Shinbone Alley."

* * *

Angelique laughed with delight as they passed the shops and bars on the street. Gaudily dressed women seemed to fill every doorway, trying to entice the many longshoremen and blockade runners looking to spend their money on gambling or whoring. One of the women approached Damian and whispered something to him.

"What did she say, Damian?" Angelique asked innocently when they were away from the woman.

"She wanted to know if we just came to port? Come one, we have a lot to see yet."

"Aren't we going to go into one of those bars, Damian," Angelique asked after they had been in the area for at least a half-hour.

"I didn't know you wanted to go in."

"Oh yes, I want to see everything."

"All right, Angel, but don't say I didn't warn you."

Damian ordered brandy for both of them, then sat back and watched Angelique as she tasted the amber liquid.

"Oh my. Oh my," she gasped and sputtered. "You should have warned me. It is like liquid fire."

Damian laughed and pushed a glass of water toward her. "I tried to warn you about this whole expedition, but you wouldn't listen."

A moment later a drunken longshoreman stumbled to the table. "May I have this dance, missy?"

Angelique looked at Damian, her eyes wide and questioning. "The lady is busy, friend."

"But she is the prettiest lady I've ever seen," the

man persisted.

"I agree, but that doesn't change a thing. She belongs to me. Now shove off."

"You don't have to get nasty," he said throwing up his hands. "You ain't very sociable."

"Come on, Angel, it's time we got out of here."

"Why did he want to dance with me?" Angelique asked as Damian led her through the crowd.

"Just like he said," Damian answered. "You're the prettiest lady he'd ever seen."

"That's silly," Angelique giggled. "Oh, Damian, look," she pointed to one of the shop windows. "Isn't it beautiful," she said staring at a gaudy red satin dress with a slit up the side.

"Oh no you don't," he said pulling her along behind him. "I'm ready for that walk on the beach."

Angelique sat on the beach drawing patterns in the sand with her finger. She was so exquisitely lovely, he thought, she was sophisticated, yet natural, complex, yet child-like.

"I used to be pretty," she said out of the clear blue.

"You still are," Damian said confused by her statement.

"That man said I was pretty. He must not have seen the scar on my face."

"It isn't a bad scar. I hardly noticed it."

Angelique ran her finger over the long white line. "I use to worry that Joshua would be afraid of it, but he isn't."

"Do you remember how you got the scar?"

"No. How did you get yours" she asked touching the thin white line at his temple.

"It was a gunshot wound I received when I was trying to escape from a Union prison."

"You've led an exciting life."

"Too exciting at times."

Suddenly Angel laughed. "I enjoyed Shinbone Alley. It was exciting."

She had the most disconcerting way of changing the subject when it did not suit her, Damian thought. "Don't ever go there alone. It's a dangerous place for a lady."

"Why, Damian?" she asked innocently.

"Because you're a very beautiful, desirable woman, Angel. The women who go there know what to expect from the men there, but you're different."

"I don't understand, but I won't go back."

"Good. It's no place for a lady."

Damian sat watching his wife, trying to find some reason and logic why they were strangers to one another. He wanted to kiss her, tell her he loved her, but instead they sat making idle chatter.

The hell with Simon Maclean, he thought. He had to try something different.

"Tell me what you remember about your life?"

"I don't remember anything before Simon."

"What are your dreams about?" he persisted.

Angelique stared at him, confused by his questions.

"Caitlin said you have bad dreams."

"Yes, but I don't want to talk about them."

"It may help. Has Simon told you that?"

"No. He says it is better to forget."

"Don't you want to remember your past? You could have family worrying about you."

Angelique looked away from him, as if considering.

"I have thought of that, but I am afraid," she answered, still not looking at him.

"Whatever you suffered is over and will never happen again." She wouldn't look at him, and he wondered if she even heard him.

"No pain is unbearable," he said, "except that of regret. You are alive and well, and have a beautiful child. It's time you put the past behind you."

She shook her head no, concentrating on a bird that chased a sand-fiddler.

"What about Joshua. Don't you think he'd like to know something about his father?"

"Do you ever wish that you could change what has been so that what is to come will be more to your liking?" she asked, ignoring his question.

Damian knew it was useless to question her further now. He rolled over on his back and stared at the cloudless blue sky. "I don't imagine a day goes by that I don't wish I could change the way things happened in my life." He leaned up on one elbow and looked Angelique in the face. "But you must not give up. Things may look bad one day, but the next day might be the best you ever had."

"That is true. It was a good day when you came to

isit Simon."

"Good for you, Angel?"

"Yes," she smiled, her face turning slightly pink.

"I'm glad because I certainly consider finding you one of the best things that has ever happened to me."

Damian moved from his prone position to sit beside Angelique. "Caitlin tells me that Simon has asked you to marry him." She shook her head yes. "Did you ever think about marriage to him before?"

"My heavens, no! I've thought of him as a father."

"Could you think about marriage to me?"

"I . . . I don't know. But Simon would never approve."

"Simon has no say in the matter."

Angelique suddenly stood up, taking Damian by surprise. "Don't you think we should get Joshua now?"

In one easy motion Damian was on his feet. "Not yet, Angel." He touched his lips to hers in a gentle kiss. She placed her hands against his chest, but did not push him away.

When he lifted his head he looked down into her violet eyes. "Do you remember that, sweet Angel?"

"Remember what?"

"Kissing a man. You had to have done that and more to have given birth to Joshua. I want you to trust me, Angel. I have only two days to convince you not to marry Simon. I want to help you put the demons in your past to rest forever."

"You ask too much, Damian."

Putting his hand under her chin, he lifted her face.

"No one can promise happiness to another, no matter how much he wishes it, but I think I can make you happy, Angel. I can almost guarantee it if you just try to remember."

He gave her every opportunity to turn away from him, but she didn't. From the first time they had met she had been drawn to him and she knew there must be a reason.

"I will try, Damian."

"Good girl. Let's go back to my house where we can be comfortable."

They walked hand in hand down the beach to the pink house. Damian was thinking about how to proceed without frightening her. He was tempted to tell her he was her husband, but he changed his mind, afraid that might be too much for her to handle. Instead he would talk about Beau, Adam and Lacey.

When they reached the house Angelique was too nervous to sit down. She paced the room while Damian sat on the sofa and watched her.

"I'm scared, Damian."

"Well, I have just the remedy for being scared," he said trying to lighten her mood.

"You have something that helps you not to be scared?"

"Sure. Gingerbread cookies."

Angelique laughed. "Gingerbread cookies? You are crazy, Damian Legare."

"I've been told that a time or two. Come on, you need to stop worrying. This could be one of the best days in your life."

"I'll try, but I still want to try the gingerbread cookies."

As they headed for the kitchen Damian noticed a letter on the table. He picked it up and stared at it for a moment. "Give me just a moment, Angel. This message is from Charleston."

Reading the signature he found the letter was from Kate. It seemed she had come to be the owner of Enchanteur. Damian closed his eyes and leaned his head back against the chair. She was asking him to come back to her. She had claimed his family home so she could share it with him. He forced himself to read more. She also owned Bellemeade and planned to make both plantations the largest estate in South Carolina. She needed his help.

Damian's laughter frightened Angelique. She stared at him, wondering if he had gone crazy.

"Life is strange, Angel."

"What is in your letter, Damian?"

"I knew a woman in Charleston who always wanted to be mistress of Enchanteur. That was my home. She always thought I would marry her, but I never had any intention of doing so. Well, I just received a letter from her saying that she now owns Enchanteur. Apparently the Federals gave it to her for services well done."

"I am sorry, Damian."

"It doesn't really matter, Angel. I was never very happy there. This is my home now."

"And it is a lovely home."

"Come here, Angel." When she was close enough Damian pulled her onto his lap. "You know, a week ago that letter would have devastated me. Now I have other things on my mind."

"Like what?"

"Like making you remember your past so you can love me."

"Does it have to be that way? Do I have to remember what happened before I can love you?"

Damian nibbled at her neck. "You smell so sweet."

"Damian, you didn't answer me. I feel the special attraction we have for one another, but I don't see why I have to remember my past for that feeling to grow."

Moving his hand up her side, Damian tentatively touched her breast, but Angelique quickly jumped up. "You promised gingerbread cookies."

While she ate cookies Damian put his plan into motion. "I had a friend when I was a child. His name was Beau Charbonne and he lived in Brittany with his mother, Genevieve and his father, Michel, and a brat of a sister named Angelique."

"Why was she a brat?"

"Because she was always following us. One time Beau and I were swimming in a creek and she stole all our clothes."

Angelique laughed. "I think she sounds delightful."

"You would. She had a lot of wonderful qualities though. She had a way with animals that was amazing. It was as if she could talk to them. I was with her once when she delivered a foal. It was a very difficult time, but she handled it beautifully." Damian continued to watch her face, but there was no indication she was remembering anything.

"When Angelique was eighteen, Genevieve and Michel decided it was time for her to get married. They chose a man named Andre LaFrancois. They didn't know it, but he was a very evil man, and when they found out and tried to put a stop to the wedding, Andre LaFrancois killed Michel and Genevieve."

"Oh, no," Angelique exclaimed. "Oh, Damian, that is terrible."

"Yes, it was terrible," Damian said as he got up to get a glass of water. This wasn't getting him any place. He had to try something else.

"Have you ever been on a ship during a storm?" Before she answered he went on. "It is terrible. The wind howls and water rushes over the decks, sometime washing people into the sea."

He thought he saw a look of pain on Angelique's face, but he wasn't sure. "I was in a storm like that once. I was put into a longboat and before my wife could get in the boat broke away from the ship and I was cast out on the sea alone."

Angelique began pacing the floor, but Damian continued. "My wife was put in another boat with a friend of mind named Joshua Maxwell." Angelique turned and stared at him.

"Joshua Maxwell was my husband."

"Simon assumed Joshua was your husband."

Angelique began rubbing her temples. "Please, Damian, I am getting a terrible headache. I really think I should go now. Joshua will be up from his nap."

"All right, Angel," Damian said, giving up for the moment. "I'll take you back. Caitlin said she would have something for us to eat."

"Oh, good. I am famished."

Damian shook his head. This wasn't going to be easy. She was fighting him every step. She really didn't want to remember.

A storm did come that evening, bringing wind and rain and a cold chill with it. Angelique lay staring at the ceiling, watching the flashes of lightning as it danced around her room. She was frightened, but not of the storm—of the flashes of people's faces and of the voices that were coming back to her—and always Damian's face was among them.

She shook her head as a man with dark hair and dark eyes shouted at her. He was holding the wheel of a ship as the rain and wind battered him . . . "I hope you don't regret this . . . I hope you don't regret this . . ." the voice said over and over. Damian's face, white and bloody, telling her she was in great danger appeared.

"No, no, please," she shook her head back and forth as another face appeared. "I won't let you die . . . for God's sake, Angelique, run, run . . . I won't let you die . . ."

Though the faces were vivid the names would not come to her. "Angel . . . I love you, Angel . . . You are a fire in my blood." Angelique reached out to touch the phantom face that wandered through the depths of her mind. She was confused. Damian didn't belong in her past. He was the present. A blond woman appeared. "You may have his name, but he comes to my bed . . . he comes to my bed . . ." A wedding and a funeral blended together with a storm at sea. "No, no, no!" Angelique screamed as a leering face stared at her. *Bruja . . . bruja . . .*"

Damian was sitting in front of Angelique's portrait, wondering if he had made a mistake trying to force her to remember, when he heard a commotion. For a moment he thought one of the shutters had broken loose, but when the sound came again he realized someone was at the door.

A young black child stood at the door, drenched to the skin, his eyes wide and frightened. "Miss Cat says you better come quick," he said before turning and running back toward the white house.

"Wait," Damian shouted, but the child kept going.

"Damn," he swore, rushing out into the storm behind the boy. He didn't need to be told something was wrong when he saw Caitlin's white face.

" 'Tis my fault, oh 'tis my fault," she cried. "I should have left well enough alone. Jesus, Mary and Joseph," she said crossing herself, "don't let any harm come to them."

Damian shook her till she stopped wailing. "Caitlin, what is it? What has happened?"

"She's gone. She and Joshua are gone. I heard her scream and before I got to her she was gone."

"Jesus, I've done it again," Damian said, his voice filled with anguish. "Every time I become involved in her life I end up hurting her." Damian forced his attention back to the problem at hand. "How long ago did this happen? How long ago did you hear her scream?"

"Fifteen or twenty minutes ago. I found the boy right away and sent him after you. The boy's family are looking for her around the house. Oh, Damian, where could she have gone?"

"Was Shadow with her?"

"He must have been. He was here in the house and now he's gone."

"You stay here. If they are close enough for Shadow to hear me he'll lead me to them."

Holding the lantern above his head, Damian searched the stables and outbuildings, then headed down the pathway toward the beach. There was no sign of them anywhere. He whistled for Shadow again, but still there was no response. "Please don't let anything happen to them," he prayed as he searched.

This was his fault. He should have listened to Maclean instead of being so selfish. If he really loved his wife he would have been more concerned with her well-being than having her remember him. "Fool . . . fool . . ." he said over and over. He stood on the bluff overlooking the harbor, shouting Angelique's name, Chantel's name, and then called Shadow again, but still no one responded. He was soaked to the skin and knew they must be. They would have pneumonia if he didn't find them soon.

"I'm going to town," he shouted to Caitlin. "She may have gone back to Shinbone Alley." Suddenly Damian stopped. He could hear something running through the brush between the houses. "Shadow. Come here, boy." The dog bounded out of the shadows and greeted Damian excitedly.

"Where are they, boy? Where is Angelique and Joshua?" Shadow danced around in circles and then headed back toward Damian's house. He turned once and looked back at Damian, then ran on ahead.

Let them be there, Damian prayed silently.

Damian opening the door, he stared around the room and found it empty. Why had Shadow led him here, he wondered.

"Are they there," Caitlin asked breathlessly.

Damian looked in the kitchen, then took the steps by two to the bedroom. He froze when he reached the door. There lying sound asleep on his bed were Angelique and Joshua.

He stood in the doorway staring at them until Caitlin came up behind him. "She must remember," she smiled.

"And she has come home," Damian said softly. "They have come home."

"Let me take the bairn back to the house. You and Chantel . . . You and Angelique need some time alone. Besides, all his things are there and he will need to be changed before long."

"Will you be all right going back by yourself?"

"Aye, I'll be fine. I'll take Shadow with me. He deserves a reward tonight. You could have been out all night looking for them if it hadn't been for him."

Joshua never opened his eyes as Caitlin bundled him up. "I'll bring him back in the morning."

"I need to talk to Simon," Damian said. "I hope we can work things out. I don't want to deprive him of Joshua and Angelique's company. I know he has been good to them. If he'll just accept this situation he can have them living right next door to him."

"I don't see that he has a choice, lad. Don't worry about that now. You have a wife to take care of."

Damian smiled and kissed Caitlin on the cheek. "I don't know what I would have done without you, Caitlin."

"Get on with you now," she laughed as she left the room.

Damian studied his wife on the bed. She had the sheet tangled about her, exposing one long, bare leg. When he sat beside her she opened her eyes.

Damian moaned in despair when she moved away from him, her eyes wide with fear. He had been wrong. She didn't remember she was his wife.

She looked around the room, as if just realizing where she was. "Where is Joshua, and where were you?" she asked.

"Where was I?" he laughed. "I was out looking for you, and Joshua is with Caitlin."

"Your clothes are wet."

"Angelique," he moaned, "will you stop talking about the state of my clothes and tell me what you are doing here."

She looked hurt. "I thought after all we'd been through you would want me here."

"Oh, God, Angel, I want you here with me more than you'll ever know." Still he was reluctant to ask her if she remembered. "Angel, what happened tonight?"

"When we were on the beach today I kept getting the feeling that I knew you from before. It was so strong that it frightened me. Then when I went home I laid down and it all started coming back to me."

"You mean you remember it all. You remember that you're my wife and that Joshua is my son?"

"Damian, do you think I would be lying here in your bed with no clothes on if I hadn't remembered?"

Damian didn't move or take his eyes off his wife. The world and storm faded away. "It has been a lifetime, my beautiful wife, but now that you are mine again, I'm going to show you in every way possible how much I love you."

Moaning softly that she loved him, that she wanted him, Angelique began to remove his wet clothes. His strong muscled body was just as she remembered, and she became aroused by just the feel of his firm flesh. Love words were whispered in her ear as he laid beside her, his hands gently moving over her soft skin, caressing her velvet breasts, and sending tremors of pleasure throughout her entire being.

"I can't believe you are here in my arms," he whispered. "God has granted me a miracle."

"God has granted *us* a miracle, my husband."

As their bodies molded into one there wasn't any need for more words.

Epilog

April 1865

Angelique was packing for their trip to Europe when John Bourne came with a paper full of the news of Lee's surrender. The war was finally over. Officers and men of the army would be given paroles, but nothing was said about the blockade runners.

Damian had known it was coming, but still it left him with an empty feeling. They had sacrificed so much.

"I know it makes you sad, Damian, but now the soldiers can return to their families and start over."

"They really will be starting over. Every major city in the South has been destroyed."

"It is a time to put bitterness behind us. If we don't live in peace together we will eventually kill each other off."

Damian pulled her into his lap. "How did you get

so wise?"

"I guess it's the company I keep." She gave him a quick kiss then became serious. "I'll understand if you want to postpone our trip."

"There isn't any reason to do that. Besides, if I don't get you to Europe soon I'm going to have Beau, Adam, Lacey and Mother as house guests, and I don't want that. This way, when we are ready to come home we can. I can't share you with everyone for too long, you know."

"I'm glad you feel that way, love, but it will be wonderful seeing everyone, particularly Beau."

"I know it will, love. I'm looking forward to seeing them myself. Simon is going to take care of the house while we're gone, and I've arranged to have Emily come back to work just as soon as we return."

"There is a little jealousy going on between Emily and Caitlin over Joshua. Our son is going to be spoiled rotten before too long."

"Not if we give him a new brother or sister to play with."

Angelique laughed. "Damian, what are you talking about? I'm not pregnant."

Damian stood up, lifting his wife with him, and capturing her lips in long lingering kiss. "But you may well be before we leave, my love," he whispered.